"Your job will be to work with the secret serving down these four suspects . . . but also to look after
our interests. Getting involved with . . . those people, I
agree, was, ah, ill-advised. But we may yet need those . . .
unpleasant resources."

"Bob, these 'unpleasant resources' are your collaborators, on the one hand, and on the other, you're trying to
stick them in stir."

"We made no promises otherwise. In addition to Hoffa,
we've got Carlos Marcello in the crosshairs. Finally, we will
deport that slippery bastard."

"That slippery bastard is part of your anti-Castro efforts,
too, Bob."

"We don't need him. We have made a lot of people
unhappy. Sam Giancana, assorted Cubans, right-wing
fanatics, certain elements within the CIA, and it's possible—just possible—two or more of these groups are coming together on this . . . and taking some of the very tactics we developed to, ah, eliminate Castro, and turning
them around on us."

"Well then tell Jack to stay away from exploding
cigars," I said, referring to one of the more arcane attempts
to kill the Beard.

Bobby was not amused. In fact, his expression turned
grave.

*Should I tell him? That right after I ran into an old
West Side buddy, a client of mine had been murdered—a
client with a Hoffa tie, and therefore a Mob tie? After all,
that old buddy had a shirttail connection to the anti-
Castro effort . . . but what the hell could a nobody like
Jack Ruby have to do with something like this?*

I kept it to myself—Bobby was already halfway out the
door.

"I haven't said I'd do this," I said.

"Sure you have," he said.

I just sat there listening to the muffled roar of planes
taking off without me, waiting to drive back to Chicago.

And to my new job at the Secret Service.

**Turn the page for rave reviews.**

Readers with a taste for hard-boiled roman à clef will hope that more Heller is in the offing."

—*Publishers Weekly* on
*Bye Bye, Baby*

"A compelling talent for flowing narrative and concise, believable dialogue . . . highly recommended."

—*Library Journal* on
*Bye Bye, Baby*

"Max Allan Collins can lay claim to being the master of true-crime fiction. . . . A seamless juxtaposition of narrative cunning and historical cross-referencing."

—*Chicago* magazine on
*Bye, Bye Baby*

"Collins's witty, hard-boiled prose would make Raymond Chandler proud."          —*Entertainment Weekly*

"Collins doesn't see the past through rose-colored glasses but rather down the sight lines of a 9mm automatic. Excellent hard-boiled fare."

—*Booklist* on
*Chicago Confidential*

"When it comes to noirish hard-boiled PI thrillers, few writers can compete with Collins; the sex is hot and the killings are cold. What else could you ask for? Recommended for all mystery collections."

—*Library Journal* on
*Chicago Confidential*

"The entertainment here is largely in watching Mr. Collins twist his story to accommodate his imagined Winchell and Capone, etc., his imagined Great Depression, and his imagined Chicago gangland."

—*The New York Times* on
*True Detective*

# BOOKS BY MAX ALLAN COLLINS

THE MEMOIRS OF NATHAN
HELLER

Ask Not*
Target Lancer*
Bye Bye, Baby*
Chicago Confidential
Angel in Black
Kisses of Death
Majic Man
Flying Blind
Damned in Paradise
Blood and Thunder
Carnal Hours
Stolen Away
Dying in the Post-War
   World
Neon Mirage
The Million-Dollar Wound
True Crime
True Detective

THE ROAD TO PERDITION
SAGA

Return to Perdition
   (graphic novel)
Road to Paradise
Road to Purgatory
Road to Perdition 2: On
   the Road (graphic novel)
Road to Perdition (graphic
   novel)

WITH MICKEY SPILLANE

Complex 90
Lady, Go Die!

Kiss Her Goodbye
The Big Bang
The Goliath Bone
Dead Street

WITH BARBARA COLLINS
(AS BARBARA ALLAN)

Antiques Chop
Antiques Disposal
Antiques Knock-off
Antiques Bizarre
Antiques Flee Market
Antiques Maul
Antiques Roadkill

QUARRY NOVELS

Quarry's Ex
Quarry in the Middle
The First Quarry
The Last Quarry
Quarry's Vote (aka Primary
   Target)
Quarry's Cut (aka The
   Slasher)
Quarry's Deal (aka The
   Dealer)
Quarry's List (aka The
   Broker's Wife)
Quarry (aka The Broker)

WRITING AS PATRICK
CULHANE

Red Sky in Morning
Black Hats

*A Tom Doherty Associates book

# Target Lancer

MAX ALLAN COLLINS

A TOM DOHERTY ASSOCIATES BOOK · NEW YORK

Although the historical incidents in this novel are portrayed as accurately as the passage of time and contradictory source material will allow, fact, speculation, and fiction are freely mixed here; historical personages exist side by side with composite characters and wholly fictional ones—all of whom are summoned, act, and speak at the author's whim.

TARGET LANCER

Copyright © 2012 by Max Allan Collins

Edited by James Frenkel

A Forge Book
Published by Tom Doherty Associates, LLC
175 Fifth Avenue
New York, NY 10010

www.tor-forge.com

Forge® is a registered trademark of Tom Doherty Associates, LLC.

ISBN 978-0-7653-6147-9

Forge books may be purchased for educational, business, or promotional use. For information on bulk purchases, please contact Macmillan Corporate and Premium Sales Department at 1-800-221-7945, extension 5442, or write specialmarkets@macmillan.com.

First Edition: November 2012
First Mass Market Edition: October 2013

Printed in the United States of America

0  9  8  7  6  5  4  3  2  1

*For Jon L. Breen*
*His generation's Anthony Boucher*

You never know what's hit you. A gunshot is the perfect way.

—JFK

My own feeling was that Bobby was worried that there might be some conspiracy . . . worried that the investigation would somehow point back to him.

—Nicholas Katzenbach,
RFK's deputy attorney general

*Do you remember where you were when President Kennedy was killed? Even if you weren't alive at the time, you surely know that a sniper in a high window was waiting for JFK to ride by on that infamous day in November.*

*In Chicago.*

**Friday, October 25, 1963**

The city's oldest, most famous strip joint was just a storefront with 606 CLUB emblazoned in neon over its lighted-up canopied walkway. Another, smaller 606 neon sign crooked its summoning finger into the street, while windows promised delight by way of posters of Lili St. Cyr, Ann Corio, and Tempest Storm, none of whom was appearing right now.

The 606 opened in 1932, back when strippers were called burlesque queens, and it hadn't changed much in all that time. Sure, the walls got washed on occasion, the floors swept, the dishes scrubbed; but otherwise it remained a cozy, smoky, naughty retreat for businessmen, college boys, and in particular conventioneers.

The latter were the lifeblood of the joint, as the 606 was mere blocks from some of Chicago's best-known, most commodious hotels. On the other hand, South Wabash was old Capone turf, not far from the site of Johnny Torrio's Four Deuces, and within spitting distance of Skid Row.

This made the 606 just the kind of joint, in just the type of dicey neighborhood, where an out-of-town businessman carrying a fat wad of cash might think taking a bodyguard along wasn't such a bad idea.

I couldn't remember when I'd last done a bodyguard job. I was too old, too rich, and too famous for such piddling work. Well, maybe I wasn't *that* old—let's call it my well-preserved fifties—and "rich" might be overstating it, though ironically any fame of mine had rubbed off from such front-page clients as Mayor Anton Cermak, Huey Long, and Amelia Earhart.

None of whom, come to think of it, had benefitted particularly from my bodyguard services.

But I was on the spot, because this client was an old friend who had done some flack jobs for me when he worked for a local agency before moving to Milwaukee, where he had built a small PR empire out of several big beer accounts.

As for me—Nathan Heller—I was president and founder of the A-1 Detective Agency, which took up much of the seventh floor of the fabled Monadnock Building. *My* small empire included fourteen local agents (that's what we were calling operatives these days) and branch offices in LA and Manhattan.

We'd met for beer at the Berghoff on West Adams, in the venerable German restaurant's bar. It was the kind of place where cigar smoke trumped cigarette, the long narrow space sporting a polished wooden counter extending the entire length of the east wall, bowing out at the north end. This was a male preserve, literally so—like Spanky and Alfalfa's clubhouse, no girls were allowed, other than the two female minstrels that were part of an ancient hand-carved clock behind the bar, amid old-world murals.

Mid–Friday afternoon, the bar busy but not crazy, we managed to negotiate a quiet corner toward the end of the counter. We had the Berghoff's own Dortmunder-style beer, from one of its twelve taps—no other options, except for the private-stock single-barrel Kentucky bourbon on the back shelf.

Beer would do fine.

"Nate," Tom Ellison said, "you're a stand-up guy, meeting me at such short notice."

Tom was easily ten years my junior, a Korean War veteran who had once been an athlete and still had the broad-shouldered six-foot frame to prove it. He wore a breezy-looking plaid jacket with a blue vest, blue-striped shirt, and blue tie. In case you're wondering, I was in a dark-blue Botany 500 suit with a blue patterned tie. Tom was hatless, but I wore a narrow-brimmed shag-finish felt hat. From Dobbs.

"Everybody in the Berghoff bar is a stand-up guy," I reminded him. There were no stools at the counter, just a brass rail for resting one foot at time.

Tom grinned and chuckled, which was more than my remark deserved. He was the upbeat type, perfect for the puffery racket, boyish with that blond crew cut, those sky-blue eyes, pug nose, and dimpled jaw. He might have been Kirk Douglas's kid brother.

"I just mean," he said, putting something serious into his tone, "I know you're a busy guy, an important guy. Hell, they call you the 'Private Eye to the Stars.'"

That was a *Life* magazine spread, and not a very big one.

"Only when I'm working out of the Hollywood office," I said, and sipped the cold beer. It had a nice bite to it. You had to hand it to the Germans. They could make war, and they could make beer.

He leaned in and smiled the PR-guy smile. "Is it true they based James Bond on you?"

"It's gospel. Ian Fleming has to send me a nickel for every book he sells."

This he laughed at much too hard.

"Is it your wife?" I asked, on the outskirts of irritation. Half my agents worked domestic.

"No! No, hell, Jean is great. Jean is wonderful."

"You don't have to sell me on it."

"Nothing to do with Jean. It's probably . . . nothing at all."

Now I was approaching the city limits. "Tom, we're not standing in the dark drinking beer in the middle of the afternoon because we're alcoholics. At least I'm not. You didn't want to meet at my office. Why?"

My bluntness made him wince. "Well, I didn't want to make this . . . official. I wanted it more social. More like a favor. Although I'll pay you! I don't expect you to listen to my stupid situation for free."

Not his wife. Business, then.

"I'll listen for free," I said, and had another sip of the nicely sharp brew. "But when you did PR work for me, I paid for it. If I have to step up to the plate for you, *you'll* pay for it. Fair enough?"

"Perfectly fair." He glanced around.

No one was close by, and there were enough other mid-afternoon patrons in the Berghoff bar, lost in their conversations—plus the restaurant bleed-in of bustling waiters with the clink and clank of dishes—to give us privacy in this public place.

"You know, Nate, a guy in the press-agent game can come in contact with a lot of . . . *colorful* types."

*That* I got. I pressed my nose to make it go sideways. The universal symbol for mob types.

He nodded, lifted his blond, almost invisible eyebrows. "Right. I guess I'd put Harry Gordon in that camp, though I didn't know it at first. I met Harry in London, at the Savoy of all places. Met at high tea, would you believe it?"

I said nothing, hoping to encourage less travelogue and more pertinence.

"Harry was doing business with some fellas from France, who needed American representation, and it all just kind of fell into place. Thanks to Harry, I got more business in Europe than ever before."

"Good for Harry. Good for you."

Tom sighed as if that were anything but the case. "Later, here in Chicago, Harry introduced me to somebody that I think you know—Jimmy Hoffa?"

That got my attention.

I knew Hoffa, all right. I had worked for him when I was also employed by Bobby Kennedy and the Senate rackets committee. That double-agent period of my life was one I'd been lucky to survive. To this day, Hoffa thought I was his pal. I hoped.

"I was staying at the Bismarck Hotel," Tom was saying, "trying to land an account with a furniture chain here. Harry took me up to Hoffa's suite, also in the Bismarck, introduced us, and we chatted about why I was in town, and before I knew it, Hoffa had called up the furniture chain's owner and . . ." He shrugged.

"And you had a new profitable client."

"I did. Before long, I realized that furniture firm was in the pocket of the Teamsters. And those European clients also had ties to the Teamsters. Then there was a fleet of trucks in Florida that I represented that—"

"I get the picture."

Had he figured out that Harry striking up a conversation with him at high tea hadn't been serendipity? I didn't bother asking.

Instead I just said, "So you're having a case of conscience. You like to think of yourself as a legitimate businessman, and now you're doing business with Jimmy Hoffa, who has more mob ties than you have silk ones."

But Tom was shaking his head. "I'm a big boy. I *am* legitimate. Nothing I've done for Hoffa or any of the firms he's hooked me up with has been remotely shady. Hoffa of course doesn't like having his associations advertised, but that's not a problem. I know how to get attention for my clients. But I'm also happy to be discreet."

I shifted feet on the brass rail. "So what *is* the problem?"

"Well . . ." His boyish face clenched in thought; his eyes were searching. ". . . I'm a football fan."

I pretended that wasn't a non sequitur. "If you're a Bears fan, you're in luck. Looks like they're on their way to an NFL championship."

His eyes brightened. "The Bears are playing the Philadelphia Eagles this weekend."

"Are they?" I was a fight fan.

"Well, like you said, they're on a roll, and good seats for any home game are at a premium. Particularly at late notice. So this morning, at the Bismarck, I had breakfast with Harry Gordon."

"Okay," I said, like I was following him, which I wasn't.

"I figured for once it was nice that I had this kind of, well, underworld connection . . .'cause who else could get me Bears tickets at this late notice?"

"Ah." Now I was following. But I was wondering who Harry Gordon was. Not that I knew everybody Hoffa worked with—he had an army. Make that *armies*.

Tom held out his hands, palms up. "So I ask Harry if he can land me some tickets, and he says, 'Piece of cake.'

Then he gets thoughtful, actually thinks for maybe twenty, thirty seconds before he says, 'But there's a favor *you* can do *me*.'"

"Which was?"

"Well, he takes this number-ten business envelope out of his inside jacket pocket, and he holds it down between us, where only we can see it, opens the flap, and runs his thumb through a stack of crisp one-hundred-dollar bills . . . at least an inch thick worth."

That was my cue to whistle, but I didn't.

Tom paused for a gulp of beer. Then: "After that, he brings the envelope up and licks the flap shut and hands me the fat thing and smiles like a kid sharing a secret. 'Deliver that to the 606 Club tonight,' he says. 'To a guy named Jake who will approach you after you sit down and order a drink. He'll be a stocky little guy in a nice dark suit with a white carnation.'"

Maybe Ian Fleming should have been sending those nickels to Harry Gordon.

Tom was saying, "I asked him how this Jake character would know me, and he said, 'You're a distinctive-looking fella, Tommy. I'll describe you. Not to worry.' Not to worry, he says." He shuddered.

I said, "What did you tell your pal Harry?"

"I told him . . . fine. What else could I say? I was out on business all morning, but then after lunch, when I stopped at the desk at the Pick? Another envelope was waiting—this one with a Bears ticket in it. Fifty-yard line, Nate."

"Expensive seating."

Tom rolled his eyes. "Yeah, but *how* expensive? What the hell have I got myself into? The 606 . . . I've never been there, but isn't that some kind of strip joint? A dive over by Skid Row?"

"It's only a few blocks from here, really. Normally I'd say it wouldn't be that dangerous."

"Normally. This isn't 'normally.' "

"No. You're by yourself, packing an envelope with maybe—seven to ten grand in it? No. And that's why you're buying me another beer, right? Because you want me to back you up?"

"I'd feel safer with you as my bodyguard, yes."

Obviously he hadn't checked in with Mayor Cermak or Huey Long. Not that he could have, short of a Ouija board.

"I haven't seen a naked woman in over a week," I said. "Be my pleasure."

The plan was I'd arrive at the 606 ten minutes in advance of Tom. We'd both take cabs (staggering the departure time) from the Pick-Congress, where the PR exec was staying.

A chill rain had let up, but the street in front of the neon-announced nightery was as slick and shiny as black patent-leather shoes. I stepped from the cab with an olive Cortefiel double-breasted raincoat over my nifty charcoal-gray worsted, tailored to conceal the nine-millimeter shoulder-holstered under my left arm. Browning, for those of you keeping track of brand names.

I didn't often carry the nine-mil, these days. It was damn near as much of an antique as I was, being the gun I'd carried as a kid back on the Pickpocket Detail in the early thirties. It was also the gun my leftist father had used to blow his brains out in disappointment after I joined the Chicago PD. I'd never carried any other gun regularly, since I viewed it as the only conscience I had.

"Nathan Heller!" a familiar gravelly voice called out.

I wheeled to see the white-haired dwarf-like owner of the 606, Lou Nathan, trotting over. He wore a snappy brown suit, too-wide-for-the-fashion tie, and his trademark fedora with its unturned brim (to my knowledge, no one had ever seen him out of that hat), with his friendly features—slit eyes, knob of a nose, and slit mouth—aimed right at me.

Lou was one of those guys who always seemed to be headed somewhere else. On his way to chat up patrons, check on the bar, supervise the kitchen downstairs, make a surprise inspection of the communal dressing room (in the basement, where the strippers tried to avoid the heating pipes).

His favorite haunt, however, was the taxi stand out front of the club, where he would chin animatedly with the cabbies till his restless feet got the best of him.

Right now those feet were bringing the gregarious little guy over to me.

"Whatever have I done for such an honor?" Lou asked facetiously. "To have the famous Nate Heller drop by my humble establishment."

I shook his firm little hand. "Been too long, Lou."

"I thought maybe my girls weren't good enough for you anymore," Lou said. "They say these days you only date the showgirls at the Chez Paree and Empire Room."

I grinned at him. "Maybe I just know you watch your fillies too close for a guy like me to ever get lucky."

Lou didn't allow his dancers to hustle for drinks between sets. A rarity in Chicago strip joints.

"With that handsome mug of yours," Lou said, pawing the air, "all you ever have to do is flash a smile, and their legs spread like a wishbone. . . . Come on in, I'll buy you your first drink."

He did, and sat with me.

Patting my shoulder, he asked, "I ever tell you about how Jackie Gleason used to come in, every night, looking for cooze and watching my comics?"

"You mean, how the Great One wanted a job, only you turned him down because you didn't think he was funny?"

"Yeah!"

"No, I don't believe you ever did."

He laughed, though that gag setup went out with the Bowery Boys. Then the slitted eyes gave my torso a glance, and I didn't figure he was checking me out for a slot on the bill.

"That suit's cut vurry nice."

"Yeah. M.L. Rothschild's top guy tailored it for me."

"Vurry nice job. But a guy who's been around, like possibly . . . me? He looks at you close and hopes that's something harmless under your left armpit. Like maybe a tumor."

"It's nothing to sweat about, Lou."

"You wouldn't kid a guy?"

"Naw." I gave my suit coat a gentle pat over the nine-millimeter. "Just happened to drop in for a drink after a job where I needed the comfort."

"You say so," he said cheerfully.

He stayed another thirty seconds, which made this a near two-minute conversation, possibly a new record, before he went scurrying off to his next stop.

I had asked for and received a booth in back, close to the door and well away from the stage, in the packed little joint. I turned my eyes loose. More women patrons than there used to be—female conventioneers, or open-minded wives or girlfriends. I figured the gals were letting the overly lipsticked, somewhat over-the-hill cuties up there working their way down to pasties and G-strings warm their guys up for them. Less work to do back home or at the hotel.

This former grocery was just a single room, maybe forty feet wide and two hundred feet deep. On one side was a long bar edging three tiers of tables accommodating perhaps seventy small tables facing a postage-stamp stage where one stripper after another was accompanied by a four-piece band: drums, guitar,

accordion, and bass guitar. The room was dark, with a
curtain nailed to the back wall, the ceiling-mounted
lighting over the stage as nakedly visible as its subjects.

There was no cover, and the rum-and-Coke Lou
bought me covered half of the two-drink minimum.
Not watered down, either, unless that was special treatment courtesy of the management. I let my eyes slowly
travel through the fog of smoke and across the jammed-
in patrons at the tables, but the backs of all these heads
didn't do much for me, despite my detective skills.

I didn't spot anybody who looked suspicious or
dangerous or in any way out of the ordinary, at least
not until Tom Ellison came in, looking pinched and
anxious.

A raincoat over his arm, hatless, with his blond crew
cut standing up as if in fright, he was in a camel-color
suit with a plaid vest—I'd suggested he wear something that stood out, to help his contact spot him, and
he hadn't let me down. Gus, the pudgy, balding manager who acted as a sort of headwaiter, came up to tell
him no seating was available except at the bar, and
Tom nodded and thanked him and found a stool over
there.

I just sat and sipped my drink and pretended to
watch a skinny redhead with more breastworks than
seemed likely prance around in a filmy harem costume.
Really, I was keeping an eye on Tom, who wasn't any
more nervous than a first-time father in a maternity-
ward waiting room.

The PR exec had fulfilled his two-drink minimum by
way of a couple of martinis when a figure rose from a
front-row seat and half turned to knife his way through
the many tables to the bar—a burly-looking little guy
with black hair whose color may have come from
a bottle, and black shark eyes that searched out Tom.

No mistaking him—this was the contact, stocky, in a

nice blue suit with red-white-and-blue tie, very snappy-looking, but not enough to offset his pasty barroom complexion or his rather blank-featured oval face with its five-o'clock-shadowed jowls. He looked like a Li'l Abner caricature that Al Capp hadn't quite finished with.

I couldn't hear the conversation. It was brief. Appeared friendly, the contact affable, Tom stilted. Smiles were exchanged, and the envelope handed over, casually, nothing surreptitious about it. Nobody was watching them but me. Everybody else was enjoying the redhead, who was down to her pasties now, tiny annoyances on the cantaloupe breasts, with the filmy harem pants next on the going-going-gone list.

The stocky contact guy nodded, smiled again, shook hands with Tom, patted him on the shoulder, and threaded back through the smoke and the crowd to his waiting table. Tom had been good about not acknowledging my presence, but now he looked right at me, and I nodded as imperceptibly as possible.

When the crowd burst into applause at the final reveal—Red plucked off her pasties and got a standing ovation out of a lot of guys, probably even those still sitting down—Tom gave the bartender a generous five-spot, and headed out.

I waited till the next stripper, a busty brunette, had shed a few garments, then slipped out of the club myself.

It was drizzling a little. Tom was waiting at a cab, about to get in, but pausing as I'd instructed him till he got the high-sign from me.

I nodded at him, indicating all was well with the world, and he disappeared off into the rain-slick night.

Me, I turned to go back into the 606.

I knew that little guy, that contact with the nice suit and the shark eyes. I knew him to be a Hoffa associate, but more than that I just . . . well, *knew* him. He was Jake Rubinstein, from the West Side, an old acquaintance but not exactly a friend.

He knew me, too, of course.

Which wouldn't have mattered, but I was pretty sure he'd spotted me.

So I needed to go back in there and deal with him. I could start by asking him what he was doing back in Chicago. He'd been in Dallas for years, running his own strip clubs.

Under the name Jack Ruby.

The little combo was doing as jazzy a version of "Harlem Nocturne" as possible with an accordion in the lineup, the drummer giving the big exotic brunette plenty to grind to. Her name was Tura Satana and she'd come out in a Japanese kimono but was down to pasties and a skirt that was just a couple fore-and-aft wispy swatches. I was on my second rum-and-Coke and ready to forgive the Japanese for Pearl Harbor when I saw the stocky figure in the dark suit and narrow dark tie rise from his front table and make his way toward the rear of the club.

He made a big show of noticing me, grinning and pointing his finger at me like a gun.

I gave him a smile, and waved him over to the back booth I was hogging. He skirted the cluster of tables and made a beeline, his hand extended. I half rose on my side of what was really a semi-booth, its back to the wall, with a table and two chairs making it easier for patrons to angle toward the stage. Even from here, tucked in the corner, the view wasn't bad.

After we shook hands, his grip show-off tight, Jake indeed angled his chair so that he could alternate his attention between me and the bosomy Japanese stripper, who put a lot of energy into her bumps and grinds, legs spread so far that her flimsy skirt flapped and snapped between them.

"*Her* I gotta book," Jake said, as if we were in the middle of a conversation, not the start. "Gotta hand it to ol' Lou—he's got an eye for talent. 'Made in Japan' is right!"

I was just thinking about apologizing to Miss Satana for Hiroshima myself. "Still in the club business, huh, Jake?"

He nodded. His thinning black hair was slicked back, and his tiny black eyes glittered. Close up, his pasty face lost some of its blankness, and you could see a certain enthusiasm for living there. Also, he seemed a little nuts.

"Oh yeah. The Carousel is my baby. Right downtown. But I'm gonna move it to a bigger, even better location before long. Thinking about having two runways, to bring the girls closer to the customers."

"Worked for Jolson. So, just the one club now? Thought you had several."

He pawed the air like a bored lion. "Yeah, got another joint called the Vegas, where we put on these amateur nights. The yahoos love that stuff, half-drunk college girls and secretaries gettin' up and strippin' off. No class, them broads. But what are you gonna do? Gotta give the public what it wants."

We'd once known each other pretty well, growing up on the West Side and sharing a friend in Barney Ross, who'd gone from tough kid to welterweight boxing champ. Barney always had more patience with Jake Rubinstein than I could ever muster. I considered Sparky (his long-ago street name) a hotheaded little shakedown artist; but Jake was jake in Barney's eyes. After all, hadn't they run errands a buck a pop together, for the Capone gang?

Tom Ellison had played bagman tonight, delivering a packet of cash to a guy who had, ironically enough, served his first jail term for scalping football tickets, and who'd first risen to mob prominence in the late thirties by acting as bagman for the Scrap Iron and Junk Handlers union.

Jake eventually got caught in a struggle between two union leaders, one of whom was shot and killed in an incident where the union's chief bagman became a principal player in a cover-up that resulted in the Teamsters taking over the union. I'd been in the middle of that and had been happy to come out of it without anybody's blood on me, especially my own.

I knew Jake Rubinstein, all right. But I'd had little to do with Jack Ruby.

I'd seen him in Dallas a few times—the Outfit had sent him there in the late forties, as part of a Chicago takeover attempt on that wide-open town's gambling, prostitution, and other rackets. But the Lone Star State coppers didn't want to play, and it fizzled. Ruby had stayed on, in the strip-club business, a sort of exile. I presumed he'd continued to do the Outfit's bidding, from time to time, but knew no details.

That left Jake and me in an awkward position. We knew each other well but hadn't talked in years. Add to that, if he'd spotted me, he was wondering what the fuck I was doing here. Like I'd spotted him and was wondering what the fuck he was doing here.

So it started with small talk.

"What do you hear from Barney?" I asked.

"Quite a bit, really. You know, them amateur nights? I was trying to get Barney's help and advice in shutting some of the competition down, with this non-pro stripper bullshit. He has an in with the AGVA."

That was the American Guild of Variety Artists. Somewhere in there among the violinists and sopranos

and ballet dancers they represented were strippers. That
is, "exotic dancers."

Barney worked for the Milton Blackstone Advertis-
ing Agency in New York, where his celebrity had made
him a successful press agent. Like Tom Ellison, though
Tom never won a welterweight championship.

The music way up front wasn't loud enough to make
conversation difficult, but we did have to lean in a little to talk.

"So, what," I said, "you're trying to get these amateur nights banned?"

"Fucking A. Then maybe I can turn the Vegas back
into a respectable joint. You know, I'm hoping to book
Candy Barr in there. When her parole's up on that pot
bust, anyway. Broad's got two of the most famous busts
in America, huh?" He cackled at that.

"Sounds like Dallas is doing right by you."

"*I'm* doin' right by *it*. Place's a shithole. When the
boys sent me down there, fuck—why not California,
or Florida? I had to make my own way, Nate. But you
can *do* that in America, can't you?"

"Sure. Look at me. Horatio Alger, eat your heart out."

"Who?"

"Nothing. Can I buy you a drink, Jake?"

"Sure. But it's Jack now. Jake's history."

I grinned at him. "Like Sparky?"

He grinned back. "Well, there's still *some* spark left
in the old kid yet, Nate."

I waved a waiter over. Half a dozen guys in white
shirts with black ties and black trousers handled all
two-hundred-some customers in the 606, no female
staff other than onstage. I ordered a Coke minus the
rum this time, and Jake—Jack—asked for tomato juice.

"You don't drink, either?" he said with an impish
smile.

"I had two rum-and-Cokes already. But I'm not a

big boozer. Don't tell me a club man like you is a teetotaler?"

He squinted his little black eyes, shook his head. "Bad for you. Like cigarettes. Don't touch 'em. I don't see *you* draggin' on one, neither."

"Only time I ever really smoked," I said, "was in the service."

"When you and Barney shared a foxhole."

"That's right."

"On Guadalcanal."

"Skip it, Jack."

"Well, you're a true hero, Nate."

"A true hero who got out on a Section Eight."

"Don't give me that fuckin' noise. Barney told me. You got the Silver Star. They mentioned that in that *Life* article, too, right?"

Jack had been following my storied career, apparently.

"Hell," he said, "me? I spent the whole damn war in the South."

"Well, my understanding is the Japs never got past Birmingham, so you did fine."

He didn't find that funny. He damn near looked like he might cry. "Only action I saw was when I punched out a fucking sergeant."

"You punched out a sergeant?"

"Goddamn right! He called me a Jew bastard! Wouldn't *you* punch him?"

Jake was a lot more Jewish than me, despite my last name. With my reddish-brown hair and blue eyes, I took after my Irish mother, not my Jewish pop, who had been apostate and raised me that way. But I would have given that sergeant his due beating, all right—just not where or when I could be made for it.

My Coke and Jake's tomato juice arrived.

He raised his red-brimming glass in a toast and I

clinked my Coke with it as he said, "*L'Chayim*," and we nodded at each other, then sipped.

Another dancer was onstage now, visible through the blue-smoke haze. The little combo was doing its best with David Rose's big-band "The Stripper." Didn't really make it, but nobody cared—the blonde onstage, Leslee Lynn, had a nice smile and nicer legs in mesh stockings that showed under the fox-fur stole she'd strutted out in, and would soon be ridding herself of.

"So what brings you to Chicago, Jack? Talent hunt?"

He was turned toward the blonde, nodding as he took in her graceful, sexy moves to the clumsy music. "Yeah, a guy has to keep a finger on the pulse."

"Is that what he has to keep his finger on."

The bullet head turned my way. His smile was boyish, in a sleazy kind of way. "Lou says this girl is a class act. She's a University of Chicago grad, he tells me."

"What healthy male wouldn't want to see *her* diploma? So you'll hit a lot of the clubs in town, looking for dancers?"

"Sure." He shrugged. "You go where the best shows are, at least in the Midwest and South. There are some talented gals in Frisco and Hollywood, but why ship them in, when there's Fort Worth and New Orleans in my own backyard?"

We both watched the fox stole as it drifted to the floor and got dragged behind Leslee's confident stride. She wasn't as busty as the other girls, but she knew how to work the crowd.

"Class," Jack said admiringly. "Your average stripper? Just ain't got no class." Without looking at me, he added, "And how about you, Nate? What brings you to the 606?"

So he *had* made me.

You didn't need to ask a Chicagoan like Nate Heller

what he was doing in a joint where good-looking girls took off their clothes. No. He'd seen me, all right.

"I met a client here earlier," I said.

*Had he seen me duck out, after Tom? And come back in?*

"We finished our business," I said, "and I decided to stick around and partake in a little culture."

"You and Lou Nathan go way back."

"That we do. But truth be told, nowadays the Chez Paree is more my speed."

He nodded, half smiled, then sighed dreamily. "Someday. Someday that'll be me, booking Sinatra and Sammy Davis."

"Booking Sammy Davis in Dallas? You *are* ambitious."

He found that real funny, or pretended to.

The combo moved onto "My Heart Belongs to Daddy" in honor of Leslee's heart-shaped pasties (I may have been in my fifties, but I had twenty-twenty vision).

Jack turned his back on the stripper and showed me a different kind of smile. The kind with no teeth. Accompanied by hooded eyes.

"We been friends a long time, Nate," he said.

Not really, but I gave him another little half toast and said, "Maxwell Street days."

He didn't bother clinking my glass. The beady black eyes were like buttons trying to sew themselves on me. "So, you . . . you'd *tell* me, wouldn't you?"

"Tell you what, Jake?"

"Jack. It's Jack."

"Yeah, like the president. Tell you what?"

"You'd tell me, somebody sent you? Was having you check up on me? You know, keeping tabs?"

"Who would be keeping tabs on you, Jack?"

He sighed. Shook his head. "When it's Nate Heller

sitting there? That's the thing. You're connected to more places than AT and T. Could be Outfit. Could be union. Could be . . . company."

*Did he mean what I thought he meant?*

I didn't ask, but he answered anyway: "Company as in . . ." And this he whispered. ". . . Mongoose."

That made the back of my neck prickle, and that didn't happen very often these days.

But I didn't play along. I played dumb. He wouldn't buy it, but I played dumb.

"Mongoose, Jack?" I was whispering, too. That probably gave it away. Just the same, I said, "What the hell's Mongoose?"

"Operation Mongoose," he said, and he touched thumb and forefinger to his lips and made the twisting, locking motion that meant his lips were sealed. Like one teenage girl assuring another at a slumber party.

Operation Mongoose was not a phrase I heard every day. It was in fact a phrase I wished I'd never heard. Several years ago, following a high-level request, I had put the CIA in touch with various organized-crime figures, so they could pursue a common goal: eliminating Fidel Castro.

I sipped the Coke. "I'm not part of that anymore, Jack."

"You *were* a big part of it, though." The black eyes glistened now; it was almost like there was life in them. "You didn't think a small cog like me would know, huh? Ha."

I managed not to say, *Fuck no, I didn't think an insignificant worm like you, Jake, would be involved in a top secret government assassination mission.*

Instead, I just said, "No, I can see where you'd be a major player."

For example, picking up a few grand in an envelope in a strip club.

"But I do wonder," I went on, "who would have shared that information with you? I mean, discretion being the better part of valor and all."

"Not important," he said, shrugged, and sipped tomato juice. "Thing is, we're both patriots, Nate. Heroes. We saw something evil, a cancer growing too close to our borders, and we did something about it."

"Okay. Fine." I found it best not to mention that Fidel was alive and well. "But it has nothing to do with why I'm here tonight."

"You were here to meet a client, I heard you the first time." He leaned in. "You wanna know what the sick joke is, Nate? The sick fucking joke?"

*Other than that, how did you enjoy the play, Mrs. Lincoln?*

"Sure," I said.

"Once upon a sorry damn time, we . . . *I* . . . helped transport guns and jeeps and you-name-the-fucking-arms into Cuba *for* Castro. To help him take out that prick Batista."

Well, that wasn't quite right, was it? The idea surely had been to get on Castro's good side *just in case* he got rid of Batista, who the mob guys already had in their pocket. To make sure the casinos stayed open, the narcotics kept moving, with the money still flowing, no matter which Cuban prick was in power.

Hadn't worked out that way.

I said, "Guys like us, Jack, aren't cut out for politics."

He shook his head, but he was agreeing with me. "Naw, hell, you're right. We're just the foot soldiers. Who only make the whole fucking thing possible. Where would democracy be without guys like us, Nate?"

"Good question."

"But I made up for it." He leaned in again, deeper, and he went sotto voce: "You would not believe how many trips back to Cuba I made since. This time

helping out *real* freedom fighters. Also . . ." He
thumbed his chest. ". . . I'm the guy who kept Santo
in touch, when that bearded bastard had him cooped
up."

I hoped he didn't mean Santo Trafficante. The Tampa
don who was among the most powerful and nastiest
alive. Or dead, for that matter.

Jack wasn't whispering now, but nobody else could
hear. The band was playing a spirited "Peppermint
Twist," and a tall acrobatic redhead in a green bikini
was doing an equally spirited twist.

"After all Santo done for Castro," Jack was saying,
"he locks him up like a common criminal. Keeps him
in for damn near two years! Without me makin' the occasional trip, Santo wouldn'ta knowed what the fuck
was goin' on back stateside."

Jack was telling me more than I wanted to know. I
had to wonder why anybody would ever trust this
chatty, overactive little screwball with anything more
important than a trip to the grocery store. And then it
better be with a detailed damn list.

I raised a tentative hand, like a schoolkid reluctantly
answering his teacher's question. "Jack—nobody from
the Company sent me to check up on you. Not from the
Outfit, either. Nobody. I really was here to meet a client. I'm not going to tell you who that client is, because it's privileged information."

He thought about that. "Like with a lawyer."

"Exactly."

". . . Okay." The shark eyes blinked in the pasty, five-
o'clock-shadowed face. Then he half smiled, suddenly
cocky. "Anyway, why should the Outfit wanna keep
tabs on me?"

"Why would they?"

"I can be trusted, can't I?"

"Sure you can."

The half smile turned full and feral, just the upper teeth showing as he leaned way across the table. "They were just down to see me, Nate, couple months ago. They're gonna try again."

I could have asked, *Who? What are they going to try?* Instead I said, "That right?"

He nodded, and the smile evolved into something just slightly maniacal. "Last June, they met at the Carousel, top Outfit boys, you don't need to know their names, Nate."

"No I don't."

"They're gonna do what they wanted to back in '47—Chicago finally takin' hold of the rackets in Dallas. And the cops down there, I got them in my pocket now. They love me. They come to my club, their money's no good there."

I just smiled and nodded. I wanted out of here. I felt I'd convinced him that I wasn't here to check up on him for either gangsters or spooks or any combination thereof. And that seemed plenty for one evening.

But had he linked my unnamed "client" to Tom Ellison?

I could not think of a graceful way to ask.

Then I said something that may have been stupid. But it was the best I could come up with, spur of the moment: "Just so you know . . ." And I nodded toward the bar. ". . . I didn't see anything. Not a damn thing, Jack."

"Huh? What?"

Shit.

That high forehead ridged in thought. Then he said, "Could you be more specific, Nate?"

I'd dug this hole. Might as well jump in.

"That handoff at the bar," I said quietly. "To that civilian-looking guy. Amnesia. It's a real problem for me."

And I smiled and winked at him.

Yes, goddamnit, I winked. Sue my ass.

He was studying me, his face as blank as a grape; then he smiled, small and tight, and winked back.

Yes he did.

So I had finally found my exit line when somebody came in. Maybe half a dozen patrons had entered while we'd been talking, but this one looked around (with no apparent interest in the current stripper, a Latin type working "Tea for Two Cha Cha") and quickly spotted us and came over.

He stood there like one of the waiters, a nebbishy guy in his early twenties, maybe five nine, with rain-damp brown hair brushed to one side. Despite the weather, he looked neat in a navy water-pearled Windbreaker over a white shirt and black tie, black narrow-leg slacks, and black loafers. A slightly squashed oval face was home to a high forehead, blue-gray eyes, a slightly prominent nose, and a small, smirky mouth over a cleft chin.

He didn't say anything, just stood there clenching his fists, looking at Jack, raising his eyebrows several times, and giving me a sideways glance, his manner accusatory.

Jack grinned up at the young man. "No, no, no, Lee—this is Nate Heller. He's one of us. It'll be fine. Here—take this chair."

Lee sat next to Jack, gave me a nod. He wasn't sure he wanted me to be "one of us."

That much we had in common.

Jack gestured with an open palm. "Nate, this is Lee. Lee Os—"

"Osborne," the young man said, his voice slightly high-pitched, about a second tenor. He extended his hand. I took it, for a quick, perfunctory shake. The hand was damp, maybe perspiration, maybe rain.

"Nate's that famous private eye you probably read about," Jack said.

I winced. You know how modest I am.

Lee shrugged, shook his head. Then he turned to Jack and said, "We should talk."

"You can talk in front of Nate." Ruby grinned. He was showing off. "Jesus, Lee—you really don't know who this guy is! . . . This is the fixer who put Mongoose together."

*Jesus! How much did this screwy bastard know?*

Lee turned his gaze on me now, the smirk gone, then smiled just a little and half nodded. "Pleasure, sir. Honor. Didn't mean to be rude or anything."

"Hey," Jack said, "you two should get along famously! You're both Marines."

I gave the kid a reassuring little smile. "Semper fi, Mac."

Now Lee grinned. Shyly, but he grinned. "Semper fi. Were you in the big one?"

"Mmmm-hmmm."

"Where'd you serve?"

"Pacific Theater."

Jack whispered, "Silver Star, kid. This character won the Silver Star."

"Shut up, Jack," I said pleasantly.

"Wow," Lee said. His expression was somber now. "It's a real honor, sir. I, uh, served in the Pacific, too, but nothing so . . . so perilous."

"Where, son?"

"Japan." He lowered his voice. "Radar operator. U-2 base."

"Impressive." That put this kid in the CIA's lap. "So you're, uh . . . involved in some of Jack's anti-Castro activities?"

Suddenly Lee's face blossomed into a smile so boyish, he might have been auditioning to play Henry Aldrich. "You might say that."

Jack leaned over toward me, chummily conspiratorial.

"Let me tell you what this kid is good at, Nate. He goes onto these colleges campuses—University of Illinois, today . . ."

"Urbana," Lee put in.

". . . and he puts on this big pro-Castro act. Gives out pamphlets, gets in with any pro-Castro student organizations, looks into any leftist student activities at all, and . . . well, *you* tell him, kid."

The smug smile was back. "Let's just say we come up with a lot of names."

I frowned. "You care about which students lean left?"

Jack interceded. "It's more . . . professors with those kind of leanings."

"Guys, I hate to spoil the party, but I vote Democrat."

Jack squinted at me, openly irritated. "This isn't about Democrat and Republican, Nate. It's about anti-Communist. Come on, Nate! You of all people."

A waiter came over and Lee ordered a ginger ale. That was us—just three clean-cut American veterans avoiding liquor in a strip club.

Lee said, "Mr. Heller, I voted for JFK. I admire him. And his family. They're interesting Americans."

"I'm sure they'd be flattered."

Jack said, "Hell, I voted for him, too. I see he's coming to visit you, Nate."

That threw me. I knew Jack Kennedy a little, though it was his brother I'd been close to, until we had a falling-out last year. I hardly expected a "visit" from either one of them.

I said, "What do you mean?"

"Oh, it's been in all the papers. Week from tomorrow, he's coming to town. Gonna see Army beat the shit out of Navy, at Soldier Field. Be a big motorcade and everything."

"Is that right?" I said, not really giving a damn.

Standing on a crowded street waving at Jack Kennedy was not my idea of a good time.

I nodded at the kid. "Nice meeting you, Lee. Some free advice? I would try not to be led too far astray by this old racetrack hustler."

"Nate, you never change," Jack said, smiling, shaking his head.

I slid out of the booth, then paused next to them before heading out. "You gonna be in town long, fellas?"

Jack said, "Few days. Couple more clubs I wanna check out. Lee's heading back tonight—friend of his has a private plane. Wish *I* rated. Hey! . . . Wish I could afford *her*."

Up onstage, the headliner—Evelyn West, "the Girl with the Chest"—was parading around to "Buttons and Bows" in a cowboy hat, riding a kid's stick horse with her trademarks hanging out.

"Yeah, Jack," I said, heading to the door, putting on my own non–cowboy hat, giving the pair a little salute of a wave. "Just the kind of class act that's perfect for you."

**Fall 1960**

My limited if key role in Operation Mongoose had, ironically enough, begun just a stone's throw from the 606 Club on South Wabash, at George Diamond's Steak House, where businessmen and families dined, with not a stripper in sight.

I was in a back booth with Edward "Shep" Shepherd, and we were studying menus with George Diamond's mug on the cover, his chef's hat diamond-shaped against a deep red that I suspected was CIA-style mind control to coerce customers into ordering their steaks rare. Much as I agreed with that philosophy, those means would never have occurred to me if my dinner companion hadn't been the Agency's top security chief.

Or I should say the Company's. That's what everybody was calling the CIA these days. Back when I'd tangled asses with them, about ten years ago, they were still the Agency. And I'd hated those fuckers, with the exception of Shepherd, who had probably talked his fellow spooks out of tossing me from a high window or poisoning my Ovaltine.

George Diamond's was a masculine expanse of dark paneling, red carpet, and framed paintings of the sad

big-eyed kid and harlequin variety, trying misguidedly
for a taste of class. No matter, it was the taste of char-
broiled steaks—cooked by colored chefs right in the
midst of the place, providing a smoky ambiance where
meat trumped tobacco—that made this the most popular steak house in the Loop.

"The filets here are the size of footballs," I said by
way of recommendation.

Shep made a face. He reminded me of Bobby Morse
in *How to Succeed in Business Without Really Trying*,
only twenty or thirty years older, but with that same
sly gap-toothed charm, his dark blond hair going gray,
his dark-blue eyes getting pouchy. Well dressed—light-
gray Brooks Brothers, dark-gray tie—he was already
on his second Gibson. He always went straight for the
pickled onion.

"I suggested George Diamond's," he said, a touch of
the South in his lilting drawl, "for its vicarious plea-
sures. You will sympathetically note that I will be ordering the broiled chicken. You have *heard* of this
cholesterol horse shit?"

And it *was* "horse shit," as he spoke it—two words.

"I read something about it," I admitted.

"Well, my doctor says I have it. So I'm off red meat.
Least the ol' pecker still works."

"Very glad to hear it, Shep. I'll sleep better tonight
knowing."

He gave me the gap-toothed grin. "If we weren't in a
public place, Heller, I'd suggest you go fuck yourself."

That made me smile. "Well, prepare to get plenty of
vicarious pleasure, Shep, because I'm having the king
filet. You *can* eat salad, can't you?"

"Jesus, Mary, and Joseph, can I have salad."

"Well, you'll want to mix the three homemade dressings they'll bring."

"Homemade? Why, do those colored cooks live in

the kitchen?" He sighed. "Getting older is a bitch, ain't it, Heller? But it does beat the alternative."

Was that his way of reminding me that my life had once been in his hands? Or maybe that it still was?

Not that there was necessarily a point to this meeting. Shep had on occasion—maybe four or five times in ten years—called to let me know he was in town, and to suggest we dine somewhere, and catch up. Since he was a CIA security chief, the catching up was limited to what I'd been doing, of course. That and innocuous family talk.

Hearing from him always seemed friendly enough when he called. Or perhaps Shep thought he might need me someday for something, and even just staying in touch had a hidden agenda.

The phone call at my office this afternoon had seemed innocent, but I'd noticed Shep passing two twenties to the maitre d' to help us avoid the standard half-hour wait at the bar, and that we'd been delivered to a booth way in back.

With the adjacent booth empty.

Small talk saw us through the salad—we were each served half a head of crisp, cold, crushed-crouton-coated lettuce, which I smothered in the three dressings from the carousel. It turned out both his son and daughter were in eastern schools, and his wife was up to her "pretty hips" in charity work. They lived in Alexandria, Virginia. Nobody *really* lived in D.C., he confided.

Shep ate his chicken slowly, dutifully, while watching me make an obscenely large, barbarically rare filet disappear. At one point, he said, "You are cruel man, Nathan Heller. A true villain."

I thanked him, and we both passed on dessert. He was on his fourth Gibson, and I was on my second gimlet, taking it slow. Never paid to be high around a spy.

"Suppose," Shep said, eyes squinty, smile gap-toothy, "you knew what bunker Hitler was hiding in—the *very* one—durin' the war? Would you have hesitated to kill the sumbitch?"

"Hey, if I could climb on board a time machine, I'd push his baby buggy in front of a truck. So what?"

"Well, it's the same with Castro."

"He's a little big for a baby buggy."

Shep looked at that fourth, half-imbibed Gibson, as if noticing it for the first time. He pushed it aside, said, "Coffee?" I said sure, and he flagged a waiter down.

While we waited for the coffee to arrive, Shep withdrew about six inches of cigar from an inside coat pocket, and lighted it up with a match.

"Havana," he said, waving out the flame, grinning around the cigar, letting out fragrant smoke, then Groucho-ing his eyebrows. "I *still* have my sources."

"Do you? This is sort of like school, right? Demonstrating with objects so that the slower kids maybe can follow it?"

He twitched half of his upper lip. "Castro is a pain in the ass. Smuggling out our damn cigars ain't the worst of it. He shut down the tourist trade, which is goddamn dumb. He's a friggin' liar who pretended to be anti-Commie when in fact he's redder than the king of hearts."

"If you had a playing card to hold up, right now? That might help me stay focused."

He lowered his gaze and held the cigar between his fingers like a cornpone Churchill. "But it's a lot worse than that, Nate. It's war. And it's a *just* war. Since that day in January, when that bearded bastard chased Batista out, he's been goin' back on his promises. Renegin'."

"Watch your language, Shep. The chefs will hear."

"No open elections, no sharin' power, no civil

liberties. Shit, this bad boy has got a direct line to the Kremlin, and that gives him all the military might he'd ever need."

"Isn't there a chart or a graph or something to go along with this?"

Shep ignored me. "Nate, Castro's pushing his weight around the Caribbean and Central America. Aiding subversive activities in Panama, Nicaragua, the Dominican Republic, out to undermine our interests any*where* and any *way* he can."

"You convinced me. He's a skunk. Right now I'm thinking maybe *I* should get the check. . . ."

He reached out and gripped my forearm. "Nathan, I need your help. *We* need your help. Your *country* needs your help."

I skipped the Uncle Sam Needs You crack, because suddenly this seemed past clowning, what with that salad and steak curdling in my belly about now.

"You've decided, then," I said, knowing.

Shep let go of my arm. Sat back. Sucked on the cigar. Let smoke out. Nodded. "Bastard has *got* to go."

He didn't exactly seem to be asking for my opinion. But I gave it to him, anyway.

"I'm not against it." I shrugged. "In fact, I'd say I'm for it."

"You have no religious reservations, no moral qualms, about . . ."

"Killing the prick? No. That doesn't mean I want to be involved—not that I can see where a middle-aged Chicago private detective might fit into it."

The coffee arrived. He put sugar and cream in his, I took mine black.

Shep was still stirring his coffee when he said, "We cannot be seen as the perpetrators of such a thing . . . not the Company, specifically, nor our country, generally. This is one of those . . . sensitive, covert operations in which we can't have an Agency or government person get caught."

I sipped coffee. Strong at George Diamond's. "I get that. But I still don't see where *I* come into this."

The blue eyes were unblinking as they fixed themselves on me. "Don't you, Nate? Who, outside of our government, could have the means and the motive to take out the Beard? And limit your speculation to those you might be able to . . . personally approach."

And it came to me.

Before *Life* had tagged me "Private Eye to the Stars," I'd been best known—in Chicagoland, anyway—as Private Eye to the Outfit. It was an exaggeration that flowed from a long-ago favor I had done Al Capone's successor, Frank Nitti.

But the fact was, I'd always made sure to stay in the Outfit's good graces. I had, from time to time, done them favors. And they me. They were unaware that I had, on occasion, been less than a friend to them, as when I worked undercover with Jimmy Hoffa for Bobby Kennedy's rackets committee.

Still, to much of Chicago in the know, Nate Heller was "that mobbed-up private dick." Not a badge of honor, exactly, though it had in several instances kept me breathing.

"We don't want to approach these folks directly," he said.

Yes, he said "folks," Southern boy that he was.

He waved the cigar like a wand. "We need a, uh . . . an intermediary . . . to test the waters. We're aware you are close to Sam Giancana, and to John Rosselli, here in Chicago."

"You have an exaggerated notion of my status with the Knights of Columbus," I said. "Anyway, Rosselli works out of Hollywood and Vegas, these days. And Mooney I generally steer clear of."

Mooney was Sam Giancana, who currently ran the Chicago Outfit.

"Talk to Rossclli, then," Shep said offhandedly. "We understand he has access to the highest levels of the Mafia, nationwide."

That was true, though they didn't use the term "Mafia" much. Rosselli was a kind of roving ambassador for the different national crime families.

"I think I better pass, old buddy," I said.

"I am trying to appeal to your sense of patriotism, Nate."

I gave him half a grin. "First of all, whenever somebody talks about patriotism, I put one hand over my wallet. Second, I vaguely remember already serving in the Pacific."

"You're the perfect person for this job, Nate."

"The perfect patsy, if anything goes wrong. Caught in the middle between two armed camps who hate each other's guts? And I got a son, Shep, remember? In junior high? *He* may want to go to college, too, someday, like your precious progeny. He can't do that if I'm dead. Or, for that matter, if *he's* dead."

"I thought these people stayed away from family."

"As a generality. I'm more attuned to specifics."

Shep let out a weight-of-the-world sigh—also a cloud of Havana smoke. He leaned across the table.

"Nate, all you have to do is play emissary. Once. Test the waters for us. One of ours will take the second meet. Tell them there's $150,000 in it for them, if they take the Beard out."

"Really? You think that kind of money impresses the likes of Giancana or Rosselli? Giancana spills that kind of cash when he's taking a crap with his pants down around his ankles."

Shep frowned at me. Motioned me to keep my voice down. I guess I was getting a little worked up. Did I mention that the adjacent booth had stayed empty? With the restaurant otherwise filled, and probably an hour wait?

"Of course," he said, in a throwaway tone, "there'd be fifty thousand in it for you, plus expenses." He shrugged grandly, drew on the cigar again. "You could use it to put Sam through college."

He didn't mean Giancana. This "Sam" was my thirteen-year-old son.

I didn't say anything. The gap-toothed smile was back—Shep knew money was my weak spot.

And I had to admit (to myself, if not Shep) that there was a stroke of genius in this: who would believe that the CIA would ever be in league with the Mob?

Plus, the Mob had plenty of reason to want Castro dead. He had taken their money and guns for years, when he was a revolutionary, then when he was president, chased them out of their casinos and seized their funds. Organized crime had long depended on their twin sin cities—Vegas and Havana—for their major cash cows. With the Beard gone, maybe the boys could reclaim their Caribbean citadel of sin. . . .

Then something else occurred to me and I frowned. "Wait a minute. I get it. I know what this is about."

This seemed to genuinely confuse Shep. "You do?"

"It's the ol' October surprise. Tricky Dick and Jack Kennedy are neck and neck in the polls about now, and if the Eisenhower administration gets credit for bagging Castro, then Nixon wins the White House."

He was waving the hand with the cigar, making smoke trails. "No, no, Nate, that's not it. . . . I told you, the government doesn't want credit for this kind of operation."

"Oh, but if it's timed right—if Castro is done in, in the waning days of the election, Nixon can get just the boost he needs before Ike's administration gets around to denying having anything to do with something as nasty as political assassination."

Shep abandoned that fine Havana to an ashtray. His gaze was unblinking but not unkind. "You're wrong. This can't happen fast enough to help Nixon. It really can't. This will take weeks, maybe months of negotiation and planning."

I was shaking my head. My arms were folded.

"Nate . . . I know you and the Kennedy boys are *tight*."

I kept shaking my head. "Not Jack. I don't know Jack that well. But I worked for Bobby on—"

"The rackets committee, I know. And I also know that the Outfit doesn't hold that against you. Which means you likely played both ends against the middle, and that's why you're on the grassy side of the ground, at the moment."

At the moment.

"But know *this*," he went on, some edge in his voice, the Southern drawl damn near gone. "The Company doesn't work for any political party. We work for *America's* interests. This plan has the blessing of both Nixon and Dulles, yes . . . but also Jack and Bobby."

"What?"

He nodded. "We brought them in on this. The potential next president and his chief adviser. And they *approve*. They are *not* fans of Fidel, Nate. You can check with Bobby yourself, and see."


I did.

And three days later I was again discussing murder over a linen tablecloth. This time at the Brown Derby in LA.

With Johnny Rosselli.

They called him the Silver Fox, a study in flashing

teeth, manicured nails, and gleaming Italian loafers, looking more like a movie producer than a mob guy with his perfectly cut silver-gray hair and blue-gray eyes against a deep tan. His gray hound's-tooth jacket, like the one Paul Drake wore on *Perry Mason*, went swell with the gray silk tie, a matching silk handkerchief in the breast pocket.

He made a piker out of me in my pencil-striped brown lightweight tropical worsted. But plenty of starlet-age girls batted their eyes at me, too, so maybe I was holding up in my declining years, or looked like a producer myself.

That made sense in the bustling hat-shaped restaurant, with its framed caricatures of stars—our booth was overseen by James Cagney and Joan Crawford, both veterans of crime movies. And all around us, in the yellow glow of derby-shaded lamps, film folks were talking about ideas for movies, but none wilder than our plot.

We disposed of our respective orders—I had corned-beef hash, Rosselli the Cobb salad, both signature Derby fare—as well as any small talk.

I waited till coffee to lay it out for him. I started by saying "high government officials" wanted his help, and that anything said today would be strictly between us.

He started laughing about halfway through my little opening speech.

"Me?" He had a cigarette in a holder perched between heavily jeweled fingers. "You want Johnny Rosselli to get in bed with the feds? Would this be the same feds who are following me wherever I go? Checking with my tailor, my shirtmaker, seein' if I pay in cash?"

"This isn't the IRS, John. It's . . . the Company. You know, the Agency."

That stopped him, but only momentarily. He

shrugged, like a bad impressionist doing Ed Sullivan. "Spooks. Yeah, okay. But that's foreign, ain't it? They're strictly overseas, those guys."

"They're supposed to be. And anyway, this *is* overseas, John. Well . . . ninety miles overseas."

His smile froze, then disappeared. Suddenly he looked his age, which was around mine (every year of which I felt, by the way), as he put the pieces together.

He squinted, trying to bring me into focus. Over his shoulder, the cartoon Cagney was giving me the you-dirty-rat look. "They want *my* help doing . . . ?"

"Just what you think, John. Getting rid of Castro."

His jaw dropped. Actually, it was kind of fun, or anyway amusing, to see a mob guy look flabbergasted like that. A guy who had hung around with top gangsters and who had killed people as casually as you might slap a mosquito, responding to me with the expression of an eight-year-old viewing Mount Rushmore.

I said, "Can you see where this would be of mutual benefit to certain parties that might otherwise seem at odds?"

He placed the cigarette-in-holder in an ashtray. Then he sipped his coffee as delicately as if taking Communion. His hand was shaking—just a little, but shaking.

"Nate . . . you are serious."

"Very goddamn."

He began drumming his fingers on the table, making tiny thumps against the cloth. "How would we go about this?"

"That would be up to you. You would have whatever support you needed, understanding that this is what they're calling a 'black bag' operation. Enlist anybody's aid you like. But it's got to be set up that Uncle Sam had no part of it. And the spooks get . . . 'total deniability,' is the phrase."

He nodded, the gray-blue eyes moving fast, like a guy watching a Ping-Pong tournament. I could almost hear him thinking how he'd like to be the guy responsible for getting Havana back for the boys.

"This ever gets connected to the government," I said, "understand that they will deny it. Just like *I* will deny any role. You say Nate Heller was your contact man, I'll say you're out of your gourd. That you're a fucking liar trying to save his ass. I leave anything out?"

"I think you about covered it," he said. His eyes had stopped moving. He looked vaguely shell-shocked now.

A red-jacketed waiter came and refilled our coffee cups.

I said, "I'm gonna guess you'll need to talk to Mooney about this."

Rosselli nodded and kept nodding for a while, like a bobblehead doll. "That's right. This is not something I can decide. Sam'll need to hear this from you."

I shook my head. "This is my only contact. I'm just the matchmaker, I don't go out on the dates. If you're interested in pursuing this opportunity, I'll give a number to call, and—"

He held up a stop hand. "*No.* This ends here, goes no fucking further, unless you take the first meeting. I don't carry something like this to Mooney second-hand."

I thought about it, but not long. Didn't see I had a choice.

"Okay," I said.

He extended his hand across the table, and I shook it. I could say it was as clammy as death and gave me a chill, but it was just a handshake, firm and dry.

Before we left, he said, "Just so you know, Heller—the only reason why I'm doing this is because I am a good American."

I didn't know what else to say, so I said, "Sure, John."

"I'm an immigrant, and whatever hassle the G has dumped on me, I still got a great life, and I love my country. You can say I'm a corny wop son of a bitch, if you like . . ."

I probably wouldn't.

". . . but I am doing this out of patriotic impulse."

"Cool," I said.

So by early October, I found myself lapping up Miami Beach sunshine outside that sleekly curving giant wedding cake called the Fontainebleau Hotel. I was in swim trunks and Ray-Bans in a lounge-type deck chair next to an ugly gnome called Sam Giancana.

The top mob boss of Chicago had a tan so dark he was damn near black, the hair on his scrawny chest and little pot belly starkly white against that tan. He was in swim trunks, too, plaid ones, and sunglasses that hid his tiny dark eyes, with a narrow-brimmed straw Panama concealing his thinning gray hair. Nothing could be done to disguise the lumpy nose and the unhealed slash that was his mouth.

Giancana had flown down on a private plane with only one bodyguard, who was also the driver of his rental car. He had left the bodyguard behind in one of the five rooms of the top-floor suite where Giancana and Rosselli were staying, with one other guest. I had my own room, to give these peers their privacy and in hopes of exiting as soon as I'd played emissary, leaving them to talk and think about the Company's request.

As for the "one other guest," that was Santo Trafficante, who had brought along three bodyguards, plus a chauffeur/bodyguard, who had driven his boss down from Tampa in a Lincoln with bulletproof windows.

I was not thrilled that another top mobster had joined the party, but was in no position to protest. I assured myself that this Miami Beach meeting would end this mission where I was concerned. Maybe I even believed it.

At any rate, I understood, without being told, why Trafficante's presence was necessary. The Florida mob boss still had the kind of connections in Cuba that would make getting to Castro possible. Also, Rosselli was really middle management, and could only approach a man of Trafficante's stature through another don, like Giancana. Politics and respect made the world go round. The underworld, too.

Right now Giancana was pissing and moaning about Trafficante's bodyguard contingent.

"What is he, a fuckin' pussy? Who the fuck is gonna bother us down here? Anyway, nobody's at war. We're all one big happy fucking family." His laugh was like the sound a guy makes when the doctor says turn your head and cough. "It's all because they tried to take him out when he was cooped up down in Cuba. Ever since then, he's . . . what's that shrink term, Heller?"

"Crazy?"

"Naw! Paranoid. That's what he is, Santo. A paranoid pussy!"

He cackled.

Giancana was on his third tropical drink. It was almost amusing to see a tough top hood like Sam sip at a straw stuck in a pineapple sprouting umbrellas and fruit and plastic.

Almost.

"I brought *one* man, Heller. One *man*! All the way from Chicago. Listen, this hotel here, I love it, this fabulous fucking place . . . they got a small army of hotel dicks. Normally, hotel dicks might give me a pain in the ass. But these guys, they look after us. So what I'm sayin' is, there are bodyguards on fuckin' *staff*.

Why bring a platoon down from Tampa? Look at that one!"

Giancana was not pointing out a hotel security staffer or one of Trafficante's bodyguards, either. Rather he was pointing out—literally—the latest of dozens of good-looking girls in bathing suits, bikinis mostly, that had caught his attention, and caused him to comment loudly on their charms. In a dignified manner, of course, like, "The tits on that one!" and "I would eat *breakfast* off that ass!"

At a little table under an umbrella next to me was Johnny Rosselli. He was in a white hotel terry-cloth robe and sandals and his own Ray-Bans. I believe he felt he had enough of a tan. I could feel the uneasiness coming off him like heat shimmer.

Rosselli caught my glance and said, "Nate? Let's get another round."

His eyes said that what he wanted was a word away from Giancana, who was sipping his fruity drink, and seeing us go said, "Get me another of these Zombie fuckers!"

This kind of language was not generally heard in a public place, where children and families frolicked among the palms, even if the outdoor walls *were* adorned with sculptures of centaurs and bathing maidens. We got a lot of dirty looks, but Giancana either didn't notice or didn't care.

At the thatched bar, Rosselli and I ordered another round, and while we waited, he said, "We got a problem with Sam."

"Oh, I think he's delightful when he drinks too much. Takes the edge off his being a psychopath. That's a shrink term, you know."

"Heller, if he doesn't go up and start talking to Santo, then Santo is gonna get pissed, and I don't mean drunk. It's disrespectful. This whole . . . *enterprise*, it's gonna go belly-up."

"I'm a trained detective, John. I already put that together. What the hell is going on?"

Rosselli sighed. "Momo got word that his Phyllis is, you know, being untrue."

"Momo" was yet another Giancana nickname. "Phyllis" was Sam's mistress, Phyllis McGuire of the singing sisters, and Rosselli referring to her "being untrue" in that ridiculous high-school sense meant that Sam (who was married, by the way) thought somebody else was fucking her.

"Okay," I said. "And *this* is what's putting him in a foul mood?"

"It is. She's in Vegas right now, and word is, she's banging Dan Rowan."

"Of Rowan and Martin. The comedy team?"

"Yeah. Shit, they ain't even that big. I mean, if it was Martin of Martin and Lewis, that'd be another thing."

"Yeah, it'd all be in the family. Also, it would mean Martin and Lewis were back together."

"It's not funny, Heller. She's the love of his life, this broad."

I sighed. "Look, maybe there's something I can do."

Rosselli's eyes sparked with hope. "That would be fucking fantastic, Nate. What?"

I didn't answer him, just took my share of the drink refills and led him back.

"Sam," I said, handing the mobster a carved pineapple full of liquor and doodads, "I heard about your problem."

His nostrils flared. "I don't *have* any problem! . . . Rosselli, you got a big fuckin' mouth, you know that?"

A muscular kid about twenty, with a swarthy cast to his features, was striding over in a small, bulging bathing suit. He was tan, or maybe just Italian.

"Excuse me, mister," he said, looming over Giancana, throwing shadow on him. Despite the words, this was not delivered in a respectful manner.

"Yeah?" Nor was this.

"I don't appreciate the comments or the language. This is a respectable place, and if you don't cut out the filthy talk and the rude remarks about nice girls, you and I are going to have a problem. Do we understand each other?"

You have to give Giancana credit. He waited till the kid was finished with his speech before flying off the deck chair and grabbing him by the neck with both hands and strangling him to his knees.

"I eat little boys like you for breakfast. Get your fuckin' ass out of here before I get hungry! Do *we* understand each other?"

The guy managed to nod, despite Giancana's death grip. Out of nowhere, guys in tan suits and sunglasses had appeared, but they were not interceding for this unfortunate guest. They were serving to keep anybody back. To keep Mr. Giancana from being disturbed.

Giancana let the kid get up. The boy clutched his throat and ran off.

"No running around the pool!" Giancana cackled at him. "No *running*, you little prick!"

When he sat down, I said, "Sam, how about I have one of my guys bug a couple of rooms in Vegas, and see what's really going on? Just for your peace of mind."

"Could you do that for me, Nate? Would you do that?"

"Sure, Sam."

Giancana smiled, sighed in a good way, put the latest pineapple drink aside, and suggested we head on up to the suite, where we finally assembled for a conversation.

Santo Trafficante was a no-nonsense man in his late forties, with almost as dark a tan as Giancana, who he was bigger than at five ten and maybe 180 pounds. The Tampa boss looked like an accountant in his black-rimmed glasses, with his bland features and high forehead and thinning black hair. He was conservatively attired—white short-sleeve shirt, black tie, black slacks. He might have been a waiter.

Giancana did his fellow don the respect of exchanging the swim trunks for a yellow Ban-Lon sport shirt and tan trousers. Rosselli also changed into a sport shirt and slacks, as had I, stopping at my room to do so. We sat at a round poker-style table in the living room area, with windows on the Atlantic.

Soon everybody but me was smoking, cigarettes not cigars. A shoulder-holster bodyguard was serving drinks and snacks. Right now we were all having soft drinks. Since Giancana had to be half in the bag already, I was fine with that.

I figured they already knew the basics, that Rosselli would have filled them in. They listened quietly, with an occasional nod, and no questions. Then I broached new territory.

"What the CIA wants," I said, no euphemisms necessary among this crew and in a room that was certainly free of bugs, "is for a standard gangland hit. They want the bastard blown away. That simple."

Giancana was shaking his head. "Too dangerous, Heller. How the hell do you recruit a shooter for a suicide mission like that?"

"It's been done."

"Yeah, well, even down here, Zangaras don't grow on trees."

Giancana was referring to the cancer-ridden Sicilian stooge who had taken out Chicago Mayor Cermak in nearby Miami, decades before, a mob hit written off as an attempt on president-elect FDR's life.

Trafficante gestured with an open palm. "Something clean. Something neat."

"Nothin' wrong with poison," Giancana offered.

Trafficante liked the sound of that. His smile made him look like a sinister Jack Benny. "Eliminates the need for an ambush." He turned his bland gaze on me. "Don't they have their own scientists, the CIA?"

"Yeah," I said. "They got their Dr. Feelgoods. But they also got their Dr. Feelbads."

"What we need," Trafficante said, "is a pill. Some kind of capsule with a gel coating that dissolves. Something that can be slipped into . . ." He raised his glass of Coca-Cola. ". . . his drink. Or emptied into his food."

I raised my hands, rose. "I'll let you gentlemen discuss this. I frankly only need one thing from you—a decision on whether you're game. I don't need to be privy to any of the details."

"Understood," Trafficante said solemnly.

Giancana grinned. "Got it."

"If it's a go," I said, "you'll meet with a real CIA contact. In the meantime, I need to put something unrelated in motion for Sam."

Giancana liked hearing that. "You go do that, Heller. We'll have an answer for you by dark."

And they did.

It was a go, all right. But that Vegas thing almost got me arrested. The Vegas op my LA partner, Fred Rubinski, lined up got busted for wiretapping Dan Rowan's hotel-room phone.

The good news was Phyllis wasn't playing "Sugartime" on Rowan's skin flute. The bad news was I had to get Shep Shepherd to pull strings to keep the A-1 out of hot water.

There of course was no October surprise for Richard Nixon, just the November one of having the presidency snatched from him by JFK (with some help from Mayor Daley, Sam Giancana, and assorted other patriots).

And when the Kennedy brothers took over the Cuban mission, they only stepped things up—the ongoing attempts to kill Castro by way of poisoned drink, food, and cigars part of an overall scheme to (as Bobby put it) "stir things up on the island with espionage, sabotage, and general disorder."

They dubbed the overall operation "Mongoose."

The baby I'd been midwife to finally had a name.

**Saturday, October 26, 1963**

A couple years back, when I was still living in my fifteenth-floor apartment at the St. Clair hotel, I got a lead from a well-heeled client that urban renewal would soon be leveling an area from Chicago Avenue to near North Avenue. A model high-rise for low-income housing called Cabrini Green was going in at the west end for the residents displaced when the slums got demolished. It was Negro poor now, but once upon a time it had been Sicilians, and Hell's Corner, where violence and murder hung out.

With Old Town starting to clean up its act, I took advantage and picked up an old ripe-for-rehab brick three-story on Eugenie Street, one block north of North Avenue, with a stable-turned-garage in back for my Jaguar 3.8 town car. The main building, typical for this side street, was narrow but deep; there was not much of a backyard, with a garden I'd let go wild.

I lived on the upper two floors, with the ground level turned into a spartanly furnished apartment (with its own entrance) that the A-1 used for visiting clients and as a witness safe house. So when I say *I* picked up the place, I mean the A-1 did. Anything to keep the tax boys guessing.

Historic preservation defined the neighborhood as something special, and I lived in a kind of artist's oasis surrounded by the high-income high-rises along Michigan Avenue and the cheap rooming houses (and the hookers and junkies) of Clark, LaSalle, and Wells (south of Division), with the Puerto Rican ghetto at the west end of Old Town as close by as the Playboy Mansion on State.

I liked Old Town with its newly put in old-fashioned lampposts and narrow, shade-tree-lined one-way side streets that would twist only to end unexpectedly, with their baroque renovated 1800s houses, some frame, others brick, with the occasional walled garden patio; and the wide boulevard of North Avenue, home to offbeat bars and restaurants, quirky boutiques and coffee houses, and even a Buddhist temple. Somebody had fired the starting gun on what they were calling the Sexual Revolution—probably Hefner, come to think of it—and I liked having the singles bars and nightclubs close at hand, where females gave away what used to be for sale in the same Rush and Division Street area.

As for work, if I didn't feel like driving there, the El could drop me within a block of the Monadnock Building, and a bus or cab down LaSalle would do just as well.

Or maybe I was getting nostalgic in my middle age. I was just slightly north of what had been Tower Town, the Greenwich Village of Chicago in the twenties and thirties, where I'd once fallen in love with an actress. And not too far from me was the building where the guy they shot down outside the Biograph Theater had been hiding out. We'll call him Dillinger, for simplicity's sake.

I'm about to give a tour of an aging bachelor's pad,

and you are free to skip it. Just wait till some dialogue
kicks in. On the other hand, as a trained investigator, I
have found that the living quarters of a missing person
or for that matter a suspected felon can tell you everything you need to know about the individual in question.

You entered from the cast-iron porch into the living room, with a jut of closet to the right and a big
open room with off-white wall-to-wall carpet everywhere else. The plaster walls, painted a rust orange, had
select framed artwork to break things up—black-and-
blue-and-white spatter by Jackson Pollock (a Hef-
suggested investment), a small melting clock by Dalí, a
Picasso lithograph called *Still Life,* a big Vegas-theme
oil by LeRoy Neiman (a gift from the artist), and a little
Shel Silverstein cartoon of a dancing nude girl (a gift
from that artist).

The right wall was a white bookcase—my taste, I'm
afraid, running to popular fiction like Harold Robbins
and Ian Fleming, with a dab of Steinbeck and Hemingway, and some nonfiction: Ted White's *Making of the
President,* Sandburg's Lincoln, Shirer's *Rise and Fall of
the Third Reich.* The shelves were deep enough to address an LP collection that was further evidence of my
middlebrow tastes—suspects included Henry Mancini
(*Peter Gunn*), Julie London (*Julie Is Her Name*), Johnny
Mathis (*Greatest Hits*), Dave Brubeck (*Take Five*),
Bobby Darin (*That's All*). No Sinatra (I knew him too
well).

The furnishings ran to overstuffed couches and chairs,
some brown, some green, with throw pillows of those
same colors. My brown-leather recliner, its back to the
bookcase wall, faced the RCA color console TV, with
its whopping twenty-one-inch screen, next to a walnut
Grundig Majestic stereo console (compliments of the
Wilcox-Gay Corp on LaSalle Street, a client). A little

Danish modern teakwood bar tucked itself near the corner where what might have been an abstract sculpture was really the spiral staircase to the upstairs, where awaited a bedroom with the de rigueur round bed plus a home office and a shower.

Beyond the living room was a dining room that didn't get used much, except when parties needed a long table where food could be laid out. A short hall with the other bathroom at left and more closet at right led into the kitchen, a white, fully modern affair vaguely reminiscent of an operating room. I'd been living alone long enough to get good in there. My specialty was breakfast for attractive young women before sending them home in a cab.

Right now I was sitting on a couch next to an attractive woman named Helen Beck, not young. You will be relieved to learn that I was not in a silk smoking jacket. Looked fairly dapper, though, in an olive Cricketeer blazer, light-green Van Heusen button-down with Webley shantung-silk dark-brown tie, and dark-brown Sansabelt slacks. Helen was in a tan jumper over a black turtleneck, a very young-looking outfit for a woman who was around my age, but she pulled it off.

Helen Beck's stage name was Sally Rand, and I'd met her when I was in charge of pickpocket security at the Chicago World's Fair. She had caused a sensation there with her nude fan dance in '33, and a bubble dance encore in '34. She had been a small, pretty, curvy blonde, and still was.

Her long blonde Lady Godiva tresses had always been a wig, the hair beneath a darker blonde now, shorter and worn up. She had lovely blue-green eyes, pretty features with a mouth that was probably too wide by most standards, but not mine.

The indirect lighting in my bachelor pad was subdued—Mancini jazz was playing (*Mr. Lucky*)—so neither one of us looked our age. But she was doing so well at staying youthful that boys were still paying good money to see a woman who was old enough to be their mother dance in the buff.

Helen and I were friends and occasional lovers, though I hadn't seen her for a long time—at least ten years. I sometimes called her Sally, by the way, but usually Helen . . . *always* Helen in bed.

She'd phoned out of the blue, this morning, catching me at the office where I often put in a couple of hours on Saturday. She wondered what I was doing tonight.

"I hope I'm seeing you," I told her.

"Giving you such short notice, Nate. I'm really sorry."

"Are you between marriages?"

"As it happens, I am."

"Then don't be sorry. Where do I pick you up?"

"I'll come to you," she said. "What time? And where are you these days?"

I told her, then said, "Hey, I can probably get us tickets to Second City."

"But that's a popular show, isn't it? Won't they be sold out?"

"Yeah, but I have my ways."

I'd done a job for the comedy coffee house's founder Bernie Sahlins, getting one of his performers, Del Close, out of a jam.

"Make it here by six," I suggested, "and we'll have a chance to grab a bite first."

That all sounded fine to her, and we'd had a fun evening starting with steakburgers at Chances R, where it was a little too loud for us to talk, really. This was followed by several hours of wild humor in the black-walled, table-crammed little venue on Wells that was the Second City.

Helen's favorite sketch: bully kicks sand in weakling's face, bully walks off with weakling's girlfriend, weakling bodybuilds, returns to beach, slugs unfaithful girlfriend, and walks off arm in arm with . . . bully. My favorite part was a musical number, the Mayor Daley Twist: "*Vote for Mayor Daley and we'll throw in for free, A trip to Cal City on your Gaslight Key!*"

Now we were back at my place. Helen was a nondrinker, part of her health regimen, but I'd put a few beers away. I made us coffee and we headed for the couch by the front windows, where we could finally get around to some real conversation.

"So what brings you to town, Helen? You're usually working on a Saturday night."

"I'm between bookings," she said, too casually. She sipped at her coffee cup, then set it on the nearby coffee table. "Actually, I'm here to drum up some business."

"So where are you staying?"

"The Lorraine."

That spoke volumes. The Lorraine in the Loop was known as a stripper hotel. No fleabag, but at four bucks daily . . .

"Not exactly the Drake," she sighed, then forced a little laugh. "Remember that all-white suite I sublet from that flamer? Right out of a Harlow movie, remember?"

"I recall the bedroom. The rest is a little blurry."

She patted my arm. "Were we really that young?"

"You look young to me right now."

"How much have you had to drink, Nate?"

"Not that much."

I kissed her. It was lingering, trying to make up for lost time. We weren't finished when she pulled away.

"I must taste like coffee," she said.

"I like coffee. Who doesn't like coffee?"

"But also cigarettes. I smoke too much."

She smoked at Chances R and at Second City, too, pretty much nonstop. And right now she was lighting up a cigarette with a silver Zippo from her purse, from the coffee table.

"When I started," she said, waving out the match, "the ads said it was good for you. Relaxing."

"Helen, do you need my help?"

The blue-gray eyes flashed. "You mean financially? No. I'm okay. I'm not flush, but . . . the setback I had, it was more career than financial."

"Career setbacks *are* financial."

She let out smoke, then said, "Hasn't caught up to me yet. But it did . . . I admit this particular setback hurt my confidence."

"You're still a very beautiful woman, Helen."

She gave me a sly look. "I saw your picture in *Playboy*."

"The one where I was covering myself with a towel?"

She slapped my shoulder playfully. "No. You weren't identified. You're not famous enough. But you were at some party, hobnobbing at the . . . *what* does he call it?"

She meant Hef, obviously.

"His mansion," I said.

"You and all those young girls. Walking around half naked."

"I swear I was fully clothed."

"Do you date them, these overdeveloped children?"

"Sometimes," I said.

Truth was, for the last several years, Bunnies from the Playboy Club downtown and Playmates in town for their photo shoots and young actresses who flowed through the mansion and the club had been just about the only women I'd dated. One of them, Krista, had been with me six months and would have broken my heart if it hadn't been misplaced some time ago. She was out in Hollywood now, engaged to a producer of Saturday-morning kiddie shows.

"Do they have staples in their tummies, Nate?"

"Why, yes they do. And they're airbrushed all over."

That made her laugh. She drew in more smoke, let it out. "How much work do you do for that guy, anyway?"

Again, she meant Hef.

"The A-1 is on yearly retainer with his company. They get threatened by all kinds of suits and blackmail schemes. We handle it."

"And you two are pals?"

"Nobody's Hefner's pal. He's very self-contained. But we're friendly. Like you saw in the magazine, I go to his parties now and then."

She gestured vaguely around my little world. "And are you happy, Nate?"

"No, I'm miserable. Can't you tell?"

"You might be at that. You're like me—you've been on a hamster wheel of a career forever, and all we've got to show for it is busted marriages."

"Only one busted marriage for me, Helen, and I have a son."

"Yeah, so do I, and a mother to support, looking after him." Her tone softened. "You get to see Sam often?"

"School breaks, including most of the summer. He's coming in a few weeks for Thanksgiving vacation."

"In high school, like my boy, right?"

I nodded.

"So, Nate . . . what *is* your life like, really?"

"It's not bad. I work hard . . . not much investigating anymore, but I'm the face of the agency, and really am kind of famous, Helen. So the clients always want to meet with me first, before I delegate whatever it is they've brought me."

"No more true detective stuff, huh?"

"Now and then. A couple of criminal lawyers locally

like having me handle things personally. And they pay for the privilege. But mostly . . . I'm just another executive."

"With a fuck-bunny pad."

That made me laugh.

"Yeah," I admitted. "With a fuck-bunny pad."

I was used to hearing her talk that way—she could make a stevedore blush. But not me.

Her eyes were traveling. "They *are* some digs."

"They are."

"I bet you get more tail than Sinatra."

"I bet I don't."

"Has there ever been a naked woman in this place over thirty?"

I thought about it. "Not over thirty-five."

"Would you like to see one?"

I didn't have to think about that. I stood and held my hand out to her.

I said, "I haven't shown you my round bed, have I?"

The lighting upstairs was suitably dim for a pair of lovers in their fifties. Sally Rand had never been a stripper—she was a dancer, who with balletic grace gave glimpses of heaven from behind huge ostrich feathers or that diaphanous balloon she bounced around.

So there was no striptease to it, at all. She just pulled that too-young jumper over her head, then the turtleneck, kicked out of her half-heels, and stood there with sheer panties worn over nylons and garter belt, in good Girl Scout be-prepared readiness. A push-up bra emphasized breasts that had gained prominence with the passage of time.

"So far so good?" she said, with a truck driver's grin.

"So far so good," I admitted, and got out of my trousers with as much grace as a guy my age with a raging hard-on could manage.

She slipped off the panties, leaving the nylons and

garter belt on—her pubic triangle was trimmed and dyed blonde, for onstage purposes, but it worked just fine in private. The bra came away and the breasts did not droop at all. Her nipples were erect within aureoles as round and big as a lucky silver dollar.

For some reason, I'd got out of the loafers and trousers and underwear first, and I was standing there still in my blazer and shirt and tie with my dick sticking out between the front halves of my shirt like a coat-tree prong when she came over smiling wickedly and grabbed me, not by the hand, and led me over to the full-length mirror between closets. She did not have a fitting in mind. Or maybe she did.

She looked small, a curvaceous little thing, like the White Rock mineral water fairy, as she got on her knees on the off-white carpet, positioning herself before me. The blue-green eyes gleamed up at me.

"Go ahead and take off your coat and shirt. You look a little silly."

I had no comment. Just did as I was told. I did still have my black socks on, which gave the tableau a stag-film ambiance.

She began to suck me.

I was feeling a little drunk, not from anything I'd imbibed, and would glance down at her, then at her reflection in the mirror, as her pretty face took the length of me in and out of her full, smiling mouth.

She would now and then pause for a remark between smooth, wet strokes. Once she said, "You *like* watching?"

I managed a nod.

"Even though I'm not a little fuck-bunny?"

She had me so damn close. . . .

I said, "Hell you aren't," and we didn't make it to the round bed. I knelt worshipfully and buried my face in that moist muff till she moaned for the real thing. Then fucked her on the floor, on the carpet, where I could still glance over at our reflection where two lovers in their twenties or maybe thirties were humping like crazy, not a couple in their late fifties trying to recapture something, no, two lovers in their goddamn fucking prime.

Still, out of deference to our bones and lower backs—which did not entirely share our enthusiasm, at least at the postcoital stage—we did find our way to the round bed, after she'd made a stop at the bathroom, and got under the covers and she sat sheet-draped with her lovely breasts showing and pillows propped behind her and smoked a Lucky Strike. She'd brought them and the Zippo along, in anticipation of the postgame recap.

"Not bad for a couple of old farts, huh, Heller?"

"Not bad at all. So. What was the career setback?"

"The world's fair."

"What world's fair? Century of Progress has been over a while, you know."

"Not *that* fair. And not the one on Treasure Island at San Fran a lifetime ago. This *current* one."

New York World's Fair.

She blew a smoke ring and watched it dissipate. "There was a lot of talk, a lot of press, about me appearing there. Bringing everything full circle, you know? I was the toast of Chicago, probably the one thing everybody remembers about that fair. And people associated with the new fair . . ."

She gestured grandly, and her tone grew arch as she spoke an official name.

". . . the New York City *Planning* Commission . . . were talking to me about it. I had that booking right in my fingertips when that stuffy prick Robert Moses snatched it away. I wasn't dignified enough. I would . . . 'send the wrong message.'"

"Shame, Sal." She was Sally Rand at the moment, so that's what I called her.

"Now, they aren't even gonna *have* a damn midway! This Moses character may know how to build a bridge, but he knows jack shit about putting on a world's fair. People go to a fair to have fucking *fun*! And the midway is where the most fun is."

"Their loss."

She sighed smoke. "It's gotten a little tough, Nate. I'm still working forty weeks a year, you know . . . mostly one-night stands. But not once in all that time a strip joint. Not *once*—always legit theaters and supper clubs and nightspots. You know, I always travel with half a dozen girls, trained dancers, who do a fan-dance ballet before I come out. Real lookers. I *know* I look good for my age . . ."

"Yes you do."

". . . but it doesn't hurt to give the younger fellas some nice fresh firm female flesh to look at, before I do my classic routine."

"I take it bookings are slow."

"Yeah. Well, that's how this setback hurt. I got a lot of publicity about being considered for the new fair . . . but also a lot for being rejected. Plus, the landscape out there's changed, Nate. Lot of venues dead and dying."

"What can I do?"

The blue-green eyes batted at me. "What about your pal Hefner?"

Suddenly she remembered his name.

"Maybe," she said, anxious, eager, "he'd do a layout on the living legend that is Sally Rand. He seems to have a sense of history. Nostalgia's a big thing lately."

"I don't know, Helen. Hef's all about the girl next door. Sweet young things who wanna fuck you silly. I don't know if he's capable of admitting a woman your age can still be sexually appealing."

She smirked. "You're probably right." Her eyes tightened. "But you know, Nate, this is the thirtieth anniversary of the *real* world's fair. The Century of Progress. Maybe that still means something in this town. Maybe you could . . . could you . . . *think* of something?"

Had I been used? Had Helen—or rather Sally Rand—blewed, screwed, and tattooed her old pal just to get his help in landing some decent Windy City bookings?

Probably, but I didn't give a damn. I was glad to help her out. And I was glad to have that kind of wild sex, at any age.

"I could talk to the guy at the Chez Paree," I said. Michael Satariano was running it for the Outfit, and I knew him pretty well. "And the Empire Room's always a possibility."

She brightened, her smile splitting her face, but in a good way. "Would you do that, Nate? Could you *do* that?"

That was when the sound of somebody banging on the door downstairs interrupted us.

"What the hell," I said.

The banging, clearly a fist hammering at the door, continued. Rattling the hell out of it.

I got out of bed, tossed on my slacks without my shorts, and got the nine-millimeter off the dresser.

"Nate!" she said.

"Just a precaution." That business with Tom Ellison and Jack Ruby had made me paranoid, I guess. "You stay."

I padded down the spiral staircase into the living room, as the banging kept up, but realizing now that whoever it was was not at the front door of my apartment, rather the door below, to the safe house.

Which nobody was staying in right now.

Somebody was assuming that *that* door was mine—it was ground-level, after all, snugged under the wrought-iron stairway that led to my actual entry.

I went to the front row of windows, kneeling on the couch where Helen and I had earlier sat. Drew back the curtain. I could get an angle down on the guy knocking.

And he was still going at it, hammering.

"I *know* you're in there, Heller!" he said, speaking for the first time. His voice was low-pitched and not happy. Also not elegant.

Very quietly, I opened my front door, sticking my head out into the crisp fall night, looking down through the crosshatch of the wrought-iron porch to see if my caller noticed me coming out.

He didn't.

Who he was remained a mystery—the top of his hatless head wasn't all that expressive—but he was yelling at me to answer him, loud enough for me not to be heard slipping down those stairs to come up behind him in my bare chest and bare feet and hastily half-zipped trousers and put the nose of the nine-millimeter in the back of his neck.

"You wanted something?" I said.

". . . Is that a gun?"

"Part of one. The part the fire and bullet come out."

"Are you Heller?"

"Yeah. Who are you?"

He put his hands up. He was just a big dark shape in a big dark topcoat. His hair was black and cropped short and his neck was no bigger around than an oak tree.

In his upraised left hand was an envelope.

"What the hell," I said. "Are you a process server?"

"No," he said. "I'm just an unlucky working stiff who got tagged for an errand on a Saturday night."

"Stop or I'll bust out crying. Who the fuck are you?"

"We ain't met. I'm just a guy that works for a mutual friend. Could I please turn around? And could you
please take that gun out of my fuckin' neck? Please?"

I did, and he did.

He was right—I didn't recognize him. He was just a
goon with a nose that had been broken frequently
enough to call into question it being a nose at all anymore. His eyes were big and wide-set and his mouth
was tiny, giving him an odd look, like the Keane kid
paintings at George Diamond's.

"This envelope is for you," he said.

I took it with my left hand.

Very carefully, still with my left, I opened it, the nine-
mil trained on my guest. He seemed relaxed now, but I
wasn't.

I peeked in at its contents.

"Tickets?" I said.

"Tickets, yeah."

"To the *Bears* game tomorrow?"

The guy grinned, as much as his tiny mouth allowed,
anyway. "That's two tickets, you will note. In case you
should wanna bring somebody with."

"Who sent these?"

"Didn't I say? That's completely my fault. Those are
box seats, Mr. Heller. You'll be joining the boss with
his compliments."

I winced and said, "Don't *tell* me . . ."

But, right before he put his hands down and slipped
by me with a jaunty little salute, he did.

"Mr. Hoffa looks forward to seein' you there."

# 5

## Sunday, October 27, 1963

Late morning at Wrigley Field, sunny but cool with typical gusts off the lake, made for perfect football weather—about sixty degrees, pleasantly crisp, just right for light jackets. But with a noon game, you saw plenty of guys salted around the stands in ties and suits or sport coats, having come directly from church. And everybody, including me, wore a hat.

Everybody but our host, who wore his butch haircut like a badge of honor.

Jimmy Hoffa's box seat worth of questionable cronies—with a row of their overdressed, overly made-up wives at the back of the metal railed-off area—had not come from church. Neither had my date and I.

Her dark-blonde hair up and in curls, Helen was in a navy-blue dress with a white Peter Pan collar with cameo brooch, looking more like a particularly demure sorority sister than the world's most famous fan dancer. I was in a collarless gray McGregor woolen jacket, zipped to my throat, looking like a priest in some very modern, nonexistent sect.

About a dozen of us were snugged into these box

seats, which did not belong to the Teamsters, exactly—
they were courtesy of attorney Allen Dorfman's insurance agency, which handled the union's pension fund.
A slim, solemn, hawkish-looking guy with Groucho
eyebrows, Dorfman was the son of Red Dorfman (not
present), a longtime Outfit crony currently playing on
Giancana's team.

Red's son Allen was one of the few of this little group
in a sport coat, but without tie, shirt open, if button-
down. Most of the rest were in heavy jackets and caps,
attire you might unload a truck in. But for the cap, the
same was true of Hoffa, his coat a lumberjack red-and-
black plaid.

Maybe that was image. Hoffa was an everyman by
nature and inclination, and anybody stopping by the
box to say hello and wave—whether calling him a respectful "Mr. Hoffa" or a too-familiar "Jimmy"—got
a smile and a wave back.

People were always surprised by Hoffa—by his size,
which despite his broad-shouldered brawn added up
only to five feet five and maybe 150 pounds; but also
by his friendliness, since TV watchers had often seen
him mad, like when he battled reporters or alternately
smirked and snarled at Bobby Kennedy in that famous
rackets committee hearing.

Hoffa, who was about fifty, was sitting next to me.
He'd been happy to meet Helen ("Sally Rand! You
was my first crush!") before she got shuttled to the
back row with the wives. Around us was an array of
lawyers and thieves—with considerable crossover—
including not just Dorfman but heavy-set, bespecta-
cled, respectable-looking attorney William Bufalino, a
master at telling Jim what he wanted to hear; and fat,
frog-like Joey Glimco, a scowling Outfit killer turned
labor leader. None of them spoke to me, though Dorfman nodded.

Absent was Hoffa's menacing three-hundred-plus-pound bodyguard, Barney Baker, convicted extortionist, the terms of whose parole prevented participation in anything union-related. Apparently including football games.

"So whaddya think of these seats?" Hoffa asked.

His grin was hard to read. Funny thing about that vaguely Oriental mug of his—the features were those of a roughneck, all right, but there was a pixie sparkle to his eyes and his smile.

I did not play yes-man to Jim, unless it really mattered. If my livelihood, say, or maybe my life wasn't on the line, I played the role of trusted truth sayer.

So I said, "Well, they stink, Jim. If this was the Cubs playing, we'd be in clover."

"I know, I know."

He shook his head like it was a naughty child, the glistening black chopped-off porcupine quills of his butch impervious to the motion or for that matter the wind off Lake Michigan.

"Blame Dorfman," he said, loud enough for the lawyer to hear. "What the fuck are they playin' football for at Wrigley Field, anyway? Do they play basketball in a swimming pool?"

Hoffa had a point. Even if that famous red sign out front was changed from HOME OF THE CUBS to HOME OF THE BEARS for football season, this was still a baseball park. To go gridiron meant reconfiguring the field, leaving us with box seats that were heaven for baseball season—right behind home plate—but hell for football, where those same seats put us at a corner of the end zone. That made the cheap seats—temporary bleachers out in right field—worthy of envy.

Not that I gave a damn. I was not a football fan, neither college nor pro, and I wasn't even a baseball fan, really. And to the degree that I did care about the latter,

I preferred the White Sox, if for no other reason than owner Bill Veeck was a pal who occasionally threw a job the A-1's way.

But I knew enough to follow the game, even if I was already bored. We were still in the first quarter, and the only excitement so far, if you could call it that, was a forty-five-yard field goal for the Bears by Roger LeClerc. But they'd been down at the other end of the field, so whoop de do.

Hoffa seemed in pretty high spirits, though, a small miracle considering he had two major federal indictments hanging over him, one for fraud, the other for jury tampering. I'd seen him twice this year, and both times he had seemed short-tempered and moody, even for him.

Not that I ever really had any trouble with Hoffa.

We had hit it off right from the start—he was Dutch-Irish, I was half Irish, half German Jew. My father had been a West Side unionist whose rabble-rousing activities in Chicago were legend. That sat well with Jim, who often spoke as if he'd known my old man (he hadn't, and my father would have abhorred Hoffa's shady dealings).

So Jim had never suspected, a few years back, that I was working as a double agent for the rackets committee. Well, he had a good reason for that: he *thought* I was working as *his* double agent.

I know, I know . . . it's hard to believe he actually figured he could buy off a Chicago detective. . . .

Still, there was much to admire about James Riddle Hoffa. His background had been (to use one of my old man's favorite expressions) rougher than a cob, his coal miner father dying young, his hardworking mother making ends meet by polishing radiator caps in an auto plant.

As a teenager Jim pulled down fifteen bucks a week

unloading trucks for a grocery chain. But it pissed him off that he didn't get paid for the time he spent waiting for the truckloads of fruits and vegetables to arrive . . . so he organized a wildcat strike. He was sixteen. Soon he was on the Teamsters payroll where, obviously, he still was.

Say what you will, the little bulldog was one effective union leader, negotiating any number of generous contracts for his members. But his ties to the mob—not to mention the Republicans—had made him a target for the Kennedys. And soon Jack and particularly Bobby became this working-class Ahab's white whale.

And, funny thing—he was theirs.

"Booby's entire fucking law experience," Hoffa had once ranted to me, "Booby" being his contemptuous way of referring to Robert Kennedy, "was servin' as counsel on that one fucking candy-ass committee! And his *brother* appoints him attorney goddamn general? Hypocritical little silver-spoon shits! And their *old man* was the biggest bootlegger of 'em all!"

Indeed, Bobby's first big action as AG was to start up the "Get Hoffa Squad." More than twenty prosecutors and investigators were on staff full-time to make cases against Hoffa, and not just recent offenses, but going back and opening up cases the Eisenhower administration had dropped.

What I knew that perhaps Hoffa did not was that the "Get Hoffa Squad" was merely part of Bobby's overall campaign, Operation Big Squeeze, aimed at the Mafia and their allies.

Like the Teamsters.

"You know who has good seats?" Hoffa asked.

"No. Who?"

He wiggled a finger toward the fifty-yard line. "That pal of yours. From Milwaukee."

Hoffa turned his face to the field, but I kept looking

his way. The Teamster boss was still smiling, if faintly. Around us, his guys were drinking beer and gnawing hot dogs and enjoying the game despite the shitty seats, and the women in their private row were chattering, ignoring the game, asking Sally Rand lots of questions, Helen obviously charming them. A gust of wind came up and I was chilled but I'd been chilled before the gust.

*So—Ruby really had made me as Tom Ellison's chaperone.*

And Jake or Jack or whatever the fuck you want to call him had reported back to somebody who had got word to Hoffa—how many steps that had taken, how many somebodies, I had no idea.

But Hoffa *knew*.

From the moment I'd looked in the envelope his goon had delivered last night, I had wondered if the job for Tom was why I'd been invited today, hoping of course that it wasn't. That Hoffa had happened to be in Chicago, where after all the fraud case was to be tried, maybe here to confer with his legal team, and thought of his old Chicago buddy Nate Heller, and sent a couple of tickets over, and . . . not really. My gut had told me Hoffa *had* to know.

Just the same, having him look at me and so casually mention Tom, sitting on the fifty-yard line, scared the crap out of me.

"This game sucks green donkey dick," Hoffa pronounced. "I gotta pee. How about you, Heller? You probably gotta pee, too."

"Now that you mention it."

I slid out of the seats and moved to the opening in the railing, stepped out and then waited for Hoffa, because he would, of course, lead the way. Up the steps he went, often pausing and shaking hands, even stopping to talk, a confident, even cocky little figure in his workingman's jacket, high-water pants, and white socks. And every guy he shook hands with winced, which did not surprise me, because that banty rooster had a grip like a vise.

Me, I just followed along like the flunky I was.

At the top of the steps, at the mouth of the inner stadium, he said, "Let's go to my office," and then I was following him down the high-ceilinged cement walkway, footsteps echoing, until we were inside a large men's room with its troughs and stalls. You would think the game was exciting, because right now no one else was in there, just the president of the International Brotherhood of Teamsters.

And me.

We stood in the middle of the echoey chamber, but we didn't echo. He kept his voice down, and I did the same, in case anybody came in, and more than a few did, during our brief discussion. About half of them seemed to recognize Jim, but nobody had the nerve to interrupt; one even backed out. Anyway, you don't ask for an autograph or shake a celebrity's hand in the john.

This occasional company, however, did not take any of the edge out of Hoffa's voice.

"This is where you explain yourself," he said. He was smiling, but it was the smile of a father meeting his daughter's date at the door an hour after curfew.

"Jim," I said evenly, "you're gonna have to be more specific."

The smile disappeared and he seemed to be trying to swallow both his upper and lower lip. His fists were clenched. Not a good sign. At all.

Then he said, "This PR guy from Milwaukee, what's his name, Elliot, Ellison, what the fuck was you doing at the 606 with him Friday night? *That* specific enough for you?"

It was.

Now I had the choice of softening and shaping the truth into something that made it more palatable. But then we were in a big men's room, redolent of piss, shit, disinfectant, and urine cake, where nothing palatable got served up.

So I gave it to him fairly straight. "Tom's an old friend of mine. He said he'd been doing some PR work for you and some friends of yours. He's an honest businessman, and when one of your guys asked him to make a money drop . . . he got understandably nervous."

"Why?" Indignant. Nostrils flaring. Fists clenched again. "Does he think we're a bunch of fuckin' crooks?"

That was like Polly Adler saying, "What, do you think I run a whorehouse?"

"It just wasn't . . . business as usual," I said, gesturing with an open, soothing hand. "He's a straight citizen, Jim. He doesn't usually go into strip clubs passing an envelope to the likes of Jack Ruby. Who, let's face it, is a mobbed-up little piece of shit."

Rather than make Hoffa angry, this actually settled him down. The truth, oddly, did that sometimes. I had often been in a room of his sycophants and caught the moment in Hoffa's eyes where he got fed up with having his dick stroked.

The union boss hunched his shoulders like Jimmy Cagney in an old gangster movie—a familiar tic of his. "So, he come to you? For help."

"Yes."

"And you didn't call *me*, or one of mine?"

"What for? Your guy didn't hide the fact the envelope was full of money. Probably ten grand. Tom was asked to hand it over to somebody in a strip club a block away from Skid Fucking Row. Tom and me go way back. He thought he might need a bodyguard. Wouldn't you think the same?"

Hoffa was squinting, considering that. "Like . . . should some asshole try to mug him or such shit."

"Exactly."

He raised his chin, looked down at me, which was tricky at his height. "You saw the transaction go down?"

"I wouldn't call it a transaction, Jim. Tom did what he was told—he handed off the envelope to Ruby. And he left."

He pointed at me with a blunt-tipped finger. "And your friend Tom—did you tell him later that you knew Ruby, and what his name was and so on?"

"No! Why would I? All Tom wanted was to do you a favor and not get his ass handed to him, in the process. What's wrong with that?"

Hoffa thought about it.

"Nothing," he admitted.

I shrugged. "It's a coincidence that the guy picking up the envelope happened to be Ruby, who I happen to know."

"Happen to know *how*?"

"We go back to the West Side. Way back. He grew up with Barney Ross and me. His real name is Jake Rubinstein."

There was no question about Hoffa knowing Ruby. His box-seat pal Allen Dorfman's father, Red, had taken over the Scrap Iron and Junk Handlers Union back in '39, after that shooting Ruby had helped cover up. Right when the Teamsters stepped in and took over.

Hoffa said, very low-key, "At the 606, did you speak to your old West Side buddy?"

Surely he knew I had.

"Yeah. Sat and talked with him a while. Nothing about the envelope he'd been handed. He didn't indicate he knew I'd seen the handoff. Or even suspected my being at the club had anything to do with Tom."

"What did you talk about?"

"This and that. Discussed which strippers he might want to book in his club. He has a club in Dallas, you know."

"And that's it?"

*Should I tell him?*

I told him. "Funny thing was . . . he mentioned Cuba."

His eyes tightened. "Cuba?"

"Yes . . . you know . . . how certain people have been helping certain other people with certain Cuban problems. . . ."

Hoffa grunted something that was not exactly a laugh. "This Mongoose deal."

I hated that he knew the name of it. But I wasn't surprised. He'd bragged to me before about helping Uncle Sam try to take Castro out. And he'd complained that "Booby" had cut him no slack for his patriotic efforts.

He cocked his head, like a deaf guy trying to hear better. "So you just talked to Ruby a while, shot the shit, nothing else . . . memorable?"

"Some kid stopped and talked with us," I said, figuring I better not leave anything out.

"This kid have a name?"

"Osborne, I think."

Hoffa shrugged. "Don't mean nothing to me."

Some guy came in and entered a stall. We moved to the other side of the chamber—for privacy, not to avoid potential unpleasant odor.

Hoffa's eyebrows went up, his expression indicating that if I hadn't been entirely straight with him, now was the time.

"Heller, you're saying nothing you talked to Ruby about had anything to do with your Milwaukee friend. With the . . . favor he done us."

"Nothing."

Ruby talking to me at all meant he'd suspected I'd been there to back Tom up, or Hoffa and I wouldn't be having this conversation. But I didn't point that out.

I went on: "Jake always did run his mouth. He was bragging to this kid that I'd been a Marine hero, that kind of bullshit. Showing off. That's how Cuba came up. Telling this kid how I was the guy that first put things in motion."

A john flushed. A guy came out, used the sink, left.

Hoffa was studying me. "You're saying . . . this was a straight-up bodyguard job. Your friend had all that cash, got jumpy about it, and wanted some protection. That simple?"

"That simple. Jim, I don't know why Tom gave that envelope to Ruby, and I don't want to know. Not interested. And neither is Tom."

". . . Okay." He did the Cagney shoulder hunch again. "Might as well piss while we're here."

"Might as well."

So we stood at the metal trough and pissed . . .

. . . though I was a little surprised I could, figuring it had already been scared out of me.

The game never turned into anything special, but the Bears did win—16 to 7. That made seven wins and one loss.

Still in contention.

That evening Helen and I sat in a booth at Pizzeria Uno and shared a small tomato pie.

"How long will you be in town?" I asked her.

We were both eating slices with forks—the stuff was just too formidable to do otherwise, half the sauce on the North Side piled on the little pie, on top of just as much cheese.

"I was thinking maybe a week," she said, with a little shrug. "If you can get me meetings at the Chez Paree and Empire Room, and something comes of it . . . a little shorter stay. Otherwise, I plan to make the rounds of the other spots." She made a face. "And there's always the strip joints."

"Well, even so, we can't have you staying at the Lorraine."

"Oh, I don't mind it, Nate, really. Lot of nice girls there."

"Why don't you bunk in at my place? You can take the client apartment downstairs. You'll have your own key. That way you can come and go as you please, and spend as much time with me as both our schedules allow."

"That's generous. That does sound nice."

"And taking all these cabs, you'll go broke. The A-1 has a small fleet of half a dozen cars. You can have one for the week. There's room for it next to my Jag in the old horse stable I use for a garage, behind my building."

Her eyes were moist. I thought for a second there this hard-boiled dame might cry on me.

"Nathan . . . this is very sweet of you. I hope I can repay you in some way. . . ."

"I don't bother with straight lines that obvious," I told her.

We were having coffee when she brought Hoffa up.

"He surprised me," she said.

"Shorter than you figured."

"That, and he . . . seemed so nice. So affable. Just a regular fella, although, you know . . . larger than life, no matter *how* short he is. I noticed he didn't drink. There was beer and booze flasks all around, but all he had was Pepsi."

"He's a teetotaler like you, Helen."

She sipped her coffee, thinking. "Tell me, Nathan—is he a bad man?"

"Depends."

"Explain."

"I think he genuinely cares about the working stiff. But he's also fine with lining his own pockets, and if you're his enemy? Let's just say some of those nice women you were sitting gabbing with, this afternoon, have husbands who have committed some of the most vicious murders Chicago has ever seen. And Chicago has seen some."

She lifted her eyebrows. "Well, they say he's a crook, and I don't have anything good to say about unions myself, so I can't say any of that surprises me."

But she had surprised me. "You're against unions? An old bleeding-heart FDR liberal like you?"

She waved a hand like a child bidding good-bye. "Never had a union be anything but trouble for me, on the road. The entertainment unions either side with the management, or tell me I can't play someplace 'cause it's blacklisted, or side with one of the little dancers I travel with on some pay dispute."

"Sounds like showbiz has taken its toll."

Shaking her head, the piled-up blonde curls bouncing some, she said, "No more bleeding heart for me, Heller. Strictly a free-enterprise girl these days. Hell, Kennedy was the first Democrat I voted for since Roosevelt. I *like* seeing his brother go after a bent union."

I gave her a kidding grin. "If you're turning so reactionary in your second childhood, Helen, why didn't you vote for Tricky Dick?"

She shuddered. "Didn't you see the debates? All that sweat and five-o'clock shadow. Nixon looked like half the fucking club owners I deal with."

That made me laugh.

"Anyway," she said, "Jack Kennedy is cute."

"You make me so proud we gave you girls the vote."

"Still a wise guy. You haven't changed much."

She shook her head, smiled, and began fishing in her purse for her cigarettes.

"Your life, Nate, even now, it's still like something out of, I don't know, Sam Spade. Last night, when you grabbed your gun and went running outside, bare-chested? I was frightened, Nate, but also . . . excited. Reminded me of the world's fair days. Kind of thrilling to know a man like you."

"Ah, well, everyone thinks so."

A tiny laugh. "Even after all these years, you still live on that dangerous edge, don't you?"

"Not by choice."

A bigger laugh, as she lit up a Lucky. "Well, *certainly* by choice. You don't *have* to hang around with people like Jimmy Hoffa."

"Really?"

"Really."

I grinned at her. "Okay, smart girl. Those tickets last night? You think they were a gift?"

"Weren't they?"

"No, Helen. They weren't."

"What were they, then?"

"A summons."

We slept together that night, with no interruptions from any dese-dem-and-dozer wanting to kill me or offer me tickets to a sporting event, either. My world seemed peaceful, damn near idyllic with Helen back in my life (and bed), an existence not at all dangerous, and it only took me about half an hour before I got to sleep wondering what it was about Jack Ruby and that packet of cash that had made me the object of Jimmy Hoffa's Sunday-afternoon attention.

Monday, October 28, 1963

At the first hint of a ring, I snagged the receiver off the bedside phone before Helen could be disturbed. The few bedroom windows had venetian blinds, which were drawn nice and tight, making it easy to sleep in, and that's what we were doing.

Not an infrequent practice of mine, after a late night out with a lady—a privilege of age and rank. Unless I had an appointment, I didn't bother going in to the A-1 till around ten, and the only thing scheduled on this Monday was a staff meeting at 2:00 P.M.

I felt awake enough, if sluggish after an excessive nine hours—the clock radio read 9:45 A.M. But my thick, whispered hello—actually "Yeah?"—must have been a tip-off.

A familiar voice on the other end of the line said, "Don't tell me you're still in bed."

"Gimme a second."

In just my boxers, I carried the phone on its long cord across the room, out of consideration for the slumbering Helen.

"I'm an executive, Dick. I go in to work when I

please. Anyway, I didn't know I had to clear it with you."

Dick was Chief Richard Cain of the Cook County Sheriff's Special Investigations Unit.

"Well, rise and shine and get over to the Pick-Congress, toot sweet. Room 318."

"Any special reason?"

"No reason. Maybe I'm just in the mood for a romantic liaison with your ancient ass. Also, there's a murdered guy with your business card in his wallet."

"Oh." Now I was wide awake. "Be right there."

I roused Helen just enough to let her know I had to leave for a while. We planned to move her out of the Lorraine Hotel this morning, into the client's apartment downstairs; but now that might have to wait. Business.

She just nodded and nestled into her pillow and didn't stir at all as I quickly shaved and showered and got into a two-piece gray worsted by Louis Goldsmith. Wanted to look my best for Dick Cain, and whoever this dead body was.

I had a sick feeling I knew the answer to the latter already, or maybe that was just the slightly stale doughnut I washed down with orange juice. Anyway, I didn't remember giving Tom Ellison my business card, so it couldn't be him. Shouldn't be him.

But beyond that possibility, I had no idea who this stiff might be.

And I hadn't bothered to ask Dick Cain what a sheriff's man was doing on a city homicide—I figured I'd find out soon enough. My hunch was Dick was looking after my best interests, which was something he habitually did.

Dick had been my inside man at the Chicago PD for a number of years, until he quit to go into private practice himself. For a while he was in Mexico City, doing Christ knows what, but when he got back to Chicago, I used him for various A-1 work, mostly lie-detector testing, which he was damn good at. He had studied with my old friend Leonarde Keeler, who was only the guy who invented the lie box.

For the last year or so, Dick had been chief of the SIU for Sheriff Richard Ogilvie, a reformer who made a frankly odd fit with Dick. I had no illusions about the fact that Dick wasn't the most honest copper in town—on the PD, he had played bagman, delivering mob graft to other coppers—but he was also a smart, tough detective who had an admirable arrest and conviction rate.

Right now, the SIU's stated mission was to crack down on vice in Chicago and Cook County, and I had no doubt Dick was using that position to alternately line his pockets with payoffs and make splashy arrest headlines.

Understand that not every cop in Chicago was bent. But understand also that I had no real use for an honest cop in my life. A guy like Dick Cain, with some Outfit ties, on the inside of law enforcement, made a very handy resource for Nate Heller. And if I talk about myself in the third person again, you have my blessing to slap me.

Anyway, I accepted bent cops as a part of Mayor Daley's fabled City That Works. The system may have been riddled with corruption, but things got done, and the voters kept putting the same aldermen—and for that matter mayor—in charge.

I drove the little Jag into the parking ramp next to the Pick-Congress Hotel, across from the Auditorium Theatre, and went in a side door and used one of the corner stairwells to go up to the third floor.

Moving down a narrow, nondescript corridor, I passed a black-and-tan team of homicide dicks,

Mulrooney and Washington, about to knock on a hotel room door. They looked bored.

The Negro cop nodded at me and jerked a hitchhiker's thumb, indicating I was wanted farther down the hall.

The white cop smirked and said, "Your brother's waiting for you, Heller."

That was police humor pertaining to the common department knowledge that Cain and I were tight, but also indicating that we bore each other a faint resemblance.

Despite their obvious preference for me to be somewhere else, I paused for conversation. "What are you ladies up to?"

"Canvassing the hotel guests on this floor," redheaded Mulrooney said. If he'd been any more Irish-looking, he'd have worn a green top hat and been knocking with a shillelagh.

Washington shook his head and said, "Hopeless goddamn task, seeing who mighta seen what, last night. They're either checked out or off doing business somewhere."

"This is one of those dirty jobs you hear so much about," I said pleasantly, "that somebody's gotta do."

Then I gave them a little wave and moved on, sensing their exchange of *who-needs-that-asshole* glances behind me.

Two uniformed officers were posted at the door to 318. I introduced myself, and the older of the pair said I was expected, the younger opening the door for me, and shutting it behind me.

The room was small and, with its pale-green wallpaper and mid-fifties Sears and Roebuck "modern" furnishings, damn near as nondescript as the corridor. The Pick-Congress had a fancy lobby but God help the guests.

Particularly this one.

Tom Ellison—*goddamnit!*—was on his back on the bed, sprawled diagonally, feet over the edge, a stiff so stiff it was like he was standing at attention lying down. The bed was made—he was on top of the spread, the pillows still tucked under.

He was in a white T-shirt and white boxers with blue polka dots and dark-brown socks, with an apparent puncture wound in his chest with the T-shirt bearing minimal rusty-brown dried dribbles of blood. His eyes stared upward, his expression saying, *What the fuck?*

I knew the feeling.

"Full rigor," Dick Cain said from the bathroom doorway, where he was lighting up a Dunhill cigarette. "You missed the police photographer."

Dick was in his early thirties, five eight or nine and about 160 pounds, a nearly handsome guy who might be taken for the 1940s Dana Andrews, from a distance. He wore black-rimmed glasses over green eyes, the left of which was milky, and his reddish-brown hair—the same color as mine—was worn just long enough to comb. His suit was charcoal, his tie silver gray, typical of his standard conservative look. You might have mistaken him for a Harvard Business School grad.

I asked, "Coroner?"

"We're waiting. But the homicide team thinks he's been dead since sometime last night, or very early morning hours."

"Discovered how?"

"Housekeeping. There was no DO NOT DISTURB on the door. Maid knocked at around eight-fifteen, got no answer, figured the guest had either checked out or gone off to some business meeting . . . and found a mess she wasn't qualified to clean up."

"Could have been messier."

"Yes it could."

He came over, and we finally shook hands. I hadn't seen him in a couple of months, so the ritual seemed called for.

"Client of yours, Nate?"

"I was a client of his. Former client, actually. He was a press agent out of Milwaukee."

"Thomas Todd Ellison, yeah. His wallet was here, but no money in it. Found it by the bed, right in front of the nightstand. Homicide boys already put it in an envelope, but there's still enough evidence around here to justify a nickel tour, if you like."

"If you can make change for a dime," I said glumly.

He moved nearer the bed, and I fell in alongside him. "Let's start with how your friend got himself killed."

"Did I say he was my friend?"

"Your business associate." Dick exhaled smoke, gestured to the john behind him. "Found a Trojan wrapper on the floor—just missed the wastebasket in there."

"Okay."

"Over at the sheriff's office, we consider that a strong indication sexual intercourse took place."

"You guys are just that sharp."

"Now take a look at the nightstand."

I did so—two hotel water glasses with the Pick-Congress crest, both with amber liquid residue, one with lipstick smudges. Nearby a little ceramic ashtray sported three filter cigarette butts, also lipstick-marked.

Falling in next to me, Cain said, "A trained detective like me adds all this up to there being a woman in the room. My guess is not his wife."

I gave him a sharp glance. "Has Jean been notified?"

"You *do* know this isn't my case? That I work for the sheriff? I would imagine she hasn't been notified yet. Chicago PD policy on an out-of-towner DOA is to contact the local police, so that somebody from the Milwaukee department can deliver the news personally. Not cold, over the phone. He *was* your friend, wasn't he?"

I sighed, nodded. "Not a buddy. You can see I'm not shedding any tears. Not like the one I'd shed for you, Dick."

This earned me a wicked half smile. "Single solitary tear? That's what I'd rate?"

"I think a tear would cover it." I nodded to the grotesque display that was all that remained of Tom Ellison. "But this was a nice guy, an honest guy, particularly compared to the two of us . . . and I don't make him for the type who'd have a doxy up to his room."

"'There are more things in heaven and on earth, Horatio,'" Cain said, "'than are dreamed of in your philosophy.'"

"That's 'dreamt,' Dick, and fuck you."

He laughed a little, not overdoing it. He spread an arm, like a ringmaster introducing a high-wire act, the hand with the Dunhill making smoke trails.

"Well, Nate, let's look at the evidence. Over on the dresser, that's an ice bucket and an empty bottle of champagne. In the john, there's a rubber wrapper. On the nightstand, lipstick traces on a glass and ciggies. At the foot of the bed, trousers apparently taken off hastily, dumped. On the bed a guy in his shorts who is dead and not of natural causes."

"What story does that supposedly tell?"

"The lead homicide dick, Mulrooney, thinks your friend had a girl up to his room . . . not a very nice girl . . . and they shared champagne, and they played some night baseball, after which Mr. Ellison nodded off to sleep."

"So a pickup, then, maybe in the hotel bar. Not a call girl?"

"Right. A hustler who plays lonely secretary or stranded stewardess or whatever the hell, and they go upstairs for nookie, have some, and cuddle up."

"And while Tom dozes, in postcoital exhaustion, the not-nice girl is helping herself to his wallet, and then Tom wakes up . . ."

". . . and is displeased, and gets physical, and his little guest grabs an ice pick, and punches his time clock."

I thought about that. It stunk, but I didn't say so.

He read me, though: "Hey, it's not my theory. It's just what the homicide boys came up with to close out the case in ten seconds."

"Least they're making an effort. Have they bagged the ice pick?"

"Wasn't here."

"Then what makes them so sure an ice pick was the murder weapon?"

Dick smirked at me, the milky eye taking the edge off his otherwise handsome face. "It's what we call in the trade an educated guess, Nate, based on a couple of things. . . . Don't tell the coroner's guys I did this."

He leaned in and over and lifted Tom's T-shirt, having to tug it up some to get past—and expose—the fatal wound. It was a small puncture in the midst of blondish chest hair with very little blood—a stab right through the sternum. Dick let me study the wound a while, then pulled the T-shirt down back into place.

"Add to this," he said, "the fact that every ice bucket in this hotel is delivered with an ice pick. Only here we have an ice bucket, but no pick."

"And they figure she took the ice pick with her, when she skedaddled, to dispose of."

"Isn't that what sewer drains are for?"

From the door, a mellow, world-weary voice intoned, "Excuse me, gentlemen—would you mind clearing the crime scene while I have a look?"

The slender, somber, narrow-faced, retirement-age guy in glasses—tortoiseshell frames—apparently knew Dick Cain, and assumed I was just another cop. After all, plenty of cops in Chicago could afford a Louis Goldsmith suit.

"Not at all, doc," Cain said. "I'm just a kibitzer from the sheriff's department. Heller here has confirmed identification of the body."

The doctor nodded at us and came in. He had a black medical bag handy. Like it would do Tom any good.

I said, "Doctor, uh . . . ?"

"Owens," he said. "Clarence Owens."

We skipped the handshake ritual. He was standing just inside the door with the Gladstone bag fig-leafed before him, held in both fists.

"Dr. Owens," I said, "when you run the postmortem I'd like to know what the angle is on that wound. Chief Cain here thinks it's an ice-pick wound."

Owlish eyes blinked behind the glasses. "I don't recognize you, detective."

"I'm Nate Heller."

"Oh. *Nathan* Heller. The private detective."

"Forgive the dumb question, doctor, but can you tell whether the deceased had sex recently before he died?"

He went over near the bed and the corpse. "Well, there seems to be dried semen residue on the front of his shorts."

"So he *did* have sex shortly before he died."

His tone and expression were dry as day-old toast. "A lot of men in hotel rooms alone ejaculate, Mr. Heller."

Cain offered, "There's a *Playboy* on the dresser."

"Some of us read it for the articles," I said.

"But," the doctor put in, "we *can* check the deceased's pubic region for female pubic hairs and secretions."

Cain said, "We believe a condom was used. Wrapper found on the john floor."

"Even so, there might be evidence of intercourse. Still, it's an inexact science."

"Sounds pretty exact to me," I said.

The doctor shook his head. "We don't know that the deceased didn't bathe or wash himself off, after having sex."

"The homicide detectives think a prostitute did this, and he would probably have waited till she left to wash up."

The owlish eyes were unimpressed. "We can't know that. But I can see that you have an interest in this case, Mr. Heller. When I have anything, I'll give you a call at your office."

"If I'm not in, ask for Lou Sapperstein."

That got something resembling a smile out of him. "I remember Lou from the old days. Is he still working?"

"When he feels like it."

"Sure, Mr. Heller. Glad to. Friend of yours, the victim?"

"Business acquaintance. A very nice guy."

"In my job, whether they were nice or not is, sadly, seldom relevant. You'll be hearing from me, Mr. Heller."

I thanked him, and then I suggested to Dick that we get out of the way of the investigators whose job this actually was. He agreed.

Soon we were sitting in the Coffee House, the blandly modern Pick-Congress eatery off the fancy lobby. A no-nonsense waitress with a lady-wrestler demeanor immediately tried to force coffee on us, but we were spoilsports—being strictly an after-dinner coffee drinker, I had iced tea; and Dick, who I'd never seen touch java, had a bottle of Coke with a glass of ice. She was not happy with us—the lunch crowd would be here soon, and we were taking up a booth.

"So," I said, "my business card was in his wallet."

"That's right. Had you seen Tom Ellison lately?"

"I had, but it was strictly social," I lied. "We had a beer at the Berghoff Friday afternoon, and just caught up with each other. I think maybe he was fishing for some business."

"But in a sociable way."

"That's right. I hadn't used him for publicity for a couple years—why go to Milwaukee, when there are so many good people here at home?" I squeezed a lemon slice into the iced tea. "Will I be hearing from those homicide dicks? Will they want a statement?"

"Not unless I advise them to." He shrugged. "That guy Mulrooney, he knows you and me are Siamese twins. He saw that business card and gave me a call, and I came right over. I just wanted to make sure you weren't jammed up in this thing, somehow."

"I appreciate that."

He nodded, *no big deal*. "Are you going to look into it?"

"I don't think so, Dick. But I would like to know a few things. . . ."

"Like the angle of penetration. I'm talking about the ice pick, of course."

"Of course." My tone was casual, matter-of-fact. "And I'd like to know what the latent print guys have to say."

He laughed once, a harsh blurt. "You really think some hustler left her fingerprints? Surely she rubbed everything down."

"You'd think so, since damn near every hooker and B-girl in town has an arrest record with prints on file. But in that case, wouldn't she clean the lipstick off that glass, and flush the lipstick butts, too?"

He waved that off. "In too big a hurry to get the hell out, probably."

"Which means, if she exists, she *would* leave finger-prints. Too panicky to be bothered with niceties."

Cain thought about that. Filled the rest of his glass of ice with Coke—it was one of those new ten-ounce bottles.

"And," I said, "how about that DO NOT DISTURB hanger?"

"*What* DO NOT DISTURB hanger?"

"Exactly."

It came to him. "You mean, if Ellison had been entertaining, he'd have hung one on his door."

"You would think. And this supposed doxy turned killer, if she were taking time to tidy up, wouldn't she have left the DO NOT DISTURB on the knob, exiting? To keep the deceased undiscovered for as long as possible?"

The sheriff's man had a thoughtful expression now. When he did that, the milky eye went half lidded. "So Chicago Homicide's theory is horseshit. Do we care? He was your friend. How do you read this thing, anyway?"

"Do you know how hard it is to punch an ice pick through somebody's sternum?"

He nodded. "Pretty fucking hard. On the other hand, adrenaline can inspire many a superhuman feat. Like a mom lifting the front of a Buick off her child."

"Yeah, that's an event I keep hearing about, but for some reason you never see any pictures. Look, if I were you, and wanted a feather in my cap, I might go a different way."

Dick grinned. He was a guy whose grins always had a frowny cast, his mouth a half moon with the corners down. "You know me, Nate. I never shy away from a good headline, and I don't mind the PD boys owing me."

"What you may have here is a guy robbing hotel guests."

His eyebrows rose over the dark frames. "Well, there's no shortage of that on the books. Unsolved or otherwise. But I don't know of any recent surge of that particular pastime."

I leaned in. "What if some sleazeball has snagged himself a bellboy's outfit? That and a bucket of champagne and an ice pick . . . he can fill the bucket with ice from a machine on any floor, right? He knocks on the door, and if there's no answer, maybe he goes on in."

"Using a jimmy or a passkey he's finagled," Dick said, going along.

"If somebody does answer, the 'bellboy' says he's delivering a complimentary bottle of champagne from the management, and is of course allowed in to set the bucket down."

"What if there's more than one person in the room?"

"Well, he probably fades. But if it's a room with just one person in it, a guy like Tom Ellison, say . . . maybe our bogus bellboy sticks up the guest."

His expression had turned half appalled, half amused. "With an *ice* pick?"

I raised my hands chest-high, like a robbery victim. "Maybe our bellboy has a gun. But for some reason, this particular mark—Tom Ellison—puts up a fight, and rather than fire off a noisy gun, the bellboy grabs that ice pick and . . . hammers Tom in the chest with it."

Dick's expression had settled back down; he was playing along again. "A *man* ice-pick stabbing somebody in the chest, deep enough to kill, does seem more likely than some little prostitute doing it."

"Yes it does."

"We're ruling out an underhand stab?"

"For a sternum blow? The assailant would have to be seven feet tall. No, this is strictly a *Psycho* stab, and a man."

Dick tilted his head. "Some of these broads are good size, Nate. And a lot of 'em work with guys who rob a would-be john *after* the doll makes entry, but before

the *john* does, if you get my drift. And anyway, how do
you explain the lipstick?"

"Well, maybe our thief in the bellboy outfit has
thought ahead to the possibility of something going
wrong. And he's brought along some lipstick and a
Trojan wrapper, just in case. To lead the cops astray."

He was smirking again. "Oh, Christ, Heller, you're
watching way too much television. Ever since you got
that color TV. *Listen* to yourself."

"Yeah, I know," I admitted. "It's thin."

*But it wasn't so thin, if you considered that Tom's
slaying might have been a hit, not a robbery.*

My far-fetched scenario got goddamn probable, if
all some killer had to do—in or out of a bellboy
uniform—was gain access to that hotel room, kill Tom,
and stage it to look like a hooker robbery gone wrong.

*Had somebody tied off Tom Ellison as a loose end?
Because of that money drop he'd made? And if so,
what the hell did that make me, but another loose end?*

Plus, there was always the possibility that somebody
had seen Tom with that envelope of cash, not knowing
he'd passed it to Jack Ruby at the 606, and my bellboy
theory—right down to preparing for the hooker
ploy—seemed suddenly less preposterous.

I did not, however, share any of that with Dick Cain.
He was a friend, as far as it went, but there was no
way I would ever let him know about the job I'd done
for Tom, not unless he confronted me with an eyewit-
ness. His presence today could have less to do with
him covering for me, out of friendship, and more to do
with somebody—*Hoffa? Giancana?*—checking up on
me, to see if I'd spill what I knew about Tom and Ruby
to a copper.

From the Outfit's point of view, my pal Dick would
be the perfect cop to send my way. . . .

Still, Dick's dealings with the Outfit always seemed

to be at arm's length—he was doing business with them because he had to, to make it in Chicago. Which was an attitude I well understood, because it was my own. You have to swim in the waters you find yourself in.

And the sheriff's top investigator had expressed his disgust with the Outfit to me many times—though everybody seemed to think of Dick as Irish, his father had been Italian . . . and had been murdered by the Black Hand.

"Do you want me to keep an eye on this thing?" Dick asked. Considering that he only had one good eye, that was damn near a joke. He was lighting up another Dunhill.

"Let's see what the coroner comes up with," I said casually. "The trajectory of the pick will help pin down whether it's a man or a woman who swung it."

He shook his head, sighing smoke. "Not sure I see that."

"Well, it's obvious Tom was standing up when he was killed."

"Is it?"

"The angle of his body on the bed. His feet hanging over. He started out standing near the bed, got stabbed, fell backward . . . and that's why there's so little blood."

"There's never a lot of blood with an ice pick."

"But more blood than *that!* After he fell backward, gravity took care of the rest—making for damn little bleeding. Anyway, the angle of the ice-pick wound will give us the height of the killer."

"All right. I'll buy that."

"And that bed, Dick—didn't you notice? It was tidy, except for Tom's body, on *top* of the spread. Didn't look to me like anybody'd been riding bareback on it lately. He was in his T-shirt, boxers, and socks—a guy relaxing in his hotel room, not a guy who just got laid.

If somebody came to the door, Tom probably pulled his trousers on and answered, and let his murderer in. Post-kill, the guy yanked Tom's trousers off and dumped them on the floor."

Now Dick was nodding, clearly with me. "Okay, Nate. Maybe you got something. We'll see what latent prints comes up with."

"Good. That's all I ask."

"Is it?" The milky eye made his gaze unsettling. "You've been known to even scores, Nate. Business, schmizness—this was a friend of yours. Are you really content to let law enforcement handle it?"

"I'm old and respectable now, Dick. I don't play Wild West anymore. That's for you young go-getters."

He'd shot a few bad guys in his time—sometimes coming under criticism for the same. Probably had led to his resignation from the PD.

But my remark only made him smile.

"You know, Nate, I think I'm gonna choose to believe you," he said. "Here comes that waitress again. Maybe we better order lunch before she puts coffee down us with a funnel. You'll be getting the check, by the way."

After lunch, I decided to leave the Jag in the Pick-Congress parking ramp and shrugged on my Cortefiel raincoat, snugged on the Dobbs narrow-brim hat, and took a brisk, overcast walk over to the Monadnock Building.

Once upon a time it had been the largest office building in the world; today the Monadnock was a sixteen-story curiosity among its taller, often less-distinguished offspring. Even now the soot-gray brick structure with its flaring base and dramatic bay windows struck a moody yet modern pose that made it a good fit for a detective agency.

I went in the main entrance on West Jackson, walked down a corridor consisting of the ass-end display windows of stores facing Dearborn and Federal, ignored the distinctive open winding stairwells, and took the elevator to seven.

Though we'd taken over much of the office space on this floor, our main area remained the corner suite where the frosted glass-and-wood exterior had stayed the same for decades. The door had been revised slightly:

**A-1 Detective Agency**
**Criminal and Civil Investigations**

Nathan S. Heller
President

with in smaller lettering,

Louis K. Sapperstein
Vice President

Like Fred Rubinski out in Hollywood, Lou was a
full partner now. Just not full enough to have his name
in letters the size of mine.

There were no customers in the reception area, which
made me sorry we'd expanded it. The walls bore the
framed vintage Century of Progress posters that had
been part of the agency since 1934, the furnishings
blond Heywood-Wakefield numbers. The reading matter on the end tables included the usual suspects—
*Time, Newsweek, Redbook, Sports Illustrated*—with a
few battered ringers mixed in. Like a certain *Life* issue
and a few decade-old true detective–type mags, covering cases of mine. I still got written up in such periodi-
cals, but the covers had grown so sleazy of late, they no
longer sent the right waiting-room message.

Our receptionist was a dark-haired looker in her
late twenties called Mildred, a name that had always
struck me as a bad parental joke. Mildred had a nice
smile, was not stupid, but wanted to be Jackie Kennedy so bad I just couldn't take her seriously. Today
she wore a pale-pink dress with a cowl collar. She'd
have worn a pillbox hat if I let her get away with it.

"Mr. Heller," she said, giving me a bright-eyed welcome.

"Mildred," I said, nodding.

A fairly typical conversation between Mildred and me.

The bullpen was mostly full, only a few agents out
in the field—we always had a Monday staff meeting,

and unless a case dictated otherwise, everybody was here. My fourteen agents were a wide range of ages and sexes, and we had a Negro and a Chinese guy, too.

Every A-1 detective had a police or military police background. Those not working a case were in business clothes, with those taking a break from fieldwork in street clothes. Their modern metal desks were widely spaced, because I didn't care for cubicles. Most of the agents did not need privacy with clients because either Lou or I took the first meetings. A wall of windows provided a view onto Jackson Street showcasing the Federal Building, and another wall was strictly metal four-drawer files.

The office was run by Gladys Sapperstein, Lou's wife. Gladys had been a gorgeous young woman when I hired her in the early '40s, who had interviewed warm but proved a cold fish, dashing any Hollywood fantasies I might have harbored about a private eye and his sexy secretary. I'd been made to suffer for my error by way of decades of Gladys's business acumen and efficiency.

Several years into my employ, Gladys had married one of our operatives, a kid named Fortunato, and when he died in the war, she thawed out some. Not that she and I were ever an item, not by a long shot; and I thought she would never remarry, but then about ten years ago, she and my partner Lou announced that they'd gotten married by a judge over the lunch hour.

I suspected a longtime office affair, but said nothing, since I didn't give a damn, other than my ego being bruised by the beautiful Gladys never having been tempted by my masculine charms. Lou was a strapping guy, sure, but a dozen years older than me—he'd been my boss on the Pickpocket Detail in the early thirties—and he was bald and bulbous-nosed and be-spectacled, and what the hell was wrong with me? Well, I knew. Gladys saw me for the randy, unreliable fucker I was, and Lou for the right guy that he was.

She had her own office now—between Lou's and mine—and remained attractive, a busty, pleasingly plump brunette in her late fifties wearing jeweled cat's-eye glasses.

I was about to step into my office when she emerged from hers, looking primly pretty in an orange and green cotton print dress.

She crooked her little finger. That was only slightly less intimidating than a cop turning his siren on.

"Good afternoon, Gladys," I said, going to her. She rarely came to me.

"Nice to see you made it in."

"I'm the boss, Gladys. I show up when I feel like it."

"Oh. Well, that's interesting. Lou is supposed to be semi-retired, and he's here more often than you are."

She never referred to Lou as "my husband" in the office. You would never guess they were married. In fact, she nagged me a hell of a lot more than she ever did Lou.

"Well, this is a surprisingly warm greeting for a Monday, I admit," I said to her through a strained smile. "Was there something?"

"Don't slip out after the staff meeting. You have a five-o'clock appointment."

"That's a little late for an appointment."

"Well, she might get here earlier. But she's driving down from Milwaukee, and has to stop at the morgue on her way, to make some arrangements."

Gladys paused to cast me a condescending look.

"Oh shit," I said. "You're talking about Jean Ellison. My God, she just found out this morning her husband is dead, and she's driving down here? That's terrible. You should have talked her out of it."

She just stared at me. She might have been a stone statue at Easter Island, albeit better-looking. I might have been a bug crawling across the wall.

"Mrs. Ellison," Gladys said finally, "said that she felt sure you would see her."

"She's right, of course. You know who she is?"

"Yes. Her husband did some publicity for us, a few years ago. Very nice man. I take it he's recently deceased?"

"Murdered. That's where I was this morning—over at the Pick-Congress, having a look at the crime scene. Killed in his hotel room, money stolen."

Something flared in her eyes. "Surely that's a police matter."

Gladys, ever since being promoted from receptionist to office manager, took a stern, proprietary interest in how I allocated my time.

I put a hand on her shoulder and she winced, just a little. "I want to promise you, Gladys, that if someone ever murders you in the night, I will not stray from my duty. I will continue to serve the clients of the A-1 and allow the honest, hardworking police of Chicago, Illinois, to bring in your killer."

That made her laugh.

When I got to her like that, she would say, "Oh, you," and slap my chest.

You now understand my relationship with Gladys Sapperstein in all its complex glory.

She was almost in her office when I said, "Lou here?"

"Yes. You want him?"

"Please."

In my private office, I hung up my raincoat and hat in the closet. My inner sanctum was a spacious preserve immune to the changes of the outer world—even the outer office area. The central feature was the old scarred desk that dated back to my one room over the Dill Pickle in Barney Ross's building on Van Buren. But there were also padded leather client chairs, a comfortable couch, wooden filing cabinets, and walls arrayed with framed, often signed photos of celebrities, sometimes celebrity clients, sometimes with me in the shots.

There was Helen, in full Sally Rand persona, standing coyly behind a fan, next to a shot of Marilyn Monroe in a white bathing suit, both signed to me with love. Funny to think Helen was still here, and Marilyn was gone.

"Nate?" Lou said. He was leaning in—I'd left the door open for him. No black rims for his glasses, strictly wire-frame. "You wanted me?"

"Yeah. Shut us in and sit yourself down. We have almost half an hour before the staff meeting. I need to fill you in."

He settled his big, muscular frame into the chair opposite me as I got into my swivel number. He had on a white shirt with its sleeves rolled up to the elbow, navy-blue suspenders, and a matching clip-on tie. His fashion sense left something to be desired, but he was a hell of a detective. And partner.

"You heard that Tom Ellison was murdered," I said.

"Yeah. Shame. Last night?"

"Apparently. I did a job for him Friday—it's off the A-1 books, okay?"

He nodded.

I had no secrets from Lou. Or anyway few secrets. He even knew at least the vague outlines of Operation Mongoose. So he listened patiently as I filled him in about the 606 Club money drop, my talk with Jimmy Hoffa in a Wrigley Field men's room, and the gist of what Dick Cain and I had discussed at the Pick-Congress this morning.

"The question is," Lou said, "are *you* a loose end now? Or was this something else? Tom getting himself killed may have no connection to that errand he ran."

"It's possible. Also possible that he got himself killed because he didn't just run the damn errand, like he was told—instead getting in touch with a private eye pal of his to back him up."

Lou nodded. "So what's the plan?"

"I don't know if Gladys mentioned it to you, but—"

"Mrs. Ellison has an appointment at five. Yes, I know."

"Well, I want you to sit in on that meeting, and hang around after."

He was nodding again. "Done. Anything else?"

"Yeah. If you wind up one of my pallbearers, wear a real tie, for Chrissake."

Lou grunted a laugh, got up, and ambled out—he was graceful for a big athletic guy, and you'd make him for his mid-fifties, not early seventies.

I called Helen at my place.

"Listen," I said, "I apologize, but I don't think we should move you in right now."

"Oh, don't worry about it." Her voice had a nice lightness to it. "We can just head over to the Lorraine this evening, and get my bags, whenever you're done with business. We're past checkout anyway."

"No, Helen. You don't follow. I think maybe somebody else might drop around to see me, unannounced . . . and this time not to deliver football tickets."

I told her briefly that a client I'd done a job for recently had been murdered.

"I don't have any intention of putting you at risk," I said.

"Don't be a pussy, Heller. We'll make the move

tonight. Then you can take me out for a nice meal. Who knows, you might get lucky again."

And the click in my ear said that was the end of it.

If I was so tough, why could all these women push me around?

After the staff meeting—two hours that ran to reports on the status of current cases and potential new clients—I headed back to my office. I was barely behind my desk when Mildred rang through.

"Your five o'clock is here," Mildred said quietly.

"It's not even four-thirty."

"I know. She says she'll wait."

"I'll be right out."

There was a bathroom off my office, and I went in, took a piss, washed my hands, brushed my teeth, tossed some cold water on my face, and looked at myself, wishing a younger face would look back at me. I toweled off and let out the kind of sigh only a man well past forty can muster.

Time to greet my murdered client's wife.

She was a petite honey blonde, thirtyish, with a Janet Leigh hairdo, wearing a simple gray dress with a rounded collar and a pleated skirt. Subdued clothing, but not widow's weeds—only her pumps were black. Her pretty, rather delicate features were highlighted by understated makeup. Her white-gloved hands were in her lap, holding a small dark-gray purse. She looked as composed as a prospective teacher waiting for her interview with the superintendent of schools.

As I stepped into the reception area, I said, "Jean, I'm so very sorry. . . ."

She rose, smiled, and said, "It's very nice to see you, Nathan. It's been too long."

She extended a gloved hand, as if being introduced to me at a cotillion, and I went over and took it, gently.

Only the barest crinkling of her chin gave anything away. Her cornflower-blue eyes were not red and did not look particularly moist.

I wanted to take her in my arms and hold her and comfort her and let her cry her heart out. But I didn't know her that well. She and Tom and I probably had dinner out, in a vaguely business-related way, half a dozen times, and that was several years ago. I'd been to their house in Milwaukee once, when I'd promised Tom I would keep my PR business with him, despite the move, which I hadn't.

She might have been battling back tears or in shock or even not that devastated—how could I know what the state of their marriage had been?

So I said nothing more, and she said nothing more, as I took her gently by an arm and led her through the bullpen. My agents did not look up—they were well-trained to ignore clients heading back for a meeting with the boss, particularly clients personally escorted *by* the boss.

Just outside my door, I said, "I'm going to ask my partner, Lou Sapperstein, to sit in on our meeting. I trust him, and you can, too. Is that all right?"

"Certainly."

I walked her to the client's chair, and Lou—who'd been tipped off either by Mildred or Gladys or both—slipped into the office, shut the door, and went directly to Jean Ellison.

He extended his hand to her and she gave him a gloved one. "Lou Sapperstein, Mrs. Ellison. I am so sorry for your loss. I knew Tom and he was a fine man."

"Thank you."

I sat and asked if she would like coffee or tea or perhaps water, as Lou stood poised to take our orders. She declined.

Then I said, "I understand you had to come down

here for . . . official matters. But if this is difficult for you, I could come to you in Milwaukee, later in the week. It's not a problem. If you'd like some time to sort things out."

"No. I'm here. I'm . . . I believe I'm rather in a sort of stunned state, Nathan. I haven't cried yet. I feel something more like . . . anger than grief. Something that feels like it's, I guess, bubbling up down deep." She laughed and it was awful. "Like a volcano, I guess."

I forced a small smile. "You have a son and daughter, I know. I apologize for not remembering their names. . . ."

"Mike is in junior high, Susie's in the sixth grade. My parents live in Milwaukee—that's one of the reasons Tom and I moved there, Dad had some very good connections with the Miller people. . . . Anyway, I'm afraid I did something very cowardly."

A woman alone who had driven the hour plus from Milwaukee to Chicago, within hours or maybe minutes of hearing of her husband's death, did not strike me as cowardly. But I didn't say that. I didn't know what to say.

Nor did Lou, who had positioned himself in a chair just in back of and to the right of her.

She explained without prompting: "I left it to Mom and Dad to tell the kids. That's terrible of me, I know. But I left it to them. They seem . . . more stable, more reliable, than me right now. I couldn't think of how I could tell the kids. Just couldn't. What would I say? *Mike!* Dad can't make it to your football game Friday night. *Susie!* You won't see Dad at the school musical."

Another short, awful laugh.

I said, "How can we help?"

She leaned toward me, just a little. "Before we speak, I must ask you, uh—your friend, Mr. Sapperstein?"

She glanced back at him and smiled politely. Then her dry-eyed gaze fixed itself on me: "Is he aware of why my husband contacted you on Friday?"

That gave me a chill. A goddamn chill.

*She knew.*

Her husband had confided in her about his worries, the situation he'd got himself into trying to get into that unmemorable Bears game.

I had not seen this one coming. I figured she might be here to ask me to look into Tom's death, because I was their former client, their sort of friend who was a private investigator . . . maybe at most Tom might have mentioned to her he was going to see me Friday, but *this*?

"Jean," I said, sitting forward, "how much do you know?"

"I know about the football ticket and the envelope of money and the burlesque house and hiring you to go along, to *protect* him. I think I know all of it."

The emphasis on *protect* had been the only sign that she perhaps blamed me a little. I'd been hired as Tom's bodyguard Friday, and two nights later he was dead.

Trying not to sound at all defensive, I said, "I didn't see Tom after the 606 Club. Everything appeared to go well—he passed along the envelope and left."

I didn't tell her the guy on the receiving end of the money drop was Jack Ruby, a little mobster I'd known for years. And I didn't say I'd been invited to that Bears game, too, by Jimmy Hoffa himself.

"I blame myself," she said.

"Pardon?"

"Blame myself." She settled back and sighed. The only sign of inner turmoil was the way she held onto that purse. Maybe she had a gun in it and was going to shoot me for letting Tom die. Maybe I wouldn't blame her.

But she went on: "We don't hide things, Tom and I. Even in business, he always runs things past me. We are close. We are still . . . sweethearts. Soppy as that sounds. He is a very loving husband, and a wonderful, attentive father. He does have to travel sometimes, but . . . he is the best husband a woman could ever dream of having, and the best father our kids could ever hope to have."

Okay, so she was talking in the present tense. That was how she was handling it. Tom wasn't dead yet. Even if she had just read me his obituary.

She was saying, "When he got the chance to take on those questionable clients, with the connections to this Hoffa gangster, I could have said no. But the money was good. The money was very good. We bought a new home. We put money away for Mike and Susie's college. If I had just said, 'No, Tom, not those people.' If I had said that, I wouldn't have had to go to that nasty-smelling place today and look at him on a tray with a tiny hole in his chest."

I thought that might unleash the torrent, but it didn't. The gloved hands strangled the purse.

"Do you think," she said, "that this big shot Hoffa or the gangsters he runs with are responsible for Tom's death?"

"I don't know. It's possible."

"May I tell you what's not possible? A Chicago police detective, and to his credit he tried to be as gentle as he could, indicated the official theory is that Tom had a woman in his room, and that she robbed and killed him."

"Yeah. I don't buy that."

"I would understand if you did. Businessmen on out-of-town trips, they sometimes see women. Girls they meet in a hotel bar. Girls they pay for it. Sluts. Whores. But not Tom. You see, we're still very . . . this is embarrassing to say . . . but there is . . . there's nothing wrong with our sex life."

I raised a hand to indicate she needn't say more. "Jean, normally I might tell you that anything is possible, even in a good marriage. Good men slip, the best husband can make a mistake. But I don't believe Tom was killed by a woman."

"You seem very sure."

"The evidence indicates a male assailant, no matter what the Chicago police may say. But it *is* possible that it was a robbery."

"How so?"

I explained my bellboy theory.

"That seems a little . . . elaborate," she said. "The planting of the glass with the lipstick, the Trojan wrapper and so on. Improbable, but not impossible."

"No argument."

"Still, Nathan . . ." Her eyes had a glint now. "It could have been something *else* . . . couldn't it?"

She was smart. Tom had married a beautiful woman but she was much more than that.

"Yes," I said. "A professional killer might well plan to leave behind a false trail . . . like the lipstick glass, the prophylactic wrapper. That's not improbable at all."

"A cold-blooded, premeditated murder, you mean."

"I do. If the errand Tom ran on Friday night turned him into a loose end, then . . . that's very possible."

She nodded, as if I had just told her, *Your car needs an oil change.*

"What kind of loose end had Tom become?"

"I don't know. I really don't. Possibly that money being traceable back to Hoffa's man may pose somebody a problem. That's just a guess. And I may be a loose end now myself."

Neither of us said anything for a while.

Lou filled the silence with a question I should have

asked. "Mrs. Ellison, when did you last speak to your husband?"

"Sunday evening. He'd eaten at the hotel. Must have been around seven. We didn't talk long. He just said he felt stupid, this mess with the Bears ticket, especially how dull the game had been. We talked about the kids, some events coming up."

A football game. A school musical.

She was saying, "I talked to him Friday night, too. After that burlesque club fiasco. And we spoke Saturday night. He'd taken a client and his wife to a matinee at the Shubert. I forget what was playing."

They'd spoken every night he was away. I believed they really were still sweethearts. And it didn't seem soppy to me. Not at all.

She turned from Lou to me. Sitting straight, business-like, purse firm in two hands. "All right, Nathan—what can we do?"

"Jean, it's not going to be easy. If he was killed by a professional, for the kind of people we're talking about . . . it can be hard, even impossible, to prove."

She raised an eyebrow. "Tom says you're an interesting man. He says people tell stories about you."

Lou gave me a look, and I said, "Really. What kind of stories?"

"Tom says that you are a very tough hombre. That's what he said, isn't it funny? Tough *hombre*. That you sit in a fancy office in Chicago, but you're more like some kind of . . . Bogart kind of detective."

Lou grinned.

"I really don't know what Tom meant by that," I said.

"Tom meant that you have your own sense of justice. Your own way of doing things. That people you don't like have been known to . . . just kind of go away."

Lou stopped grinning.

I could have dissuaded her. I'm not sure why I didn't. I could have said those were silly rumors, and just talk, people's imaginations running away with them.

But I didn't.

"Let me just say," I replied gently, "that if the long arms of the law prove a little . . . short . . . I might sometimes find a way of evening a score. In certain situations."

Lou's eyes were wide. He was obviously surprised by what I was saying—not by the content of it, but that I uttered it out loud.

"I like the sound of that," she said.

"You need to understand that I wouldn't be able to tell you about it. And it might take years. Sometimes many years, before a score can be settled."

"But maybe you could call me on the phone some night."

"Maybe."

"And just say, I don't know, something like, 'I think Tom would be pleased.' Just something like that."

I half smiled at the new widow. "I think that's a phone call I might be able to make. Someday."

She smiled back at me.

Then she lifted her chin, her expression regal now. "Well, I would very much like to hire you, Nathan. Things are obviously a little topsy-turvy right now, but I feel confident I'm well off. Tom has a big insurance policy, you know, his business is flourishing, and—"

I raised a stop hand. "Jean, no. This investigation was already paid for, by Tom."

"No, I insist—"

"I'll let you pay any expenses I incur. How's that?"

". . . All right."

"And I'll need your full cooperation. If any of my people come around wanting information about Tom or access to his private papers or anything at all, you have to provide it."

"All right."

"Good," I said, rising. "I need to discuss the particulars of this assignment with Mr. Sapperstein . . . so for now, I'll just show you out."

I came around and helped her out of her chair, and she looked up at me and her lower lip began quivering. "Please, Nathan. *Do* something about this."

"Count on it," I said.

I walked her through the bullpen, which had cleared out by now. Lou trailed after. Gladys was framed in her office door, watching.

The reception area was empty, just a faint hint of Mildred's perfume remaining—Joy, Jackie Kennedy's favorite.

"Do you need someone to drive you?" I asked.

"No, I've done quite well today."

"You have. But it's going to hit you."

"Oh, I know," she said.

She took my hand, squeezed it, and—the picture of composure—stepped out into the hall, shutting the door behind her.

Lou was at my side suddenly. "Somebody should drive her back to Milwaukee. You want me to?"

"She says no. She seems strong."

That was when I heard something fall.

I went into the hall and she'd collapsed, she was curled up against the wall, one shoe off, the purse discarded, weeping, moaning, grief coming up out of her in wrenching wails. I picked the little thing up in my arms like a bride and crossed the office's threshold and rested her on the reception-area couch.

I sat next to her and she crawled over and hugged me, hard, and wept into my clothes.

"I'll drive her," Lou said.

"You do that," I said. "We'll talk later."

Anyway, I had someone to see.

The big, burly Bismarck Hotel, on the corner of LaSalle and Randolph, hadn't changed much since it was rebuilt in 1926. Oh, during World War II its celebrated dining room became the Swiss Chalet, but then even the Berghoff turned magically Swiss when Hitler suddenly made Wiener schnitzel unpatriotic.

Squatting on the edge of the Loop near the northwest corner of the El tracks, the venerable Bismarck had seen the city around it shift. German Square, over which it once ruled, was a term nobody used anymore, the *deutsche* shops, steamship office, and clubs largely gone. And the real downtown center of social activity was a few blocks away—famous restaurants, ritzy hotels, movie palaces, and legit theaters.

Yet the Bismarck survived and even thrived. Located across from City Hall as it was, the hotel made the perfect place for politicians, businessmen, gangsters, union leaders, and assorted combinations thereof to hold meetings or maybe lunch in the Walnut Room or (for you out-of-towners) even book a room.

The overcast sky decided to spit at me as I walked over to the old hotel; I just tugged my hat brim down and hunkered, walking against the wind like a goddamn mime. At only six-thirty, the darkening sky made it seem like night was getting impatient, and maybe something bad was coming.

I wasn't heeled, as we of the lower class used to say, my nine-millimeter and shoulder holster back in my bedroom, and I hadn't availed myself of any of the other artillery in the A-1 safe. My suit wasn't cut for hardware, anyway. And why would I need a firearm to protect myself in the Bismarck Hotel?

On the other hand, Tom Ellison could have used one at the Pick-Congress.

I nodded to George the doorman in his Victor Herbert operetta uniform, got a hat-touch nod back that said I mattered, spun through the revolving door into the modest entryway, and trotted up the double-width, red-carpeted stairs into the wider world of the lobby. My raincoat wasn't wet enough to climb out of, but I did take off my hat and shake some droplets off. Then I moved across the high-ceilinged, elaborate chalet-like chamber, dodging overstuffed chairs and potted plants, footsteps echoing off marble.

The elevator I shared with half a dozen others, a mix of tourists and business types. When you pushed a floor button, a sultry female voice talked to you: "*Lobby . . . second floor . . .*" This was a relatively new feature, and I hadn't decided yet whether to be amused or spooked.

I went up to seven, took a left turn down the carpeted hallway to the Presidential Suite. The gentleman I was calling on usually stayed here, though sometimes you would find him in the Conrad Hilton's Presidential Suite, which at a thousand dollars a night was twice the rate here, such a bargain.

Anyway, I had called the Bismarck first, and got lucky. I had not asked to be connected to this famous guest's room, merely saying I needed to have something messengered over to Mr. Hoffa, and was he in?

He was.

At the end of the hall was a little vestibule with a door within that said 737 over a small golden plaque that read PRESIDENTIAL SUITE. The numbers and plaque looked new, but their predecessors had read the same, back when I would come to this suite in the 1930s and early '40s to call on another powerful man—Frank Nitti, Al Capone's successor and my sometime benefactor. Gone since 1943 but a presence still felt.

I'd met with Hoffa here a couple of times before, so the resonance of this having been Nitti's suite was nothing new. But somehow, this evening, it seemed more pronounced.

There was a gold knocker. I used it.

I stood and waited while, presumably, a guardian of the gate eyed me through the peephole. The door cracked open, the night latch in place. A part of a chubby face with half a flat nose and half a mouthful of bad teeth revealed itself. Also in that lineup was a bulgy orb (under a hairy eyebrow) that stared out at me like I was an apparition. Maybe the Virgin Mary, or the Ghost of Christmas Past.

"Nate Heller," I said. "To see . . ." Shit, I damn near said *Mr. Nitti*. ". . . Jimmy."

"You don't have no appointment."

The rough-hewn low-pitched voice was familiar. I believed this was the put-upon lackey who had delivered my football tickets the other night.

"Tell Mr. Hoffa I apologize for coming unannounced," I said, the "Jimmy" familiarity not having worked, "but that it's important."

"You gotta have an appointment."

"If I leave? Be sure not to tell Jim I was here, and you sent me away, because he'll kick you in the ass."

The bulgy eye blinked. The door shut. I waited. The door opened.

It was indeed my pal from the other night. He was in a brown suit that was too baggy with a blue tie that was too short. I figured the bagginess was to make the gun under his left shoulder not show. You'd think the Teamsters could afford a decent tailor.

"Nice to see you again," I said with a nod, as he opened the door, stepped aside, and I went in. "The game was lousy, by the way."

"You gotta stand for a frisk."

"I'm not armed."

"Rules is rules."

Before I let him pat me down, I gave him my damp raincoat and hat to dispose of, just out of general disrespect, thinking this would have been an excellent time to shoot him, if that was why I was here.

As he did his job, I glanced around the spacious suite. The living room still had a Victorian look, as in Nitti days, but had been remodeled, and they'd brought in new fake antiques about five years ago. In all its incarnations, the suite maintained a lavish, gold-leaf look that would impress politicians and whores, if you'll forgive the redundancy.

Two thugs also in baggy suits and ill-knotted ties were sitting on a fancy couch reading *Ring* magazine and *Modern Man* respectively. A versatile pair, they were also watching a rerun of *My Little Margie*. Same model color TV as I had, I noticed. But Margie remained in black-and-white. They looked up at me, wishing I were room service.

I was wondering if I should find something fancy and uncomfortable to sit on in there when I heard Hoffa call, "*Heller*! Nate! Come on in here. Come on, come on, come on."

I followed the machine-gunning voice into a lavish bedroom with its own color TV. On the bed, like the Invisible Man taking a nap, a suit was laid out—just a standard off-the-rack pinstriped blue business suit, with a white shirt on a hanger inside the coat. Some well-shined shoes were on the floor nearby, a pair of the white socks he always wore waiting next to them.

Hoffa was in the bathroom, with the door open, shaving with a straight razor, about half the lather on his face gone. Black head of hair bristling with butch wax, the broad-shouldered little man was in an athletic-style T-shirt that showed off his massively muscular arms, and yellow-and-white-striped boxer shorts that revealed somewhat less muscular legs. He was in his bare feet.

"I have to meet some fuckin' lawyers downstairs at seven," he said, chin out, shaving his neck. "We don't have much time to talk. But it must be important, or you wouldn't barge in on me like this."

And the blade paused for the half-lathered face to turn and grin at me, to take the edge off; but I knew he was kidding on the square.

I stood near the bathroom door, not too near. "I apologize for busting in on you, Jim. But it *is* important."

As he watched himself shave, now and then his Chinaman eyes would flick toward me, catching me in the mirror. "We got maybe ten minutes, kiddo. Go, man, go."

"Jim, are you aware of what happened to Tom Ellison?"

"No. What happened to Tom Ellison?"

*Okay. So that was how he was going to play it. He didn't know about it.*

But the hell of it was, maybe he didn't. I had seen the papers, and only the afternoon editions had anything about Tom's murder, and those had been squibs, buried deep.

If Hoffa was innocent in this thing, he really *wouldn't* know.

"Tom was murdered last night, Jim. In his hotel room."

If he was acting, he was good. The razor jogged, then froze, and when he wiped the lather from his face, I saw a little blood come away on the towel. He hadn't really finished the shave, but he threw some water on his face, toweled off, stuck a little piece of toilet paper where he'd nicked himself, and exited the john.

"I do not mean to downplay the import of this thing," Hoffa said, "but you talk while I get ready."

He got dressed, initially sitting on the edge of the bed to pull the white socks on. He'd motioned me to sit across from him, which took pulling a chair around, which I did. I gave him a condensed, factual report, including the police suspecting a hooker robbery gone awry, and my own feeling that this was a horseshit theory, and that in all likelihood a man had committed the act. Hoffa was ready for his dinner engagement by the time I finished.

But he didn't stir. He just sat on the edge of the bed facing me, big hands on his small knees.

"I'm gonna save you the trouble," he said. His face was serious, even somber, his eyes hard but not cold. He gestured with a karate chop. "I can see where you could think this thing may be related to that other thing."

Apparently Hoffa was not convinced the Bismarck was free of bugs, and I don't mean bedbugs.

"It seems suspicious to me, yes. You were unhappy with Tom, because he hired me to go along on that handoff."

I was doing my best to be cryptic myself, in case cops or FBI were listening.

"I think you have a valid concern," Hoffa said.

This surprised me.

Then he stood, gave me the finger crook like Gladys

(not as ominous, strangely, coming from him), said, "In my office," and I followed him back into the bathroom.

He turned on both faucets, all the way, letting them run hard and loud. He gestured to the toilet, which had the seat down. I sat. He stood near the sink with his arms folded and a piece of toilet paper on his face.

Well, it appeared once again we were going to talk in the can.

"If Tom became a loose end that somebody decided to cut off," he said softly but forcefully, "it was done without my knowing, and is not something I would have approved. Something like that when I am in *town*, doing business? Jesus H. Fucking Christ. I have already seriously reprimanded the individual who involved a civilian in this thing in the first place."

"Jim, a reprimand doesn't go far with a widow and two young kids."

"No, it don't." He looked grave. Nothing seemed phony about it. "If I gave you, say, ten grand for the family, would you pass it along?"

That was funny. Well, not hilarious, but sick-joke funny: that had been the amount of cash in the envelope Tom gave Ruby at the 606.

He cocked his head, raised an eyebrow. "You would have to accept that it comes out of genuine concern for the family of a trusted business associate, and is not in no way an admission of guilt. Nate, I swear on my mother's grave I had nothing to do with this goddamn thing."

"That's good to hear." I had no idea if he was telling me the truth or not.

"That will come out of my personal funds," he said, tapping his chest, allowing himself just a touch of magnanimity.

The running water seemed to be shushing us.

"I'll get the ten grand to them," I said. "I'll say it's from an anonymous friend of Tom's."

"Good. I would appreciate it."

I'd keep the ten grand. Jean Ellison wouldn't accept it, and I could use it to fund the investigation. That way I could spare her the expenses.

He rocked on his heels; standing there in that suit, he might have been a cut-rate after-dinner speaker, or the headwaiter at a hash house.

"What are your intentions in this thing, Nate? Are you going to let this thing lie?"

The sink noise wanted to know, too.

I met his unblinking gaze, wondering if my life depended on my answer.

"Here's what I'm thinking of doing, Jim—I will put agents on the case here and in Milwaukee, and see if this murder really was a robbery gone wrong, whether a hooker or some asshole robbing hotel rooms. I'll also see if there's anything else going on in Tom's life that could have got him killed. You never know—some people have secret lives. He could have a girlfriend who had a boyfriend who decided to get rid of the competition. He could have a business partner who is embezzling that wanted him gone. Anything's possible."

Hoffa said, "Anything's possible."

"But if you tell me not to look into this, I won't. *I* don't want to be a loose end, Jim."

I might have been lying about the former, but I was telling the God's honest truth about the latter.

And after several moments' thought, Hoffa said something interesting: "Would it make the little woman feel better, you looking into it?"

"I think it probably would . . . unless I come up with an answer that doesn't sit well."

"Another woman kinda thing."

"Right."

He shook his head, made a sympathetic clicking sound in his cheek. "I can't see any reason why you shouldn't do this investigation and bring some peace of mind to the little lady."

"All right."

"But I can't promise you this ain't connected."

That shook me but I tried not to show it. "No?"

"No. Sometimes subordinates do things that they think they should do—you know? Sometimes these sons of bitches think too much on their own. They take the goddamn fucking initiative, the ass-kissing jack-asses. Guys like me, you know how it is, Nate—we're insulated. So I will not lie to you. It is possible Tom getting killed was a by-product of that favor he did."

I wasn't sure I should ask, but heard myself saying, "Would you be willing to ask around? If some subordinate of yours was responsible . . . and you're unhappy with him . . . maybe I could . . . fire him for you."

That got a big smile out of Hoffa. "Kiddo, you are one of a kind. You always never fail to surprise me. Goddamn right, I will ask around. Anything else? I'm five minutes late. I fucking hate being late."

I raised a hand, gesturing for just another moment. "There is one other thing. If somebody under or . . . over you? If there *is* such a person? If somebody considers me a loose end that needs tying off, would you . . . please discourage them?"

He nodded with a big, reassuring smile, and he patted the air with his palms to indicate, No *problem*.

Then he added, "If I can't discourage them, how about I warn your ass?"

"Please."

"Okay? We done?"

"I can see taking a guy like Tom out," I said, ignoring

the dismissal. "I hate it, and I don't think it was smart or necessary. But he was a civilian, and the mistake was enlisting a civilian."

"I one hunnerd percent agree."

"I don't know what makes that little bagman exercise at the 606 worth killing somebody over. . . ."

"We don't know that it was," Hoffa reminded me.

I rose from toilet lid. "Right. But if it *was* worth killing somebody over? I don't want to know. I don't want to know why, and I don't want to know what it's about. I don't want to know *anything* about it. I just want to live long enough to happily retire and see my son grow up and get rich enough to support me in my old age."

The running water sounded like applause now.

"I hear ya!" he chortled. "Come on, come on."

Then he turned off the faucets, slipped an arm around my shoulder, and showed me out of his "office."

"I'm not a civilian, Jim," I said, as he escorted me into the living room. "Look back over my history, and think about everything I've seen, everything I know, and see if you can find me ever testifying about any of it."

*He didn't need to know about all the information I had, once upon a time, passed along to Bobby Kennedy and the rackets committee.*

"You *do* know where the bodies are buried," he said pleasantly, getting bored with me.

My hairy-eyebrow doorman and the two other baggy-suit thugs were playing nickel-dime poker now, at a card table in a corner of the Victorian living room. Seeing me, the doorman threw in his hand, scurried to get my coat and hat, gave them to me, and scurried back to the game.

Hoffa and I went down in the elevator together, having it to ourselves. None of his bodyguards had made the trip, probably because their boss was dining in the hotel, with those lawyers, and there was no need.

He was rocking on his heels again, looking at the floor indicator, having forgotten I was there, though I was at his side.

I said, "I wouldn't ever insult you with that old wheeze, of course."

Hoffa frowned. "What old wheeze?"

"Oh, that I've written a bunch of stuff down and left it with my lawyer or in a safety deposit box . . . or both. If something should happen to me. You know, the original one place, the carbon another?"

He had the expression of a clown that just got hit by a pie.

I patted him on the shoulder. "Wouldn't insult your intelligence that way, Jim."

The elevator said in its seductive female voice, "*Lobby floor. . . .*"

I headed quickly across the lobby's marble expanse, but when I glanced back at him he was standing near the elevator, possibly waiting for his party, or maybe I'd slowed him down a little.

I called out, "Jim! If you're eating at the Swiss Chalet, and you never tried the pork shanks and sauerkraut? Do."

**Tuesday, October 29, 1963**

When I rolled in at just past ten, I found Lou Sapperstein—as ever, in shirtsleeves, suspenders, and wireframe glasses—seated in our little break room off the bullpen. This was just a glorified cubbyhole with counter, coffee machine, sink, a few cabinets, and refrigerator. The bulk of the space was taken up by a Formica table whose centerpiece was a cardboard container offering the remnants of what had undoubtedly once been a proud selection of pastries and doughnuts. Lou sat drinking coffee, nibbling on one of the latter.

I joined him, but just for talk—I'd had juice and toast at home. "You get Jean Ellison home okay?"

It was one of those questions you knew the answer to but had to ask.

He nodded, chewing. He swallowed. "I drove her in her car. Gladys followed in ours. We were back by midnight."

"Appreciate that. How did Jean do?"

"She was very quiet. No more crying, at least not that I saw or heard. She was turned away from me, resting against her window. Think maybe she even slept a little. You could transcribe our conversation on the head of a pin."

I leaned back in the kitchen-style chair. "She's brave and she's smart, but this would be a rough one for anybody."

He sighed, nodded again. "Her parents were at her place. They seem pretty solid. Kids were already in bed. There was no melodrama."

"None is needed when you got actual drama." A sigh seemed called for. "I appreciate you handling that, Lou."

"Sure. But I'll stop short of saying 'my pleasure.'"

"I'll need you to represent the A-1 at the funeral."

"No problem." He sipped his coffee. "Your pal Dick Cain called right at nine. Said he had a big meeting this morning, something about Kennedy's visit this weekend, and might not be free for a while, so I should give you a message."

"So give."

"Said to tell you the latent print guys say the drinking glass with the lipstick traces was otherwise clean—probably *wiped* clean. Interesting, huh? Somebody takes the time to wipe off a glass but leaves the lipstick?"

"Doesn't surprise me. There hasn't been a more obviously staged crime scene since Basil Rathbone last made a monkey out of Nigel Bruce."

Lou smiled at that. He appreciated it when I made an effort.

"Dick say whether the latent print guys found *anything* useful?"

"No." He smirked. "It's a hotel room. There's gonna be all kinds of prints—recent guests, hotel employees, not to mention cops."

I frowned. "Not *that* tough an exercise—the hotel knows who stayed in the room lately. You print the hotel staff for elimination, or to see if anybody working there pops up with a prior."

My indignation amused Lou. "Listen to yourself, Nate. The homicide boys already have their theory, and that's what they'll try to prove—they'll compare whatever prints *do* turn up to known hookers, and known hookers only. Some poor schmuck is probably flipping through ten-print file cards on that hopeless mission right now."

Two glazed doughnuts were staring at me. I started eating one of them.

Lou was saying, "The fingerprint aspect of what we'll call a police investigation, just to have *something* to call it, will begin and end there."

I knew he was right. I got up and got myself a glass of orange juice. My second of the day.

But Lou wasn't through: "I also heard from Doc Owens. Nice guy, Clarence. Surprised you haven't run into him before. Anyway, he confirms the weapon was likely an ice pick. He said to tell you that the killer was probably five nine or ten, due to the angle and depth of the wound."

"Five nine or ten," I said, sitting back down with the glass of juice in hand. "Probably a man but still possibly a woman. Did salt-of-the-earth Clarence comment on whether a woman might be capable of a blow with that kind of force?"

Lou shrugged. "Wasn't part of Doc's message for ya. I have his number, if you want to follow up."

I waved him off. "No. No need. The cops will just say it's a big strong gal that did it. Let's not waste our time on that."

He nodded—that was fine with him. "So what about *our* investigation of the Ellison death? Since it will be the only real one."

I sipped juice, flipped a hand. "You don't need me to outline it for you."

"Do, anyway. You're the boss, after all."

I chewed. Swallowed. "Okay, let's put two agents, male and female, on the Milwaukee end. Have the female deal with Mrs. Ellison, whenever contact with her is necessary. Both ops need to dig through the Ellisons' lives—neighbors, friends. We want to know if Tom had any skeletons in the closet."

"Particularly skeletons in skirts."

"Or if any of Jean's friends wear trousers. I don't suspect her but that has to be looked at. And let's see if Tom's murder grew out of his PR business."

"Associates and clients?"

"Yeah. Short of the Teamsters-related ones."

Lou took the other glazed doughnut. "I'd suggest we put *three* agents on the business end. Reynolds has an accounting background. Might come in handy."

"Good. Use him. Then locally, we want to hit that hotel. Put one guy on that, somebody good—Donaldson, maybe."

Lou had a free hand; he gestured with it. "How about I do that myself?"

"Perfect. See if any B-girls are known to be working the Pick-Congress bar. Talk to the staff, from janitor to desk. Find out what phone calls Tom made, if he had any meals in his room, anything you can."

"All right." Lou sipped his coffee. "So how did your meeting with your pal Jim go?"

Even at this late date, the son of a bitch could surprise me. I hadn't mentioned anything last night other than I needed to talk to somebody. He just put it together. He just *knew*.

"Finish your breakfast," I said, "and we'll continue this in my office. A little too public here."

He nodded, and I left him—he had half a doughnut to go. I'd finished mine.

I crossed the bullpen—maybe half our agents were out in the field, which pleased me, because that meant income—and Gladys stopped me just outside my office. She was in a blue and white print dress and that body, even in her fifties, even with a few pounds on it, was worth hating Lou over.

"I took the liberty of making an appointment for you," she said.

"Imagine that." As if she hadn't done that thousands of times.

"Two o'clock. It's an old friend of ours—Eben Boldt."

"Really. Did he say what about?"

"He asked if you had the entire afternoon clear, and I said yes."

"Anything else?"

"No. Very closemouthed, our Eben. I always found him a little humorless. Didn't you?"

That was like Jefferson on Mount Rushmore saying that Washington character seemed kind of stoic.

"Hadn't noticed," I said.

A few minutes later, Lou stepped into my private office, shut the door behind him, and settled into the client's chair. I was already behind my desk.

"Where were we?" he asked.

With no further preamble, I gave him a straight report on the conversation with Hoffa.

Lou sat blank-faced throughout. When I'd wrapped it up, he said, "Do you believe him?"

"I don't *not* believe him. That he didn't deny the possibility one of his people did it, on their own initiative, says something."

He considered that, then asked, "Are you satisfied that *he's* satisfied?"

"That I'm not a loose end? Well, I don't think I am

to him. But if one of his guys did take it upon himself to remove Tom, it's possible they might try the same with me."

Behind the lenses, his eyes were almost gone, just cuts in his face. "Doesn't have to be one of *his* guys, you know."

"True. Could be the Outfit, on their own, or even . . ."

I didn't say it, but Lou just nodded, slowly. The word we both skipped was CIA. Operation Mongoose cast a long fucking shadow.

I said, "Make a discreet call down to Dallas to see if Jack Ruby is back. His club's called the Carousel. Nothing direct—if there's some agency we work with down there who can check this out without getting Ruby's attention, that would be perfect."

"We do have a guy down there."

"Good. If Ruby isn't deep in the heart of Texas yet, check our local hotels and see if you come up with him. He might be staying under Jake Rubinstein."

"Okay. Figure to have a chat with your old West Side compadre?"

"If he's in town. If he's back home . . . we'll see."

Neither of us said anything for a few seconds.

"If you *are* a loose end," Lou said, "that means somebody's weaving something goddamn serious. How the hell could a small-change payoff to a nobody like Jake Rubinstein get Tom Ellison killed? And put you on the spot?"

I laughed softly. "'On the spot.' There's an old Chicago term for you. Going back to Capone days. . . ."

"What kind of steps can you take?"

"Well, I slept downstairs with Sally last night," I said, shrugging one shoulder, "as a kind of half-ass precaution."

Nobody called Sally "Helen" except me, and maybe her mother, so I stuck with the familiar.

"You got her moved in okay?" he asked, his turn to pose a question he knew the answer to but asked anyway.

I nodded. "I love having her around, but this is a lousy time. If I'm reading Hoffa wrong, I'm putting her at serious risk."

"She's a big girl, Nate."

"Actually, she's a little wisp of a tough-as-nails thing."

Lou smiled a little. "She take those meetings you lined up at the Chez Paree and Empire Room?"

"Yeah," I said, relieved to have the subject changed. "Nice response, some apparent interest, particularly from Mike Satariano. But no bookings yet. I set her up with meets with the managers at the Ivanhoe Club, this morning, and the Gaslight, this afternoon."

"I wish her luck," he said, crossing his arms, but his expression said he thought she had a rough road ahead of her. "Cabaret and theater aren't what they used to be in this town. Sally's probably going to have to go the strip club route. Even at her age, she's a name in that world."

"She doesn't look her age," I reminded him.

"No, and neither do I, and neither do you, but we are still old fuckers. Never forget that."

"Where Sally has it over on us," I said, "is nobody would pay a nickel to see us in our birthday suits."

That made him chuckle, and he rose. "I hear Eben Boldt's stopping by today. If you can make *him* smile, I'll buy lunch two days running. Make him laugh, I'll spot you, my missus, and Sally to supper at the Café de Paris."

"Honor system?"

"Sure. You wouldn't lie to me."

"Only because you'd know."

He shut the door—like all invaders of other people's privacy, I prized my own—leaving me smiling, because he was right about Eben Boldt. What it took to make that guy laugh was a mystery this detective had never cracked.

Nice guy, though, and smart, and if I might be allowed, I was proud of him.

Eben Boldt was the only Negro Secret Service agent in the Chicago office, one of a handful in the nation, and had even spent a number of months on the White House detail, the first Secret Service agent of his race.

Boldt had grown up in East St. Louis, Illinois, his father a railroad worker, his mother a strict disciplinarian. He'd been raised around Dixieland and jazz music, which was the part of his personality I liked best, and he'd earned a college degree in music.

So in the summer of 1957, when he showed up on the A-1's doorstep, saying he was interested in a career in criminal investigation, I said, "Hum a few bars and I'll fake it." That marked the first of many times I looked into the sharp-eyed chocolate oval of his face and got no reaction.

"I'm serious about this, Mr. Heller," he said.

He'd been twenty-two years old, a handsome kid—not Sidney Poitier handsome maybe, but close enough, a slender, highly presentable exemplar of his people.

We ran a regular advertisement seeking investigators but had never had a Negro apply before. I thought a young colored operative would come in very handy in Chicago, and based on his professional if somber demeanor, and his impressive grade average at Lincoln University, I took him on.

Boldt was with us only a year, however, before he applied to the Illinois State Highway Police. It was clear the A-1 had just been a stepping-stone into what I'm sure he figured would be "real" police work, but I took no offense. He'd done an excellent job for us, mostly working undercover on gambling-related cases in

Bronzeville, and I had been happy to give him a glow-ing letter of recommendation.

His work experience for the A-1 probably helped Eben move quickly out of traffic into the then brand-new Illinois Criminal Investigation Division. He'd been noticed there by the head of the Springfield office of the Secret Service, and encouraged to apply—which he did, passing the civil service test and entering the Secret Service in 1960.

Eben and I had not been friends exactly—I'd been his employer, and much older—but we encoun-tered each other from time to time, when the A-1 had occasion to interact with the local Secret Service office.

And he had shared with me the story of how he got invited to be on the White House detail. He had a very somber, grandiose way of telling it, which on the sev-eral occasions I'd heard it had never failed to make me laugh. He took no apparent offense but never saw the humor.

Jack Kennedy had been in Chicago at McCormick Place for a banquet designed as a thank-you for Mayor Daley and his political machine, who'd helped put the Prez over the top in Illinois, through means that might best be described as imaginative. Boldt's role had been to stand guard in the basement at a restroom set aside for the President's personal use. When Kennedy and an entourage including the mayor, the governor, various congressional leaders, and local pols trooped past Boldt's post, the President raised a hand like Ward Bond halt-ing the wagon train. Seemed the leader of the free world needed to heed nature's call.

Nevertheless, Kennedy paused to speak to Boldt, the President seeming to the agent "strangely shy." He asked the Negro, "Are you one of Mayor Daley's finest, young man?"

"I'm a Secret Service agent, Mr. President."

An agent accompanying the group called out, "He's assigned to the Chicago office, sir! His name is Eben Boldt."

Kennedy said to the doorman, "Do you know if there has ever been a Negro agent on the Secret Service White House detail, Mr. Boldt?"

"Not to my knowledge, Mr. President."

"How would you like to be the first?"

"Yes, sir, Mr. President!"

The next day, Eben had his new marching orders.

"That's how I became the first Negro Secret Service agent to serve at the White House," he said, the first time I heard the story.

"What you are," I said, laughing, "is the first bathroom attendant ever promoted to the White House staff."

Eben had not seen the humor.

Nor had he fit in well on the White House detail. He had gotten along famously with JFK and Bobby, but there was friction with the other agents. They made continual racial digs, and Eben wasn't the kind of guy who could roll with punches like that. I'm not saying he should have, just that he couldn't. He reported his fellow agents for racial comments, as well as drinking and carousing when on the road with the President, and was generally not popular.

Eben requested a return to the Chicago office, after a three-month probationary tour, and permission was granted.

Lou and I discussed the A-1's talented if tight-assed graduate over lunch at Binyon's.

"He's a good man," Lou said. "Think of the shit we've got as Jews, over the years, and just try to imagine what his life is like."

"I'm not a Jew," I said, over my finnan haddie. "I'm

just a Mick with an unfortunate last name. Anyway, his life would be easier if he knew how to laugh."

"See? You *are* a Jew."

Lou also reported to me that he'd assigned various men (and one woman) to the Ellison case, as I'd outlined earlier.

When we got back at one forty-five, Eben Boldt was already there, seated in the waiting room, hands folded in his lap, as immobile as a cigar-store Indian.

Seeing Lou and me, he shot to his feet. He was in a crisply tailored dark-gray suit with a white button-down shirt and a black tie with a restrained red pattern; his black wingtips were mirror-shined. A charcoal green-feathered hat was on the seat cushion next to him.

And he immediately proved me wrong—he smiled at us both. Not a big smile, but he was obviously pleased to see us, and shook both our hands, a firm, perspiration-free grip.

"Mr. Sapperstein," he said, with nods to both of us. "Mr. Heller."

"You know us too well for that, Eben," I said. "It's Nate and Lou, okay? And just because you work for the government, don't expect me to call you 'mister.'"

He gave me a blank look. He *could* smile—it was just humor that he missed.

I led Eben through the bullpen and he nodded and said hello to a couple of agents who'd worked here when he did. No stopping for conversation, though. We moved right into my office, he took the client chair and I got behind my desk, and we had one of the shortest conversations on (or off) record at the A-1.

"Someone wants to see you," he said. He stood. "I'll drive."

I stayed put. "What, you're taking me for a ride? To a Chicago guy, that has a kind of nasty ring."

Nothing.

"Okay," I said, getting up and coming around the desk. "Why don't *you* drive, then?"

He frowned a little, but politely opened my door for me.

Soon the Secret Service man was behind the wheel of a dark-blue Chevy Impala with me in the passenger seat. No other agent had made the trip with Eben—it was just the two of us. On this cool, overcast day, both in raincoat and hat, we headed a few blocks west to the Northwest Highway, and before long were at Foster Avenue, where the road split; keeping left took you to O'Hare, but Eben headed north onto the Edens Expressway.

He hadn't said anything since telling me somebody wanted to see me.

We got off the expressway at Lake Street, heading west past ranch-style houses and other nice but not pricey middle-class residences.

Finally he broke the ice. "I was in an interesting meeting this morning."

"Really. What kind of meeting, Eben?"

"Coordination meeting. They held it in the anteroom of Mayor Daley's office. Fifth floor of City Hall?"

I knew where Mayor Daley's office was, but didn't point that out, just saying, "Ah. You were representing the Secret Service at this meeting?"

Whatever the hell it was about.

He steered with two tight hands. Wouldn't want that Impala to get away from him like a bucking bronco. "I was there with Special Agent in Charge Martineau. I think the SAIC may have resented my presence, but the White House apparently requested it."

And he smiled again. Just a little. Eben obviously got a kick out of the boss getting trumped by the Negro's connections in high places.

I, on the other, was not smiling. The White House?

Eben was saying, "There were three deputy chiefs of police on hand, and Captain Linsky, security liaison between the PD and the SS."

He meant Secret Service, not Hitler's elite.

"Your friend Chief Cain was there, Nate, serving in the same capacity as Captain Linksy, but for the sheriff's department. Lasted a good four hours, the meeting."

"Did it? Is it a breach of security for you to tell me what the meeting was about?"

Since we'd been discussing it for five minutes.

"Oh. Sorry. Thought I'd covered that. We were mapping out the security plans for the President's visit Saturday. He's scheduled to attend the Army–Air Force game at Soldier Field."

"Yeah, I noticed that on the front page on my way to do the Jumble."

He ignored that, which was okay—it didn't really merit anything. "Each deputy chief was assigned an area of responsibility. Patrol Deputy Rochford, the airport. Traffic Deputy Madi, the motorcade route. Captain Linsky, the Conrad Hilton—where the President's motorcade ends up, and where he and his staff will headquarter for the trip. Chief Cain has the stadium, and various street security functions. The mayor's special events man, Jack Reilly, was there, too. Extended His Honor's best wishes for a safe visit."

We were passing through a section of middle-class businesses, currently gliding by Scott Foresman, the textbook publisher, home of the Dick and Jane primers. See Nate. See Nate ride. See Nate wonder what the fuck was up.

"For a few hours yesterday," Eben said, eyes on the road, "I was ranking agent in the office. So I was the one who took the call."

I frowned at him. "What call?"

"From the FBI. Phoning from Washington. The agent on the line said they had information from an informant warning of an attempt to assassinate the President by a four-man team using high-powered rifles."

"What?"

"The attempt would be made on his way to the Army–Air Force game."

Eben took a curve and I knocked against my door as Lake Street opened up on the north side into a vast open space—an airfield that pre-dated most of the neighborhood we'd just passed through.

The agent was saying, "The suspects are reportedly right-wing military paramilitary fanatics . . . armed with rifles with telescopic sights. The assassination itself would likely be attempted at one of the Northwest Highway overpasses."

"The FBI considers this credible intel?"

"Yes. But I don't know anything about the informant, except that the agent on the phone mentioned his name is 'Lee.' "

*That college-campus rabble-rouser with Ruby had been named Lee. Coincidence, surely.*

"Shortly after the phone call," Eben continued, "a telex came in, confirming it. A long, detailed telex that went straight to Martineau, who was back in the office by then. I have to admit it surprised me."

"I would think so. An assassination plot . . ."

"Well, yes, that does get one's attention. But, Nate, the FBI seldom cooperates with the Secret Service. We're rival entities. Yet for some reason, Mr. Hoover seems eager to pass this one along to us."

That *was* odd: that aging iguana who ran the FBI would normally relish the opportunity to reap the rewards of the positive publicity saving the President's life would bring. On the other hand, maybe J. Edgar figured if somebody failed to save the President, let that somebody be the Secret Service.

Eben was shaking his head, rather glumly. "I'm not normally one to pass the buck, but I admit I would prefer this had stayed with the FBI. We're really understaffed, Nate. *Critically* understaffed. We have only *thirteen* men in the Chicago office—many with other assignments. I got pulled off a counterfeiting job, for example. The idea of a group conspiring to do something like this . . . it blindsides us."

"Why is that? It's your job, isn't it?"

"Well . . . we frankly are more used to dealing with the cranks who write their crazy letters and make their threatening phone calls. We pull them in, and they're usually mental cases, perhaps with a cheap handgun and some irrational score to settle. If the President is coming to town, we just keep them locked up till he leaves again."

The airfield was bordered by a mix of chain-link and solid fencing. A Navy helicopter was on the runway among fighter planes and prop jobs—no jets. A huge old hanger and a control tower loomed.

"Eben, what does any of this have to do with me? And what the hell are we doing at Glenview Naval Air Station?"

The Negro turned onto an access road and headed toward a guard gate.

"You'll have to ask the man I've brought you to see," he said.

With a faint smile.

# 10

Naval Air Station Glenview—NASG, to military types—
had begun as a civilian enterprise, the Curtiss-Wright
airfield, 450 acres of farmland purchased to build a
modern airport outside Chicago's so-called "smoke
belt" of coal-burning industrial plants, railroads, and
homes. A grand dedication in October 1929 was followed almost immediately by the stock market crash,
from which the facility never recovered.

The Curtiss corporation had given it the old college
try, though, like hosting the International Air Races of
'33, an offshoot of the same Century of Progress
World's Fair where Sally Rand had flashed her fans
and fanny to fame. I'd supervised the security team for
the event, sharing my Pickpocket Detail training with
them, as there was a huge crowd attracted by the attending aviation luminaries—the likes of Charles Lind-
bergh (who I knew well), Jimmy Doolittle, Wiley Post,
and Eddie Rickenbacker. Amelia Earhart had to cancel,
due to engine trouble in Kansas, but I got to meet her
later.

It took the war to make a real go of the airfield, after
the Navy purchased the property for a fraction of the
$2 million Curtiss-Wright had spent on it in pre-
Depression dollars. The massive, famous Hangar One

was joined by more hangars, administration buildings, ground schools, barracks, dining halls, and more, as the private airport turned into an in-land training base, taking advantage of Lake Michigan for simulated aircraft carrier landings.

Today NASG was a Navy Reserve training center, still bustling with men and aircraft, if nothing compared to the war years. Now the Navy Reserve units were joined by Marines, Army, and Seabees, as well as a Coast Guard search-and-rescue team.

Eben Boldt parked near the control tower, which rose from lower-slung buildings still resembling a modest commercial airport, with its late twenties/early thirties art moderne touches. Eben led me down a corridor of military personnel going efficiently in every direction until we were through a door and moving across a bullpen of uniformed aides and civilian secretaries at their desks, typewriter clack providing urgency to a static tableau.

We took a left down a bland hallway to where two men in dark suits were standing on either side of a nondescript door to a room whose outer wall was windows that venetian blinds concealed. The two government men—more Secret Service? FBI maybe?—had the expressionless watchfulness you would expect, hands at their sides, not tucked behind their backs, suit coats unbuttoned for fast, easy access to the .38s that would ride their hips.

Eben's nod to them was barely perceptible, as were theirs back to him—maybe these were local SS. If so, I didn't recognize them. The Negro agent made a gesture toward the door, not opening it for me but indicating I was to go in. Then he positioned himself against the opposite wall.

I went in.

And was in another break room, twice the size of

the A-1's, with a fairly impressive facing wall of vending machines, including a sandwich dispenser and one that served up coffee. The side walls had framed photos—a World War II–era photo of fighter planes in formation, a not dissimilar shot of jets circa the Korean conflict, another of the control tower, another inside a busy hangar. Two tables that would each seat half a dozen office workers took up most of the space. The tables were between me and a slim male figure in a white shirt and navy-blue trousers with his back to me—he was getting himself a cup of the terrible coffee such machines served up for your dime and nickel, when they were in the mood.

Bobby Kennedy looked over his shoulder at me and, with his rather shy, slightly bucktoothed grin adding to the Tom Sawyer effect, asked, "Coffee, Nate? It's swill but it's, ah, the best I can do."

"No thanks," I said, in no mood to whitewash a fence.

His suit coat was slung over a chair at the farthest table, a manila envelope positioned like a place mat, and I went over and sat next to where he'd be.

I said, "But I will let you buy me a Coke."

"My pleasure," he said, playing gracious host. He was actually pretty good at that, with all the wingdings he and wife Ethel threw at Hickory Hill, their home in McLean, Virginia.

He deposited his cardboard cup of coffee at the table and I watched him selflessly dig change from his pocket and get me my very own Dixie cup of caffeinated swill from one of the machines. It was like when Jesus went around washing the feet of the poor.

He delivered my beverage, sat, and extended his hand for a quick, perfunctory shake. His manner was vaguely embarrassed. I hadn't seen him in over a year, but he had aged much more—he looked skinny to me, new, deeper lines carved into his boyish face, that sandy mop flecked with gray. His tie was red. So were the whites around his blue eyes.

The muffled rumble of an aircraft taking off was like a roar so far off in the jungle, you couldn't tell what beast it belonged to. Such sounds were fairly continual as we spoke, never loud enough to interfere with even the most soft-spoken segments of our conversation.

Sitting next to me—with military craft taking the sky, just outside—was the President's top legal adviser, chief political adviser, foreign affairs aide, most dogged protector, tireless campaign manager, and best friend. And they were all this one slight, not terribly experienced lawyer who wouldn't be forty for several years.

"Sorry about the cloak-and-dagger routine," he said. He folded his arms. "I'm not, ah, officially in town. On my way to North Dakota to assure some Indians that their treatment by the federal government is a, uh, national disgrace."

"You expect this to be news to them?"

"I expect to get a polite welcome and maybe a war bonnet to take home and impress *my* tribe."

"No Mayor Daley this trip?"

He shook his head. "I made the, ah, political rounds not long ago, and talked to the local prosecutors and FBI. We have a Hoffa case coming up, you know."

"Really."

His smirk was humorless. "Would it surprise you that I don't find Chicago a shining example of what America might hope to one day achieve?"

"I'm about as surprised as those Indians."

He shook his head, sipped the coffee, made a face. I couldn't tell whether that expression reflected the vending-machine coffee or my hometown.

"On my prior trip here," he said, "Daley arranged for a limo, courtesy of some Chicago captain of industry. I turned it down, had local FBI agents pick me up and give me a *real* tour, the kind the mayor, ah, wouldn't have liked—slums, low-cost housing projects, a mental hospital where on a sunny day the inmates, and that's what they were, ah, inmates, were inside staring at blank walls. A disgrace. And *this* from a Democratic administration."

"You sold me. I'll vote straight-ticket Republican next time around."

That got a little smile out of him. He was easier to make laugh than Eben Boldt, but just barely.

Then his smile turned sideways. He spoke softly, to imply both intimacy and confidentiality: "I could've used you lately, Nate, I'll tell you that."

"Oh?"

"You've seen this crap in the papers, about Bobby Baker and his call girls?"

"Don't tell me Jack has suddenly taken an interest in the fairer sex."

He smirked. "How about a German lass with connections to their Communist party?"

The press boys had always kept hands-off where JFK's sexual escapades were concerned, but in the wake of Great Britain's headline-making Profumo Scandal, they might well have a change of heart. A German Mata Hari in bed with the President would make goddamn good copy.

Plus, it was getting toward the end of JFK's term, which encouraged a little good old-fashioned muckraking—outside the bedroom, the Kennedys were already considered fair game. Headlines in Chicago recently lambasted Bobby for going after Sam Giancana with tactics a federal judge had termed "Russian spy–type pursuit"; and nationally, stories embarrassingly revealed some of Bobby's secret Cuban operations, specifically his anti-Castro guerrilla bases in Central America.

"I hope she was a looker," I said, referring to this German variation on Christine Keeler, knowing Bobby's brother wasn't always picky.

"A ringer for Elizabeth Taylor."

"Hell, why not just go after Liz herself? Unless Marilyn has given him second thoughts."

Bobby didn't get angry, which considering his hot temper said something; he didn't even frown. His eyes were, if anything, sad suddenly.

The reason we hadn't seen each other—or spoken—in over year grew out of the falling-out we'd had over the murder of Marilyn Monroe. Bobby hadn't been responsible, nor had Jack, but people looking out for their best interests had been. Sound familiar?

And Bobby, the attorney general of this great land of ours, helped cover it up.

Which was why I'd told him, in no uncertain terms, that I was no longer available to the Camelot crowd for government work.

"I have to ask you," he said, quietly, "to put that aside. I don't expect your forgiveness, but I do request your forbearance."

I said nothing.

He tried again. He touched my arm, a remarkable gesture coming from a guy about as demonstrative as a bust of Napoleon.

"Nate, I need your help. I understand your wish not to be involved with us, in any way, anymore. But you are in a unique position to help us out in a very tough situation."

"Is it an opening in the Peace Corps? I always wanted to dig wells and teach in developing nations. Plus I hear it's a good way to meet chicks."

An aircraft was taking off—big enough to make the framed pictures nervous.

"You're not going to make this easy, are you, Nate?"

I sipped the Coke. God it was awful. Too much syrup. Ice floating like glass chips, flat as Audrey Hepburn.

I asked, "What did you do about the German streusel?"

The slightest twinkle in those bloodshot blue eyes. "What do you think we did?"

"Deported her and paid her off."

Another small smile. "Actually, ah, I understand she *has* come into money. I do know she was escorted overseas by LaVern Duffy."

Another investigator from rackets committee days.

Bob was saying, "I think he, ah, got along quite *well* with Miss Rometsch."

"For that gig, I might have made an exception."

I twitched a smile at him, and he knew he had me.

With a relieved sigh, a business-like Bobby pushed the coffee away. I had already done that with the Coke.

"I trust Mr. Boldt has briefed you, at least in broad strokes. Very reliable man, Mr. Boldt. Jack misses having him on the White House detail."

I frowned. "Is that what this is about? This planned attack on Jack next Saturday? Why don't you just cancel the fucking trip?"

I already knew at least one answer: if every time a death threat came in before a public appearance by the President, the leader of the free world would never stick his head out of the Oval Office.

But, as Eben had indicated, most of those threats came from lunatics with a handgun and a grudge—not a trained assassination squad.

The latter might have been Bobby's answer, but it wasn't.

Instead, he said, "My brother is probably the most loved man in America. And possibly the most hated."

"No," I said, "*you're* the most hated. But he's probably second."

That got a real smile out of him. His sense of humor was wry and dark, so I wasn't surprised by that toothy display.

"This month, we've lined up several high-profile trips for Jack—motorcades preceding political events . . . not just this Chicago one, but to Florida and Texas."

"The *South*?" I looked at him sideways. "That's where they *really* hate you Kennedy boys. Remember what they used to say back in WW Two—is this trip really necessary?"

Though Bobby actually had a precarious relationship with Negro leaders—especially Martin Luther King—he was viewed in the Deep South as the "nigger-loving" attorney general who had forced Governor George Wallace to get out of that schoolhouse doorway and let the colored kids in.

"Florida and Texas are the only two Southern states we are likely to carry," Bobby was saying. "And we *need* them. Much as he may sicken us, Lyndon being on the ticket again gives us a decent shot at Texas."

"Isn't Lyndon enough to swing it?"

"I wish he were. But the party down there is at war with itself—Governor Connally might as well be a Republican, and Senator Yarborough's a liberal maverick. Jack has to go down there and spread the charm around." He shook his head, smiled ruefully. "Shitty way to make a living, isn't it?"

"Well, at least there's plenty of retired Democrats living in Florida."

"Can't even take that for granted. Retirees are by

nature conservative." His eyebrows went up. "And, of course, we *really* need Illinois, and all those lovely electoral votes. Canceling is *not* an option, Nate."

I sat forward. "It should be. Bob, your Secret Service contingent in the Loop numbers an underwhelming dozen or so. That would be a joke if it wasn't so sad."

His hands were folded on the table now, on top of the manila folder, almost prayerfully. "We have support from the Chicago PD and sheriff's department, but your point is valid. We'll be bringing in agents from Secret Service offices all over the country, on Saturday. But in the meantime, I would like to bolster the local bunch with some, ah, outside help."

"What outside help are you thinking of?"

"You."

I am fairly fast with my mouth, and my brain is usually only a second or two behind it. But I had nothing to say.

"I want you there, Nate, on the inside of this thing. First of all, you know this town better than, ah, any of these local agents. Only a handful of them grew up in Chicago. Mr. Boldt's from St. Louis, I believe. That's reason enough."

I was starting to get it. Something was crawling up my spine on its way to my neck, where it would lay goose bumps.

"But that isn't *the* reason," I said.

"No." He pushed the manila folder toward me. Turned out it wasn't a place mat.

I opened it and shook out four 5-by-7-inch photos, blurry, grainy color surveillance-type photos, taken on the street at various indistinct locations.

Two were of Latin types, a trimly bearded guy maybe in his late twenties, the other a mustached old pro who was probably mid-thirties. Both were in sport shirts, the older man in sunglasses. Nothing distinctive about them, really—they could have been hacienda owners or members of a mariachi band, but somehow I didn't think they were either.

The other photos were of pasty-looking white guys, both wearing crew cuts, both in their mid-twenties, both in sunglasses, one blond chewing a toothpick, the other black-haired with a cigarette frozen near his lips as the hidden camera snapped him. They had lean faces but what showed of their upper torsos appeared trimly muscular. One was in a T-shirt, the other in a blue plaid shirt.

"The white guys are either military or ex," I said. "What's the story on the Cubans?"

Bobby almost blinked. "Did I say they were Cubans?"

"No, but I don't think I'd be sitting here if they weren't. Two of these shooters are Cuban exiles who might have ties, vague or not so vague, back to Operation Mongoose. Which is why you want me sitting in on this."

He just stared momentarily, then nodded.

"What the hell is going on, Bob?"

"We don't know." He tapped the bearded guy's photo. "That's Gonzales." He tapped the older, mustached guy's photo. "That's Rodriguez."

"No first names?"

"Not yet."

"No background?"

"Nothing specific. FBI intel indicates the Cubans are dissidents."

"Exiles, yeah. And the soldiers?"

"No names at all. FBI believes they are right-wing paramilitary fanatics. Southern boys."

"Racist white trash I believe is the term. If the intel is coming from the FBI, why aren't the fabled G-men who took down Dillinger on top of this thing?"

Bobby shrugged, gestured with an open hand. "Mr. Hoover says this is clearly a Secret Service matter. After all, it's not a federal crime to attempt the murder of a President—not even a federal crime to succeed."

"Just another run-of-the-mill murder," I said dryly, over the muffled roar of yet another takeoff.

"It's the Secret Service's job to protect the President, and Mr. Hoover says it would be 'inappropriate, even illegal' for the FBI to participate in this investigation."

As the attorney general, Bobby was Hoover's boss, and he should have been able to tell him what to do in this, or any, instance. But that fat old fucker had too much on the Kennedy brothers in his legendary (but real) secret files to make that possible, or anyway advisable. As much as Jack and Bobby hated J. Edgar, they had to keep hiring him back on as head Bureau mucky-muck. Why didn't they hire me to get a photo of that old queen getting buggered or blown?

Some of my best ideas are just too advanced. . . .

Bobby leaned back in the hard plastic-and-metal chair. "Nate, this has to be, ah, handled. There is so much at stake. We are close in Cuba, *very* close . . . we finally have someone next to Castro. Someone who can eliminate this problem without stooping to any of the more fanciful means our, uh, friends at the CIA have come up with."

"Like using the mob?"

"Without using that kind of resource, yes. A lot of things have been set in motion in recent years, too many things, that seem, ah, in hindsight poorly judged."

"Like exploding cigars? I always thought the CIA should try one of those trick lapel flowers. Squirt acid in the Beard's kisser and see how he likes it."

Bobby laughed lightly. "Well, I can top that. How about an exploding seashell? Or a poison-lined wet suit? The CIA says Castro enjoys skin-diving, you see.

Well, we're finally at the end of this comic-opera non-sense. But goddamnit, if we have to go the whole hog to take care of this thing, we'll do that, too."

I took that to mean mount or anyway fund a violent overthrow of Castro, of the sort the abortive Bay of Pigs represented; but I didn't ask for clarification.

"You know that's not my preference," he clarified anyway, raising a hand as if being sworn in. "Jack and I much prefer to encourage counterinsurgency in these countries, and make use of spy operations."

"You guys do know that Ian Fleming is a fiction writer, right?"

"Actually, he was a real-life spy before he became a fiction writer. Maybe you didn't know that."

Actually, I did.

Bobby was saying, "Subversion and sabotage, not all-out war, *that's* our preference. I think you know that. You would be shocked, and I know you aren't easily shocked, by the pressure Jack is getting to engage in a full-scale ground war in Vietnam. We want nothing to do with that kind of insanity. We're going the other way."

"Black operations."

His shrug was a yes.

"Like Mongoose."

He damn near winced. "Getting involved with . . . those *people*, I agree that was, ah, ill-advised. But Mongoose is still operational, Nate."

"The curtain isn't down yet on the comic opera?"

"Not quite. If all goes as planned, yes . . . but as of now, not quite. We still need options. We may yet need those . . . unpleasant resources."

We had come to something that I had never understood, and could never get a good answer for. "Bob, these 'unpleasant resources' are your collaborators, on the one hand, and on the other, you're trying to stick them in stir."

"We made them no promises otherwise." His eyes glittered and his bucktooth grin turned feral. "In addition to Hoffa, we've got Carlos Marcello in the crosshairs. We have him in a federal courtroom in New Orleans, *right now*. Finally, we will deport that slippery bastard."

"That slippery bastard is part of Mongoose, too, Bob—through Trafficante."

He was shaking his head. "We don't need him. Doing something for his country doesn't buy him a 'Get Out of Jail Free' card. You don't buy your way out of wholesale murder and dope-trafficking."

Bobby had tried to deport Marcello before—notably when he had the FBI kidnap the don of New Orleans and dump his ass unceremoniously in a Guatemalan jungle.

"What I want from you, Nate, is to work with the Secret Service on tracking down these four suspects. Obviously, you have Saturday morning as a deadline— Jack arrives at O'Hare at eleven A.M."

"That's less than four days, Bob."

"If I'm able to squeeze more information from Edgar on their identities, and the source of this intel, I will. And you'll hear from me."

"How will the Secret Service feel about taking on a slightly overage recruit?"

He reached into his suit-coat pocket and withdrew a small black wallet, skimming it over to me across the tabletop.

"These are your credentials. You're a special investigator attached to the Justice Department on loan to the Treasury Department. I have spoken to Chief Martineau personally, and he's been instructed to give you every courtesy."

"Am I working for myself or Martineau?" I knew the guy a little, and wasn't wild about the prospect of being under his thumb.

"You're working for me," Bobby said, "but give the chief his due respect. Work within the unit. Your job is to help find these four . . ." He pointed to the photos. ". . . but also to look after our interests."

That "our" was vague as hell, but I understood it: his interests, his brother's interests, and my interests . . . as collaborators in Operation Mongoose.

"We have made a lot of people unhappy, Nate, Jack and I. Sam Giancana, assorted Cubans, right-wing fanatics, certain elements within the CIA, and it's possible—just possible—two or more of these groups are coming together on this . . . and taking some of the very tactics we developed to, ah, eliminate Castro, and turning them around on us."

"Well, then tell Jack to stay away from cigars and seashells."

Bobby was not amused. In fact, his expression turned grave.

He said, "There is a plan that includes taking Fidel out via high-power rifle with a scope from a high building while he rides in an open vehicle, a Jeep. That plan has never been attempted, never carried out, obviously . . . but it's, ah, a scenario the various players in this little comedy did in fact develop."

"Do you think the Cubans, if they're captured, will spill about Mongoose? Will they use that knowledge to barter themselves out of captivity?"

The disaster that implied—not just politically but internationally—was staggering to contemplate.

"They might," Bobby said. His tone seemed casual but expression remained grave. "That's why I would recommend, if given the opportunity, considering your options."

That was also vague, but I got it.

*Kill the bastards, if you get the chance.*

"How about the white guys?" I asked.

"That's up to you, Nate. This kind of individual, young soldier or ex-soldier, doesn't usually know much. They tend to have CIA handlers who manipulate them, control them. But if you, ah, don't deal with them?"

"Yeah?"

"Their handlers likely will."

Bobby rose, leaving the photos with me. "Martineau has copies of those. He'll be handing them out to his agents. They have the names, too, Gonzales, Rodriguez. The only thing you know that Martineau doesn't is the possible Mongoose tie-in."

*Should I tell him about Tom Ellison? His murder, and the strip club payoff that proceeded it? There was a Hoffa tie, and therefore an Outfit tie. But what the hell could a nobody like Jack Ruby have to do with something like this? He was a shirttail Mongoose connection himself, sure, but . . .*

I kept it to myself—Bobby was already halfway out the door.

"I haven't said I'd do this," I said.

"Sure you have," he said.

He went on out.

Me, I just sat there not drinking the cup of Coke, listening to the muffled roar of planes taking off without me, till Eben Boldt collected me. To drive me back to Chicago, where the mental patients stared at blank walls on sunny days.

And to my new job with the Secret Service.

Just catercorner from the Monadnock Building on Dearborn, between Adams and Jackson, the Federal Building was one of those massive, magnificent classical buildings designed to outlive the pyramids.

But this was Chicago, and the wrecking ball would be coming before long, to make room for another glass-and-steel Mies van der Rohe slab like the nearly completed federal courthouse across the street, already casting its thirty-story shadow on the Federal Building's meager sixteen (counting the dome, anyway).

Eben Boldt and I clip-clopped across the three-hundred-foot-high octagonal rotunda, surrounded by polished granite, white and Siena marble, elaborate mosaics, gilded bronze, and government drones. An elevator with a uniformed attendant (you were seeing less and less of that now) took us up to the ninth floor, where the various federal offices were as utilitarian as the lower area was imposing.

On the ride back from Glenview, Boldt and I had not discussed my confab with the attorney general—in fact, the meeting wasn't mentioned at all, Bobby Kennedy's presence unacknowledged. We knew each other well enough to rustle up some small talk about his wife and their two grade-school-age children, and about my boy Sam, and how I was looking forward to spending time with him over Thanksgiving vacation.

The only reference to the little trip we'd just taken came when we were already in the Loop, with Eben saying, "It will be good having you work with us on this."

And I said, "Yeah. How will Martineau feel about that? We mildly butted heads a while back."

I had worked for an attorney defending a guy who had passed some counterfeit money, innocently as it turned out (at least according to the jury), and Martineau—who had not appreciated my testimony— asked me after, "How do you sleep at night?"

"With my eyes closed," I'd said.

"SAIC Martineau and I," Eben said, pulling into the Federal Building parking ramp, "maintain an uneasy truce."

I didn't pursue that.

Moving through an area half the size of the A-1's waiting room, past a stern-looking but not unattractive brunette receptionist with mannish eyeglass frames, we entered at the midpoint of a rectangular bullpen of perhaps a dozen gray-metal desks. The layout— courtesy of substantial squared-off pillars and walllike arrangements of filing cabinets—divided itself into numerous sub-areas, giving each desk some work space and even privacy. Down to my right, one end had a glassed-in area of telex machines with a door on either side marked INTERVIEW ONE and INTERVIEW TWO, and down at my left, that end was home to two glass-and-wood-faced offices, the glass blotted out by venetian blinds.

Eben walked me through and I nodded to a couple of agents I recognized, though most were as anonymous as monks hunkered over calligraphy. These servants of a higher power wore not shaved skulls and robes but crew cuts, dark-rimmed glasses, and white shirts with dark ties (suit coats slung over chairs). They seemed to either be on the phone or at their typewriters, the latter on stands that extended from the right of metal desks arrayed with gooseneck lamps, blotters, multiple-line phones, and disturbingly neat piles of paperwork. Clipboards hung on pillars with high-mounted black-bladed fans and the occasional clocks. This was an institutional world of gray-green plaster trimmed in dark wood, accented by bulletin boards bearing circulars, existing under fluorescent lighting that gave everything and everyone a ghostly pallor.

At the end with the two offices, Eben ushered me to the door at right, which was stenciled in gold:

### SPECIAL AGENT IN CHARGE
#### Maurice G. Martineau

the implication being that the position was more important than the mere man who held it.

Eben knocked, waited for the "Yes," and said, "Mr. Heller is here, sir."

"Send him in, Ebe."

This was apparently Eben's nickname around the office, sounding vaguely like "Abe," and news to me.

The Negro agent opened the door for me, I stepped in, and he shut it behind me, not joining us.

This was a good-size office, also rectangular but in the opposite direction as the outer area, putting Martineau at his glass-topped mahogany desk at right with a blinds-shrouded window behind him, facing a small conference table all the way across the office, by a wall bearing a big map of the United States. The furnishings were not the gray metal of the bullpen, but dark woods, Mediterranean style. A framed picture of Kennedy overlooked a bookcase of law books opposite as you entered, with the wall adjacent to Martineau's work area dominated by a bronze Department of the Treasury seal.

Martineau did not rise. He was in fact on the phone—had two multiple-line jobs on the desk, which held many stacks of papers and files, nearly as neat as those of his minions. The desk itself wasn't any bigger than a Buick, and instead of a gooseneck lamp, he had a green-shaded banker's number, the shade the same color as his blotter. No ashtray.

Maurice G. Martineau was a sturdy-looking fifty or so, not in his shirtsleeves—his charcoal suit tailored, his tie striped blue and black. His oval mug was well-grooved but otherwise as anonymous as those faces in the crowd out in the bullpen. No crew cut for Martineau, though—his salt-and-pepper hair was neatly parted and combed and a Little-Dab'll-Do-Ya'ed, and the only thing unruly about him were wiggle-worm eyebrows over deceptively bland blue eyes.

He raised a hand while he finished his phone call. I took in a few other details—the American flag behind him and to his right, the framed family photos (wife, boy, girl) arrayed on another smaller bookcase under the Treasury seal. Also a pitcher of ice water and several glasses.

Call finished, Martineau leaned back in his dimpled-brown-leather swivel chair and extended his hand. It was an odd example of gamesmanship, because this required me to rise from the visitor's chair to accept the handshake, which proved firm and perspiration-free.

Sitting back down, I said, "I'll try not to get in anybody's way, Mr. Martineau. I'm just here to help."

His smile might have seemed genuine to somebody who couldn't read eyes.

"Make it 'Marty,'" he said. "We don't stand on ceremony around here. I know the Service has a reputation for stuffiness, but when your job is to lay your life on the line, the people you work with become your friends."

"Fine. So then make it 'Nate,' and just let me know how I can lend a hand."

"Let's start with why you're here." He was rocking a little. "All I've been told is that you're on loan from Justice, as . . ." He checked a paper on his desk. ". . . an investigative assistant courtesy of the Attorney General. But to my knowledge . . ." He gestured in the vague direction of the Monadnock Building. ". . . you work across the street. For yourself."

I wasn't crazy about justifying my presence to this bureaucrat, but I could see I needed to.

"I was an investigator on the rackets committee," I said. "Worked for Bob Kennedy, and became an occasional asset to him, ever since. About an hour ago, he asked me to help you out for the next few days. Because of this situation with these potential assassins. And I said yes."

His smile couldn't have been more stuck on if he'd used Scotch tape. He put a lightness in his tone that didn't quite do the trick when he said: "Then you're not a spy?"

"What, for Bobby Kennedy? No. He just knows you're shorthanded. And meaning no disrespect to that young crew of yours out there, most of whom were not raised in this town, I do know my way around Chicago."

He thought about that for two seconds. "All right. Then I'll treat you as just another agent."

"Fine by me."

"With one exception. You'll take the office next door. For one thing, I don't have a free desk. For another, I want the men to understand that you have a certain standing in this investigation. That you represent the AG."

"Oh, that's not really a card I want to play. . . ."

"Then don't play it. But it's how I'll present you, and . . ." He gestured toward the wall dividing this office from its neighbor. ". . . that's the available space I have for you. Used to be my office, when I was deputy SAIC. But when I got moved up, I didn't get assigned a second-in-command."

So I had a private office. I didn't think any further argument was necessary.

He drummed the fingers of one hand lightly on mahogany. "How well do you know Mr. Boldt?"

Interesting. He had called the agent "Ebe," and made a point of how informal the guys around the office were. But now it was "Mr. Boldt."

"He worked for me at the A-1 for a year. Before he got that investigative post with the Illinois troopers."

He was nodding. "Yes, yes, that's right, isn't it? How did you find him as an employee?"

"A good agent. With a stick up his ass."

That made Martineau smile. Whatever artifices were hanging between us had just been broken through.

"He is a very good investigator," Martineau said. "But he's not popular here. About half my staff comes from the South, you know."

"Not surprising," I said. "Washington, D.C., is damn near Dixieland."

"Right. Well, Mr. Boldt is . . . racially sensitive. I would say oversensitive. If he hears his co-workers telling some innocent jigaboo joke, he files a complaint. We had a kind of unfortunate incident when he came back to work here, after his sojourn on the White House detail. He came in that first morning back, and somebody had hung a little noose from the nail where his clipboard hangs. By his desk?"

"That doesn't sound so innocent."

"Nate, do I have to tell you that when men do this kind of work, they develop a dark sense of humor?"

"No, but I don't think a darkie sense of humor is called for."

He raised his palms and patted the air. "I quite agree. But where you or I might shrug it off, and maybe even throw a punch after working hours, Mr. Boldt makes formal complaints—he did the same thing on the White House detail, which is why he didn't make it there. So he's never really been accepted. Never been . . . one of the guys."

"That's a shame," I said, sort of meaning it, "but what does it have to do with me?"

"When I break this down into two-man teams, I'll be assigning Mr. Boldt to you. I wanted you to know that in advance, in case you might take offense."

"Why would I take offense? Anyway, of the guys out there, Eben's the only one I really know at all."

"Good. Good. Then there's no problem."

"Not as far as I'm concerned."

"Good," he said again. Then he sighed in a *that's-that* manner. "Well, go check your office out, and be back here in fifteen minutes, for the briefing. Only a handful in the branch are aware of what's in store for us, and it's time to clue in the rest."

I rose, and this time Martineau did as well, and we shook again. I was glad that bullshit was over.

My new home-away-from-home was half the size of Martineau's office, but it had the same pricey dark Mediterranean furnishings, the desk only slightly smaller. No American flag, but another bronze Treasury seal reigned over an empty bookcase. The walls were otherwise pretty bare, though there was one interesting thing: a framed presidential portrait of Eisenhower, not Kennedy. And it had a bumper sticker plastered across the bottom: I STILL LIKE IKE. A comment on Kennedy, dating back to when this was Martineau's office? I never asked.

Soon, around the conference table in the SAIC's office, six agents joined Eben Boldt, Martineau, and me. They were an assortment of crew cuts, about half in dark-rimmed glasses, and I would be lying if I said I ever got their names straight. The water pitcher had moved to the table and two ashtrays were present, and three of the agents smoked during the meeting, but not Martineau. Or Eben or myself, for that matter. At each of the seats a manila folder waited. On the wall behind Martineau as he sat at the head of the table was a big framed city of Chicago map.

All of us were in shirtsleeves. A couple had theirs rolled up, apparently the office rebels. And every eye was on Martineau.

"We have a serious threat to the President on Saturday," he said, solemn yet matter-of-fact. "Some of you know Nathan Heller here. He has a distinguished record as an investigator with work on some of the most famous cases in this city's history—actually, in American history."

All eyes were on me now.

"We'll agree not to mention his bodyguard assignments for Mayor Cermak or Huey Long," Martineau said joshingly.

That got smiles and laughs, from me as well.

"We'll hope for a better outcome this time," I said.

Martineau continued: "Nate worked with the AG back in rackets committee days, and the AG asked him to trot across the street over here to pitch in. We couldn't be more short-staffed, so we're happy for the help. Welcome, Nate."

I actually got a polite little hand out of the boys.

"Glad to be here," I said, rising. "I'm in the office next door, but I have no special status. If anything, I'm low man on the totem pole. Just want to do my bit."

I sat.

"We appreciate that," Martineau said. "We'll start with Ebe here . . ."

Eben was on one side of Martineau, I was on the other.

". . . who will fill you in about the phone call he got yesterday afternoon."

The Negro agent gave his fellow officers the same rundown I'd received on the ride out to Glenview—the FBI agent passing along the warning of a possible assassination attempt on the President by a four-man team using high-powered rifles.

Martineau picked up: "That phone call was confirmed by a lengthy telex from the FBI in D.C. You won't be surprised that they've bounced this over to us. They would like nothing better than for us to screw the pooch, and give them an opening to snatch presidential protection away."

Half the agents nodded; the rest just stared at their boss in stoic agreement.

"We have basically three days," Martineau said, "to deal with this threat."

An agent asked, "*Is* it just a threat, Marty? Meaning no disrespect to our brothers at the FBI, but we deal with crank assassination calls every day."

"Not just a threat. Look in your folders."

They did, and each checked the photos. I had a folder, too, and unlike the photos from Kennedy, these were labeled: *Gonzales* (the younger Cuban), *Rodriguez* (the older), the white guys both tagged: *Unknown Subject*.

"You now know everything available on these suspects," Martineau said. "These photos are to be shown around but not copied. Not passed out. Understood?"

Nods.

"This morning I spoke with Chief Rowley, who had very specific instructions for me, and for you."

Rowley was the head of the Secret Service in Washington.

"There are to be no written reports on this investigation," Martineau said. "Any reports are to be given to me directly—orally. Nothing is to be sent to Chief Rowley—no interoffice teletext communication, either. Phone calls to me, or eyeball to eyeball, nothing else. And this case is to be given no file number."

These instructions seemed odd as hell, and even in this group—where questioning authority was not on the menu—I saw agents exchanging wary, confused glances. But nobody said anything.

"Understand that there are political implications here," Martineau said. "Last October, because of the missile crisis, the President had to stand Mayor Daley up. His Honor didn't appreciate that."

"Yeah," I said, "acted like it was the end of the world or something."

That got some smiles. Still, it was a tough room.

"So it's unlikely the President will cancel this trip," Martineau said. "He has political fences to mend and next year's election on his mind. We need to operate from the assumption that he is, in fact, coming."

Martineau got up and went to the wall map of the city. He indicated the various locations as he discussed them.

"We have an eleven-mile parade route from O'Hare Airport to Soldier Field. Chief Rowley says this route gives him considerable misgivings, and I have to agree. Most of it is in relatively open areas, and we can guard overpasses on the Northwest Expressway, as we did last March—we have enough support from the Chicago PD and the sheriff's department to pull that off."

An agent asked, "So where is the problem?"

"Jackson Street," Martineau said, tapping the map. "The President's limo will have to lumber up the ramp and then make a difficult ninety-degree turn that will slow the vehicle to practically a stop."

"That's a warehouse district," I said. It was just half a dozen blocks from where we sat, actually.

Eben said, "Any warehouse district is far more hazardous than a standard corridor of office buildings."

Martineau said, "No argument, Ebe. On top of that, we have no fewer than forty-five local school and civic organizations who'll be on hand at that exit, eagerly awaiting a chance to see their president."

"And if shots are fired," I said, "with a crowd like that? You'll have panic that could easily cover the escape of the assassins."

"We won't allow any shots to be fired," Martineau said sternly.

Another agent said, "We don't begin to have enough men to cover that Jackson area. Marty, this is a nightmare."

Martineau raised his hands, palms out, in a calming gesture. "We *will* have more agents by Saturday morning. I don't know how many, but Nate here isn't our only support."

"Thank God," I said.

A few smiles.

Eben asked, "So—where, when, and how do we start?"

Martineau got up again, and resumed pointing to the map. He assigned groups of two agents to three heavily Latino neighborhoods: Pilsen on the Lower West Side, West Town northwest of the Loop, and South Lincoln Park.

"I'm leaving Heller and Boldt free to run down leads you guys come up with," Martineau said, "and to follow any other leads that may develop from tips. Questions?"

There were a few, but nothing worth reporting here. That was still going on when the receptionist stuck her head in.

"I'm sorry to interrupt, sir," she said, eyes worried behind her masculine glasses, "but you weren't answering your phone."

"That's because we're in conference, Miss Kundel," Martineau said rather stiffly.

"I know, but there's a Chicago police detective in the waiting area, and he says it's important. It's a Lieutenant Moyland . . . ?"

I said, "I know him. Want me to take it?"

Martineau nodded, and the meeting resumed while I followed the receptionist back to her post. She was about thirty-five and her gray suit was as mannish as the glasses; she seemed to be working hard not to sway her very nice hips. But I am a trained detective and noticed them anyway.

Lieutenant Berkeley Moyland was about thirty-five, a freckled-face, red-haired copper who might have been my cousin, though I took him for a strictly Irish heritage. Pacing a small patch of carpet, he was in a rumpled raincoat and was turning a brown fedora around in his hands like a bumper-car steering wheel. He looked anxious, but his frown disappeared when he saw me coming forward to shake hands with him.

"Nate Heller?" he said, in his pleasant tenor. "What the hell are you doing at the Secret Service office?"

"It was either this or pay up my back taxes."

"I can almost believe that."

"Actually, I'm doing a temporary tour of duty for this presidential trip Saturday."

"That's why *I'm* here," he said, the frown returning.

So I showed him to my new office.

He sat opposite me at my big empty desk and said, "How does the town's most notorious private dick wind up with an office at the Secret Service?"

"Thanks for the vote of confidence. Don't you remember I used to work for Bobby Kennedy?"

"Oh, that's right—the rackets committee." He tossed his hat on my desk, sat forward on his brown-leather chair. "Listen, there's a little cafeteria I grab breakfast at, over on Wilson Street—the Eat Rite. I go in about seven. I know the manager there pretty well. Today he pulls me over and points out this other customer, a regular he says, though I never noticed him. Kid called Vallee. Muscular little schlemiel with a butch haircut."

Maybe Berkeley had a little Hebrew in him, after all.

I asked, "What about him?"

"Well, my manager pal says this kid's been talking about wanting to kill the President. Even saying this weekend would be a good time to do it."

"You have my attention."

"Yeah, it got my attention, too. So I went over and sat down and talked to the kid. I said I heard he was no Kennedy fan, and he starts in bad-mouthing the guy, saying how he'd like to do something about it. I cautioned him against that kind of talk. Told him I was a cop and that it could get him in trouble."

"How'd he take this advice?"

"At first he said it was a free country and he had a right to his opinions. Then I told him that kind of talk had serious consequences, and that nothing good could come from it. And he quieted down. Just got quiet."

"How do you read him?"

"I think he's nuts. He had a USMC tattoo on his forearm, so he's obviously one of these ex-service guys who can't adjust. Kind of a shrimp, not physically, but short. Like, five five. How the hell he made the Marine minimum height requirement is a mystery beyond me."

"You make him as unstable?"

"I do. If this guy doesn't have a gun collection that would give Hemingway a hard-on, I'll eat my fuckin' badge. Nate, I been thinking about this all day. I probably shoulda called it in sooner. But I decided, as soon as my shift was over, to come tell the Secret Service about it, in person. I mean, it's their job, right?"

"Right." The manila folder Kennedy had left with me was on the desk—about the only thing other than Moyland's fedora. "Something I want you to look at, Berk."

I showed him the photos of the two white suspects, and asked, "Is either one of these guys your boy Vallee?"

"No. Mine has a kind of prominent forehead, and a dimpled chin. Same kind of Marine base haircut, though."

"Okay." I tucked the photos away.

His eyes were earnest. This was a hard-bitten, seen-everything copper, but talk of killing presidents got him going. "Do I need to make a formal statement about this? You want to have it taken down by a secretary or something?"

"No. I'll follow it up myself."

"I don't know where this kid lives or anything. I could snoop around for you."

"No. I'll do the snooping. You've done plenty."

I walked him out, and along the way we chatted about family and so forth. Shook hands with him, thanked him, and sent him on his way, winked at the receptionist, who pretended not to like it, then reported the conversation to Martineau in his office.

"Why don't you let me take this," I said. "I'll grab

some breakfast at the Eat Rite on my way in tomorrow morning."

Martineau nodded. "Doesn't seem to be one of our assassination team, though."

"No, I figure them for imports, even the rednecks, and this guy is local. But somebody's got to check. Not terribly far from where I live."

"Do it," Martineau said. "Young ex-Marine, mentally unstable. Sounds like a dangerous type."

"Sounds like me in 1943," I said, and went out.

Wednesday, October 30, 1963

The Eat Rite cafeteria on Wilson was just a couple of miles northwest of my Old Town town house. I took Clark Street through Uptown, its many cemeteries lending a general aura of death to yet another overcast day. This was about where Uptown turned into Ravenswood, or anyway started thinking about it, an area dominated by its tallest building, a looming Sears store. A lot of DPs—that is, displaced persons—lived around here, German and Greek refugees of the Second World War, well-assimilated by now, a very frugal, blue-collar, lower-middle-class bunch.

The cafeteria, on the first floor of an apartment building, was no bigger than your average luncheonette, just a modest food-serving counter with a diner-style window on the kitchen and a cluster of Formica tables on its linoleum floor. A few white-collar workers were mixed in with the blue-collar, more men than women. A bouquet of scrambled eggs and syrup wafted, and the clatter of dishes, silverware, serving containers, and trays mingled with morning conversation to make nonmelodic, percussive music.

I went to the skinny cashier in his white shirt and black bow tie and asked to see the manager, got a bald guy in a brown suit, whispered that I was following up on Lieutenant Moyland's suspicious character, and got nodded toward a table for four where a pale, muscular little guy with a butch haircut sat solo.

That's who I'd figured for the role, but confirmation was always appreciated. I slid a tray along the counter, got some scrambled eggs, bacon, hash browns, toast, and orange juice from unhappy women in hairnets, left a buck with the morticianish cashier, and threaded through the well-populated little place, heading for the butch haircut by the backward EAT RITE painted on the front window.

As I pretended to move past the guy, I paused and noticed the USMC eagle-and-anchor tattoo on his left forearm, the sleeves of his tan work shirt rolled to the elbow.

He was looking at his own plate of eggs and bacon and potatoes and toast, but I grinned at him as if I already had his attention and said, "Semper fi, Mac."

He glanced up into my waiting smile. His face was oval, but the butch gave it a squared-off look, his eyes big and blue and dull under a shelf of high forehead and cartoonish ink-slash eyebrows, his nose pug, his mouth small and pinched, chin dimpled, ears sticking out like an afterthought. His initially blank expression blossomed into a small smile—small because of the size of his mouth.

"You an ex-Marine, too?" His voice was high-pitched, his words rushed, tumbling onto each other.

"Are you ever really an *ex*-Marine?" I asked. "Mind if I join you?"

"Not at all! Sit right down. Always up for jawin' with a fellow jarhead."

I set my tray down opposite and sat, then extended

my hand across our breakfasts. "My name's Heller. Nate Heller."

He clasped it. Firm. "Thomas Vallee. Friends call me Tommy. You must be local—I can hear the Chicago in your voice."

"There's some in yours, too."

He shrugged, picked up a piece of bacon, snapped it in two, munched. "I grew up northwest of here. Just moved back from New York after a couple years away."

"Work in Uptown or maybe Ravenswood?"

"Naw. Downtown, in the Loop. Printing plant. I'm a lithographer. You?"

"I'm in sales." I nibbled a corner of burnt toast. "So where did you serve?"

Some pride came into his expression. "Korea," he said, and shoveled some eggs in.

"You don't look old enough."

"I'm almost thirty."

"That's still not old enough for that war."

He got a goofy little grin going. "So I lied about my age. I said I was eighteen but I was only fifteen."

I laughed, sipped some juice. "I lied, too—but I had to shave some years *off*, to get in. I was in the big one."

The dullness had left the blue eyes; they glittered with interest now. "Yeah? Where did *you* serve?"

"The Pacific. Guadalcanal."

"No shit. You must have seen some real action."

"Some," I said, as casual as Audie Murphy trying to impress a starlet. I had a bite of eggs, then added, "I'd be lying if I said I had an easy time of it."

"Nobody does. You get wounded?"

"Nothing serious, but, uh . . . they sent me home on a Section Eight. I went a little Asiatic."

All of that was true, by the way. I'd gone home due to what they used to call shell shock and later termed battle fatigue, but was really just good old-fashioned crazy.

He was nodding. "Yeah, I got discharged, too. Didn't get a Section Eight, but I talked to my share of Marine Corps shrinks, I'll tell ya."

My frankness had opened him up.

He was saying, "See, a mortar went off, right by me, and I got a concussion." He tapped his head. "Got myself a steel plate in my scalp."

"That's rough."

"You think *that's* rough? Right after I get out, I manage to get myself into a damn *car* crash . . . not sayin' I wasn't partly to blame. I'd knocked back a few, and was out of sorts, 'cause I'd just been in, well, a kind of bar fight. Anyway, I wound up in a coma for three months."

"You're kidding. That *is* rough."

"Tellin' *me*? Hell, I came out of it like a baby. Had to learn to walk, talk . . ." He held up his knife. ". . . even how to use a knife and fork. My old man had to teach me every basic skill of livin', all over again. And you know what? It . . . it killed him."

His eyes were moist.

"How do you mean, Tommy?"

"Hard to talk about. Day, very damn day, that I felt like I was myself again, like I could go out in the world and be a real man . . . he falls down dead with a god-damn heart attack. It just ain't fair. Ain't fuckin' fair . . . excuse the French."

A busboy stopped to collect our trays. Vallee exchanged smiles with the kid.

"That's a lousy break, Tommy. What did you do?"

"I'll tell you what I did. In '55, I re-upped, is what I did. Got myself a second hitch."

"After a *medical* discharge?" And a plate in the head?

He shrugged. "I must've healed up, at least enough to suit them. Not to say I didn't hit my share of potholes, and, like I said, those shrinks made a hobby out of my ass. . . . Only served another year and a half or so before I got discharged, once and for all."

"Any medals for your trouble?"

His chin raised a little, propelled by pride. "Purple Heart and oak-leaf cluster. How about you, Nate?"

"Purple Heart. Silver Star." Also true. Not a card I like to play, but perfect for this game.

His eyes popped. "Silver Star! You're the genuine article, man! That is goddamn impressive. I have to shake your hand."

We already had, hadn't we? But we did it again.

"Tommy, what made you enlist so young?"

"Oh, I always wanted to be Marine, long as I can remember. My older cousin, Mike, he was a Marine. He was a great guy. And I guess I was like every kid who watched Hopalong Cassidy and Roy Rogers on TV—I *loved* to play guns."

"Still like guns?"

"Oh yeah. I still go shooting. I, even, uh . . . well, I own a few. How about you?"

"I do a little shooting now and then." I finished the orange juice. Breakfast hadn't been bad, for cafeteria food. "Good to hear you have a trade, Tommy. Some military guys can't seem to readjust to civilian life. They just can't let go."

He shrugged, his eyes twinkling. Yes, twinkling. "I keep my hand in."

"Yeah? How is that possible?"

He leaned in, conspiratorially. "In New York . . . just between us gyrenes? . . . Would you believe I trained anti-Castro guerrillas?"

"This was before the Bay of Pigs?"

"Naw! We lost a hell of a lot of good men there, though, didn't we?"

"Who were you training exactly?"

"Cuban exiles. They want their country back. They want a free Cuba! Don't you?"

"Where in New York did you train guerrillas?"

"Well, not in Manhattan!" He giggled. That's right, giggled. "Long Island. Ever hear of Levittown?"

I had heard of Levittown, and a more unlikely place for guerrilla warfare training I could not picture.

Vallee was saying, "No, this is *today*, Nate, this is going on right now. There's a war going on, you know. A secret war. Against the Communists. You ever hear of the John Birch Society?"

"I'm a member in good standing," I lied.

The John Birch Society was an ultra-right-wing movement started by candy mogul Robert Welch, who deemed Dwight D. Eisenhower an agent of the Commies. For a bunch of screwballs, they had attracted considerable mainstream attention.

Vallee was talking very fast now, his high-pitched voice almost shrill. "Then you *get* it, Nate—you know we have to be vigilant. We have to be *more* than vigilant . . . we have to take action. What would you say if I told you another Cuban invasion was coming? And not to be surprised if you look in the papers someday soon and see somebody took care of that son of a bitch Castro."

*This little lunatic, if he'd been training guerrillas on Long Island, was—whether he knew it or not—a pawn of the CIA, and likely had been for some time. How else would a plate-in-the-head medical reject get to re-enlist in the Marines? And the guerrilla training he'd done in fucking Levittown, aimed at taking Castro down, meant he was a part of Operation Mongoose, too . . . though he'd likely never heard the phrase.*

"You're right about the Bay of Pigs," I said, quietly goading him. "It's that bastard Kennedy's fault."

"*Yes!* Yes, exactly. He's the primary obstacle." If he'd

opened his eyes any wider, they'd have rolled out of his head onto the Formica. "He's surrendering our military forces, our security, into Communist hands. We have to eliminate the Communist influences in Washington, Nate, and we need to start with Jay Fucking Kay, pardon the French."

"You know, he's coming to town this Saturday— Kennedy."

Vallee smiled his small smile. "I know. I know. He'll be near where I work. . . ."

Mention of work made him think to check his watch. "Hell, I'm gonna be late! Nice meeting you, Nate."

His breakfast gone, he rose, we shook hands again, and he was gone.

He was gone, all right.


The Eat Rite manager didn't know where Tommy Vallee lived, but he thought that one of his busboys might, which turned out to be the case. The address was on Paulina, less than two blocks away, so I left the Jag parked on the street near the cafeteria and hoofed it over.

Once past a block of nondescript brick apartment buildings, this was a nice enough neighborhood, with plenty of trees and expansive lawns, in what many decades ago had been a well-to-do community, a small town that the city engulfed.

In less than five minutes, I was on the sidewalk outside the three-story paint-peeling-off white frame house where Vallee lived. Three stories was generous, since the top floor was the peaked-roofed attic. An open but roof-sheltered porch fronted what had once been a big one-family residence; acknowledging the structure's current rooming-house status was a metal fire escape that climbed one side all the way to the attic.

I took the eight steps to the porch where several old worn wooden chairs sat, not yet hauled in for winter. In summer around neighborhoods like this, people sat out and watched kids, fireflies, and the world going by. The door I knocked on was an echo of the handsome residence this once had been—a solid if weathered well-crafted door with cut-glass decorations in an arc above with narrow stained-glass panels on either side. The only sign this still wasn't a one-family dwelling was the oversize mailbox.

The woman who answered was slender and hand-some in a severe, time-carved way, with very pretty light-blue eyes; probably in her mid-fifties. She wore a brown-and-orange-print housedress with an apron, her graying blonde hair tucked under a yellow scarf. No makeup, but you could tell she could have once given Leni Riefenstahl a run for the money back at the cabaret.

I think she liked my looks, too, because instead of frowning and beating me with that broom she was leaning on, she cast something my way that had the makings of a smile in it.

Her voice was a kind of guttural purr. "Yes, young man?"

Young man, huh? I was easily her age. She *did* like me.

I flashed her my credentials. I tried to make it quick enough that she wouldn't catch the name "Heller." Some people are known to hold grudges.

"I'm here on a confidential matter for the govern-ment," I said. "May I step in?"

"Certainly." She had the kind of accent that made each syllable seem considered.

I stepped inside and she closed the door behind us. She rested the broom against a wall and casually removed the scarf from beauty-shop hair, and the apron, too, setting them on a small table with tenant mail piled up on it.

The foyer was enclosed, with several apartment doors on either side, a spindle-banister stairway rising to more doors. No framed paintings or family pictures were on the uncluttered wallpapered walls to remind you that this had been a home, before it got chopped up into flats.

"My name is Peters. How may I help you, Mr. Heller?"

She *had* seen the name.

"*Miss* Peters?"

"Missus, I am a widow."

"Sorry."

"It has been twenty years. He drove a bus and had a heart attack in the intersection at State and Randolph. No condolences are necessary."

"Oh. All right."

"Do we need to go somewhere and sit, Mr. Heller? Would you like coffee, tea?"

"I don't think so, no thank you. You have a roomer named Vallee? Thomas Vallee?"

Thin curves of eyebrow arched. "I do. He is a polite, strange little man. Is the government interested in him?"

Not *why* is the government interested in him—*is* the government interested in him. She'd been in Germany during the war, all right.

"This is fairly routine," I said, going the Jack Webb route, "but Mr. Vallee is known to have made threatening remarks about the President. And since Mr. Kennedy is coming to town on Saturday, we would like to check up on him."

Her nicely carved face was placid. "Of him I know very little. He pays his rent on time. He sometimes has

men in his room. But I do not judge. Not when he pays
his rent on time."

The way she said that made me think less of
co-conspirators than of something sexual. Maybe I
was just remembering the glance Vallee and that busboy exchanged.

I asked straight out: "Is he a homosexual?"

"I have my suspicions."

I found myself recalling that the homosexuals had
been in line right next to the Jews at those very special
showers. Still, I kind of dug her. She was a nice-looking
middle-aged gal, and she couldn't help being a German
any more than I could being a sort of Jew.

"Do you know his place of employment?"

"It is a printing business. Downtown. Where it is
exactly, I do not know."

We'd have to find that out. According to Vallee, it was
on the parade route.

"What I'd like to do, Mrs. Peters, is have a look at
your tenant's flat."

"Certainly."

She did not ask if I had a search warrant or any official document justifying such a request. *Boy*, had she
been in Germany during the war. . . .

As I followed her up the stairs, she glanced back at
me and said, "I hope you will not be critical of me to
your people."

"Why is that?"

"Because there are things in Mr. Vallee's room."

"Things in his room?"

We were on the landing now.

She said, "Things that I find troubling. Things that
perhaps I should have alerted you of."

"Okay. Well, I guess I'll see for myself."

Vallee's room was unremarkable in most ways—a
good-size single room with a living area and a bedroom

area, no kitchenette, just a place to stay. Furniture dating back twenty years or more, faded floral wallpaper of similar vintage. A small rabbit-ears portable TV perched on a stand near his bed, and a plank-and-brick bookcase under a window bore paperbacks by Fleming, Robbins, and Spillane—not far removed from my own reading habits. The muscle-building magazines on his nightstand wasn't my scene, but to each his own.

Where our tastes really differed was the collage on the wall next to his bed—a homemade artistic masterpiece consisting of newspaper and magazines clippings, all pertaining to JFK, whose face was inevitably doctored in various ways: red ink turning him into a devil, or an X through his face, or just plain scribbled out. Various threats were scrawled in margins, not that subtle—for example, "Bastard must die!" and that oldie but goodie by the ever-popular John Wilkes Booth, "Sic Semper Tyrannis." Vallee misspelled the latter, however, as "Tyrranous." Dinosaurs, presidents—just so they're extinct, right?

Frau Peters was at my side suddenly. "Will he pay?"

I said, "Well, he has to actually try something before he can be arrested. This kind of thing is covered by freedom of speech."

"No, I mean, will he pay for ruining my wallpaper?"

I almost laughed. "That's between you and him, Mrs. Peters."

She nodded, filing that away. She pointed, like the Wicked Queen in "Snow White" indicating which direction the huntsman should go. "There is something you should see in the closet."

I figured one thing in the closet was Vallee himself, only not literally. But our Germanic landlady seemed to have a pretty good fix on what was in her tenants' apartments.

And she was right to call it to my attention. In the

closet, among Vallee's spare work boots, a few other shoes, work clothes, and a single suit, were two rifles, leaned against the back wall.

I parted the clothes on their rung to get a better look.

The rifles were both M-1's, the standard implement of war for the infantry. Gas-operated, semi-automatic, clip-fed. Using .30-06 rounds, in clips of eight. Speaking of which, on either side of the rifles were stacked ammunition boxes, twenty rounds per oblong box. About half Winchester, the other half Remington. Like maybe he'd bought out a store's supply of one brand and had to start in on another.

Kneeling there, I counted fifty boxes.

On my feet again, I turned to see Mrs. Peters pointing to a dresser, the Ghost of Christmas Future indicating Scrooge's gravestone.

She was right again. In the dresser, I found a .22 revolver. A Smith and Wesson model 22. Just one box of ammo, though, Remington brand . . .

. . . of 2,500 rounds.

"You will take away all of this contraband," she said, at my side again.

"No. Actually, it's not illegal, owning this stuff. It's not even illegal to say you want to kill the President, though it does get the attention of certain people."

"I no longer care that he pays his rent on time. I wish you to take him away."

"You have every right to throw him out on his tail, you know. You don't need a reason to ask a tenant to leave."

Those curves of eyebrow were diagonals now, trying to form an upside-down V together. "What, and have that nice little man shoot me? I do not think so."

I smiled. "Anyway, please don't throw him out until after this weekend. We like knowing where he is."

At the door, I gave her my card, after adding the Secret Service number under my regular ones.

"If you witness anything else suspicious regarding Mr. Vallee," I said, "or odd in any way . . . you let me know."

"Oh yes, Mr. Heller. If this happens, you will hear from me."

She smiled, and the light blue eyes sparkled like sunlight on Lake Königssee. At Berchtesgaden.

You may think that's a cheap shot, but before I left, I let my hostess talk me into a cup of tea in her kitchen, which was down a hallway where family photos finally kicked in, and I swear I glimpsed a framed Hitler Youth photo. You could never be quite sure about these German DP's.

But I still kind of dug her.

When I got back to the Secret Service office, I found Chief Martineau with my friend Dick Cain in the former's office. They were preparing to go to another presidential trip meeting, this one in the auditorium of police HQ at Eleventh and State.

"It's a special security coordination conference," Martineau said, "with the sheriff, PD and us. I really don't have time to hear your report right now, Nate."

I pulled up a chair next to Dick and sat.

"Yes, you do," I said, and filled him in quickly and thoroughly about the breakfast conversation with Vallee and my visit to his rooming house.

"It does sound serious," Martineau allowed. "But your loon is *not* one of the suspects the FBI gave us that your friend the AG wants us to concentrate on."

"Well, I can see ignoring this," I said lightly. "It's just a guy with a kill-Kennedy collage on his walls and a couple of M-1 rifles in his closet and thousands of rounds of ammo. Nothing to sweat bullets over, right?"

Dick—who'd been studying me with that disconcerting gaze of his, with the one milky eye—said, "Nate's right, Marty. You need to put this joker under surveillance."

"I can't spare the men," Martineau said, his frustration palpable. "How about loaning me a couple of your guys from the SIU, Dick?"

The sheriff's man shook his head. "No—we're short-staffed, too, working on stadium and street security. But I know a couple of guys from your old bailiwick, Nate—the Pickpocket Detail? Dan Gross and Pete Shoppa. I could get them for you."

"I know them a little," I said. "But they're way after my time on the Pickpocket Detail. . . . Still, anybody with that kind of training is perfect for surveillance."

Martineau seemed almost amused. "The sheriff's chief investigator is making PD assignments now?"

I reminded him, "Dick was on the PD for a lot of years."

Cain was sitting forward. "I can approach Captain Linsky about it—*he'd* have to make the assignment. But I'm sure I can swing it."

"Swing it then," Martineau said, rising to go out. Dick was also on his feet. "And when I get back, I'll get the Washington office on rounding up information for us on this Vallee character. We have till Saturday, after all."

Right.

Less than three days.

In downtown Chicago, after dark, the two most brightly illuminated buildings were easily the Wrigley Building and the Silver Frolics nightclub, unlikely neighbors on the north bank of the Chicago River. Unlikely but fitting, since what was more American than chewing gum and sex? Particularly when you factored in the Doublemint Twins.

And if the Wrigley Building on Michigan Avenue was the heart of Chicago commerce, the Silver Frolics—in its shadow to the west—was the city's navel, or the glittering costume jewel in it, anyway.

That jewel liked to call itself "Paris in Chicago," but "Chicago in Paris" was more like it. The gaudy neons outside and the billboard-like come-on painted on the former warehouse's side promised FOLLIES INTERNATIONAL, 35 ARTISTS, GLAMOUROUS GIRL REVUE, and (best of all) NO COVER, NO ADMISSION. Thousands of conventioneers and small-town visitors, and even the occasional local, learned soon enough that the ballyhoo omitted the four-buck minimum. And the only resemblance to the French capital would be limited to froufrou decor and one Parisian production number per show.

Few complained, however, as the Silver Frolics' exotic dancers were unanimously considered the best-looking in town—young, well-built, and pretty, and exclusive to the venue, appearing in a revue elaborate enough to rival Broadway, including a chorus line and the kind of acts (comic magician, contortionist, ventriloquist) that Ed Sullivan on TV made you sit through Sunday night waiting for the really big show.

This was no 606 Club—nothing so crowded or poorly ventilated, no pockmarked tables or pockmarked dancers, either, the former wearing white linen, the latter elaborate costumes, to start with, at least. The clientele was classy for a strip joint, too, men in suits, the few women in smart dresses, attire appropriate for the most plush legit nightclub. Which the Frolics resembled, seating perhaps 250, tables for four arranged so that none was more than two or three rows away from the large stage, which bumped up against a dozen ringside seats.

Still, there was something about the place that felt quaint, even old-fashioned—especially compared to the plush Playboy Club on Walton Street, with its Bunnies spilling their beauty-contestant bosoms from sleek, satiny, colorful, cottontail costumes, cut thigh-high to expose lushly nyloned legs. The Silver Frolics, from its ornate hoop-skirted floor-show costumes to the inevitable pasties and G-strings (never more, or rather never less, not at the refined Frolics), seemed damn near nostalgic in its approach to naughtiness. Strippers teased. Bunnies promised.

Working on a rum-and-Coke, I was seated somewhat away from the stage and relieved to be, as right now dark-haired yuck-it-up stripper Tinki DeCarlo was dumping various items of discarded clothing on the heads of ringside customers. It was a Christmas routine, and she came out Mrs. Santa Claus and was down to electric pasties that glowed red like Rudolph's nose and a bunch of sleigh bells dangling off her G-string.

"She's good," I said to Helen, able to converse easily over the small orchestra, "but I don't care for funny strip acts. Maybe I take sex too seriously."

We were two at one of the four-seat tables.

"It makes men feel uncomfortable," Helen said, with a knowledgeable nod; she was between sips of her Champagne cocktail. "They're already a little embarrassed, just coming to a place like this. But you're right, for that kind of thing, she's not bad."

Helen was flying under the radar tonight, nothing overtly Sally Rand about her, in her navy-blue dress with white Peter Pan collar and her blondeness pinned up in curls—an extremely attractive middle-aged woman who might still turn heads, anywhere except a club where girls in their twenties were peeling down to their most appealing.

I wore a dark-green Stanley Blacker hopsack blazer, my tie striped dark orange and white, shirt a very light orange. My slacks were brown H.I.S., and my shoes darker brown Hush Puppies. But the most distinctive aspect of my dressed-to-kill ensemble was the shoulder-holstered Browning, Lytton's in the Loop having tailored the blazer without spoiling the line.

Because I wasn't going anywhere now without the nine-mil.

We had arrived around ten P.M.—the place didn't open until nine-thirty—and were here to talk to manager Ben Orloff about the possibility of a booking for the world's most famous fan dancer. This had taken a good deal of discussion, since the Frolics was, for all its pretensions, a strip club. But none of the legitimate nightclubs in town had offered Helen a firm date, despite half a dozen meetings and gracious reception from all concerned. Nobody wanted to insult a living legend in the burlesque biz. Just seemed like nobody wanted to hire one, either.

I had frankly little hope for the Frolics, as they had never hired the big-name exotic dancers like Gypsy Rose Lee or Tempest Storm, preferring to stick to their own stable of younger unknowns, none older than early thirties. But Sally Rand was a Chicago institution, and I'd done a couple of jobs for Orloff, so when I called him, he issued a positive response in his gruff baritone: "Stop by tonight."

Helen and I had dinner at the Cape Cod Room at the Drake, in part because it was the best seafood in Chicago (narrowly edging out Ireland's) and also because back in 1934, when we had first become friendly, Helen had lived in a suite at the hotel. Some very friendly times, in fact, were spent in that suite.

The show ran two hours, and would start back up in half an hour, lengthy enough a break to clear some of the tables out for newcomers. During the hiatus, Ben Orloff came trundling over, all smiles. He was short, balding, heavy-set, in a well-tailored brown suit with a brown and green tie a little too wide for the fashion—like his club, he looked fine but out of step.

He bowed to the seated Sally Rand and took her hand with respect, as behooved such flesh-trade royalty. She liked that and beamed at her host.

"Miss Rand, a real, genuine honor. Where would any of us be without you?"

I know he meant this nicely, but it reminded her that she was a museum piece, and anyway, lovely as Helen had been in her prime, I had a hunch if she'd never existed, guys would still be paying to see good-looking women take their clothes off.

"Mr. Orloff," she said, "I can't believe we've never

met. This has to be the most beautiful club of its kind. And your girls are stunning."

Orloff took the chair nearest Helen. There had been a nod between us that sufficed.

"Please call me Ben. And is Sally okay?"

"Sally is fine."

"I guess you know," he said with a shrug, "we don't normally book big acts in here. *But* . . . we might consider an exception for a star of your stature. And with your special connection to Chicago."

"At risk of reminding you that I've been around a while," she said, her smile as broad as it was beautiful, "we *are* celebrating the thirtieth anniversary of the fair."

He grinned and his eyes damn near popped. "I'll never forget going to that wingding! I was still in high school, and had to lie about my age to get in to see you."

Her smile remained, but turned strained. She was aware of an inescapable fact—like the Frolics itself, she was an anachronism. Like strippers.

Like private eyes.

I was wishing I'd never suggested this, but the club manager surprised me.

"I will tell you right now," he said, taking her hand and patting it, "no beating around the bush whatsoever, that I am prepared to book you in here."

Nothing strained about her smile now.

"That's wonderful, Ben," she said, almost purring.

He raised a cautionary finger. "But here's the thing—we may not be here long."

"What? Why?"

Her question got an answer out of him, but he aimed it at me: "Nate, it's that son of a bitch Wilson. Do I have to tell you he's shuttered half the clubs in town?"

I shook my head—very old news. Plenty of the other strip joints had converted to movie houses, showing nudie-cutie fare like *The Immoral Mr. Teas* and *Not Tonight, Henry*. Apparently Mayor Daley's reform police commissioner, Orlando Wilson, had less objection to cinematic skin than the genuine article.

The Summerdale police scandal a couple years back—eight cops had formed a burglary ring in their off hours—had forced Hizzoner to finally do something about police graft here in the City That Worked, hence Commissioner Wilson and his new broom. (Wilson's presence probably had something to do with Dick Cain leaving the PD and winding up with the sheriff's department.) I didn't mind this Wilson character cracking down on some of the rampant police department corruption, but enough was enough. A guy might want to get a parking ticket fixed.

Ben was talking to both of us now. "We had a bad incident last month, and the hammer could fall any time."

"Yeah?" I said. "Anything I can do?"

He shook his head glumly. "We had a bunch of doctors in here. I don't know if you know much about doctors, when they decide to let their hair down, but they go wild, turn into one nasty bunch of assholes, in my experience. They caused a lot of trouble, got very plastered, threw tables and chairs around like a bar fight in a John Wayne picture, and played the kind of grab ass with our girls that we don't put up with in a respectable club like the Frolics."

"What did you do about it?"

"Our bouncers dragged them outside, beat the shit out of them, and dumped them in the gutter. What would you have done?"

Maybe something a little more diplomatic.

"Anyway, they filed a complaint," Ben said, in a

*whaddaya-gonna-do* manner, "and that gives Wilson just the ammunition he needs. Meaning we may be in the last days of this grand establishment."

Helen said, "That's awful news."

He leaned toward her, his broad face apologetic, hands folded as if in prayer. "I only confide in you like this, Miss Rand, because if I give you a booking, and we sign a contract, and I don't have this place no more . . . well, you have to be prepared for that, and agree not to sue my ass."

"That sounds fair."

"I think it *is* fair . . . and speaking of fair, we will make a big deal out of your appearance commemorating the thirtieth anniversary of the great Chicago World's Fair. We'll get Irv Kupcinet and Bill Leonard and Herb Lyon and all the big press guys on it, and if it turns out the Frolic is on its last legs, we will go out kicking."

That was when I noticed Jack Ruby sitting up at a front table.

I sat forward and had to work not to put anything into my voice. "Ben, excuse me for changing the subject, but isn't that Jake Rubinstein up there? I grew up on the West Side with him."

"Yeah, you and Barney Ross. That's Jake, all right. Jack, he's called now. Jack Ruby. Last few days, he's been going around town checking out the few of us that Wilson hasn't snuffed out. Looking for talent for his club. Even went out to Cal City, scoping out the girls. He's got clubs down in Dallas, you know."

"So I hear." I rose. "You and Sally have business to conduct. If you'll excuse me, I'll leave you two to it, and go say hello to my old friend."

Helen gave me a smile that said, *Thank you,* giving me maybe more credit for this booking than I deserved.

Ben grinned. "Wait'll you see who ol' Jake is sitting with."

I grinned back. "Ben, right now, nothing would surprise me."

But I *was* a little surprised, because when I made my way to Ruby's ringside table, his companion—whose tight, beaded white dress had a neckline exposing a shelf of bosom that you could rest a couple of martinis on, with little fear of spillage—was that platinum-blonde, blue-eyed, baby-faced stripper, Candy Barr.

Her presence was surprising because I thought she was in stir. Candy, who was maybe twenty-five, had several years ago drawn a stupidly harsh marijuana charge deep in the heart of Jack Ruby's Texas. The well-known stripper, nude model, and occasional blue-movie star was also a former mistress of gangster Mickey Cohen, another old friend. The kind of old friend you don't mind never running into again.

Ruby didn't see me at first. The beauty-and-beast-type couple were talking—or anyway Ruby was talking while she blankly endured it—and there was no way not to interrupt. Sporting a dark-gray sharkskin suit with a lighter gray silk tie, he was gesturing with his left hand, which was missing the tip of its forefinger. Bit off in a fight.

I leaned in, a hand flat on the linen tablecloth, and said, "Jack, sorry to bust in, but I just had to say hello."

Candy frowned after I used the word "bust"—I had a feeling she had suffered a lot of bad bosom jokes, so she was apparently always watchful. Like the men eyeballing her in that low-cut dress.

Ruby looked up, and his smile seemed genuine until I noticed the corners of his dark little eyes tightening. "Nate! Didn't expect to see you again this trip."

"I didn't figure you'd still be in town," I admitted.

Actually, I knew it was a possibility, because Lou

Sapperstein had reported today that our sources in Dallas could not place Ruby either at the Carousel Club or his apartment. That only meant he was on the road, however, not that he was still in Chicago.

Turned out he was still in Chicago.

"Candy, this is Nate Heller. The famous detective? Nate, this is the famous Candy Barr."

"We've met," she said without enthusiasm.

That lack of enthusiasm did not reflect any bad blood between us. She just didn't seem to have much enthusiasm, period. What she had was the best body I ever saw on a female and you may have noticed that I have an unseemly way of keeping track of such things.

Her real name was Juanita Slusher, by the way. If you thought she was born Candy Barr, we should probably part ways right now.

"Nice to see you, Candy," I said, meaning it. Seeing Candy was always a treat. Talking to her was more like a toothache, but that doesn't keep a kid from wanting candy, does it?

"Sit down, join us," Ruby said, pulling a chair out for me.

I did. "I didn't know you and Miss Barr were friends."

"Oh, Candy and me, we go way back. I'm hoping to talk her into working for me at the Carousel, once her parole's up. I told you that, didn't I? At the 606?"

Was there anything pointed about the reference to the club? And the money drop?

"Maybe," I said, and shrugged. I turned to Candy. "They won't let you make a living? What kind of parole is that?"

"Well," she said, "since the fuckers gave me fifteen years, it's the kind of parole I'll take."

"Well-reasoned, Candy. What are you doing now, to pay the rent?"

"Breeding," she said.

I'm sure there are hundreds of clever comebacks to a comment like that one, especially coming from the likes of Candy Barr, but what I said was, "Ah."

"Jack gave me two dachshunds to get me started," she said. "I like dogs. They're better than people, don't you think?"

"That's kind of faint praise," I said, and she actually smiled a little. "You and Jack traveling together?"

"No," she said, "I'm opening Friday in *Will Success Spoil Rock Hunter?* at Pheasant Run."

"Oh, that's that new dinner theater in St. Charles."

About an hour outside Chicago.

"It's an easy part," she said with her trademark lack of enthusiasm. "I did it before. Mostly I walk around half naked, but it's not stripping so my parole officer said it was okay. Even let me travel out of state to do it."

"So you're doing more than just breeding."

"Girl's gotta make a living."

Having no argument with that, I turned to Ruby and said, "I think the show's about to start up again— are you staying for it?"

He nodded. "We came in late. Rumor is this place may shutter, and these girls will have to work somewhere—why not Dallas? People get tired of seeing the same old tail."

Yes sir, Jack Ruby, class all the way.

I gestured with a hand that had all its fingertips. "Could we talk out in the lobby, Jack? Just for a few minutes? Would you excuse us, Miss Barr?"

"I wish you'd make your mind up," she said to me.

"Huh?"

"Is it Candy or Miss Barr? One or the other."

That was a little bitchy, but then she *was* a dog breeder.

In the meantime, Ruby had been thinking over my request. He would surely doubt my presence here

could be coincidental, and likely assume I'd been trying to track him down. And I *had* been trying to track
him down, through Sapperstein anyway; but our meeting tonight really was a coincidence—though in fair-
ness to fate, the world of Chicago strip clubs was small
these days, in part thanks to the police commissioner.

In the lobby, we took a position near the mouth of a
hallway that led to restrooms, planting ourselves next
to a big gaudy girl-arrayed poster under glass (*Folies
Bergère! Moulin Rouge!*). We had decent privacy. Our
only company was a bouncer in a tuxedo who was
chatting up the hatcheck girl at her window, and they
were blocked from view.

"What can I do for you, Nate?" The pudgy oval of
his pasty face was smiling, except for the tiny black
eyes, which were almost as shiny as his slicked-back,
thinning hair. "I'm not really sure if we should be seen
together."

I kept my voice down but pulled no punches. "Why
is that, Jack? Operation Mongoose?"

He blinked. "Well, sure, but . . . I have to tell you,
Nate, I damn near cut out of this town, when I saw
that squib in the paper. And to hell with business."

"You mean about Tom Ellison getting murdered in
his room at the Pick? *That* squib?"

He nodded nervously. "Is that why you come looking for me, Nate?"

"I didn't come looking for you. I'm here with Sally
Rand, trying to help her get a booking."

"Maybe she'd like to work the Carousel!"

"I'll relay the interest. What kind of business has
you hanging around Chicago, Jack?"

"Checking out the local talent, like I said. Also selling a couple of items."

"Such as?"

"I designed this Twist board."

"This what?"

"It's a board you stand on when you're doing the Twist. It improves your dancing. You should try it. The chicks go wild. And then there's my specially designed pizza ovens for restaurants."

"You're selling pizza ovens in Chicago."

"Damn right. I sold two so far. How's that for ice to Eskimos?"

"Not bad." We were having a fine little chat. "Jack, what do you know about Tom Ellison's murder?"

"Nothing! Not a damn thing. What do *you* know about it?"

"I know that somebody framed it, kind of shittily, to look like a pickup or hooker kill. It was a murder, all right. And I want to know if it had anything to do with that envelope of cash—you know, Jack . . . the one Tom handed off to you?"

He had started shaking his head halfway through my little speech. "Far as I know, didn't have a *thing* to do with it. He wasn't a made guy or anything, your pal. Wasn't Outfit. He was a civilian."

"Did that make him a loose end?"

"How should I know? You should check out his private life. Maybe something in his personal life or business got him whacked."

"Or did he get to be a loose end because of me? Did *I* get him killed, by coming along with him? Did somebody think that Tom talking to me meant he couldn't be trusted?"

His eyes were wide and round, like white marbles with a big black dot at each center. "You ask me this stuff like I know the answer! I don't. If he's a loose end, then maybe *I'm* a loose end. Should I be looking over my shoulder, Nate?"

"Should *I*?"

"He got it Sunday, right? Has anybody made a move on you, since then?"

"No."

"Me neither. So maybe we ain't loose ends. It's been a few days, right?"

Either he was telling me the truth, or was a hell of a lot better an actor than I gave him credit for.

I played a tricky card. "That kid you introduced me to at the 606—Lee?"

"What about him?"

*The FBI's informant on the four Cubans had been called Lee.*

"Is there any chance he's an FBI informant?"

He laughed. "Well . . . define 'FBI informant.' Who hasn't passed along a little worthless information to those sons of bitches, just to get a pass on something or other?"

"Okay. Let's try this. You been doing any business with Cubans since you been in town?"

"Cubans? Why Cubans? I'm here looking for strippers for my club! I guess I could use a Cuban girl, if I called her exotic. Some of my patrons might just call her a nigger. I have to put up with some low-type people, you know, to make a living."

"You used to visit Cuba, didn't you, Jack? Passing messages to Santo? Not to mention a little gunrunning?"

"Ancient history."

"And there's Operation Mongoose. Lots of Cubans in that. Exile types. You got any Cuban friends, Jack? Maybe back in Dallas?"

"I don't even have any Cuban cigars!"

I kept trying. "Did you know Jimmy Hoffa is in town? Or anyway, he was."

Ruby held his palms up—*What, me worry?* "What does Jimmy Hoffa have to do with me? I never met the man. I admire him, sure, they say he's a stand-up guy, but I never met him. We got mutual friends and acquaintances, but himself? Way out of my league. What the hell is this about, Heller?"

I didn't know, really.

Seeing Ruby made me want to connect that money drop and Tom's murder and Hoffa to those missing Cubans with their high-power rifles. Nobody on the planet hated the Kennedys more than Jimmy Hoffa. But the connections were too vague—I hadn't been able to bring myself to tell Martineau about them, let alone Bob Kennedy.

Opened too many embarrassing doors on all sides.

I said to the stocky little man, "I'm not sure what the hell it's about, Jack. I accompany my client to a money drop at a club like this one. Well, not this nice, but a strip club, and two nights later, he's stabbed to death in his hotel room. You and I have both, in our time, run in some rough circles. Sometimes the same circles. If you know something, anything, about Ellison's murder, you tell me, and I'll give you a free pass. Just like the FBI."

His face got red. "Are you accusing me of something?"

"Where were *you* Sunday night, Jack?"

He threw a punch. He was that kind of guy, an impulsive hothead. But because he was that kind of guy, I was half expecting it, and ducked it.

Good thing, too, because he was a bull—thick-necked, a lot of muscle in that upper torso, enough to almost pop the seams on that Bobby Darin sharkskin suit of his.

But if I hit him back, we'd have had a brawl right there in the Silver Frolics lobby, giving the police commissioner another excuse to shut the joint down, and that wouldn't be fair to Ben Orloff.

So instead of slugging him, I slapped him. Twice.

Once per cheek. Like I was his date and he got fresh with me.

This surprised him. Stopped him, both his hands coming up to cheeks flaming with pain now, not flushed with anger. His eyes were moist.

Though no one had seen it, I'd humiliated him.

"Throw another punch at me, Jack, and see what happens. I'm not some drunk at the Carousel you can rough up to impress the customers. I'm not some stripper's lowlife leech husband you can pummel to show the girls who's boss. Get tough with me again and I will make your life miserable, or maybe just end it. Understood?"

He swallowed. His eyes weren't angry—they were frightened.

Good.

"Let's hear it, Jack."

"Understood," he muttered. His chin was quivering.

"Okay. Before we go back in and enjoy the show, is there anything else you know about this situation that I should know? That I would *like* to know? Because if you're holding out on me . . ."

I didn't have to finish it.

He shook his head. He was almost crying. He seemed hurt—not hurting . . . hurt.

"I thought we was friends," he said, and swallowed and I followed him in where the little orchestra was starting up a bump-and-grind symphony.

I was shaking my head, grinning, but kind of pissed off, too.

How I hate a fucking hothead.

**Thursday, October 31, 1963**

Just after nine A.M., at the Secret Service office, the two Pickpocket Detail cops recommended by SIU chief Dick Cain arrived for a meeting with Chief Martineau.

I knew Lieutenant Dan Gross and Sergeant Pete Shoppa, but not well. They had reputations as smart, tough detectives, both in their late thirties, with the vaguely bored yet somehow alert eyes all seasoned cops seemed to possess.

Shoppa was a blocky, pockmarked and balding cigar smoker, and his blue suit was something J.C. Penney sold him several seasons ago, the blue and white paisley tie probably a Christmas present from around '59. Horse-faced, sandy-haired Gross was tall, or at least taller, and better dressed—his brown J.C. Penney suit was this year's model, his tie properly narrow and a darker brown. No law required that Chicago detective teams always be Mutt and Jeff pairs, but if there had been, Gross and Shoppa didn't break it.

Theirs were the kind of unremarkable faces in the crowd just perfect for pickpocket work . . . and surveillance.

Gross was a friendly type, the first to offer his hand

as we stood in the no-man's-land of Martineau's office between the chief's desk area and the conference table. Martineau had stepped out to check on some telex info he was expecting, and we three Pickpocket Detail veterans had his big office momentarily to ourselves.

"You know, Nate," Gross said with a grin, "they still talk about you over on the Detail."

"They talk about me lots of places," I said, returning his smile.

Shoppa said, "Of course nobody over there ever really worked with you, Heller. I figure everybody you ever worked with on the PD is dead by now."

He offered his hand, too, and there was just enough of a smile on that stogie-pierced, pockmarked pan to tell me this was his version of friendliness, too.

I said to him, "Pete, most of the guys I *busted* are dead, too. Kind of makes the whole exercise seem a little irrelevant."

Shoppa frowned at that. A little too philosophical for his speed, I guess.

Martineau came in, the formidable chief moving with considerable energy, and in his shirtsleeves for a change—like most of the agents in the SS office, he wore a short-sleeve white shirt under his suit coat, despite the time of year. The office tended to be warm, the old steam heat in these soon-to-be former headquarters apparently having one setting: inferno.

Eben Boldt trailed in after his boss, quietly spiffy in a charcoal suit and black necktie. Introductions between Martineau and the two police detectives had already been made, but Boldt was a new addition. There was an awkward moment, then I introduced Eben as both an agent and my partner on the current investigation. Polite smiles, nods, and handshakes were traded, but no remarks, friendly or otherwise.

That didn't make the two cops bigots necessarily—more Negro cops were coming onto the Chicago force all the time, another part of Commissioner Wilson's revamping of the department, and the white cops hadn't figured out yet how to behave around these dusky interlopers.

Martineau, however, knew just what Eben's role was.

"Ebe," he said, "get us some coffee, would you?"

There was the slightest tightening around the agent's eyes, then a nod, and he went out.

Martineau had a manila folder with him, and he rested it in front of him as he took the head seat at the conference-room table, gesturing for us to find chairs.

We did.

"Has Chief Cain or Captain Linsky filled you fellows in at all?" Martineau asked.

The two cops were at Martineau's right, and I was opposite them. They both shrugged, Shoppa knocking some ashes off his stubby cigar into a glass ashtray with the Secret Service emblem in the bottom.

"The captain just said that you were shorthanded," Gross said, "what with the President coming to town Saturday."

"Said you might need some surveillance help," Shoppa said. "Implied it might have something to do with JFK's visit. But that's all."

"You'll need a full briefing, then," Martineau said.

He opened the manila folder and passed them a set of 5-by-7-inch photos of the suspects—the two Cubans and two white boys.

"We believe these men to be highly trained assassins with high-powered rifles. A hit squad. And their target is Lancer."

"Lancer?" Gross asked.

"That's Secret Service code," I said, "for President Kennedy."

I'd picked up around here quick.

Shoppa, looking over the photos, wore a smirk with a cigar stuck in it. "Jeez, a couple of spics called Gonzales and Rodriguez. *That* narrows the friggin' field. What are the white guys' names? Smith and Jones?"

Martineau's expression barely registered his displeasure with Shoppa's manner, but I caught it. I doubt Shoppa did, but if he had, he probably wouldn't give a shit.

The SS chief said, "This is not your direct assignment, gentlemen, other than to be on the alert if your surveillance subject should come in contact with any of these individuals."

"This," Gross said, tapping the picture in front him, "is why you're shorthanded. You're focusing on *this* threat, and need us to cover for you on some other bozo who's made a crank call or something."

Martineau said, "That's not wrong, but we have new background on this 'bozo' that makes it vital we take him seriously. First, however, I'll have Nate brief you on how we got where we are with Mr. Thomas Arthur Vallee."

That middle name was news to me—Martineau really did have info he hadn't yet shared.

Eben came in with a tray of cardboard cups and a pitcher of coffee, and everybody helped themselves as I told them how Lieutenant Berkeley Moyland of the Chicago PD had alerted us to Vallee's spouting off about Kennedy, and laid out in some detail the conversation I'd had with the subject at the Eat Rite yesterday, winding up with the discovery of the two M-1's, the .22 revolver, and the several thousand rounds of ammunition at his rooming house.

No wisecracks from Shoppa and no remark from Gross, either—they just exchanged dark glances at the mention of all that firepower.

And now Martineau dipped into his manila folder for a picture I hadn't seen before: a Marine Corps photo of my breakfast club buddy, Vallee, looking very young but otherwise much the same—prominent forehead, glazed eyes, tiny pinched anus of a mouth.

"Not who I want dating *my* sister," Shoppa said.

Gross grunted. "*Looks* like the kind of nut who'd want to take a potshot at the President."

"We know a lot more about him today," Martineau said. "This is all fresh intel that even Nate and Ebe are hearing for the first time."

I glanced at Ebe, seated beside me, and he shrugged. Apparently he didn't know any more than I did.

Martineau glanced at various papers that he'd extracted from the manila folder, but did not read from them, rather summarized. His ability to do so from material he'd only recently received was impressive.

"Thomas Arthur Vallee joined the Marines at age fifteen," he said. "That's right, gentlemen—he lied about his age. He's thirty now. During the Korean War, he suffered a head injury, thanks to a mortar round exploding nearby, which got him discharged from the Marines in 1952. Traumatic brain injury. Complete VA disability. This jibes with what Mr. Vallee shared with Nate in casual conversation."

I asked, "What about his claim that he re-enlisted? How does a guy with a brain injury and complete disability get back in uniform?"

"I have no idea," Martineau admitted. "But it's true that, after two G.I. Bill years at a community college, he was able to re-enlist, in 1955. He was honorably discharged in '56."

Gross frowned. "After one year?"

Martineau nodded. "It was a physical disability discharge again. Military doctors classified him . . ." And now he did read from a document. ". . . 'an extreme paranoid schizophrenic.'"

"Which is medical jargon," Shoppa said, "for screwier than a shithouse rat."

The chief did not disagree, and again referred to a sheet. "Vallee's mental condition, the psychiatric evaluation says, is 'manifested by preoccupations with homosexuality.'"

"So the kid's a queer," Shoppa said, sucking on his cigar, "as well as a nutcase."

"His landlady mentioned male guests," I said, "and he had some reading material that fits that notion. But since when does a homosexual get an honorable discharge from the Marines?"

Martineau had an answer: "His psychiatric evaluation further finds indications of 'organic difficulty' that may relate to that mortar-shell incident in Korea."

Shoppa said, "So a shell exploded and turned him homo? That's a new one."

"I'm out of my depth there," Martineau said. "But there's worse on his record than just perversion—his psychiatric evaluation also notes 'homicidal threats' and 'chronic brain syndrome associated with brain trauma.'"

"This is just peachy," Shoppa said.

"So," I said, "he gets his honorable discharge because the Marines blame themselves for his mental condition."

Gross asked, "What else do we have on this character?"

Martineau shrugged. "We know that Vallee is, or was, a member of the John Birch Society. We also know he drives a Ford Falcon with New York plates—he moved back to Chicago from Hicksville, Long Island, in March—and of course we know his home address. We don't have his work address as yet."

Eben said, "His place of employment is a printing facility of some kind in the Loop. We're checking out every possibility by phone, emphasizing any plants on the parade route. There's an agent working that angle right now."

Martineau said to the two cops, "We would like you men to get right on this. Get over to that rooming house and once Vallee shows up, stake him out, and don't let loose of him. If you can find a way to get him off the street, do it."

"You want him off the street," Shoppa said, rolling his cigar around his mouth, "he's off the street."

Martineau raised a calming hand. "Keep in mind Mr. Vallee hasn't committed a crime."

"Yet," I said.

Martineau lifted his eyebrows, then continued: "One of the saddest and most frustrating situations a Secret Service agent faces is knowing that someone threatening a president's life has not committed an illegal act. Nor is it illegal for Mr. Vallee to have those rifles, that handgun, and that ammunition. He's protected under the Second Amendment like the rest of us."

A knock at the door got our attention.

Martineau called, "Yes?"

One of the anonymous crew-cut, dark-rim-glasses-wearing agents stuck his head in. "We have Vallee's workplace, Marty. It's the IPP Litho-Plate Company."

"Good," Martineau said. "Tell me you didn't tip our hand. I don't want this getting back to Vallee. . . ."

"No," the agent said, crisply. "Nothing was given away. This was just a routine check, as far as IPP is concerned. Vallee works on the third floor as a lithographer, which apparently means he changes the paper in a big machine."

"Nice job, Fred. What's the address?"

"West Jackson Boulevard. 625 West Jackson."

Martineau whitened.

Ebe groaned, and I said, "Well, fuck a duck."

The agent in the doorway frowned and said, "That's on the motorcade route, isn't it?"

"Yes, it is," Martineau said rather numbly. "Thank you, Fred. That'll be all."

The door shut, and the two cops didn't seem to be getting it. The motorcade route was eleven miles long, after all.

I said, "That address, if I know my Loop geography at all—and we can walk right over there, gents, if you like—is a perfect place to watch the President's limo make its slow turn from the expressway off-ramp onto Jackson."

"Ideal for a sniper," Eben said.

Martineau was on his feet, looking at the map. But he wasn't saying anything.

"Any of you fellas ex-military?" I asked.

Neither Martineau nor Boldt responded, but both Gross and Shoppa nodded.

"Then maybe you already know this," I said. "But the way a sniper plans to hit a moving target is by knowing in advance where that target—in this case Lancer—is going to be. The exact point past which the target will stroll by, or maybe drive by in a car. The sniper aims his rifle at a chosen spot and just waits in his nest till the target walks or drives into the cross-hairs. That way, a sniper can keep his rifle still as hell, with his only movement the squeezing of the trigger. Saves him from having to move himself and his rifle in sync with that moving target."

Eben asked, "Does this make Vallee a bigger threat than our team of four assassins?"

Martineau, his back half turned to us as he studied that map, said, "He may be *part* of that team."

Shoppa said, "He ain't Smith or Jones, and he sure as hell ain't Gonzales or Rodriguez. Listen, we are happy to take Vallee off your hands, Chief Martineau, but are you sure you don't want your own people on this?"

Martineau was thinking.

Then he wheeled and said, "The AG says our primary suspects are those four: Gonzales, Rodriguez, and—as you put it, Sergeant Shoppa—Smith and Jones. So, yes, take over the Vallee investigation, Lieutenant Gross, which is chiefly a surveillance job at this point. But the moment you see Vallee making contact with any one of those four . . . call us immediately. Call us right fucking *now*."

That was the first time I'd heard Martineau use that kind of language.

Gross glanced at Shoppa, and Shoppa glanced back.

"All right," Gross said. He was the ranking officer, so it was his decision. "We are on it. Where on Paulina is that rooming house again?"

We gave them the address and they were off.

The cops were barely out of the door, the smell of Shoppa's cigar still lingering, when another of those crew cuts leaned in and said, "We just got an interesting tip, Marty, courtesy of the Chicago FBI."

"Yeah?"

"Seems there's a landlady on the North Side complaining about some 'spics' renting a flat from her. She says they have four rifles with telescopic sights in there."

"Where would we be today," I said, already on my feet, "without suspicious landladies?"

"Ebe, you and Nate follow this up," Martineau said.

But Ebe was right behind me, as we trailed the agent out and to his desk, to get that address, grab our raincoats, and go.

The rooming house, oddly enough, was just four blocks south and a couple of blocks east of my town house. The compact nature of the geography of this case was starting to feel weird.

The light-yellow Victorian wood-frame, peak-roofed structure dated to the teens. The landlady lived in the basement apartment of the old three-story, whose outer walls almost touched the newer brick buildings on either side—a twenties-era terra-cotta-trimmed number with offices over a Walgreens drugstore and a nondescript fifties-vintage four-story with apartments over a "New and Used" record shop. Three decades represented by three side-by-side buildings—not unusual in this part of the city.

She met us up the handful of steps on the small porch, a squat woman in her fifties wearing a floral tent and nurse's shoes, another DP but of Greek extraction. Her features were coarse in a squashed circle face, her hair gray and netted, her eyebrows thick and black with a facial mole perfect for today—Halloween.

I introduced myself, showing her my Justice Department credentials, and, wide-eyed, she pointed past me to Eben Boldt, like somebody about to yell, *Fire!*

"Is he with you?" she demanded.

"We're together," I admitted. "He's a Secret Service agent."

She folded her arms like Chief Sitting Bull. "Well, the boy waits outside. No colored allowed."

Eben's face turned hard as a carved African mask—a

frightening one, at that—also fit for All Hallows' Eve. He seemed about to verbally explode, so I stepped in.

"Ma'am, he needs to come along. I may require him to take notes for me, or maybe run errands."

Eben's eyebrows went up, but so did the heavy black ones on our witchy hostess's mug.

"Okay, then." She heaved a wary sigh, then shook a schoolmarmish finger at me. "But *you* deal with him. I don't truck with the colored."

"He'll be my responsibility," I assured her, and followed her in. I grinned back at Eben, who sneered at me. He really didn't have much of a sense of humor.

Again, there was no question of a search warrant. The landlady—whose name was Knockomus, she said, and who was the owner of the building—led us up a flight of stairs.

"They paid for a week in advance," she said. "Starting Monday."

At the landing, we followed her to the left, a short trip. You could see a bathroom at the end of the hall, door ajar.

Wondering if I should be getting the nine-millimeter out, I asked, "Is there any chance they're here now, ma'am?"

"No. I saw them go an hour ago. They never come back till late afternoon."

We were in front of a door marked 2A.

As she was unlocking it, Mrs. Knockomus said, "I don't relish this at all. I have to put up with the girls on the first floor—I got two apartments down there, they are whores, those girls—and now it comes to renting to spics."

Her description of her first-floor tenants as whores was likely less a slur than a job description—we were at Clark and Division, near Rush Street and the older Rialto area, where prostitutes plied their trade.

Mrs. Knockomus opened the door and gestured for me to go in. I did, and she moved in front of Eben, I guess to make sure he was admitted last.

This was a flat that took up the entire second floor. The rooms—there were three—were much nicer and larger than Vallee's one room. The floors here were hardwood with worn yet still handsome Oriental carpets, and the solid-looking furnishings were probably antiques, the upholstery still decent, the iron bed blessed with a "Home sweet home" comforter that looked hand sewn. Maybe our hostess had hidden depths.

"I should have sold back in the fifties," she said, scowling at nobody in particular, not even Ebe, "but I missed my chance. This urban renewal thing coming up? I'm gonna snap at that line like a mackerel. Enough of this nonsense with scum-of-the-earth tenants."

We'd been through all three rooms. No guns, not rifles, not handguns, not in the dresser, not in any of three closets.

"I mean, I don't mind the girls, really," she was saying. "The whores keep to themselves and don't bring nobody home. And I don't even mind some Outfit guy on the lam, now and then, neither. They dress nice, those type fellas, and they are . . . what's the right word? Much more *discreet* about their weapons. These spics, they just leave their guns lying around! What if one went off and was pointed at the floor and killed somebody, like me for example?"

"I don't see any weapons," I said.

She pointed at the windows onto the street. No screens, I noted; no air conditioner. Summer would be rough in this space.

"They was leaned up against there," she said, indicating the wallpapered area between the windows. "Four rifles. Had those fancy telescopes attached. Like the hunters use. . . . It's Kennedy, isn't it?"

Eben and I exchanged glances. "What makes you think that?"

"Right there," she said, and pointed to an end table by the couch, "they had a map with street names on it."

I asked, "The kind of map you get from a service station?"

"No! Hand-drawn. With street names and highways and places."

"Such as?"

"Such as Northwest Expressway and Jackson and Soldier Field."

Jesus.

She was smiling at her own cleverness. "The motorcade route, am I right?"

Eben walked over to the table. "No map here now."

Forgetting herself, she said to him: "And the newspaper is gone, too."

"What newspaper?" I asked.

"It was on that dresser, in the bedroom." Now she was pointing in that direction. "With the article about Kennedy coming, circled."

Not a wall collage, but telling enough.

I said to Eben, "Show her the photos."

He took the four suspect shots from his inside suitcoat pocket and handed them to her. She paused before accepting something from him—he might have been a Zulu handing her a shrunken head—but finally she took them.

Without hesitation, she said, "That's the two tenants. Their names on here are correct, the spics— Gonzales and Rodriguez. These other boys, the whites? They aren't staying here, but they come around in the evening."

"Often?"

"Twice, at least."

She had placed all four suspects in this flat.

I asked, "Could the two white guys be crashing here at night?"

"Crashing?"

"Staying all night. Maybe slipping out before you're up, or when you aren't looking."

She frowned, offended. "I'm up at six, mister G-man, and I don't miss nothing."

Eben asked, "They haven't checked out, have they, ma'am, your two tenants?"

"No," she said, but she was looking at me. "They're still staying here. I don't know where they go during the day. What do spics do with their time, anyway?"

"It's a mystery to me," I said. "Look, Mrs. Knockomus, you mustn't say anything to them about our being here. About you having a look in their room. Nothing at all."

"You don't have to worry about that," she said. "The only thing I ever said to them was, 'Seventy-five dollars in advance.'"

I asked her several more questions—did her tenants have a car? *Yes, green Pontiac, no idea what model or year.* Where did they park it? *On the street, best they can.* Was there a rear exit? *Not one available to the upstairs tenants, as it was off one of the downstairs apartments.*

Soon we were on the sidewalk, under a sky that remained overcast on a day cooler than the previous several.

I used the phone booth in the Walgreens next door to report in to Martineau.

After filling him in, I said, "I'm going to recommend a twenty-four-hour stakeout."

"Fine," Martineau said. "Saves me the trouble. You and Ebe take the first shift."

Before doing so, we had lunch at the drugstore

counter. Cheeseburgers and fries and Cokes. Around us, mothers were scurrying to buy their kids Halloween costumes—Yogi Bear, Popeye, Casper the Ghost. And all sorts of people were scooping up whatever candy was left for the little ghouls and goblins who'd be ringing their doorbells before too long.

"This sounds real, doesn't it?" Eben said, meaning what we'd learned at Mrs. Knockomus's place.

"Does to me." I dragged a fry through ketchup. "Is this common?"

"Is what common?"

"I've been with the Secret Service since Tuesday afternoon, and this is the second time rifles with scopes have turned up in rooming-house flats."

"There weren't any guns next door."

"No, but that sweet old gal saw them. She didn't imagine 'em or make it up—the guns were there. You know it and I know it."

He bit into his cheeseburger, chewed awhile, swallowed, then said, "No, it isn't."

"Isn't what?"

"Common."

We didn't speak any more of it as we finished lunch. We got a few dirty looks, a white guy and colored guy eating together, but we got served, didn't we? Hell of a lot better than down south. I wondered if Eben appreciated that.

On the way out, I said, "I want to stop in at that record shop."

"Why?"

"I'm gonna prove to you I'm not prejudiced."

"How?"

"I'm going to see if they have *Ray Charles Greatest Hits*."

"Are you making fun of me?"

They had a nice used copy.

We sat in the car and started our surveillance—perhaps a little too noticeable, a Negro sitting in a car on the street in this part of town; but with the Secret Service's limited man power, it would have to do.

Before long Eben asked, "Ever hear Muddy Waters?"

"Heard *of* him. Plays the blues on the South Side?"

"Yeah. After we catch these pricks, I'll take you there. Joint called Smitty's. Nothing against Ray Charles, but you haven't lived till you heard Muddy."

"Smitty's, huh? South Side? Is it safe?"

"Well, *I* won't get killed."

That made me smile.

"Looking forward to it," I said.

And the boring afternoon officially began.

Because the Secret Service office was so undermanned, Eben Boldt and I sat surveillance at the rooming house near Clark and Division till after seven P.M. We witnessed the return of the Cuban tenants at around five-fifteen—they parked a green Pontiac Bonneville on the street, a recent model and a nice ride for guys staying in a rooming house. They snagged a spot maybe half a block from the old Victorian structure, not a bad parking place, considering. It was a Cook County license plate, which Eben wrote down.

They were clearly the Gonzales and Rodriguez of the photos, though the younger man, Gonzales, had been bearded in his surveillance shot and now was clean-shaven, with a wiry look not obvious before. Rodriguez, on the other hand, had a formidable build and a mangy ball of black, slightly graying hair to go with his Zapata mustache—the effect made his head look damn near as big as the carved pumpkins on porches.

The two Cuban pals were smiling, joshing, with an easygoing spring to their step, and both were smoking—cigarettes, not cigars. They wore zippered jackets over sport shirts, and chinos and sneakers.

They went up into the rooming house. There hadn't

been a kitchenette in their flat, not even a hot plate or little refrigerator, so I figured they had to come back out and eat somewhere, sometime. But it didn't happen on our watch.

And the two white guys, the rest of the supposed hit team, never made an appearance.

Around six o'clock, trick-or-treaters started their assault, kids (with poor or maybe cheap parents) in homemade hobo getups or sheets that made them ghosts, as well as the gaudy but cheap-looking store-bought outfits, among them one Howdy Doody, two witches, and three Lone Rangers, but not a single Tonto.

By the time we got back to the Secret Service office, and reported in to Martineau (who would be working even later than we had), it was well after eight; and by the time I'd collected my Jag from the Federal Building lot, and made my way to my Old Town town house, nine was looming. The trick-or-treating in my neighborhood was winding down, the cowboys and princesses and cartoon characters replaced by older kids just wearing masks, eager as thieves to fill their brown-paper bags with goodies.

I did not park in back, in the former stable, having called Helen from the office with my plans, which were to drive us somewhere nice for a late supper. Maybe Riccardo's. She had landed a January booking at the Silver Frolics, and we had that to celebrate, plus she was leaving for California tomorrow; so I wanted it to be a special night.

Luck was with me and I found space at the curb right in front. My raincoat loose and open, I climbed out into the cool evening—the squeals of kiddie laughter and padding feet on pavement seemed distant and a little hysterical, as the spoils of Halloween were taken home for sorting, eating, and puking. Down the street, candlelit pumpkins watched me, flickering their eyes and jagged teeth, as the sugarcoated bacchanal wound down.

I headed up the walk. After this long day, I wanted to go in and shower and change clothes before going out for what was left of the evening. Helen must have been watching for me, because she opened the door to the safe-house apartment and was just stepping out—in another of those Peter Pan–collar dresses—when I heard the footsteps behind me.

Heavy ones that didn't belong to trick-or-treaters.

A low-pitched voice said, "Heller," and when I turned, the nine-millimeter was in my hand.

Behind me I heard Helen scream, "Nate!"

*"Helen, get inside!"*

I heard the door close behind me.

Standing before me, maybe five feet away, were the two scariest night creatures Chicago could ever hope to conjure on this All Hallows' Eve. One could only hope that these were two older high-school kids with a sick sense of humor and a big enough allowance to put on an incredible masquerade.

Either that, or I was facing Chuckie Nicoletti and Mad Sam DeStefano, the two most dangerous killers in Chicago. I could add, *Outfit* killers, but there were no non-Outfit killers to match them, unless maybe some young mad scientist was cooking up a batch of black plague in a basement lab in DeKalb or something.

Chuckie—at my left—was a big man, maybe six two, broad-shouldered and with hands so big they looked swollen, his features handsome but with an over-ripened look. In his late forties, he was sharply dressed—that was a tailored suit, dark enough to blend with the night, and the tie was silk, black-and-gray striped.

*Chuckie Nicoletti, when he was twelve, killed his*

*first man, his father; currently he was Sam Giancana's killer of choice. The in-between you can fill in yourself.*

His smile was faint, but genuinely amused, as he said, "You don't need that rod, Heller. Put it away."

What a ridiculous thing to call a gun! Didn't he know this was 1963? Edward G. Robinson didn't play gangsters any more, Bogart was dead, and this was real fucking life, where a guy ate and slept and sometimes even peed. Christ, I wished I didn't have to pee so bad right now.

The man standing next to Chuckie must have thought calling my Browning a rod was funny, too, because he was giggling uncontrollably. Of course, his nickname was Mad Sam, so that might have something to do with it.

Maybe five ten and in his fifties, Mad Sam had an unruly head of dark graying hair, reminiscent of Larry in the Three Stooges; his close-set eyes, lumpy nose, and unhealed wound of a mouth gave him the look of a demented clown. He wore an off-the-rack black sport coat over a white shirt, a skinny loose noose of a red tie, baggy gray trousers, and what looked to be bedroom slippers.

*Mad Sam DeStefano had not killed his own father. He had killed his own brother, in part to save his sibling from a life of drug addiction, in part because he'd been hired to kill him. A free agent, Mad Sam made his money off loan-sharking, doing his own enforcing. Still, he remained tight with Giancana and could be hired on for any job, as long as it required a sadistic maniac.*

Right now Chuckie's smile had turned kind of sideways and he held his oversize hands up chest-high, palms out, as if in surrender.

"This is a *friendly* call, Heller."

"Is it?"

"Mr. Rosselli would like to see you."

*And he sent these two killers to tell me?*

Mad Sam stopped giggling long enough to say, "You're supposed to come wid us. We're gonna drive you over so's you and Johnny can talk."

I wasn't pointing the gun at them—I'd allowed it to drift down, but not quite at my side. I was still giving serious thought to just shooting them both.

Chuckie said, "Heller, you stand around on the sidewalk, pointing guns at people, somebody may call the cops."

I said, "And that's a bad thing? Anyway, this is my private walk and it's only one gun."

Mad Sam slapped Chuckie on the back and roared with laughter. "Tough talk, but look at his eyes! He's gonna piss himself! I swear he's gonna *piss* himself!"

So he was nuts *and* psychic.

Chuckie gestured slow and casual as he said, "That Lincoln over there? That sweet ride across the way? We're just supposed to escort you over to Agostino's, where Mr. Rosselli is waiting. To talk. Just to talk."

Mad Sam snorted a laugh. "Wanna take your girlfriend along, Nate? That's Sally Rand, ain't it? Don't look half bad for a broad her age. I bet Johnny would get a kick out of that."

But Chuckie said, "No, Sam, we're just collecting Heller, here. Sorry, Nate, this is a private conference. Better you come by yourself."

"Let me get this straight," I said. "You boys want to take me for a ride? And I'm just supposed to file my 'rod' away under asshole and come along?"

Mad Sam was giggling again. "Not *that* kinda ride, Heller! Jesus, you always crack me up! This guy has always cracked me up, Chuckie. Heller, if it was *that* kinda ride, would we still be standing here, shooting the shit?"

*I* might be shooting *something*. . . .

"Fellas," I said, raising the gun just a little, "generous as the offer is, I'm going to have to pass. I'm fine with seeing Mr. Rosselli tonight. Johnny and me are old pals. But I have my own wheels. You gents just take off, and I'll be right behind you."

Chuckie was frowning. "Nate, we're supposed to bring you."

"I'm not getting in a car with you two."

Mad Sam's grin was jack-o'-lantern worthy. "No? *You're* telling *us* how this is going down?"

"I am," I said. "I have the gun out. You guys are good, but you'll both be dead and I won't go to either funeral."

Chuckie thought about that. Mad Sam's smile had curdled somewhat; he thought he was still amused, but just wasn't quite sure.

"You have my word," Chuckie said quietly. "This is just a chauffeur job."

"No," I said. "Make your play, or get the fuck out."

Now Mad Sam wasn't smiling. Not at all.

"Why won't you let us *drive* you?" he demanded. "We got *paid* to drive you!"

"Sam! I'm not getting in a car with you and Chuckie."

"Why? Chuckie give you his word! I'll give *my* word! You're gonna make us look *bad*, Heller. I don't *like* looking bad."

"I don't like looking dead. As for why I won't get in a car with you? Because Chuckie here watched Spilotro crush a guy's head in a vise till the bastard's eyes popped out onto the floor, and didn't miss a beat eating his pasta. And you, Sam? You hung Action Jackson

on a meat hook and gave him the cattle-prod treatment until you decided to get really rough with him."

Mad Sam was giggling again. "These stories you hear,
Heller. They're just so much exaggerated horseshit."

"Well, I don't wanna be a story, Sam. Chuckie, I'll
follow you in my Jag. You fellas go into the restaurant
first, and I'll trail in, and Johnny will never know I
drove myself. No loss of face and no loss of income."

Chuckie thought about that.

Finally he said, "All right, Heller. We'll shake on it."

He extended his hand.

I grinned at him. "Maybe later."

I watched them go, Mad Sam shaking his head and
chattering, Chuckie just plowing through the night like
a ship's prow, heading for the parked Lincoln.

When the car was gone, I went into the lower apartment.

Helen threw a barrage of questions at me, but all I
said was, "If I'm not back in two hours, call Dick Cain.
His home number's in my book upstairs. Tell him I
went to Agostino's to see Rosselli. Got that? Now if
you'll excuse me, I have to piss like a racehorse."


Agostino's was on the corner where Rush and State
Streets converged. The restaurant's vertical neon-
lettered sign and striped canopy were all that dressed
up a drab old building. The Sciacqua brothers, Gus
and Andy, ran the place, and I was a regular, so Johnny
Rosselli had accidentally stumbled onto comfortable
turf. Maybe somebody told him about the spaghetti
with anchovy sauce.

I parked the Jag under a streetlamp on busy Rush,
and walked about a block to the corner building that
had been a drugstore with a blind pig over it, when I
first started on the PD.

Chuckie and Mad Sam were pacing around to one side of the canopied entry, looking like the least-welcoming doormen in history, Sam in particular. Chuckie was smoking a cigarette, looking annoyed—probably as much with himself as me—and was probably about two minutes away from climbing back in that Lincoln and really coming after me when I strolled up.

Though it was fairly cool, I'd left the raincoat home, and my suit coat hung open for easy access to the Browning. I'd worn a feathered Dobbs hat and looked jaunty.

"Hi fellas," I said. "May I make a suggestion?"

Mad Sam goggled at me, rocking forward on his feet. He was three feet from me but I could smell his rancid breath. "May *I* make a suggestion, Heller? That you should go fuck yourself?"

"You took your time," Chuckie observed.

"I had to go in and pee," I said, "before coming over here. What can I say? You guys are scary."

Chuckie actually liked that remark. He had a decent sense of humor. Unlike Sam, whose idea of humor was to tie you naked to a hot radiator.

Chuckie said, "What's your suggestion?"

"We go in together. You peel off into the bar, and I'll head into the dining room. That's where John is, right? That back corner booth?"

Chuckie nodded, approving the plan.

We went in, and the two killers joined the revelry in the jammed, lively bar, where the Venta brothers strolled with guitar and mandolin, as on every night. Gus was circulating, too, and waved to me from in there. I waved back.

*Good,* I thought. I'd been seen. Noticed.

The dining room, which wasn't large, had maybe half of its twenty tables and booths filled. The decor was only lightly touched with Italian imagery, a wall mural here, some plastic vines there, a simple space with subdued lighting. I just nodded at the maitre d' as I headed for the corner booth.

Johnny Rosselli was by himself in the burgundy button-tufted booth. As always, he looked movie-star handsome, or anyway Hollywood producer handsome, with his perfect silver-gray hair and that deep tan that made his blue-gray eyes stand out and the ivory grin so dazzling. His gray Ivy-League suit was perfectly matched to a shirt of lighter gray and a narrow tie as silver as his hair.

"Nate, I'm so glad you could make it," he said, and gestured for me to join him in the booth.

We arranged ourselves so that we were sitting opposite. He had no food, just a glass of what I knew was Smirnoff on the rocks—he drank nothing else.

"Haven't ordered yet," he said genially. "Wanted to wait for you. You've been here before, right?"

"Many times. But I'm eating later with a lady friend. Don't want to spoil that."

"No, no, wouldn't want to do that."

"But you go ahead and order."

With a diamond-bedecked hand, he waved over a red-jacketed waiter, politely let me make my drink request first—I got the rum cooler—and ordered one of the house specialties, chicken cacciatore.

"Thanks for seeing me at such short notice," he said. "I hope I didn't interfere with what you got planned tonight for you and your lady friend. Is it true you've got Sally Rand bunking in with you?"

I nodded.

"That impresses an old goombah like me. But don't you usually go for the younger dolls?"

All the hoods talked Rat Pack these days.

"Sally and me are friends going way back," I said. "World's Fair days."

"Thirty years ago! Would you believe it? Anyway, thanks for coming."

"How could I resist when you send such charming emissaries?"

He smile was minuscule. "What do you mean, Nate?"

The waiter brought my rum cooler—ice, lime juice, rum, Coca-Cola in a highball glass. Agostino's did not stint on the rum, and I would be sure to have only one. I needed my wits about me, if I didn't want them in my lap.

Softly I said, "I mean Nicoletti and DeStefano."

He shrugged. "So?"

"So I get the message."

He sipped Smirnoff. "I just sent a couple of the fellas over to give you a lift, is all."

"The two most ruthless killers in town, is all, the top whack guy and the biggest whack job. Both as well known for torturing people as for putting them out of their misery."

He smiled, displaying no teeth, just puckish amusement. "All right. So it *was* a message of sorts."

"A warning. That you could send those two animals again, and not just for chauffeur service. I almost shot the bastards, John. They won't tell you, but I had the drop on them for five fucking minutes while Nicoletti played nice."

Now the toothsome dazzler of a smile came out. "I'll bet Sam didn't."

"No, he just giggled like a schoolgirl. A cop told me that's what he did when they questioned him about murdering his brother. Nice crowd you run with, John."

A tiny shrug of shoulders almost as broad as Nicoletti's. "We swim in dangerous waters, Nate, you know that. Sometimes it pays to bring your own sharks along. Trained ones. You know, domesticated."

"DeStefano is about as domesticated as a rabid mountain lion. So, you can probably have me killed if you feel like it. Okay. That's the threat. What's the point?"

He called the waiter over and ordered up another Smirnoff. I was still nursing the rum cooler.

"You ran into Jack Ruby the other night," Rosselli said.

*Did he mean at the 606 Club? Or the Silver Frolics? I couldn't be sure.*

So I said, "You mean, at that strip joint."

"Yeah. Man, I hope that Wilson character don't close it down. The Frolics is the only decent tits-and-ass palace in Chicago, should you want to take some business associate somewhere classy."

Okay. So he was referring to my more recent conversation with Ruby.

His eyebrows raised and his voice took on an avuncular tone. "Nate, you got kind of rough with him, I hear."

"I slapped him a couple times, but only after he threw a punch at me. Why, is he a friend of yours?"

That could have been taken two ways: a made Cosa Nostra guy; or . . . a friend.

"He's one of our boys," Rosselli said, with a flip of the other diamond-heavy hand. "Small fry, not even a soldier, just a . . . what do the spooks say? Asset."

That CIA jargon, coming from Rosselli, was a little disconcerting. Not as disconcerting as having Chuckie and Mad Sam show up for you at your house; but disconcerting enough.

"So he threw a punch," I said, shrugging, "and I slapped him. My read was, he's a scrapper, and better to embarrass him than start a goddamn brouhaha."

Rosselli was nodding. "That was probably wise. He's an emotional little firecracker. He left this morning, by the way—back in Dallas by now. I mention him only because of this embarrassment with your client. The press agent from Milwaukee?"

The "embarrassment" was apparently Tom Ellison's murder.

He spoke softly, his mellow voice soothing, friendly. "Listen, I'm aware he come to you for help, because of that money he had to pass along. You played bodyguard and that was that. Ruby being there, recognized by you, that maybe made somebody think a simple little handoff got turned into something . . . complicated."

*This was an admission that Tom indeed had become a loose end that got tied off.*

"Nothing was complicated," I said, "till somebody stabbed Tom Ellison in his hotel room."

"I understand the Chicago PD says it was a hooker done it, or maybe some bar pickup. A bedroom boost that got out of hand."

"Could be that."

"But you don't think so. Are you poking around because this Elliot was your friend?"

"Ellison, and no, John, I'm looking into it because the widow hired me to."

The blue-gray eyes were narrow. "And just *how* are you poking around?"

His fresh Smirnoff on ice arrived.

"I'm not seeing how this is your business, John."

"Humor me. I take an interest in my friends, Nate, particularly friends I'm involved with in, you know, various endeavors."

I took that to mean Operation Mongoose.

"We're looking into the victim's private life," I said, "and his business life, in Milwaukee mostly."

"What have you turned up?"

I shook my head. "Too early. I may get a report tomorrow. We did some checking at the Pick, and some other hotels, to see if there's a robbery ring using a female shill. Nothing on that yet, either."

"Okay. Okay." He sipped more Smirnoff. "I don't see any problem with any of that."

"You don't?"

"No. Let it play out, and then tell the widow that you've done everything you could, send her a bill, and go find yourself other clients."

"I would do that anyway, John. For a minute I thought you were saying I shouldn't look into this killing."

His gaze was thoughtful now. "No, I think you should. The police are as usual too hasty in their thinking, and you have a widow with her doubts . . . let's assuage her."

He did come up with the occasional five-buck word. Too much time in Hollywood.

"Then I don't see what you're asking," I said, but really I did. "And I don't know why you would send Dracula and Frankenstein over to see me, unless maybe you just dig Halloween."

*But really I did.*

Rosselli said, "I don't want you, and I don't want any of your people, looking into anything having to do with Jimmy's connection to him."

He meant Hoffa's connection to Ellison, of course.

"And," the Silver Fox went on, "no digging whatsoever into anything related to the kind of business dealings that I am engaged in. And Mooney."

The business dealings meant anything Outfit, and Mooney meant Giancana, the man he answered to.

"I wasn't planning to," I said.

"Good. Because the ramifications, they would stink on ice. And I don't mean to threaten. To my knowledge, nobody thinks of *you* as a loose end, and won't unless you start acting like one. And maybe I should apologize for insulting your intelligence by sending Chuckie and Sam around, to get your attention."

"Well, they got it."

"Just the same, I do apologize. The thing is, this could come back on us. And by us, I mean *us* . . . as in me and you and people we deal with. Jack Ruby, in particular. That envelope. You don't want to know what that was about. Maybe I don't even know what it was about. But that's a door you cannot fucking open."

"Okay," I said.

I hadn't asked "Why," but he answered that question anyway: "It just might touch on a certain operation, Nate, a snake-killer-type operation? And we don't want any of our connections to those kind of activities getting public scrutiny. Understood?"

"Sure."

"Then we're in agreement?"

"Yeah. I'll let the Ellison investigation die a natural death."

"You do that, and maybe you'll be the one handed the next envelope of cash. How would you like that?"

*What I would have liked was never sitting down again with the fucking likes of Johnny Rosselli. Years and years of having to deal with these Outfit psychopaths was wearing me the fuck down, and never seeing any of them again was my fondest desire.*

"That would be nice," I said.

His chicken cacciatore arrived. It smelled fantastic, but right now that marinara sauce reminded me a little too much of blood, draped as it was over dead chicken.

He asked, "I wish you would join me. Just have some minestrone soup. That won't spoil your supper."

"No thanks, John."

He began to eat. His manners weren't bad. No speaking with his mouth full, and frequent pauses to dab off red sauce with his white napkin.

"Nate, I can give you some nice reassurance, in the middle of this awkward unpleasantness tonight. I can tell you that there's a change coming. Everything that you helped put in motion on our Miami trip, there at the Fontainebleau, it's all coming to fruition. Great fucking things are coming, and you made it possible."

I finished my rum cooler.

"That sounds swell," I said. "But I do have to make one small point."

"What's that?"

"If Chuckie or Mad Sam show up on my doorstep again—alone or separate—I'll just fucking shoot them. *And* whoever sent them. I may not be as cold-blooded as Nicoletti, or as screwy as Mad Sam, but people who cross me have been known to not be around anymore."

That didn't anger him. "You do have that reputation. But, Nate, remember . . . we are not adversaries. We are in this together. And if you don't like this shit? May I remind you? *You* called *me*."

Yes I had.

Goddamnit.

On my way out, I waved to Chuckie and Mad Sam, who were standing at the bar. Sam grinned and waved and Chuckie nodded. I lingered outside for a couple of minutes, waiting to see if the pair would come out to follow me. They didn't.

Which was a relief, because had they done so, there might have been a gunfight, after all.

And as I drove back to Old Town, despite all the provocative and intimidating things Rosselli had said, all I could think of was a point I'd been careful never to raise with him.

That Mad Sam's renowned weapon of choice was an ice pick, and that he would be plenty strong enough to pierce a guy's sternum with one.

**Friday, November 1, 1963**

Sitting surveillance on a street as busy as Division has its hazards, not the least of which is finding a decent goddamn parking place. Though it wasn't ideal, each team watching that Victorian rooming house between the drugstore and the record shop was sharing the same spot, vacating it when each new team showed up. And feeding the same damn meter.

Eben Boldt and I, having taken the first shift yesterday afternoon, were taking this next afternoon shift as well. We were in a different Secret Service vehicle today, so as not to repeat ourselves—a navy-blue '62 Chrysler—and had traded in suits for casual attire, zippered Windbreakers, sport shirts, chinos, sneakers. I'd skipped shaving today, in case we ever moved from vehicular surveillance to on foot. In the latter instance, looking somewhat scruffy could be useful.

We came on at two P.M., and the team we spelled said the two Cubans hadn't come out yet today. The team before them saw the subjects enter the rooming house at one A.M., after a night of bar-hopping in the neighborhood, reported by the team before that. The night on the town did not involve the two white subjects, unseen as yet anywhere except on those Justice Department surveillance photos.

I was behind the wheel. Eben was watching the rooming house perhaps a little too intently.

"Hey," I said. "You're a chocolate guy in a vanilla part of town. Don't advertise you're casing that place. Somebody might call a cop."

He frowned over at me in irritation, then thought it over. "Good point. Maybe I should check around back."

I shook my head. "Their car's in front. We checked that alley yesterday and there's nowhere to park behind there, without blocking the way. Sit tight. Or, anyway . . . sit loose."

"Okay, Nate."

Here I was in my late fifties, successful, even relatively famous, pulling down high five figures (after expenses), owner of a detective agency with offices in three major cities, with money in the bank, a town house in Old Town, all my hair, all my teeth, and no medical problems except a few lingering scraps of shrapnel from bullets in various fleshy parts of my anatomy. What the hell was I doing at this late date sitting surveillance?

On the other hand, the President of these United States was due in town in twenty hours, and waiting for him was an unofficial reception committee of assorted malcontents with high-power rifles. So I would just have to put up with the indignity.

Last night, after I got back from Agostino's, Helen was a wreck, anxious as hell, flying into tears when I stepped through the door of the downstairs apartment. She kissed me and kissed me and kissed me some more, and pulled me down to the carpet where suddenly my underwear and pants were around my ankles, her dress pulled up and her panties pulled down, and we were screwing there, rug burn be damned, and it was frantic and quick and intense, and the best time I'd had all week.

We were both too old to be embarrassed about such impulsive behavior, but we did take time to pull ourselves together. We shared a shower upstairs, purely cleansing, put on fresh clothes, and made our way to the Erie Café on Wells. We'd discussed Riccardo's, but after Agostino's and Johnny Rosselli, I was no longer in the mood for Italian.

Helen and I ordered the Erie Café house specialty—a seven-inch-thick broiled steak with their special steak sauce. Rare, which we would share.

"Those men," Helen said, "they looked . . . awful. That one looked like the wild man from Borneo escaped from a circus."

This was the first she'd directly mentioned Chuckie and Mad Sam. I explained that the gentleman who'd summoned me had sent them to make a point, and that everything was fine now.

Her head tilted, and her gray-blue eyes took on a sad tinge. "Will you always have to deal with those kind of people in your work?"

"Probably till I retire. You deal with a lot of them, yourself."

She shrugged. "What can I do? They own the venues, and pay me to share my talents. I suppose in a way the same is true with you."

"I try not to work for them."

"Will you ever?"

"What, work for them again?"

"Retire, one of these days? As Sophie Tucker puts it."

"I think so. I'm feeling like I've about had all the fun I can stand. I'll probably go to sixty-five or so. I'm hoping when Sam gets out of college, he'll take over the business. If he wants to. How about you, Helen? Great as you look, how long can *you* shake your . . . fans?"

"Maybe not much longer," she admitted with a shrug. "Who knows? Maybe it's time that you and I . . ."

A waiter brought us Poncinos—rum in very hot coffee with a lemon twist.

"You and I what?" I asked, after a sip of the deadly stuff.

Her smile twitched and seemed to be thinking about what it wanted to settle into. What it decided on was warm and lovely.

"Nate . . . we've been friends a long time. I have a kid, you have a kid. We have both been around and then some."

"No argument."

"I'm not sure we've ever exactly been in love. I'm not sure we haven't been, either. And we've both had busted marriages, me more than my share. Still . . . maybe we should start thinking about, well . . . I mean, old age *is* coming, my darling."

"Some mornings, it's here." I saluted her with my Poncino. "If that was a proposal of marriage, I'm in."

She smiled. Patted my hand. "Maybe I'm just feeling sentimental. Maybe I'm feeling knocked around after a week of hustling from club to club trying to wrangle a booking out of guys younger than me. They look at me like . . . like I'm the Statue of Liberty or something."

"Hey, sooner or later everybody visits the Statue of Liberty. And you *did* get booked."

"Yes. At a strip club. And a strip club that is probably about to get itself shut down by the law, and in Chicago yet. Look, light of my life. Assuming the Frolics is still open in January, I'll be back in town, and maybe I can borrow that downstairs apartment again, and upstairs bedroom, too. And we can pick this conversation up where it left off."

Which is what it did—leave off. Our giant steak arrived, and our talk turned to other things, too dull for me to remember.

So now I was thinking about my fifty-something fan dancer as I sat parked in a Secret Service Chrysler on Division Street next to a Negro agent who was once again staring too conspicuously at the lodging place of our subjects.

"You're doing it again," I told him.

"They're coming out."

I sat up.

The two Cubans were in tan zippered jackets, chinos, and sneakers, same as before, but they were not joshing around with each other, not today. In fact their expressions were sober and they walked with what might be termed purpose. Or was I reading in?

Anyway, they got into their green Pontiac—Gonzales driving, Rodriguez riding—and pulled out into the light traffic. I caught a break by way of a lull that let me pull a U-turn and fall in a couple of cars behind them. They were in no rush, heading west into a run-down area, home of hookers who liked to call nearby Clark Street "the Rush Street of the Working Man."

The Pontiac crossed LaSalle where Urban Renewal was busy creating the future by displacing the present. Just to the north, Carl Sandburg Village (named for the Bohemian newsman poet) housed white-collar Loop workers. Like the moon, its towers were seen by the people around here, but they could not hope to live there.

We tailed the green Pontiac past Wells and under the Ravenswood El. Just north were the blocky towers of Cabrini Green, a modern high-rise slum replacing the Sicilian tenements of Little Hell.

Beyond Halsted, the green buggy crossed the ancient, stone-towered steel-lift bridge that led onto Goose Island, three blocks of industrial wilderness—warehouses, manufacturing lofts, scrap-metal junkyards. As we rolled by in slow pursuit of the Cubans, large chunks of iron whooshed into the air, with a rattle like the Devil trying for seven or eleven—a missed tank of compressed gas, not entirely emptied, had made its way into a crusher.

Neither Eben nor I registered any surprise at this explosion.

From Goose Island we were led below the new four-lane expressway, Mayor Daley's extension of the national highway system linking Chicago to Wisconsin and Indiana, and O'Hare to the Loop, a concrete ribbon across the North and Northwest Sides that had made fortunes for insider speculators in right-of-way property. Would have been nice if one of my wealthy clients had clued me in. Hadn't I helped save or end enough fat-cat marriages to rate that?

Soon we were in an older neighborhood, once Polish, Russian, and Jewish, now turning Puerto Rican; well-kept older storefronts with apartments above mingled with small narrow two- and three-flat buildings. Things seemed more run-down on side streets. West Town (as the area was called) was dominated by looming factories and the steeples of its many churches, mostly Catholic.

Now we entered a wide square where Ashland—a major four-lane street—bisected Division, and where another angled street, Milwaukee Avenue, also crossed. What you probably noticed first was the three-story building to the north whose huge sign announced DAILY ZGODA.

Taking that in, Eben asked, "A Polish newspaper?"

"For more Poles than Chicago," I said, "I suggest Warsaw."

A small central park featured junkies wandering, and was an old woman taking a crap in the grass? Yes, she was. And those old guys passing her on the sidewalk, hauling grocery bags, either didn't notice or didn't care.

The Pontiac turned north on Milwaukee, where block after block of stores awaited, of all types and all nations, signs in Polish, signs in Russian, signs in Spanish, even a few in English. Cuba's flag was painted on some store windows and Puerto Rico's on others. The spire of the Morris B. Sachs flatiron building, five blocks north, dominated this fiefdom of two- and three-story buildings with their storefronts below and apartments above.

"They're pulling over," Eben said.

"I see it."

The Bonneville pulled into a place near where a side street cut across, no light, no stop sign. I went on through the intersection—having to pick my way through the light traffic—and pulled into a place half a block up.

Eben, turning to watch, said, "They're getting out. Cutting over to that side street."

I shut off the engine. "I'll see where they're going."

Eben nodded, content to stay put. Not many Negroes around this part of town. Not any, right now, except him.

As I rounded the corner, the Cubans were entering a storefront in the middle of the block. Pedestrians were mostly older people and moms with little kids, apparel ranging from Sears to rummage store, Poles outnumbering Puerto Ricans two to one. A few winos, a few junkies. No Cubans to speak of—they were the area's ownership class.

I walked down to where Gonzales and Rodriguez

had disappeared and found an old kitchenette with GOOD FOOD written in big bold red cursive on the window. Through the glass, between two flags painted there (Cuba and Puerto Rico), I could see our two subjects heading toward the back. They slipped into a booth, sharing the same side.

Cozy.

I walked quickly back to the car and leaned in like a carhop, telling Eben, "Drive around and find a place opposite 'Good Food' restaurant. Middle of the block. They're in there. Keep a close watch."

"What about you?"

"I'm going to have a Coke. Haven't you heard? It's the pause that refreshes."

I headed back for the luncheonette.

Good Food's food smelled good, in a carnival kind of way. The old restaurant was just a clutter of Formica tables with kitchen chairs on linoleum, rows of wooden booths along the left and right walls. Across the rear was a counter behind which was a diner-style window onto the kitchen. This time of afternoon was slow, but about a dozen customers were seated, mostly Puerto Ricans.

Running the place was a skinny man and a plump woman, handsome Cubans in their late thirties, neatly dressed in white shirt and slacks, or in the woman's case dress. Husband and wife, most likely, with hubby at the register and the better half behind the diner counter. Behind her, dark faces scurried in the kitchen.

Over the serving window was a big wide plastic menu board, courtesy of Coke—listing sandwiches geared toward both Poles and Latinos: Polish sausage, fritas, plus typical diner fare. On the walls were Orange Crush, Green River, and 7-UP signs, but behind the register hung a huge "Old Cuba" calendar with a *magnífico* color photo of the Hotel Nacional in Havana, once owned by that great native Cuban, Meyer Lansky.

Exiles owned all the stores around here, thanks to SBA loans—seemed Uncle Sam wanted to show the Cuban DP's just how much better America was than Castroville. As Spanish speakers, they could serve the Puerto Rican customers well. But resentment was brewing, since the PR's—like the Negroes—somehow couldn't seem to wrangle those kind of loans.

At the counter, I ordered a Coke, glad to be in street clothes and unshaven, just another working stiff. The zippered Windbreaker was blousy enough to conceal the holstered nine-millimeter under my arm, and I was hardly the only white guy in the joint. For example, there was a joe in a work shirt and matching pants eating a Polish sausage sandwich just down from me. And down from him, a husky guy in a checkered shirt and black pants having chicken soup.

And two white guys just over to my left, sitting on the same side of a booth . . .

. . . across from the pair of Cubans we'd tailed here.

Not just any white guys, either—these were (as Sergeant Shoppa of the Chicago PD had dubbed them) Smith and Jones, the ex-soldier Southern boys with butch haircuts who rounded out the set of four Justice Department surveillance photos. Collect them all.

The blond guy, in a plaid shirt unbuttoned over a T-shirt, reminded me of Vallee, but with a narrower, fox-like face; he was chewing a toothpick and frowning, not irritated, just trying to think. His black-haired associate, in a well-worn gray U.S. Army sweatshirt, was listening, chewing gum, as the Cubans spoke to them in Spanish.

That impressed me. These two white-trash ex-GIs had picked up a second language, and here I was barely functional in English. I gulped some Coke from the room-temperature bottle I'd been served, while the two Cubans—the older, fright-wig character doing most of the talking—continued with what might have been a briefing.

The confab hadn't gone on long before the two white guys gave knowing nods to their booth mates, slid out, and headed back around the counter.

*Had I been made?*

Casually as possible, I unzipped the Windbreaker.

But they weren't getting behind that counter to better deal with yours truly—they did not seem to have noticed me. No, they were going out, through the kitchen, letting no grass grow. An alley was back there, and I was about to lose them.

Moments later, the two Cubans exited their booth quickly, tossing a couple of bucks on the tabletop for their own soft drinks. As they hurried out onto the street, I kept my back to them, perched on my counter stool.

Not wanting to be too damn obvious, I finished my Coke, tossed a quarter on the counter, and went outside. Looking diagonally across to Milwaukee Avenue, I could see the two Cubans getting into their Pontiac. They had hustled.

I jaywalked over to the Chrysler, where Eben sat in the passenger seat. That was good surveillance technique: stay in the driver's seat and other cars'll pull up and wait, thinking you're vacating your parking space.

Getting behind the wheel, I said, "The two white guys were in there."

"All *right*," Eben said, and then he was pointing. "Subjects are heading north on Milwaukee again."

The Pontiac indeed was on the move. But not moving fast—interesting, considering the Cubans had all but run out of the restaurant.

Then I put it together.

"They're gonna pull into the alley behind the restaurant," I said, waiting for an opening in traffic.

"Why?"

"The Caucasian Twins are back in that alley. My hunch is, it's a weapons delivery."

"Damn, I bet you're right!" Eben sat forward. "The rifles the landlady saw in that flat are in their *trunk* now! I better call this in. . . ."

The Negro agent got on the radio, and by the time I had taken the left on Milwaukee, he was saying into the hand mike, "Tell Chief Martineau we have located all four subjects, repeat, all four subjects. More information as things develop. Ten-four."

Just like Broderick Crawford on *Highway Patrol.*

Turning through the intersection, I saw no sign of the Pontiac.

"They've already pulled in," I said.

I was driving faster than I should when I swung into the alley—narrowly missing the iron pillar supporting the Elevated tracks above—and had to slam on the brakes not to bump headlights with the Pontiac parked back there.

Gonzales was again at the wheel and he reared back as our vehicles almost kissed snouts. The Bonneville trunk was up, with just the top of a bushy-haired head visible over it; then the trunk slammed shut, and revealed Rodriguez, gaping in annoyed surprise.

That lowered trunk also provided us a better view down the alley, as another car—a light-blue Ford Falcon (couldn't catch the damn plate)—was waving its ass and taillights at us from down at the other end of the alley, making a right turn and then out of sight.

*The white boys.*

From behind the wheel, I offered Gonzales a goofy grin, and shrugged in a way that proclaimed myself the dumb ass at fault here. The alarm left the Cuban's expression and he nodded, reluctantly polite. Why call attention?

That was when the damn police radio squawked: *"This is Chief Martineau. What is your location, Agent Boldt?"*

Eben lurched forward to turn down the volume, but far too late.

The message had been heard by the two Cubans—it had frozen them, in fact. But they'd thaw soon enough.

Fuck it.

I leaned out my window. *"Secret Service! Exit the vehicle with your hands up!"*

That sounded like something a real G-man would say, right? Who wouldn't wilt under that kind of verbal assault?

Well, the Cubans didn't. The bushy-haired guy yanked open the Pontiac's rear left door and threw himself inside the car, slamming that door just as Gonzales threw the vehicle into reverse, hitting the gas and backing up, fast.

I hit the gas, too, rocketing down the alley after them—they could never outrun us in reverse, though I could hardly blame them for trying.

But we would never know the outcome of such a chase, because as they neared the alley exit, another car backed in, pausing, apparently to turn around, and we were on top of the Pontiac again, headlights getting reacquainted. I threw it in Park, leapt from my side of the vehicle as Eben did the same from his, both of us with guns in hand.

Gonzales gave up immediately, getting out to stand with his hands up and his chin down, even assuming the position against a brick wall, making it easier on Eben cuffing the guy's hands behind him.

But Rodriguez wasn't so cooperative. While Eben was making his collar, the big bushy-haired bastard scrambled out of the backseat on the other side and came charging at me, like an offensive tackle rushing the line, and despite my having the Browning in hand, he practically ran me down, shoving me aside and against a brick alley wall, jarring me, overwhelming my ancient ass.

Still, I recovered quickly and picked up pursuit.

He dashed out of the alley and across the street, several cars slamming on brakes and swerving to miss him, getting himself sworn at in various languages, and I was right behind him, taking advantage of the path he'd cleared. Where the alley picked back up, he went down it. For a big man, both broad-shouldered and bulky, he was fast, or at least adrenaline was making him so.

We ran down the alley, footsteps echoing, the Elevated tracks visible above, a train rumbling by, its shadow racing across the buildings at left whose backs provided a collective wall. As the chase continued, the El started its roller-coaster dip into the subway, enclosed now by a short cement barrier topped by a wire-mesh fence on either side of the double tracks.

Huffing and puffing like a Big Bad Wolf with no house to blow down, I somehow managed to cut the distance between us. Rodriguez was younger, but also fatter, and his sprint was losing steam into distance running. The tracks were right next to us now, behind their fence, as the El continued its descent.

The nine-mil was still in my right fist—I could have shot the bastard, and maybe I should have and spared myself the aches and pains that the aftermath of all this running would bring, not to mention the burning gut-ache that was already starting. A leg shot might have brought him down, though you can kill a guy with a leg shot—there's an important artery hiding inside.

But Rodriguez didn't seem to be armed, and if this was all just some kind of royal FUBAR, and these subjects turned out not to be a paramilitary hit squad, then I'd be shooting down an unarmed Cuban exile, which would make me popular with nobody, myself included.

And if Rodriguez *was* part of such a hit squad—the two white-boy members of which were currently in the wind, maybe now carting high-powered rifles with scopes in their Falcon trunk—there might be information in that mangy-haired Cuban skull that could save the President's life.

Now the tracks were actually lower than we were, as the El headed toward the black mouth of the subway tunnel, and Rodriguez glanced at the fence, where a gaping tear yawned—locals having clipped a path to provide a cut-through to the houses beyond—and he slowed enough to clamber through it.

I was right on him, though.

He turned and shoved me, and I damn near lost my balance, knocking back against the fence with a springing effect. I was stumbling on the trash-strewn cinders of the El ditch when he caught my helplessness and decided to start throwing ham-sized fists at me, and I whapped his knuckles with the nine-mil, both hands, making him yelp and reconsider.

Then he tried another shove, and this one put me on my ass. A train was rumbling our way, but it wasn't on us, not yet, the more pressing problem being that he didn't seem to know that as he ran pell-mell across those tracks, his next step would be on the third rail.

*Didn't they have fucking electricity in Cuba?*

I threw myself at him like a desperate sweetheart and grabbed onto his jacket, and yanked him back right before his sneakered foot touched that deadly rail. I clouted him alongside the skull with the Browning barrel, and that turned him drunken woozy. I dragged him like a stubborn bag of dirty laundry back across the tracks.

When the train came roaring past, he was on his side in the cinders between the fence and the tracks, and as the beast blew by with its familiar metallic scream, I stood pointing the nine-mil down at the wild-haired, wild-eyed Cuban, who was covering his ears, the noise too much for this dainty flower.

I said, "You're welcome."

"Fuck you, *maricón*," he said.

Might have been fun at that, seeing him do the one-man rhumba on that third rail.

**Saturday, November 2, 1963**
**8:00 A.M.**

The Secret Service office was damn near empty, most of the agents already out in the field for the President's arrival; but Martineau was visible in his window, the blinds up for a change, and Eben Boldt was in there, standing opposite his boss, who was apparently issuing instructions.

Eben and I had brought the two subjects in yesterday afternoon, and Polaroid pictures had been made of them—no prints taken. This was strictly "detention for questioning," not an arrest. But the pair had already given up their names, or anyway "names"—Victor Gonzales and Ramon Rodriguez. They claimed to be from Miami. Gonzales had a driver's license backing that up. Rodriguez had various I.D., none of it official—no driver's license because he said he did not drive. The Bonneville was on loan from a friend in West Town, one Luis Garcia.

Martineau had sent both Eben and me home yesterday around seven P.M. We'd been getting a ribbing for having the radio on during surveillance and blowing our cover. They were giving Eben the worst of it. Of course, that was after I had cheerfully given him the blame. There was nothing overtly racial in the kidding, but I could tell Eben was taking it personally.

Finally I told one of the crew cuts, "On the other hand, we *did* haul those two Cuban assholes in. Kennedy's here tomorrow in the A.M., and how are you fellas doing finding those missing white boys?"

The ribbing let up at that point.

This morning I arrived showered and shaved and armed, ready to save the President—Air Force One would touch down at O'Hare in just under two hours—but without much of an idea how the hell I (or for that matter the entire Chicago branch of the Secret Service) might accomplish that.

Eben came quickly out of Martineau's office, pausing to say, "Marty wants you to stick around in case something comes up."

I fell in alongside him. "Where is it you're going without me?"

"Heading out to Soldier Field. I'm to check the area around Kennedy's seating. There are two sections reserved for him—one on the Air Force side, other on the Army. He'll switch during halftime."

"I'd just as soon not be out there. That halftime gun might make me shit myself."

He actually laughed at that. Well, he chuckled and shook his head.

I followed him to his desk, where he grabbed his raincoat from where he'd dumped it, apparently having arrived just before me.

As he shrugged into the coat, he said, "There's been a foreign development."

"Yeah?"

"Coup in South Vietnam that has the President's attention. Some kind of special communications facility is being rush-constructed under the bleachers, to keep Lancer informed."

"Maybe he'll cancel."

"I wish he would," Eben said, and went out.

Martineau called from his office doorway: "Heller! Nate! Come talk."

The sturdy SS chief was behind his mahogany boat of a desk by the time I dropped into the chair opposite him. No shirtsleeves today, strictly a crisp navy-blue suit and red-and-black-striped tie. His cuff links were little golden replicas of that Treasury Department seal on the nearby wall.

"Ebe mentioned there's a coup in Vietnam," I said.

"Yes, apparently the Diem brothers just killed themselves."

"They've been assassinated, in other words. Did we do it?"

He just gave me a look. "I had hoped this would give the President an excuse to cancel, but I was just told in no uncertain terms that the trip is on, and on schedule."

"Swell."

"I assume Ebe mentioned this communications setup they're constructing at Soldier Field."

"Yeah. If you need somebody to sweep up the candy wrappers under the bleachers for 'em, I'm not available."

He smiled a little at that. He was used to me by now. "I want you to take a crack at Gonzales and Rodriguez. We've been in steady interrogation with those two since you delivered them yesterday afternoon."

"Learning what?"

"Little and nothing. We've got Gonzales in the left booth, Rodriguez in the right, and Motto and Stocks have been in session all night with those sons of bitches.

One-on-one, two-on-one, good cop/bad cop, playing one off the other, you name it, they tried it. Goddamn nothing."

"I could always feed them the goldfish."

"What?"

"Old Chicago cop expression for the rubber hose you probably don't have around this refined establishment." I sat forward. "Glad to give it a shot—they're tired by now, and I'm fresh as a daisy. Anything we can offer them?"

"They've had two meals. There's water and coffee. They get bathroom breaks. What else?"

"How about money? What's the petty-cash situation? I doubt they're small enough fry to be bribed, but it's always worth a try."

Martineau shook his head once. "Against policy."

"The CIA topples governments, and the Secret Service doesn't pay off informants? This is why Avis never catches up with Hertz."

"Try something else, Nate. Your charm maybe. Or your wit."

I told you he was getting used to me.

First I spelled a frazzled Motto, even his crew cut looking wilted—and you can bet he was in his shirt sleeves after that long night. Interview One's narrow space with its soundproof-tile walls was all but filled by a scarred table decorated festively with cigar-butt-heavy ashtrays, an almost-empty water pitcher, and discarded Styrofoam coffee cups. The wooden chairs were just as scarred, and as comfortable as a cement block.

Gonzales wasn't so clean-shaven today. He looked up with eyes that were half-lidded, sleepy with contempt. And just plain fucking sleepy.

"Good morning, Victor," I said, sitting opposite him. "Remember me?"

He nodded.

"Boy, do I feel refreshed. Last night, after I dropped you and your pal off, I had a great meal at Rancho Grande . . . on North Clark? Then straight home for a nice long hot shower, and right to bed, must have got nine hours. I slept so goddamn long, I feel almost sleepy today. Ever have that happen?"

Nothing.

"So you're from Miami."

A nod.

"A businessman."

A nod.

"The Bonneville was loaned to you by a friend?"

A nod.

"What's your friend's name?"

"Luis Garcia. I told the other two."

"Where does Luis live?"

"I don't know."

"How did you get the car from him?"

"He had it waiting at the airport for us."

"Luis doesn't seem to have a phone, Victor."

A shrug.

"Who were those two white fellas you were talking to at the Good Eats restaurant yesterday?"

"I told Agent Motto. I told Agent Stocks."

"Tell me."

"They are real estate agents."

"Do they have names?"

"Johnson and Smith."

Sergeant Shoppa had been close, at that, with Smith and Jones.

"You're interested in property?"

"Yes. We hear there are the investment opportunities in Chicago for Cubans."

"You're Cuban?"

"Yes."

"Exiles."

"Yes."

"What did you do in Cuba?"

"We were businessmen. The Communists, they took our businesses. We start over in Florida."

"Your landlady says you had rifles in your flat."

"She is crazy. A busybody. She does not like the color of our skin."

"Well, she liked the color of your money. Enough to rent you a room, anyway. The rifles had sniper scopes, she said."

"These rifles have nothing because they do not exist."

I had a 5-by-7 of Vallee in my inside suit-coat pocket and I got it out and shoved it across the rough table-top. "You ever see this guy?"

*Did something flicker in those sleepy eyes?*

"No."

"Are you sure?"

"Gringos, they all look alike to me."

The conversation in the other interview room went no better. The droopy-mustached Rodriguez was more openly surly, due to our altercation.

"Ramon, what is your opinion of President Kennedy?"

"Better than Nixon. Much more better than Castro. I have no argument with Kennedy."

"Did I say you did?"

He shrugged.

"You handed off those rifles to the two 'real estate agents'—that's why you were standing in back of that Pontiac with the trunk lid up. Did they buy the guns?"

"I have no guns in the trunk."

"Then why were you back there? What were you looking for? You didn't have a flat tire."

"The afternoon was getting colder. I thought I had another jacket in there. I was wrong."

"You weren't *selling* weapons, you were delivering them, right? Are the two white guys the shooters? I would think three shooters is more like it, especially if you're planning for that warehouse district on Jackson. Triangulation would be the best bet."

"I don't know anything about any of what you speak."

"Are you the third shooter, Ramon, or just the driver? Probably just the driver. Big clumsy guy like you, probably not that good with weapons."

"Fuck you."

"Don't repeat yourself, Ramon. You're better than that." I pushed Vallee's photo across to him. "Is *he* the third shooter, and you and Victor strictly transport?"

"Fuck you."

"Probably strictly transport. You wouldn't want to entrust a couple of hatchet throwers with anything really important."

His big hands made big fists. The knuckles were scraped where I batted them with the nine-mil yesterday.

"You know, if there are two or three shooters out there, ready to pull this thing off? That leaves you and Victor in custody, ready to take the brunt. You really *will* fry, Ramon. And it won't be on the third rail."

He folded his arms, his scowl made comically sour by the Yosemite Sam mustache.

"Give those white boys up now, and it might go easy on you. Lead us to them, and I wouldn't be surprised if you walked out of here, later today."

Nothing.

Outside the booth, I found Martineau heading my way, climbing into a raincoat.

"Anything?" he asked, pausing to talk.

"Just their cover stories. Where are you headed?"

"Out to O'Hare to meet the President's plane."

"What's the score on Vallee?"

"He's been under twenty-four-hour surveillance by the Chicago PD—two teams on twelve-hour shifts. Shoppa and Gross are back on him this morning."

"Listen, what about that printing facility where Vallee works?"

"They're a six-day-a-week operation. All hundred-some employees will be on the job this morning, including Vallee, presumably."

"You scoped the building out."

He frowned at me. "Of course we did. Vallee works on the third floor, Nate, with another thirty-some employees. You think he could go over to the window and take a potshot at the President under those conditions?"

"What about the rooftop?"

"My understanding is Shoppa or Gross will secure that. And the eighth floor is strictly warehouse, which is another possibility, and one of them will handle that, too. Once they've followed this hero to work, anyway." He checked his watch. "They're probably already there now."

"Are you in contact with Shoppa and Gross?"

"They'll be on foot, not in their unmarked with the radio handy. Why, are you figuring to blow another surveillance with radio chatter?"

Actually, Martineau himself had blown it, but I didn't point that out.

"Marty, when the President goes by, people will rush to the windows—they may go to lower floors to get a better look. Vallee could snag an opportunity to get a shot off. Who was it checked out that site?"

He frowned, mildly irritated. "I went over there

myself with two agents. It does provide, especially from upper floors, a good view where the limo makes its slow turn onto West Jackson. But so do another half dozen or more other buildings."

"Vallee doesn't work in those other buildings."

"He's covered, Heller. The Chicago PD has him. We're stretched thin. Look. If you want to walk over there and see for yourself, you have my blessing."

He went out.

Back in my office, frustrated as hell, I just sat at my desk looking for options. The only thing that occurred to me was taking Martineau up on it and hoofing over to IPP Litho-Plate. Only six blocks. . . .

The phone rang. I pushed the Line Two button and answered it.

"This is Mrs. Peters."

Vallee's landlady.

"Hello, Mrs. Peters. You have something for me?"

"Possibly. Possibly it is unimportant. But Mr. Vallee goes out this morning. Half an hour ago."

"Is that unusual? He does work on Saturdays, right?"

"Usually. They work him very hard at the printing plant. But they are closed today."

"Our understanding is they're open."

"They decide yesterday that they would close. I hear Mr. Vallee on the hall phone talking to someone about it. He said to this person that his work was shutting down because of the . . . he said 'goddamn President' coming to town. His bosses, they say that the crowds and the parking will be bad, so they give the day off."

This had perked me up. "When Mr. Vallee went out this morning, was he carrying anything?"

"You mean his guns? No. But they will be in his car."

"Why do you say that?"

"Well, where else could they be? They are not in his room now. I check there before I call you."

"You are a rare gem, Mrs. Peters." Hitler Youth or no Hitler Youth.

She reminded me of her open invitation for me to stop by for tea, and we exchanged good-byes.

Looking like hell, Motto and Stocks were discussing whether or not to transfer the two uncooperative subjects to Federal Building holding cells. I came up and shared what I'd learned about Vallee and his place of business, and asked them to get hold of Martineau ASAP, and tell him.

"You're going over to IPP?" Stocks asked.

"Yeah. In the meantime, one of you guys try to get those Chicago coppers on the line—try to get patched through to their radio. They may be in their car, if Vallee is riding around, waiting for the right moment to sneak into his workplace."

I collected my raincoat and hat and headed over to IPP.

# *18*

**Saturday, November 2, 1963**
**9:10 A.M.**

The day was chilly but not overcast, sunlight lancing through clouds and off skyscraper glass, with some lake wind making itself known; but that hadn't discouraged the good citizens of Chicago. When I got to West Jackson, I found them by the hundreds eagerly lining both sides of the street, a mix of well-dressed and casual, men in hats or bareheaded, women in Easter-worthy hats or just scarves, some citizens standing at near military attention, others leaning on the wooden handles of homemade placards they would eventually brandish (ALL THE WAY WITH JFK!), abuzz with anticipation ("I wonder if Jackie will be with him!"). Over the next hour and a half, these hundreds would grow into thousands. And soon JFK himself would be riding in his convertible, smiling and waving to them all.

IPP Litho-Plate, on the corner of West Jackson and Des Plaines, dated to just after the turn of the century, a nondescript brown brick rectangular eight floors. The building across the way, on Des Plaines, was several stories shorter, so from the roof or a high window, a corner IPP window would (as Martineau had admitted) provide a sniper a clear view of the slowed limo making its way onto Jackson.

Another possibility was a shot from above, directly down at the President as he passed in his convertible.

I was part of the crowd, just facing the wrong way, as I knocked on the front doors, getting no response. An after-hours buzzer did no good, either. The crowd's giddy excitement—loud talk and shrill yelling and hysterical laughter—made a collective cacophony that created an anxious edge in me that I needed to shake. Glad to get away from them, I headed around to the rear of the building and found a loading dock, and climbed up there and pounded on another door.

A guy finally answered, a scrawny character in his fifties in overalls and gray stubble, who made about as good a security guard as a kid with a cap pistol, only he didn't have a cap pistol.

Of course, he wasn't a security guard at all, just a janitor, and he took about two seconds to glance at my Justice Department credentials before letting me in.

We stood in a cement stairwell and echoed at each other.

"Anybody else in the building, Pop?" I asked.

"No, sir. Just me, the rats, and the roaches."

"Nobody came around today, wanting to get in to watch the President's parade from the fifty-yard line?"

He shook his head. "That's not allowed. Maybe you know the Secret Service came by earlier in the week, had a look around, and said, on the motorcade morning? Keep anybody but employees oh-you-tee. Last minute yesterday, bosses here decided just to shut down for the day."

I gestured toward the cement stairs with their metal railing. "Can I get to every floor from these?"

"Yes, sir."

"Doors locked on the landings?"

"No, sir."

"Okay. Listen, nobody else gets in unless they have credentials that say Secret Service or Chicago PD. Got it?"

"Yes, sir."

"How do I get to the roof?"

"There's a door on the warehouse floor. That's the top floor. Eight. I can show you."

"No. But thank you, Pop."

What the hell was I calling him "Pop" for? He was probably my age. . . .

I headed up. Eight floors was a lot to search, and a sniper—depending on whether he wanted to hit Lancer coming off the expressway ramp or wait till the target moved past the building—could be just about anywhere, on just about any floor.

My hunch, however, was that the shooting post of choice would either be the warehouse floor or the roof—either should provide the kind of privacy a shooter would need. True, no other employees were around today; but when the plan had been formulated, the assumption would have been that Saturday was a workday at IPP. And they would stick to plan. Popping the President from the third-floor window, with Vallee surrounded by thirty or more other print-plant employees, would not have been a contingency.

I decided to take the warehouse floor first. As I climbed, I got out the nine-millimeter, releasing the safety.

*So we had two of the four assassins in custody—or was it five? The fifth assassin, Vallee, would be under surveillance, unless—in the confusion of the IPP plant's taking the day off at the last second—the screwed-up little ex-Marine had slipped his tail. Where better for him to make his stand than his workplace, where he either had a key or had made sure to get one. A familiar setting for him to use as the stage for his John Wilkes Booth performance.*

*Was Vallee part of the Cuban/white-trash team? Or was he acting of his own twisted accord?*

*That bothered me. Either way you read it, something seemed wrong—Vallee as another ex-soldier in bed with those Cubans, or Vallee as just another lone nut.*

*Even as a lone nut, however, a guy like Vallee was not some frenzied maniac racing across a hallway or an intersection, waving a cheap pistol, careening suicidally into the waiting armed arms of the Secret Service. No—Vallee, those Cubans, and the other ex-soldier boys were all cool, calculating, military-trained killers. With loaded rifles. With sniper scopes.*

*And the President would be here soon.*

The door opened onto a vast expanse of giant paper rolls, stacked oversize cartons, and piled metal plates, a city of paper supplies with avenues wide enough to accommodate a forklift, two of which were at rest nearby, like small slumbering dinosaurs. Also nearby were the wood-slatted doors of a big old-fashioned freight elevator.

The ceiling was high and open-beamed and the lights were off, sunshine filtering lazily through the many windows like bright mote-floating fog.

Moving slowly across the wooden floor, with the nine-mil ready, I kept my back to a wall of looming paper rolls. No ink smell up here, more like a lumberyard scent. I felt Vallee—or whoever the sniper might be—would more likely be on the roof; but I could take no chances. Down at the end of this aisle (they were aligned with the narrow sides of the building's rectangle) I could make out several of the windows onto Jackson.

No one perched to shoot down there.

And when I reached the end of that aisle, window upon window with views onto Jackson presented no Vallee, no anybody, waiting with a rifle. I didn't know whether to be relieved or disappointed.

At the left, however, down at the West corner of the building, some cartons had been piled in an orderly fashion, though not following the layout of the rest of this warehouse floor. This had a homemade, temporary look to it, like some kid had made a fort out of thirty or forty cartons, walling himself in, making a little room with six-foot paper-carton walls. Behind those walls would be the corner windows, including at least one looking across the intersection of Jackson and Des Plaines.

What you might call a sniper's nest.

I have never moved more slowly. More cautiously. More silently. I was glad to be wearing Hush Puppies with their rubber soles, though socks might have been better. If a foot chase developed, though, particularly on this wood floor, a slip in socks could put you on your ass.

So I eased down past the half-dozen mouths of aisles in IPP's paper city, until I had neared the three-walled makeshift room surrounding the corner windows. Space on both sides of the stacked-carton fortress had been left to allow entry and exit.

I did not hear any movement from another human being. I did not hear heavy breathing or a cough or a rustle of clothing, much less someone loading a weapon.

*Had this sniper's nest been prepared earlier, and the shooter not yet taken his position?*

That possibility seemed very real.

When I swung around into the open space, however, there he sat, Indian-style, his arms folded, as he watched out that window. Waiting patiently. A rifle with a scope was propped on a little stand, an M-1 like Vallee's.

But this wasn't Vallee.

Perched there maybe six feet away from me was the white soldier boy who somewhat resembled Vallee, in a white T-shirt and plaid shirt with its sleeves rolled up and blue jeans and sneakers. He had a blond butch and he was chewing a toothpick and he was wearing Ray-Bans.

White trash in blue jeans and green sunglasses.

"On your feet," I said. "Hands up. Nice and easy, son. . . ."

He just looked up at me. Bland as toast. As unconcerned as a lion regarding a cricket.

Finally he nodded, started to slowly rise, then lurched for the rifle, and damn he was fast, because that long barrel was staring right up at me when I cracked a Ray-Ban lens by putting a bullet through it.

It stood him up straight, that eyeglass lens cracking like an eggshell, weeping a single red tear, and it was damn near comical, like he was coming to attention and preparing to salute when instead he just flopped facedown at my feet and showed me the nasty wet hole where the nine-mil slug had made its exit.

I removed the M-1 from his limp grasp, then yanked him by an arm and dragged him out of the nest.

There would be at least two shooters. *Why hadn't this guy been Vallee?* This was Vallee's building. Or had the mentally disturbed ex-Marine been some sort of decoy? In which case, with the Cubans in custody, one other white–boy shooter was out there.

Just one.

I knelt in the window and looked around at the buildings of the intersection. My eyes searched windows and rooftops.

Then just across Des Plaines, on the five-story building across from me, I saw him.

Again, not Vallee.

It was the white boy with the black butch and he was emerging from a rooftop doorway, staying low, scoped rifle in hand, heading to the roof's edge.

Should I go over there?

Should I call it in?

The President wasn't due for a while yet. But what if the rooftop shooter didn't get a scheduled signal from his now-dead cohort, and decided to light out, or find some alternate position? A lot could happen by the time I left the eighth floor of IPP and got across Des Plaines and made my way to that rooftop.

I waited till he was in position near the building's edge, where the lip came up and gave him a resting place for his weapon, and I lined him up in the M-1's cross hairs.

When I fired, the report of the rifle was just a minor whip crack in the morning, probably dismissed by one and all as a festive firecracker or maybe a car backfiring or some other unidentified city sound, even the indistinct blare of a sound truck down the street, making some announcement or other, possibly for a new pizza place or perhaps *Stop the World, I Want to Get Off* at the Shubert.

That is, dismissed as such by everyone but the sniper who the M-1 round had caught in the neck. I hadn't handled a rifle since the Pacific, and been trying for his head and came close. I hadn't intended for him to die that way, rolling around unable to scream with his hands clutching his throat as he strangled in his own blood.

But it served the purpose.

I was on my feet, wondering what to do next, when I could finally make out the sound truck's blare: "*The*

*President's appearance has been canceled! We are sorry to announce, President Kennedy's Chicago trip has been canceled! A parade featuring other dignitaries will go on as scheduled. The President's appearance has been ...*"

Might have told me before I went to all this trouble.

Near the freight elevators was a little office area where I used a wall phone. No police sirens cut the air—just those sound trucks, which a glance out a window told me were actually police cars with uniformed cops hanging out rider's windows with bullhorns to announce the President's cancelation.

As for the cancelation of those two snipers, no sign that anyone had noticed any part of that episode presented itself. The warehouse area on West Jackson was really just a bunch of empty buildings—IPP working on Saturdays was the exception not the rule around here—and anybody normally in those buildings had probably been down lining the sidewalks waiting for the motorcade. As far as I could tell, no other buildings or even the expressway had a view of that rooftop, where the body of the black-butch sniper was just a vague shape near a rooftop edge, anyway.

I'd be lying if I didn't admit to considering just digging out that nine-millimeter slug from the wooden floor, where it had deposited itself after traveling through the blond assassin's Ray-Bans and brain, and wiping down the M-1 I'd borrowed to eliminate the other assassin, and fuck it, walk away. Wasn't like that janitor was liable to provide much of a description of me.

But I was law enforcement today, not the free agent I usually was, and I had a responsibility to Bobby Kennedy and even these great United States. Besides, it was odds on that this would be covered up—that neither the Justice Department nor the Secret Service would want word getting out that two assassins were killed while lying in wait for a Presidential parade. Not good press. Not good press at all.

So what to do?

I called the Cook County sheriff's office and asked for Dick Cain, knowing he'd be out in the field, maybe Soldier Field, still caught up in this presidential trip that wasn't happening.

"Patch me through," I said. "Tell him it's Nate Heller and that it's important."

Getting Cain took five minutes that only felt like five hours. The small solace was that in the meantime nobody came running up the stairs with guns to arrest me or kill me or anything. Two dead, and even the janitor hadn't noticed, which was no surprise.

"Nate," Dick said, outdoors apparently, maybe using the radio mike in his car, "what is it?"

I told him what had happened.

"First," he said, "change your story. What went down with the first sniper, don't change a thing. That's heroic stuff, my friend. But the second guy? Best say that you looked through the sniper scope, saw that other sniper aiming back at you, and fired in self-defense."

"Yeah," I said, nodding to myself. I probably would have come up with that myself on the walk back to the Federal Building, but I thanked Dick for the advice and pledged I'd take it.

"Second," he said, "why the hell are you calling me? I'm with the Cook County Sheriff, in case you forgot."

"I need these shooting scenes secured before I go

back and tell Martineau how I saved the President from getting shot on the trip he didn't take."

"Oh. See what you mean. You can't risk either of those bodies being found and this thing spiraling out of control."

I was nodding again, like the phone had eyes. "This can't go public till we know what the official story's going to be. I could go downstairs and find a cop easy enough—that motorcade's going on without Kennedy, for some reason, which means there's still crowd control down there. But I'd have to take potluck."

"And in Commissioner Wilson's brave new world, when you call a cop, how do you know what you're getting? I follow you. You want me to send some of my boys over, or reach out to dependable fellas on the PD?"

"I'll leave that to you, Dick."

"Consider it done."

"So then . . . I can just walk away?"

"Yeah. You go fill Martineau in. He's probably back by now—he left O'Hare when the call came from D.C., canceling."

"Is that where you are, O'Hare?"

"Yeah. We still have Senators Dirksen and Douglas taking the motorcade into town, plus Justice Goldberg, Bob Kennedy's guy Katzenbach, a few other dimly lit luminaries. Nice to know that even if the President can't make it, the crowds can go wild getting a load of the comptroller of the currency."

I laughed at that. "Yeah. And what teenage girl doesn't go to bed dreaming about Everett Dirksen? Listen, Dick, thanks for this. I knew you were the right guy to call."

So I took the stairs down, did not encounter the janitor on the way out, and headed back for the Federal Building. Sunny but cool, the walk felt good.

When I got to the ninth-floor offices of the Secret Service, the bullpen was about half full, guys pulled back in from duty that no longer mattered. Martineau's office blinds were down, but he proved to be home.

I stuck my head in. "Marty, got a few minutes?"

He looked none the worse for wear, after this frantic, stressful morning, working at his desk in his suit coat. Those wiggle-worm eyebrows made his frown look unfriendly, but that was more concern than anything.

"Nate, where the hell have you been?"

I shut the door behind me, went over and sat across from him, feeling very much like a juvie reporting to the high-school principal. I kept the report short and factual, except for the self-defense aspect Dick Cain had suggested, and as dry and humorless as if I'd been a Secret Service agent all my career. Easy to play it straight when the cordite is still clinging inside your nostrils.

Throughout, the broad-shouldered chief was rocking gently in his big swivel chair, his hands tented before him. His expression remained blank but for eyes that were moving in thought. When I'd finished my report, I didn't prompt him for a reaction. He would give it to me in due time.

Finally Martineau leaned forward, resting his elbows on the desk and clasping his hands, as if we were about to say grace. I hoped I wasn't the meal.

"Chief Cain has secured the scene?"

"If not, he soon will have. Either with his own SIU guys or with reliable PD."

His sigh damn near ruffled papers on his desk. "Nate, you did the right thing. You may have saved the President's life . . . yes, I know he canceled, but having two armed, trained assassins floating around out there, with Lancer as their target, would be unacceptable. We might prefer them in custody . . ."

Interesting choice: *might* prefer to have them in custody.

". . . but we certainly like having them out of the game. You did well calling Chief Cain. I didn't realize you were aware of his special status."

"What special status is that?"

Martineau shrugged. "I don't entirely know, I was just told to work with him on this Presidential visit. He apparently is a government asset. I would assume of the Company. Both the Cook County Sheriff's Department and the Chicago PD have a strong working relationship with the CIA, you know."

"I *didn't* know."

That seemed to faintly amuse him. "In this day and age, Nate? Local police in big cities routinely take specialized counterintelligence training with the spooks. Anyway, Cain will help us make this go away."

I'd been right. This would be covered up.

Martineau sighed again, not so big this time. "The President has a number of scheduled trips on the docket, and I've already spoken to your boss—Robert Kennedy, I mean—and he wants no publicity on this assassination plot."

That didn't surprise me.

"What about Vallee?" I asked. "Is he still loose out there?"

Martineau's head snapped back a little and he grinned. "No, didn't anyone tell you? He's in Interview One, right now. Lieutenant Gross and Sergeant Shoppa brought him in about fifteen minutes ago. We haven't even had time to question him."

"You mean, he's not a priority anymore?"

"Not really. Just another crank. We've had other fish

to fry—actually, we've already had an agents' meeting about the general situation."

I hadn't been able to attend, busy managing the scenes of two shootings. Of mine. Still, it must have been a short meeting.

"What did I miss, Marty?"

"Well, you're aware we've been operating on a non-documentary basis—strictly oral reports. On Monday, every agent involved in this investigation of potential motorcade assassins will spend time with Charlotte dictating oral reports."

Charlotte was the top secretary around here.

"From these typed reports," he said, "I will write an overview that will remain top secret—with our COS designation—which I will send by special courier to Chief Rowley."

"COS?"

"Central Office Secret. You can see how this benefits your situation."

I did. I had just killed two suspects and would not have to answer any detailed questions, no hearings, no shooting board, no nothing.

"And the two Cubans?"

Martineau shrugged. "They'll be released shortly."

"What the hell?"

"Nate, we don't have an iota of evidence on them. Checks we've run bring up no outstanding warrants, and only back up their cover story. The sole indication that they're dangerous comes from the FBI, who don't want any part of this. What else can we do?"

"I *saw* them with those white pricks!"

"What white pricks?"

He had a point.

"And Vallee?"

"We'll be turning him over to the Chicago police this afternoon."

"On what charge?"

"The one Shoppa and Gross hauled him in on—concealed weapons. He was making an illegal left-hand turn; they pulled him over, and saw a hunting knife on the rider's seat. When his trunk was searched, cartons of ammunition, an M-1 and a .22 revolver were found."

"Who's interrogating him?"

"Nobody. What *about,* at this point? We yanked him off the street to keep a lid on him while the President was in town. And the President isn't coming. Anyway, Vallee's just another nut. The team of four were the main attraction."

"Mind if I have a chat with Vallee?"

"Be my guest."

I got up and was halfway out when Martineau said, "We do appreciate everything you've done. That was a dangerous situation this morning, at that printer's. I think you handled it well."

"I appreciate that, Marty."

"I can't imagine how chilling it must have been, looking through that sniper scope and seeing another rifle aiming back at you." He seemed to actually shiver. "That you had the presence of mind to just . . . *take* him out, before he could do the same to you? Well, it's something not just anybody could do."

I nodded at him. That wasn't close to what really happened, but what could I say? On the other hand, the way I really handled it wasn't something just anybody could do, either.

Shoppa and Gross were standing outside Interview One. The two Pickpocket Detail cops were in street clothes, per good surveillance technique, stocky Shoppa in a who-shot-the-couch blue-and-white-speckled sport coat over a white open-neck shirt, horsey Gross in a baggy brown suit and a yellow shirt with no tie. They looked happy but beat, having logged plenty of hours babysitting Vallee. Shoppa was smoking a cigar, Gross a cigarette.

"So you nailed him on a left-hand turn, huh?" I said with a grin. "Nothing like good, solid police work."

"Some of the best goddamn arrests," Shoppa said, mildly defensive, "grow out of traffic violations."

"How'd it go down, exactly?"

Gross said, "We'd been tailing Vallee since around eight. We figured he was headed in to work, but then he was just, I don't know, driving. We didn't know what the hell he was up to. I'll be seeing the ass end of that piece of shit white Ford in my sleep."

Shoppa shrugged. "He was turning west onto Wilson from Damen, heading toward the expressway. Figured he was finally going to that printing plant."

"They were closed today," I said.

"Yeah," Shoppa said, and exhaled cheap cigar smoke. "We didn't hear about that till we hauled his ass in."

"When was that?"

Shoppa shrugged. "Must've been ten after nine." He looked at his partner. "Nine-fifteen?"

Gross shrugged, nodded. "He didn't have any firearms on his person, but his trunk was a friggin' arsenal. Seven hundred fifty rounds for that rifle of his." He grinned and looked even more like a horse. "Think we'll get a thank-you note from JFK?"

"Maybe not," I said.

"Fuck it," Shoppa said, and blew a smoke ring. "I was a Nixon man anyway."

I gestured toward the interview room. "Martineau said I could take a crack at him."

Shoppa farted with his lips. "Move in with him and pick out furniture, for all I care. I don't wanna waste *my* time with that screwball."

When I went in, the sight of Vallee gave me a little

start—seated military straight on his side of the scarred table, wearing a white T-shirt with a blue and black plaid shirt over it, damn near identical to the ensemble worn by that blond assassin I'd shot right in the Ray-Bans. Identical, too, was the military-style butch haircut, and the hair color and general Nordic cast of the features.

Vallee was smaller than the late blond, whose face had been narrower; but the resemblance did shake me some.

Settling in opposite him, I said, "Good morning, Tommy. Remember me?"

He frowned, and the big blue eyes under the slightly Neanderthal shelf of forehead narrowed but didn't blink. "We spoke at the Eat Rite. Were you undercover?"

"Guess you could say that. I was checking you out on a tip from a cop who heard you making threatening remarks about the President."

A tiny sneer on the pinched little mouth accompanied a grunt of a laugh. "I've never made a secret of how I feel about Kennedy. We'll be in serious trouble unless Goldwater is elected, you know. But I never really threatened him."

"Sure you did."

"Negative. That was all just figures of speech. Hyper boly." He meant "hyperbole."

"Okay." I had photos of the Cubans and the two white snipers in my inside jacket pocket. I got them out and pushed them across to Vallee. "Know any of these fellas?"

"Negative."

"Not either *one* of these white fellas? In the service, maybe?"

"No, sir."

I tapped the photos of Gonzales and Rodriguez.

"These other two are Cuban. And you trained Cuban exiles near Levittown, right? Maybe you met them there. Look again. Maybe you met just one of 'em."

He looked. He did look. Shook his head. "Negative."

"Where was it you served in Korea, Tom?"

"Mostly I was stationed in Japan."

"Whereabouts in Japan?"

"Camp Otsu."

That meant nothing to me.

I asked, "What did you do there?"

"That's classified, sir."

"Weren't you just a private? With no special skills? Why would what you did in Japan be classified?"

"Well . . . Camp Otsu was a U-2 base, sir. Back in those days, that was top secret stuff."

Goose bumps danced on my neck. Ruby's friend Lee had bragged to me about service at a U-2 base in Japan.

I said, "U-2—wasn't that program the CIA's baby?"

"Affirmative."

"Tommy . . . were you working for the CIA over there?"

"I'm sorry, but I was told that was classified."

"Well, since you got out of the Marines . . . have you worked with the CIA?"

"That's classified, too." His eyebrows scrunched. "Were you *really* a Marine?"

"I was."

"And your name really is Heller?"

"It is."

"So not everything was lies when we talked."

"Not at all."

"Are you with the Company, too, Mr. Heller? Are you debriefing me?"

*Christ. I didn't like where this was heading. For example, if he'd been training Cuban exiles on Long Island, that likely made him some small part, at least, of Operation Mongoose.*

"You could call it that, Tommy. Were you on your way to work when those Chicago cops stopped you today?"

"Negative. We were closed today."

"Were you heading there, anyway? To IPP? Or maybe to some other building on West Jackson?"

"Negative."

"Okay. What were you doing with all that ammunition and those guns in your trunk?"

"Could I see your ID?"

I showed him the Justice Department credentials. He frowned as he examined them—they weren't Central Intelligence Agency, but they were official, all right. And not Secret Service.

He sat and mulled that for a good thirty seconds. Then he swallowed. He'd decided what he wanted to say.

"I wasn't planning to shoot the President. I think somebody *thinks* I was. Because I work on West Jackson. And the motorcade would go right by, and getting off a shot wouldn't be hard. But that was never my intention. I think . . . I think I'm being framed for this."

"Really."

He nodded. "I got a call from someone I trust. I don't want to say more. I *can't* say more. But it was an opportunity for me to make some money this morning."

I was ahead of him. "When the cops stopped you, you were on your way somewhere to sell guns and ammunition. You had a buyer."

He nodded. "The deal was to go down at a parking lot in the Loop. I was supposed to wait there. An unspecified time. As long as it took. But I never made it—around nine-fifteen, those cops pulled me over." The big eyes grew wider. "Is he all right?"

"Is who all right?"

He seemed very earnest. Like he might cry. "The President. *Did* someone shoot him?"

"Why do you think that?"

"Because I think somebody knew about how I felt toward him. Somebody with special knowledge about me and my background and my beliefs. But I'm a good American and a former Marine and wouldn't do that. I speak my dissatisfied mind under the Freedom of Speech. But I didn't do it, Mr. Heller. I was framed."

I raised a calming palm. "Nobody did anything, Tommy. The President canceled his trip."

He blinked. Sat back. "Nobody told me."

I rose. "You relax. I don't think you'll get anything out of this arrest except maybe a fine. Maybe an overnight stay in lockup. Okay?"

"Really?"

"Really."

I went out and found Shoppa and Gross sitting at a vacant desk they'd commandeered, having coffee. Shoppa was lighting his latest noxious cigar.

I said, "Did you fellas know the President's trip had been canceled when you pulled Vallee over?"

They looked blankly at me, and then the same way at each other, and then Shoppa shrugged and waved out his match and said, "Yeah, it came over the radio right around nine."

Official word hadn't gone out till around 9:15. Those cops in squad cars with bullhorns had been at maybe 9:20 or 9:25. But law enforcement involved in motorcade security would have been told first. At nine.

I asked perhaps too casually, "Why did you wait till

after the trip had been canceled to pull Vallee off the street?"

Shoppa's expression darkened. "We didn't pull him over till he made that wrong turn! We couldn't nab him for no fuckin' *reason,* Heller!"

Like *that* had ever stopped the Chicago police.

Shoppa's cigar jutted from a corner of his mouth. "What the hell are you implying?"

"Nothing. Just that you were asked to pull Vallee off the street because he's a danger to the President, and it's interesting you didn't get around to that till the President wasn't in danger anymore."

Shoppa and Gross just laughed and waved me off, like I was a gnat too tiny to warrant swatting. Then, as if I had vanished in a cloud of pixie dust, they returned to their coffee and conversation, and one of the Secret Service crew cuts tapped me on the shoulder.

"Chief Cain of the SIU is in your office, Nate." He pointed, as if I might have forgotten the way. "Waiting to talk to you."

"Thanks."

I wanted to talk to him, too.

—CHAPTER—

## 20

I shut myself in my office with Dick Cain, who was already settled in the visitor's chair, his feet up on my desk, drinking a bottle of Coke he had wangled from somewhere. The reddish-brown-haired detective was in an olive Ivy League suit and his socks were dark green with black brogans.

"Make yourself at home, why don't you?" I said, sitting across from him.

He removed his feet, grinned at me, set the Coke on a scrap of paper, then settled back in the chair. His green-eyed gaze behind the black-rimmed Buddy Holly glasses would have been reassuring had it not been for that milky left eye.

"Everything is copasetic," he said, and gestured with two open palms. "You never shot anybody. Those two white kids never existed. You want the details?"

"Hell no." I leaned back. "But I would like to know what the fuck is *really* going on."

Dick just grinned at me. "What do you mean, what the fuck is really going on?"

"Like—what's this about you being a Company guy?"

He shrugged. "I'm not a Company guy. You mean CIA? That's bullshit."

"Utter bullshit? Complete bullshit? Or just plain bullshit?"

He smirked and batted the air dismissively. "I did some electronic jobs for them when I had my office down in Mexico—during that little hiatus between my Chicago PD time and this sheriff's office gig. So what? Lots of Chicago cops have done business with those spooks. Taken training, traded favors."

"Cops like Shoppa and Gross out there?"

"Yeah. Sure. What of it?"

I was shaking my head. "I don't know, Dick. I don't know. But some things are starting to make sense to me. A kind of a theory is forming."

He reached for the Coke, swigged it. "This oughta be good."

"That kid Thomas Arthur Vallee, sitting in Interview One right now? What if he was supposed to be the patsy today? Put in position to take the fall for the real shooters—the ones that disappeared? Remember them?"

He snorted a laugh. "My understanding is that kid is a screwball. A fag screwball at that."

"Right. And he'd have been the fag screwball ex-Marine who popped the President, all on his own. Crazy collage in his apartment, lots of big talk about killing JFK, ties to the John Birch Society, perfect."

"Nate. Really. Stop. You're embarrassing yourself."

"Why, is it an accident Vallee and the real printing-plant shooter wore the same fucking shirt today? Is it just a coincidence that the two Chicago cops assigned to bring in the nut who threatened Kennedy waited till the President's trip got canceled before doing it? I'm supposed to believe *your* handpicked dicks didn't intend to follow Vallee to that parking lot, where he was heading to a nonexistent gun sale?"

"And do what?"

"What do you think? Wait for word that JFK had been shot, after which they would bring the schmuck in to fit some early suspect description. Or maybe just force or stage a shoot-out. Didn't you leave the force 'cause they thought you'd staged a shoot-out, Dick?"

Cain's expression darkened and he sat forward and clunked the now-empty Coke bottle hard on my desk. "Are you *serious* about this?"

"I always get serious after I kill a couple of nameless assholes. I'm sensitive that way. Were those soldier boys Company, too, Dick? How about the Cubans? Are they assets? Like Vallee is an asset, only *smarter,* and up a level or two?"

"You really don't know what you're talking about."

"Has the CIA finally had it up to here with those skirt-chasing Kennedy boys? Or is this just rogue elements, still sulking over the Bay of Pigs? Gung ho to get rid of JFK, and set up some schmuck like the Vallee kid to take the fall?"

Now he laughed, or pretended to. He got out his pack of Dunhills—moving carefully, I noted—and lit one up. Sucked smoke in. Let it out.

"Quite a yarn, Nate. Why don't you go next door and try peddling it to Martineau? Wait . . . I know! It's because it's a pile of unbelievable crap. Why are you telling *me* all this? You think I'm part of it, this James Bond coup you concocted? I didn't know you smoked the same cigarettes as your musician pals."

"I have no idea who the mastermind is," I admitted. "Hoffa? Marcello? Giancana? Maybe Trafficante, or maybe take one from column A, two from column B. Probably not Johnny Rosselli. Certainly not *you.* You were a kind of point man, weren't you?"

He seemed about to rise. "If you're gonna keep this up, I've got better things to do. . . ."

"You know me, and you know me well. When I turned up as a bodyguard for Tom Ellison, at that money drop, that meant Ellison wasn't following orders. In fact, he'd pulled in Nate Heller of all people, a guy already connected to some of the players and a snoop to boot. You figured it wise to do something about it. About Ellison, anyway, who was the kind of civilian who could prove to be a problem. Me, an insider with my own dirty laundry, different story. You stayed close to me, showing up at the hotel crime scene, to see if I could be handled, or at least sent off in the wrong direction."

"I was there, Nate, because the victim had your card in his damn billfold."

"No he didn't. I never gave Ellison my card."

He was leaning far forward now, a vein throbbing in his forehead. "You think *I* killed Tom Ellison?"

"Well, Mad Sam probably killed Tom. Ice pick. Right height, too. I'd almost pay to see Sam in a bellboy outfit, though, if that's how he swung it. No, you ordered the hit, or Rosselli, or you two came to the mutual conclusion that Ellison was a loose end. What made him important enough a loose end to tie off, I still can't figure. But in a plot to kill the President—"

"You really think I orchestrated a *plot* to kill the *president*?"

"You're part of it. But it failed, didn't it? It fucking failed."

He flopped back in the chair and he was grinning, but it was forced. He did have a gun under his left shoulder—his tailor wasn't as good as mine.

"Nate—you're kidding, right? This is your idea of a Second City skit or some shit."

"No, Dick, I think I'm right on the money. Not that there's anything I can do about it. I could warn Bobby, but I don't exactly think you're gonna try again. Not with the scheme exposed. You fucked up. You failed. It's over."

He got to his feet, stubbed out the Dunhill in an ashtray on my desk. He was smiling, and it wasn't pretty, not with that milky-eyed stare a part of it. "I'm not saying there's anything to this, Nate. But keep a couple of things in mind. You shot two men today, and I covered it up for you. And do I have to whisper those two little words? The ones that guarantee you can't go public?"

*Operation Mongoose.*

I said, "Why kill Ellison over Jack Ruby getting passed ten measly grand?"

Suddenly Dick's expression carried a remarkable lack of human emotion, and it came to me that his Dana Andrews–ish features had probably never worn any actual human emotion. He was one of those guys missing a small but vital part of the machinery we call humanity—an alien from Planet X who could only imitate human feeling.

He said, "I thought you had everything figured out, Nate. But you don't, because there *is* nothing *to* figure out. You're a paranoid seeing spooks in a big dark old house. You don't have any evidence, not a shred. You're just a guy who has had a very tough week who is walkin' around delirious on his damn feet. You go around spewing crazy ideas like these, you might have problems, even though there's nothing to it."

Cain was right. And I was on dangerous ground.

"Not from *me*," he said with a grin. A practiced grin, it now seemed. "But these wild accusations, about those kind of people—Rosselli, Hoffa, and on up that ladder you mentioned—a guy can wake up dead."

*I thought about killing him right there. It might be the only way to protect myself, and—more important—my son. But alone on some deserted warehouse floor of a printing plant was one thing. Next door to the Chicago chief of the Secret Service was another.*

"You're right," I said. Sighed, shook my head, and gave him a grin as phony but I hoped believable as the one he'd just flashed me. "I don't know what the hell's wrong with me. Maybe it's the Mexican food I had last night. Maybe I should get a good night's sleep for a change."

Actually I'd slept long and well last night.

Cain seemed relieved. Whether he really was or not, who could say?

And now he summoned compassion, or a reasonable facsimile thereof. "Look, old friend—you killed a couple guys this morning. That's enough to sit anybody back on their ass. Enough to get the nuttiest thoughts going. You'll keep all this craziness to yourself?"

I grunted a laugh. "Keep what to myself? Sorry, Dick. It just all sort of seemed to fit. You're right—I sound screwier than that Vallee kid. Forget I said any of it."

"Sure." He rose and ambled to the door, then paused there, a hand on the knob. "You forget all of it, too."

"Sure."

He gave me an unfiltered smile that would have made the devil jump. "Or do you actually *believe* that load of horseshit, Nate? You wouldn't be harboring any ideas of settling up with me, would you?"

"No."

*Not today.*

I said, "I just want to get the hell out of this government job and back into the private sector. But enough of that horseshit just *might* be true, Dick, that I don't think I ever want to see you again."

"Nate . . ."

"Stay away from me and the people I care about,

amigo, and I will cut you a wide swath. We were friends long enough that I owe you that much."

*Like hell.*

"All right, Nate." He gave up an easygoing shrug. "You and I, we'll keep our distance. For now, anyway. But here's what I would say to you, if that fever dream you shared happened to have any truth in it—stay on the sidelines, and I give you my word, no reprisals. You've never been a political animal, and there are changes coming that are way out of your league. Nothing you can understand, or do anything about. If a guy wants to die, that can always be arranged. If a guy just wants to be ignored, that can be arranged, too."

Then he was gone, and I settled back in my chair and I was shaking.

Fucking shaking.

We had been friends for many years, we had done each other favors, and I had relished his loose way with the rules, always a plus in a friend in law enforcement, but now I realized, not too late I hoped, that I was Abel in this relationship and that bastard was Cain.

When I felt like myself again, I looked around this office I'd inhabited since Tuesday and realized it bore no traces of my presence whatsoever. Nothing to pack. Nothing of me in here at all.

This time Martineau's door was closed. I knocked, got permission to enter and did.

"Marty," I said from the doorway, "consider this my resignation from the Secret Service."

He smiled. "I'm glad the AG assigned you here for this case. And I appreciate everything you did for us."

I raised an eyebrow. "Everything?"

"Everything."

"Would you do me a small favor? Use your influence to make your pals in the Service keep a very damn sharp eye out on these upcoming presidential trips."

"Nate, we always do."

"I know, I know. But this isn't just the messed-up likes of Vallee anymore. Four gunmen, Marty, that's a full-blown conspiracy. And you'll be cutting two of the players loose this afternoon."

"I hear you."

"Good."

"Listen, Nate, you'll still need to come in on Monday to sit down with Charlotte and dictate your report. You know, for me to include in the overview I'll be doing for Chief Rowley."

"Sorry," I said. "I can't make it."

"You need to try. I'm sure, after almost a week away, you have matters at the A-1 that needed tending to . . . but we need to wrap this up, officially."

"Marty, I won't be in," I said. "I'm sorry, but it really doesn't matter."

"Why is that, Nate?"

"Marty, don't you know? I was never here."

*Do you remember where you were when President
Kennedy was killed? Even if you weren't alive at the
time, you surely know that a sniper in a high window
was waiting for JFK to ride by on that infamous day in
November.*

*In Dallas.*

---
**Friday, November 29, 1963**
---

In Chicago, around ten P.M., after a long day of work
and a quick bite to eat, I got on the El in the Loop, taking the subway south to Thirty-fifth and Wabash. At
the White Sox stop, I got off in what used to be called
the Section, where colored folk had wound up, coming
to Chicago in that first big northward swing after World
War I. Jazz had got its start in the Section, Chicago-style
anyway, and the area was still rife with filthy streets,
broken-down buildings, and greasy spoons. Walking
east on Thirty-fifth, the only honky around, I might
have felt scared if the nine-mil wasn't under my arm.

Since last Friday, I hadn't gone anywhere unarmed.

In my experience, you avoided trouble in Bronzeville
by not looking for it. Move easy, cool, confident. No

eye contact, not even with those two high-yellow gals in tight dresses striding your way, emphasizing their hip sway and wearing grins half come-on, half dare. If you hear footsteps on the sidewalk behind you, too fast for your taste, just half turn and walk sideways a few steps. Hardly anything really to worry about.

At Thirty-fifth and State—heart of the Section— were the dives where Jelly Roll Morton once played. At Thirty-fifth and Indiana, I wondered if I'd missed the place; but there it was on the northwest corner, a brick storefront with a Schlitz saloon sign and a banner that boldly announced MUDDY WATERS & BAND— FRI, SAT, SUN.

Inside, Smitty's was dark, crowded, and smoky. Moving through the loud bar into the club area, where the brown walls peeled paint and a sign advertised CHEEBURGERS, I spotted Eben Boldt and a good-looking Negro woman, both dressed casually but nice—dark suit, light blue dress—seated toward the front among quiet couples at checker-clothed, postage-stamp tables.

Joining Eben, I was introduced to his friendly wife, Barbara, a schoolteacher pretty enough to worry Diahann Carroll.

The show hadn't started yet, but the drums, piano, several guitars on stands, and several amplifiers were waiting up on the small stage.

"You will dig this, Nate," Eben said. "You really will."

"What's it like around the office these days?"

"A morgue, only more depressing. Martineau's had three meetings so far, reminding us to stay mum about that week you were with us."

I shook my head. "First time I saw those Dallas cops dragging Oswald through that police station, I thought he was Vallee. My God they look alike."

*And when I'd been watching Sunday morning and saw the stocky figure in the fedora lurch forward and*

*fire his gun into Lee Harvey Oswald, I knew it was
Ruby. Didn't have to see his face. Just the shape of him.*

"Here's some more cheap irony you'll enjoy," Eben
said. "Mayor Daley got the city council today to re-
name the Northwest Expressway the Kennedy Expressway."

"Yeah, I saw. They should have the ribbon cutting at
the West Jackson exit."

"Actually, they are."

"Aw, please...."

"Swear to God, Nate. Next week. There'll be a ceremony with more Irish politicians than an alderman's
wake. Bobby Kennedy was invited, but declined."

"Yeah, he's keeping his head pulled in. I don't think
you'll see him doing much traveling in the foreseeable
future."

*I had warned him. We had a talk, a late-night phone
call, from "a secure line" Bobby said, Saturday, November second. I hadn't told him chapter and verse—
I'd left out specific names, like Richard Cain and Jack
Ruby—but I did tell him what had really happened at
IPP, and that I believed Operation Mongoose was riddled with cancer cells.*

*"I know, Nate. We're looking into it. We're all
over it."*

*"Bob, do me one small favor. Convince your brother
to stay out of open cars for a while."*

*"Can't do it, Nate. You try telling him. We have an
election to win. We're okay. We know what we're dealing with."*

*"Do you?"*

Eben said, "Something else I heard, and this you will
simply *not* believe."

"Pretty sure I will. I have a low disbelief threshold
these days."

Even though nobody in this mostly Negro crowd

gave two diddleys what we were saying, Eben leaned in and damn near whispered.

"On the Monday before the assassination," Eben said, "the eighteenth? The Service was dealing with a serious threat in Tampa for the President's visit. An FBI source indicated an unidentified sniper in a high window in a tall building, with a high-power rifle with scope, would try to take JFK out."

I noticed Barbara had a rather long-suffering look on her lovely face. Who could blame her?

"They even had a suspect," her husband was saying, "a former defector named Lopez. Part of the Tampa Fair Play for Cuba Committee. Sound familiar?"

"That's who Oswald was with in New Orleans, it's claimed. So they had an Oswald . . . a Vallee . . . ready to go in Tampa, too?"

"Nate, they were stalking the President all month. All damn month."

"I figured that we'd shut the thing down," I said, with an Atlas-worthy sigh. "But Chicago was just Plan A. There was a Plan B in Tampa, and Plan C in Dallas."

Barbara said, "Third time's a charm."

A cute waitress came and took our orders; she seemed fascinated by me, like a Martian had walked in the place. I couldn't quite tell if she was flirting or afraid. We all had beer, and that was the last JFK talk for a while, unless you counted Muddy Waters singing "Sad, Sad Day."

When the band took its break, I said, "I dig this electrified blues. I think it could give rock 'n' roll a run for the money."

"When the white kids hear it," Barbara said, "they'll steal it."

Eben said, "Nate, I don't care what Martineau says. I'm going to testify at the Warren Commission."

The papers and TV had been full of that all day—LBJ

establishing the President's Commission on the assassination of President Kennedy.

"Ebe, don't even think about it. Allen Dulles is on that damn thing—former CIA director? It's a dog and pony show, full of people who hated Kennedy. Stay away from it."

"Somebody's got to come forward. What can they do to me?"

"Fire you," Barbara said.

Ebe smiled at her and patted her hand. "Honey, I can always get a job with Nate Heller."


If only it had been that easy.

The winter day in 1964 when Eben Boldt went to Washington, D.C., to testify to the Warren Commission, both about the covered-up Chicago plot and the misconduct he'd witnessed on the President's protection detail—the drinking, the carousing, the racism—he was arrested and sent back to Chicago. The accusation? He had supposedly tried to extort $50,000 out of a counterfeiter by sharing a secret file with him.

This book would be at least one-hundred pages longer if I were to share with you the work the A-1 did pro bono for Ebe's various attorneys over the years. Even when I was able to get the counterfeiter to recant, to admit having perjured himself on the stand, Eben Boldt remained behind bars. Despite the Supreme Court reviewing the serious misconduct of a judge who'd advised the jury that the defendant seemed guilty, behind bars Eben remained. The counterfeiter, by the way, was a close associate of Mad Sam DeStefano. I always suspected Dick Cain of being behind the frame-up.

When he was paroled in 1969, Eben did not return to law enforcement. He didn't even want the job I offered him. Instead he became a quality-control supervisor in the automobile industry. For forty years, he has attempted to clear his name. Documents at the Chicago Secret Service Office that might have cleared him—concerning, among other things, the Chicago assassination plot—were "routinely" destroyed in 1995. His efforts and those of others to get Congress and/or the President to restore his good name have also failed. To date.

I like to think Marty Martineau didn't have anything to do with the railroading of Eben Boldt. He continued his distinguished government service for many years, but when asked about the four-man assassination squad—or about the lone nut, Vallee—he was vague and even evasive. Still, he was one of the few Secret Service agents willing to go on record saying that the JFK assassination was a conspiracy. He died at ninety-five.

On December 3, 1963, Thomas Arthur Vallee briefly surfaced in Chicago newspapers covering the brave cops who had seized the "Gun-Toting Kennedy Foe." Charges against him were never pressed. On the rare occasions when Vallee was tracked down by a journalist—fascinated by such details as Oswald having also served at a U-2 base in Japan—the interview subject insisted he'd been framed by his CIA handlers, and seemed to realize that he'd narrowly escaped the role that Lee Harvey Oswald played in history. Still working as a printer, Vallee died in 1988 in Houston, where he lived in a ramshackle trailer with a well-oiled M-1 propped near his bedside.

Berkeley Moyland, the honest Chicago police lieutenant who alerted the Secret Service to Vallee, was instructed by the Secret Service in late 1963 never to share his knowledge of the Chicago assassination attempt. But in his final years, he told his son the story, adding that Vallee had later sent him a thank-you card. Apparently the ex-Marine believed Moyland had saved his life.

The two cops who had been so highly recommended by Sheriff's Chief Investigator Richard Cain gained notoriety in a later case. In December 1969, the pair—acting as state's attorney raiders—burst into black activist Fred Hampton's apartment, kicking the door down, showering the place with bullets, and killing Hampton and another Black Panther leader. The detectives spent years in and out of court, fighting claims that they were CIA or FBI agents on a "black op," an ironically apt euphemism for this incident, widely termed a massacre. Whether they are alive or dead, I couldn't tell you. But the last time I saw Gross, he was gray and nervous, his family life ruined under a crush of massive legal bills.

The gangsters met various well-deserved deaths: Mad Sam DeStefano, shotgunned in his garage, 1973; Sam Giancana, shot in the head while frying sausage and peppers, 1975; Jimmy Hoffa, disappeared, 1975; Johnny Rosselli, strangled, shot, dismembered, 1976; Chuckie Nicoletti, shot in the head three times, 1977.

Santo Trafficante died by the knife in 1987—the surgeon's scalpel, on an operating table at the end of a long battle with heart disease and other ailments. Carlos Marcello died in 1993, a hopeless imbecile thanks to Alzheimer's; when still of sound mind, he confessed a major role in the JFK assassination to his attorney, Frank Ragano, and also implicated Hoffa.

Awaiting a new trial, Jack Ruby died of cancer at Parkland Hospital, where JFK had been pronounced dead. Ruby felt he'd been poisoned, and during his incarceration became increasingly bold about denying full culpability in the shooting of everybody's favorite lone-nut assassin, saying shortly before his death, "I was framed to kill Oswald."

Sally Rand had a very successful engagement at the Silver Frolics in January 1964, though shortly thereafter the place was indeed shut down, then torn down, in its place a parking ramp erected for employees of the nearby *Chicago Sun-Times*. Helen gained national prominence that same year when she was invited to perform for the astronauts at the Astrodome in Houston, with new President Lyndon Johnson hosting. The event was given a certain inaccurate permanence in the Academy Award–winning 1983 film *The Right Stuff*, whose soft-focus gaze implied a much younger fan dancer. She'd have loved that.

Helen and I remained close over the years, but never moved in together, much less married. Her only lasting marriage was to her career, and she managed to keep Sally Rand in front of the public, performing her fan dance as late as 1979, the year of her death.

Richard Cain, as time passed, was revealed as a cop who was also an Outfit member—a made man who had been not just a bagman but an assassin. Some think he was involved in the Dallas hit, that perhaps he was even one of the shooters, though with his lousy eyesight, I doubt it. Cain was, however, the guy who notified the FBI where and when Oswald's infamous Mannlicher-Carcano had been purchased in Chicago.

In 1964, Cain was fired from the sheriff's department for lying to a grand jury in a stolen drugs case, serving six months for perjury, and in 1968 went to prison as an accomplice in a bank robbery. When he got out in 1971, he became Sam Giancana's right-hand man and chief courier, during Mooney's Mexico days. Returning to Chicago in '73, Cain began informing on other Outfit guys to FBI agent Bill Roemer, clearing a path for his own planned takeover.

A few days before Christmas 1973, I caught up with Dick Cain at Rose's Sandwich Shop on West Grand on the West Side. I was in my sixties now, and he was in his forties, but he looked ten years older. Sitting at a table by himself, he wore a black suit with a conservative tie. Hair longer, some silver in it, even sideburns. Hell, I had them, too.

Rose's was just a hole-in-the-wall diner, with maybe eight tables and a counter. Jelly Cozzo owned the joint, and Outfit guys were his regular clientele, probably because of his mother's recipes for spaghetti, ravioli, and lasagna. Jelly, a fairly bad dude in his day, served red wine and Zinfandel, too, though he had no liquor license.

Dick was having some spaghetti. I knew now that his real last name was Scalzitti. But he was also drinking a Coke and had a Dunhill going in an ashtray. Some things never changed. Like the dark-rimmed Buddy Holly glasses.

And the milky left eye.

I sat down. He looked up and frowned—his eyesight really was lousy, plus I looked older—and then he smiled.

"Nate Heller," he said. "What the hell."

He put his fork down and extended his hand and we shook. The waitress (there was only one, a little Annette Funicello look-alike who needed her mustache waxed) came and took my order—I had a Coke, too, and she brought it right over.

"My God," he said, "how long as it been?"

"Since the sixties, anyway. I hear you had a falling-out with Mooney."

"Naw, everything's fine there. I just decided to go my own way."

"Dick, I wanted to warn you about something."

"Really? What?"

"I still keep my hand in at the A-1. Not completely retired, you know."

"I didn't know, but . . . what's happening?"

I leaned in confidentially. "One of my guys picked up on a very dangerous rumor. It just can't be true. It's crazy."

"Try me, Nate."

"Well, it's a coup. Scheduled for New Year's Eve. Word is you've reached out to various contract guys around the country, and plan to hit every single mob boss in town, here and in Vegas and all over the place. All at the same time. Midnight, to ring in the New Year."

He laughed. "That does sound screwy. Naw, that's not me, Nate. You know I'm a stand-up guy."

"I know you been working with Marshall Caifano. Advising him what houses his burglary crew should hit. But that sounds frankly . . . small-time to me, Dick. I mean, when I heard this crazy story about an Outfit coup? On some weird level, it made sense. Just the kind of elaborate, Machiavellian kinda shit you might come up with."

"Naw. No. You heard wrong."

I finished my Coke, gave him a smile. "Well, I heard this from one of my guys, and I thought I better let you know. Wrong people hear this, you could have a problem."

He was nodding. "I appreciate it, Nate. I do appreciate it. Old times' sake, huh?"

"Well, I owe you from way back, Dick. Always like to pay my debts."

I gave him a wave, paid for the Coke, and headed out to West Grand, where a beater Ford was pulled in at a meter just down the way. I gave the two guys in the car a nice slow nod, and they started pulling on the ski masks. As I cut across the street to where my Jag was parked, I heard the crackle of a walkie-talkie: "*He's in there.*"

Over my motor starting up, I could hear screams, and yells from guys ordering patrons around, and then a blast that just had to be both barrels of a shotgun.

The papers didn't give the details, but a cop pal who had hated Dick Cain, too, reported that indeed both barrels of a shotgun had been fired up under Dick's chin, tearing away the right side of his face. The downside? That meant an instantaneous death.

I still had the building in Old Town, though several years earlier, I had converted it into three floors of living space. I'd remodeled some, but that's not the point.

The point is that around nine that evening, I got Tom Ellison's wife on the phone. We hadn't talked in a while, and we had a very nice catching-up session. Her kids were grown and fine. She hadn't remarried, and the sound of her voice was such that I thought I might one of these days drive to Milwaukee and take her out for a nice meal.

For now, though, it was time to wrap up the conversation.

"Nice talking to you, Jean. But the reason I called."

"Yes, Nate?"

"Remember how I told you, sometimes it takes years to take care of certain matters?"

". . . I do."

"Well, I just wanted you to know, something happened today."

"Oh?"

"I think Tom would be pleased."

And I hung up.

# I OWE THEM ONE

Despite its extensive basis in history, this is a work of fiction, and liberties have been taken with the facts, though as few as possible—and any blame for historical inaccuracies is my own, mitigated by the limitations of conflicting source material.

Most of the characters in this novel are real and appear under their true names, although all depictions herein must be viewed as fictionalized. Available information on the various individuals ranges from voluminous to scant. In some instances, few or no photographs were available, and for narrative purposes a description was invented—a fair amount of information was available on Maurice Martineau, for example, but research turned up no photo. Secret Service agents tend not to advertise their appearances.

Nathan Heller is, of course, a fictional character, as are the people he works with at the A-1 Detective Agency. In some cases, I have chosen not to use real names as an indication that either a surfeit of research is available on some minor historical figure, or that enough fictionalization has occurred to make that prudent. The fictional Chicago PD detectives Gross and Shoppa, for instance, have real-life counterparts, one of whom was a key player in the Fred Hampton shooting. Probably the most unbelievable character in this novel, Richard Cain, actually existed.

Eben Boldt is based on Abraham Bolden, an American hero—the Jackie Robinson of the Secret Service—who appears to have been framed due to his efforts to expose Secret Service shortcomings. These include presidential protection, racism in the ranks, and the Chicago plot itself. This is a man who only wanted to play by the rules and become a top-flight professional in service of his country. His fate is a sad footnote in the grand tragedy of the Kennedy assassination.

As far back as the first Nathan Heller novel, *True Detective* (1983), which also deals with a political assassination, I have intended that my detective would eventually delve into the Kennedy murder. Even before Heller, I had a strong interest in the case, and have a vivid memory of seeing on television Lee Harvey Oswald shuttled around the station house by Dallas cops. Oswald wore an expression any adult human being should immediately recognize, which might be described as: "*Shit*—I should have seen this coming." My gut reaction as a teenager? When Oswald said he was a patsy, he wasn't lying.

But it is my practice to come to Heller novels with an open mind. I didn't go into *Stolen Away* (1991) assuming either Bruno Hauptmann's guilt or innocence, and I wrote the Roswell novel, *Majic Man* (1999), fully prepared for Nate Heller to encounter aliens, if that's where the research led. Where JFK is concerned, however, I admit that I formed my basic opinions about the case a long time ago, based upon what I had read—and I had read a lot. Still, I was ready to change my mind.

I didn't. Both my longtime research associate George Hagenauer and I plowed through scores of books on the subject. In the last two years, the research has been intensive and intense. On no other historical fiction project have we tried to ingest and digest more material, and as the time approached for me to begin writing, my head was swimming. I had a game plan that would take Heller to Dallas shortly after the shooting and put him in the midst of everything. But it didn't feel real, or right, and the massive nature of the evidence that needed presenting overwhelmed me.

I can only shake my head when I see intelligent, well-meaning commentators from Vincent Bugliosi to Chris Matthews ignore such basics as Oswald's ties to the CIA and FBI, Jack Ruby's mob affiliation, and the Kennedy administration sanctioning the assassination of foreign heads of state. Never mind the magic bullet, the ballistics test that proved Oswald hadn't fired a rifle, the Grassy Knoll witnesses, and your own lying eyes watching the Zapruder film. Yet even at this late date, we are battered over the head with copies of the risible *Warren Commission Report,* and told that our screwball conspiracy theorizing means we simply can't accept that a great man like John F. Kennedy could be struck down by a nobody like Lee Harvey Oswald. And we're to forget that other official government report that came *after* the Warren Commission, the one from the House Select Committee on Assassinations that concluded conspiracy was probable.

Those of us who view the obvious facts and interpret them in a logical fashion can only reply to Bugliosi, Matthews, Gerald Posner, and all the rest: in the face of overwhelming evidence, you cannot accept that the Kennedy brothers, whether great men or not, were flawed and helped create the Shakespearean circumstances of their own tragedy.

That aside, my problem as a historical novelist was the potential size and shape of a Heller novel on this subject, and the possibility of bogging myself and the reader down in minutiae to prove a point that I feel is evident on its face. Add to that the many novels and films already based around the Dallas events, and I began to dread treading over such familiar ground. Finally, with Nathan Heller as my protagonist, there always has to be a Chicago door to go through. Where, other than the obvious mob aspect, was the Chicago doorway to Dallas?

I credit George Hagenauer for finding the Chicago plot—the hit-man squad, two of whom were Cuban, and the obvious patsy in Thomas Arthur Vallee. Well, I had noticed it, and made notes about it, but had not realized its full meaning or potential. George thought the book might open with the Chicago plot, which then would take us to Dallas.

But I came to realize that a new JFK assassination story was there, just waiting to be told. That the Chicago plot of November 2, 1963, was virtually unknown and yet its very outline, its stark parallels to Dallas, offered a fresh way to demonstrate the conspiracy behind JFK's murder between the mob, CIA elements, Cuban exiles, and various right-wing players. To say to the doubters, if this happened on November 2 in Chicago, how can you look at November 22 in Dallas and say, "Lone nut gunman?"

Suddenly the mass of research fell away and only a handful of sources were available that focused on this ignored, virtually forgotten piece of potentially key history. *Target Lancer* is the first book-length treatment of the Chicago plot. While perhaps a dozen Kennedy books give a paragraph or at most a page to the case, only a handful of writers have really dug in.

Investigative journalist Edwin Black did the key, groundbreaking research for his article "The Plot to Kill JFK in Chicago Nov. 2, 1963." Black, writing for the obscure *Chicago Independent* (November 1975), is a highly respected, credible reporter whose lengthy piece reflects in-depth, on-site research and remains the definitive treatment.

Perhaps the best recent Kennedy assassination book, *JFK and the Unspeakable* (2008) by James W. Douglass, takes a lengthy look at the Chicago case, weaving it into the greater fabric of the international crises then at hand, and bringing in fresh research and information that expand upon Black.

*Ultimate Sacrifice* (2005, 2006) by Lamar Waldron with Thom Hartmann is a massive work, somewhat controversial but with its own well-researched take on the assassination. In their coverage of the Chicago plot, Waldron and Hartmann draw largely upon Black but present the longest nonfiction look at the plot to date. *Legacy of Secrecy* (2009), a similarly weighty followup by the same authors, also deals with the case, but in considerably less detail.

Web research revealed the work of Vincent M. Palamara, which proved very helpful, notably chapter 17, "The Chicago Connection," from his *Survivor's Guilt* (2006). Palamara has problems with Waldron and Hartmann's handling of the Chicago plot, and goes to admirable lengths to present his research in a straightforward, unslanted manner.

Surprisingly, Abraham Bolden mentions the case only in passing in his autobiography, *The Echo from Dealey Plaza* (2008). Bolden has been far more forthcoming elsewhere, as in an ABC News article, "44 Years After JFK's Death, New Assassination Plot Revealed" (November 22, 2007).

*The Kennedy Detail* (2010) by ex–Secret Service agent Gerald Blaine with Lisa McCubbin deals with the Chicago case in a dismissive manner that includes belittling Bolden, which is typical of this insider's book designed to put the best spin on a very bad situation. The Vallee coverage, however, contained some interesting facts not found elsewhere.

The incident involving a press agent who did a favor for a Hoffa emissary—involving a ten-thousand-dollar payoff to Jack Ruby in Chicago, right down to the tickets to the Bears/Eagles game—is detailed in *Ultimate Sacrifice* (as is Lee Harvey Oswald's presence in Chicago in that time frame). Further, numerous books report Jack Ruby in a Dallas bank on the afternoon of November 22 with a similar packet of cash. The real press agent, Jim Allison, was not murdered, although his Hoffa contact man died under suspicious circumstances within several months of the JFK assassination. On November 24, 1963, Allison was (like me) watching on TV the transfer of Oswald from the Dallas police station to the county jail when he recognized Ruby as the shooter.

The major liberty I have taken with this incident, for the sake of creating an entertaining mystery thriller, is turning Allison's fictional stand-in—Tom Ellison— into the murder victim, essentially making a composite of Allison and the Hoffa contact. The other major liberty taken is Heller's fictional disposal of the two ex-soldier assassins on the morning of November 2.

But the spine of this story has a solid factual basis— from the four-man hit squad including two Cubans to the ex-Marine patsy Vallee (whose many parallels to Lee Harvey Oswald include the stunning information that both served at U-2 bases in Japan); from the very controlled Secret Service response to the threat (including the blown surveillance of the Cuban subjects because of a radio transmission from Chief Martineau) right up to the last-second cancelation of the President's Chicago visit.

Heller's role in the formation of Operation Mongoose is based upon the actual role played by Robert Maheu, as described in numerous sources but in particular his memoir, *Next to Hughes* (Robert Maheu and Richard Hack, 1992). Those who consider Nate Heller a character who strains credulity might check out the real-life career of Howard Hughes's favorite private eye.

A number of biographies proved crucial. Holly Knox's *Sally Rand: From Film to Fans* (1988) was most helpful, as was Michael J. Cain's sympathetic but unflinching look at his half brother, *The Tangled Web: The Life and Death of Richard Cain—Chicago Cop and Mafia Hitman* (2007).

My portrait of Jack Ruby was influenced by any number of books, but in particular *The Ruby Cover-Up* (1978) by Seth Kantor; *Jack Ruby* (1967, 1968) by Gary Wills and Ovid Demaris; and *Jack Ruby's Girls* (1970) by Diana Hunter and Alice Anderson.

The major Jimmy Hoffa source here is *Mob Lawyer* (1994) by Frank Ragano and Selwyn Raab. A key mob reference was *All-American Mafioso: The Johnny Rosselli Story* (1991) by Charles Rappleye and Ed Becker. Also helpful were *Mafia Kingfish: Carlos Marcello and the Assassination of John F. Kennedy* (1989), John H. Davis; *The Trafficantes: Godfathers from Tampa, Florida* (2010), Ron Chepesiuk; and *The Mafia Encyclopedia: From Accardo to Zwillman* (1987), Carl Sifakis.

Among the books on Bobby Kennedy that helped form his portrait were *Brothers: The Hidden History of the Kennedy Years* (2007), David Talbot; *The Dark Side of Camelot* (1997) by Seymour Hersh; *Robert Kennedy: His Life* (2000), Evan Thomas; and *RFK: A Candid Biography of Robert Kennedy* (1998), C. David Heyman.

Of the scores of Kennedy assassination books in

my library, those that proved most helpful were *Conspiracy* (1989 edition), Anthony Summers; *The JFK
Assassination Debates: Lone Gunman versus Conspiracy* (2006), Michael L. Kurtz; *JFK: The Dead Witnesses* (1995), Craig Roberts and John Armstrong; *To
Kill a President* (2008), M. Wesley Swearingen; *Who
Shot JFK: A Guide to the Major Conspiracy Theories*
(1993), Bob Callahan, illustrated by Mark Zingarelli;
and *Who's Who in the JFK Assassination* (1993), Michael Benson.

Works consulted that specifically explore the orga-
nized crime aspect of the assassination include *Con-
tract on America: The Mafia Murder of President John
F. Kennedy* (1988), David E. Scheim; *The Plot to Kill
the President* (1981, 1992), G. Robert Blakey and
Richard N. Billings; and *The Kennedy Contract: The
Mafia Plot to Assassinate the President* (1993), John
H. Davis.

Nate Heller's world of early '60s Chicago is reflected
in *Mr. Playboy: Hugh Hefner and the American Dream*
(2008) by Steven Watts. *Playboy* was not the only men's
magazine published in Chicago during those years, and
issues of it—as well as of its local competitors, *Rogue*
and *Cabaret*—played a big part in my re-creation of
those days in these pages, as all three carried much coverage of the Windy City scene. It seems I really have become a man reading *Playboy* for the articles, and for
the advertisements, reviews, and other material, particularly as relating to Chicago.

Several specific articles are worthy of citation: "Amer-
ica's Oldest Stripper" (Sally Rand) by Stan Holden,
*Cabaret,* December 1955; "American's Most Refined
Strip Show" (Silver Frolics) by Stan Holden, *Cabaret,*
July 1956; "The Windy City's Hottest Night Spot" (606
Club) by Henry Darling, *Cabaret,* April 1957; "Satirists
à la Sartre" (Second City) by Bruce Cook, *Rogue,*

December 1960; "Chicago: Backstreet Blues" (Smitty's) by Gabriel Favoino, *Rogue,* February 1961; and "Rogue Swings at an Art Fair" (Old Town), unsigned, *Rogue,* August 1964.

General Chicago information and color was supplied by the following books: *Chicago Confidential* (1950), Jack Lait and Lee Mortimer; *Kup's Chicago* (1962), Irv Kupcinet; *Vittles and Vice* (1952), Patricia Bronte; and *The WPA Guide to Illinois* (1939). There has of course been considerable newspaper research as well, leaning upon *The Chicago Tribune*.

Special thanks to George Hagenauer, whose many trips to Iowa for brainstorming sessions and research planning ultimately resulted in the approach taken here. George was always there to give me firsthand information on Chicago in the '60s at my last-second request.

Thanks also to my frequent collaborator, Matthew Clemens, who advised on matters of sports and forensics; my friend and agent, Dominick Abel, who has helped me keep Nathan Heller alive; and my editor, James Frenkel, who gave Heller and me the chance to finally take on the JFK case.

Of course, Barbara Collins—my wife, best friend, and valued writing collaborator—was on hand with suggestions and encouragement, on this sometimes harrowing ride.

Turn the Page for a
Secret First Look at *Ask Not*,
the Climactic Nathan Heller Novel in
Max Allan Collins's JFK Trilogy.

# *Ask Not*

## MAX ALLAN COLLINS

*Available in October 2013 from
Tom Doherty Associates*

A FORGE BOOK

—CHAPTER—

*1*

September 1964

My son's generation will always remember two key events of their teenage years—where they were when news came of President Kennedy's assassination, and seeing the Beatles on Ed Sullivan.

I learned of the former in a guest room at Hugh Hefner's Playboy Mansion in Chicago—in the company of Miss November, fittingly enough. Soon, amid beauties with their mascara running, she and I had hunkered around a portable television with a little gray picture in a big shiny white kitchen. The latter broadcast I somehow missed, but Sam has made it abundantly clear over the years that the February 9 appearance of those four Liverpool lads on *The Ed Sullivan Show* was right in there with JFK getting it.

My son once told me that that joyful noise had signaled a rebirth for his generation, the Baby Boomers, granting them permission to smile and have fun and be silly again. But it also signaled the end of barbershops as we knew them and extended the fad called rock 'n' roll through the rest of the century and beyond.

Unlike many of my contemporaries—I was a successful businessman in my well-preserved late fifties—I did not have disdain for the Beatles. They were a pretty fair combo, better than most of the little bands that had made the Twist a very big deal on Rush Street, and they seemed to have a sense of humor. Earlier this year, Sam had convinced me to take in their flick *A Hard Day's Night,* and I'd liked it. More importantly, Miss November—who you may have calculated was younger than me—loved it.

The Beatles, through no fault of their own, had created a problem for me with Sam. He lived with his mother and my ex-wife (that's one person) in Hollywood with her husband, a fitfully successful film producer. Normally Sam spent summers with me in Chicago, but he had begged off of June and July because his combo—yes, the Beatle bug had bit him hard—had a weekly pool party gig at a Bel Air country club that paid "incredible money" ($100).

"So what about August?" I'd asked him over the phone.

"August is cool. August is groovy. Everybody's going on vacation with family, so we can't take gigs anyway. Dad, are you okay with this?"

"It's cool. Maybe not groovy, but cool." I had maintained a strong relationship with my son by not insisting on having my own way. That's right. I spoiled his ass. Divorced dads get to do that.

Have to do that.

And August had been swell. At a second-run theater in Evanston, we took in *From Russia with Love,* and before the film began I bragged about having met James Bond's papa during the war.

"I doubt Ian Fleming was on Guadalcanal, Dad," Sam had said skeptically over his popcorn.

"It was on Nassau," I said. "He was doing spy stuff."

"The stories you tell! How am I supposed to know when you're bullshitting me?"

Another way I spoiled Sam was to let him swear around me. His mother hated it. Which I loved.

I sipped too-sweet Coke. "Someday you'll appreciate your old man."

"Hey, as dads go, you're one of the cooler ones."

Not cool, just one of the cooler ones. I'd settle.

Sam—actually Nathan Samuel Heller, Jr., but his mother and I decided one Nate around the house was plenty (more than enough, as it turned out)—had caught up with my six feet now. He had my late mother's Irish good looks, the Jewish half of my heritage nowhere to be seen in either of us, and we looked enough alike to be brothers. If he had a really old brother.

Oh, and he had his mother's brown hair, not my reddish variety. Cut in that Moe Howard bowl haircut the Beatles had bestowed on American males. Once upon a time I'd wished he would let that dumb crew cut grow out. Careful what you wish for.

"Listen, uh, Dad . . . I need to talk to you about college. I'm thinking about liberal arts."

"Not business?"

"No. I want to be able to take music courses."

Like the Beatles had ever studied music!

Sam was my only son. My only kid period. I had no desire to reshape him into Nathan Heller, Jr., even if that was his name. But I did have a successful business—the A-1 Detective Agency, here in Chicago and with branches in Los Angeles, New York, and more recently Las Vegas—and I hoped he'd eventually take it over.

Not as a detective—private eye days were long gone. Hell, they'd even canceled *Peter Gunn*. But the agency was a very profitable business indeed, and Sam would make a great executive—he was smart and personable and already pretty darn savvy.

"Music, huh?" I said lightly. "You'll teach, then.

What, marching band? Chorus? What's the starting salary, thirty-five hundred a year?"

"Money isn't everything, Dad."

Said the kid with two well-off parents.

"Anyway," he went on, "I don't wanna teach. I don't know what I want to do, maybe keep playing my music . . ."

*His* music. The last time I looked, "his" music was the Beach Boys, Beatles, Chuck Berry, and, what was that instrumental group? The Adventures? Surf music. Jesus God.

". . . or something else, maybe, but not . . . *business*."

He said the word the way a Republican says Democrat.

"You know I'll support you any way you want to go, son. But you might, I'm just saying *might*, want to—"

"It's starting," Sam said, meaning the movie, or anyway the previews.

And it was starting. The first major struggle between father and son, at least since back when he wanted to stay up and watch Johnny Carson on school nights.

So August flew by, and we went to the fights and to ball games and more movies and had plenty of great food with an emphasis on Gino's pizza. We loafed around my Old Town bachelor pad and watched my color TV with its impressive 21-inch screen. I even arranged for an afternoon tour of Hef's mansion, just to give Sam a little hint of what being a successful businessman might bring.

Anyway, it was September now. This was Saturday and Labor Day was Monday. Back in Beverly Hills, school had been in session a couple days already, but I'd arranged for Sam to stick around so I could give him his seventeenth birthday present.

The Beatles were performing tonight at Chicago's International Amphitheater. This was the hottest ticket in town, the latest stop on a twenty-four-city, thirty-two-day tour. Tickets were going for $2.50, $3.50, and $4.50. A really great dad, with just the right connections, might be able to score his kid one of those tickets. But I could top that.

Just like the Beatles could top Elvis Presley, whose first Amphitheater appearance had required two hundred policemen, for security—*three hundred fifty* cops were being put on for John, Paul, George, and Ringo, plus a couple hundred firemen with half a dozen ambulances standing at the ready. But celebrities like these required personal security as well, for their Midway Airport arrival, their Stock Yard Inn press conference, and the concert itself.

And that was where the A-1 Detective Agency came in. Alan Edelson, who was handling press arrangements in Chicago, said Brian Epstein himself had requested me. I pretended to be impressed, and later really was, when my son informed me that Epstein was the boy wonder who had discovered and signed the Beatles. Mr. Epstein had apparently read of me across the pond in a *News of the World* story about Hollywood's "Private Eye to the Stars."

In reality I remained Chicago's private eye to anybody with a fat wallet, and spent at most maybe three months in California spread out over an average year. But *Life* and *Look* magazine articles, focusing on star clients like Frank Sinatra, Bobby Darin, and the late Marilyn Monroe, had made a minor celebrity out of me.

Normally as president of the A-1, I would have left this job to my staff and whatever add-ons from other agencies we might require. Sure, I'd likely stop around, shake a famous hand to provide the celebrity reassurance (and the A-1 a photograph), then go on my merry way.

But attending to the Beatles personally gave me an opportunity to maybe be a hero to my son.

We skipped the madhouse at Midway Airport because I knew the best opportunity for Sam to meet his real heroes was at the Saddle and Sirloin Club, the Stock Yard Inn's restaurant. The medium-sized Tudor-style hotel itself was at Forty-second and Halsted, adjacent to the amphitheater. Sam and I were already there—half a dozen of my agents were doing the actual security work—when the Beatles arrived in a phalanx of blue uniforms.

The dining room—a replica of an old English inn with oaken paneling arrayed with hunting prints—was jammed with linen-covered tables at which only invited reporters whose credentials had been checked were allowed. Screaming teenagers outside held back by sawhorses made a kind of muffled jet roar. Blue cigarette smoke drifted lazily in contrast to a general air of tension. Every table had a photographer on his feet with flash camera ready.

They were so young, these four superstars who took chairs at a microphone-strewn banquet table on a modest platform. With the exception of Ringo Starr, who was maybe five seven, the others were around six feet, slender, smiling, amused. They wore sharp unmatching suits in the mod British style, Paul and Ringo in ties, John with his collar buttoned, George unbuttoned. A row of cops, their caps with badges on, were lined up behind them, as if not sure whether to protect or arrest.

Sam was in a suit similar to what the Beatles were wearing, but it was a Maxwell Street knockoff I bought him, not a Carnaby Street original; like George, he wore no tie and his collar was open. His shoes were something called Beatle boots that a lesbian might have worn to an S & M party. Not that anyone cared, I was in a dark-gray suit by Raleigh with a black-and-gray diamond-pattern silk tie. And Florsheims, not Bea-tle boots.

Before the questioning could begin, I approached the raised table with Sam at my side, and introduced myself to McCartney.

"You're the private eye," he said, pleasant if not overly impressed. He was smoking. They all were. My God, they were young. Not far past twenty. Just four years or so older than Sam.

I handed him my card. "These are my private num-bers, if you need anything or there's any problem at the hotel."

After the concert, they would be staying, briefly, at the O'Hare Sahara awaiting their Detroit flight later tonight.

"Obliged," McCartney said.

I took a shot. "This is my son—Sam. You mind sign-ing something for him?"

They were all agreeable, signing a cocktail napkin. Sam was frozen, so I mentioned he was in a band him-self.

"Watch what you sign, man," Lennon said, as he was autographing the napkin. He winked at Sam, who took the flimsy paper square and nodded and said thanks to all of them. They had forgotten him already, but I will always remember that they were nice to my son.

*"Have you fellas given any thought to what you're going to do when the bubble breaks?"*

"Well," Lennon said, "we're gonna have a good time."

"We never plan ahead," Harrison said.

*"How about your retirement, or buying into a big business?"*

"We already are a big business," Lennon said, "so we don't have to buy into one."

That was a smart-ass reply, which the reporter well

deserved, but Lennon's lilting accent took the edge off.
Americans were suckers for a British accent; there was
something seductive about it. I'd been with a couple
BOAC stewardesses myself.

"*What do you think of Chicago?*"

Gesturing as he spoke, McCartney said, "I'm looking forward to seeing the gangsters with their broad-
brimmed hats and wide ties."

I'm sure the cute Beatle considered that a gag, but
the day before, a restaurant got blown up on Mannheim
Road for resisting the protection racket, and two mob
factions were currently shooting at each other over
control of gambling on the North Side.

Anyway, the lads were funny and made monkeys
out of any number of smug reporters. Sam wore a big
grin throughout, holding on to that cocktail napkin
with both hands.

The concert started at 8:30, but the Beatles didn't
come on right away. The vast high-ceilinged chamber
was packed with fifteen thousand audience members,
most of them teenagers, chiefly girls, often with bee-
hive hairdos. They didn't scream much during the four
opening acts—a couple of nondescript combos, an out-
of-place R & B singer, and a long-haired blonde who
looked like she belonged in the audience—and I started
to wonder what all the fuss was.

I'd been told the audience would scream so loud, you
couldn't hear a damn thing. I was hearing these opening acts much better than I cared to. When the blonde
girl wrapped up her short set, meaning the headliners
were next, the screaming kicked in, the sound like a
burning building with flames eating away.

Finally at 9:20, the Beatles emerged, led onto the
stage by Chicago cops, coming down stairs off to one
side. Grinning and waving, the three front men strapped
on their guitars—Ringo getting behind his drums on a

little stage-on-the-stage—and the place went wild. Stark raving mad. Like the Playboy mansion the day JFK was shot, lots of mascara was running. The shrieking was unbelievable. That muffled jet roar wasn't muffled now—the damn jet was flying around in circles in the place, which was almost possible, since they held indoor drag races in here. There were six hundred thousand square feet of it, after all, currently filled by thousands of girls having a nervous breakdown.

We had front-row seats and could almost hear the music. Well, Sam seemed to hear it just fine—he was singing along to "I Saw Her Standing There" and "Twist and Shout" and all the rest.

I officially joined the older generation by covering my ears. Oddly I could hear the music better that way, particularly the bass guitar and drums. The damn thing seemed to go on forever. I thought I might weep. Finally it was over—thirty minutes that had earned these four twenty-year-olds a grand a minute.

When the Beatles fled the stage, I took advantage of my security status to enlist a cop to lead Sam and me out a side exit while the audience was still on its feet screaming and crying. As for me, my ears were ringing. It was like I had a seashell up to either ear and could hear waves pounding the shore.

We came around to an ocean of cars—the lot held four thousand and was at capacity—but the kids hadn't started to stream out yet, lingering inside in the afterglow of Beatle hysteria. All across the lot, parents were standing by cars, waiting, smoking, the little red tips bobbing like fireflies in the night.

A fairly short walk away, my car was parked across from the Stock Yard Inn on South Halsted. Short walk or not, I was well aware that this was the South Side, an area tougher than a nickel steak, not that the Saddle and Sirloin Club had served up any nickel steaks lately.

The nearby stockyards consumed a sprawling area between Pershing Road on the north, Halsted on the east, Forty-seventh on the South, and Ashland Avenue on the west—close to five hundred acres. Still, you could neither hear nor smell those thousands of doomed cattle, unless you counted the fragrant aroma wafting from the Saddle and Sirloin.

"You want me to get that napkin framed up for you?" I asked Sam.

"You won't lose it or anything, will you?"

"No. I can be trusted with evidence."

"That would be fab."

Engines starting up, mechanical coughs in the night, indicated the teenagers were finally exiting the amphitheater for their rides. The wide street was still largely empty, though, as we jaywalked across, making no effort at speed.

We paused mid-street for a car to go by in either direction. Across from us, my dark-blue Jaguar X waited patiently, with its hubcaps and everything—not bad for this part of town.

"I'll just hold on to it for now," he said, meaning the napkin. It was still in his hands like the biggest, luckiest four-leaf clover any kid ever found.

He would be seventeen later this month, but I had that same surge of feeling for him I'd first experienced holding him in my arms at the hospital. I was studying him, trying to memorize the moment, slipping an arm around his shoulders, and he tightened, hearing the engine before I did.

It came roaring up from our left, where somebody had been parked on the Stock Yard Inn side, a light-blue Pontiac Bonneville, screaming down the street like those girls at the amphitheater. The vehicle, even at this stupid speed, was no danger to us, but we began to move a little quicker across our lane.

"*Dad!*"

Headlights were bearing down on us. The Pontiac had swerved—not swerved, *swung* into our lane, as if we were its targets.

Maybe we were.

The damn beast was right on us and it clipped me a little but it would have been much worse if Sam hadn't tackled me and shoved me out of harm's way. I glimpsed a blur of a dark-complected face in the window of the Pontiac as it whipped by, dark eyes glaring at me as if I were the one who'd hit him. Well, I had, a little.

Sam and I both landed hard on the pavement, and I had taken some impact, a glancing blow but still painful, on my left hip.

I was on my other side and Sam was hovering, saying, "Dad, Dad" over and over, as I managed to sit up, pointing.

"Son! Get that license number! Can you see it?"

I was too dazed—all I could see were red halos around taillights.

But Sam was nodding. He stared after the receding vehicle. It had disappeared by the time he got a pencil out of somewhere and jotted the number down on the back of his precious cocktail napkin, which was already rumpled and wadded from when he'd clutched his fists and tackled me to safety.

He had tears in his eyes. I'll never know if it was out of fear for himself or concern for me or sorrow over his ruined Beatlemania artifact.

But I'd lay odds on the latter.

He helped me up and drunk-walked me the few steps to the Jag. Another car went by, slow, the driver giving us a dirty look. We were just a couple of lushes lurching across the street.

Nobody had seen the incident, at least nobody who

bothered to come help or anything. I told Sam to drive, fishing out the keys for him, and he helped me into the rider's side. Now the stream of amphitheater traffic was picking up, slowed by traffic cops. Like they say, where was a cop when you needed one?

"I'm going to get you to a hospital," Sam said over the purr of the Jag. "What one should I go to? I don't know this part of town."

"Just get us back to Old Town. I didn't get hit that bad."

"Dad, no!"

"Son, I'll be bruised up, and my chiropractor will make a small windfall out of me. But I'm fine. Drive."

We'd gone about half a block when he said, "Shouldn't we call the cops? We should go back to that Stock Yard hotel and call the cops."

"No."

"What was *wrong* with that guy? Was he drunk?"

"Don't know."

"It was almost like he was *trying* to hit us!"

More likely me. Sam hadn't been on the planet long enough to make my kind of enemy.

We stopped at an all-night drugstore to pick up some Anacin, four pills of which I popped, chasing them with a Coke. Despite all that caffeine, I was asleep when Sam pulled behind my brick three-story on Eugenie Street, one block north of North Avenue. I woke up just as he was pulling the Jag into my stable-turned-garage. The main building, par for this side street, was narrow and deep with not much of a backyard.

I lived on the upper two floors, the ground level a furnished apartment the A-1 used for visiting clients and as a safe house. Sam was still helping me walk as we entered in back through the kitchen and across the dining room into the living room, an open space with off-white wall-to-wall carpet and a wrought-iron spiral staircase. The plaster walls, painted a rust orange, had select framed modern artwork, and one wall was a bookcase with as many LPs as books. Furnishings ran to overstuffed couches and chairs, some brown, some green.

I settled into my brown-leather recliner and used the phone on the table where the *TV Guide* and remote control also lived.

"You know, old married people like me," my long-time partner Lou Sapperstein said gruffly, "aren't necessarily up at this hour."

"It's not even midnight. You still got friends in Motor Vehicles?"

"I have friends everywhere, Nate. Even in Old Town."

"Do you have friends in Motor Vehicles who work night shift?"

"Are you okay? You sound funny."

"Yeah, I'm a riot. Rowan and Martin got nothing on me. I'm going to give you a license plate to have your friend run. And I want to know right now. Not tomorrow."

"Okay," Lou said, no more kidding around. "I got a pencil. Go."

I gave him the number.

Twenty minutes and two glasses of rum later, I picked the phone up on first ring.

"Pontiac Bonneville," Lou said. " '61. Light blue."

"That's the one."

"Stolen earlier this evening."

"Big surprise."

"Found abandoned within the last half hour on the South Side."

"Within, say, half a mile of the International Amphitheater?"

"You are a true detective, Nathan Heller. What's this about?"

"Maybe nothing. Maybe something."

I'd already gotten the nine millimeter from the front closet and rested it on the *TV Guide*.

Lou was saying, "If there are any prints on that vehicle, we'll know tomorrow."

"Tomorrow's Sunday."

"I have friends who work Sundays. I have all sorts of friends."

"This is where I came in," I said, thanked him, and hung up.

Sam was sitting on the nearby couch, leaning forward, hands clasped. He looked worried. A little afraid. He'd watched me go to the shelf to fetch the Browning automatic and its presence in the room, near my reach, was palpable.

"What's this about, Dad?"

"I don't know. Maybe nothing. Maybe a joyrider. Or a drunk. Or a husband who didn't like the art-study photos I took of him for his wife."

Sam was well aware of what I did for a living, though we both knew it had been a long, long time since I had shot pictures through motel windows. Although my agents still did.

"Dad, are you *sure* you're all right? I think we should get you to an emergency room."

"An emergency room at a Chicago hospital on a Saturday night? That's more dangerous than that street we crossed."

He smiled a little. "That was a close one. That was terrible."

"I'm sorry about that napkin."

"It's okay."

"No. It isn't. I'm going to call that guy Epstein in London and get you a signed photo."

"You don't have to."

But something had jumped in his eyes.

And eventually I did get him the photo, personally signed to him, and another to me for the A-1 office wall.

Right now, though, more pressing matters were on my mind. Specifically, that swarthy face that blurred by in that Bonneville; but not so blurry that I didn't recognize him.

I was damn sure—well, pretty sure—that he was a Cuban who'd been arrested in November of last year by the Secret Service. I'd been working with them at the request of a friend of mine who was so famous that if I'd told my son, he would have accused me of bullshitting again.

Three weeks prior to the shooting of the President in Dallas, a similar scheme had been hatched, and thwarted, in Chicago. I had hauled in two Cuban suspects and delivered them to the Secret Service, who had let them go after JFK's motorcade through the Loop was canceled. I'd never seen either of the Cubans again.

Until tonight, anyway, when one of them tried to run me down outside the Stock Yard Inn.

## ABOUT THE AUTHOR

MAX ALLAN COLLINS has earned an unprecedented nineteen Private Eye Writers of America "Shamus" nominations, winning for his Nathan Heller novels *True Detective* (1983) and *Stolen Away* (1991), receiving the PWA life achievement award, the Eye, in 2007.

His graphic novel *Road to Perdition* (1998) is the basis of the Academy Award–winning 2002 Tom Hanks film. It was followed by two acclaimed prose sequels and a graphic novel sequel, *Return to Perdition* (2011). He has created a number of innovative suspense series, notably Quarry (the first hit-man series) and Eliot Ness (the Untouchable's Cleveland years). He is completing a number of Mike Hammer novels begun by the late Mickey Spillane; his audio novel *The New Adventures of Mickey Spillane's Mike Hammer: The Little Death* won the 2011 Audie for Best Original Work.

His many comics credits include the syndicated strip *Dick Tracy;* his own *Ms. Tree; Batman;* and *CSI: Crime Scene Investigation*, based on the hit TV series, for which he has also written ten bestselling novels. His tie-in books have appeared on the *USA Today* bestseller list nine times and the *New York Times* list three. His movie novels include *Saving Private Ryan*, *Air Force*

*One*, and *American Gangster,* which won the IAMTW Best Novel "Scribe" Award in 2008.

An independent filmmaker in the Midwest, Collins has written and directed four features, including the Lifetime movie *Mommy* (1996); he scripted *The Expert,* a 1995 HBO World Premiere, and *The Last Lullaby* (2008), based on his novel *The Last Quarry.* His documentary *Mike Hammer's Mickey Spillane* (1998/2011) appears on the Criterion Collection DVD and Blu-ray of *Kiss Me Deadly.*

His play *Eliot Ness: An Untouchable Life* was nominated for an Edgar Award in 2004 by the Mystery Writers of America; a film version, written and directed by Collins, was released on DVD in 2008 and appeared on PBS stations in 2009. His documentary *Caveman: V.T. Hamlin & Alley Oop* (2005) was also released on DVD after screening on PBS stations.

His other credits include film criticism, short fiction, songwriting, trading-card sets, and video games. His coffee-table book, *The History of Mystery,* was nominated for every major mystery award, and his *Men's Adventure Magazines* (with George Hagenauer) won the Anthony Award.

Collins lives in Muscatine, Iowa, with his wife, writer Barbara Collins; they have collaborated on nine novels, including the successful "Trash 'n' Treasures" mysteries—their *Antiques Flee Market* (2008) winning the *Romantic Times* Best Humorous Mystery Novel award in 2009. Their son, Nathan, is a Japanese-to-English translator, working on video games, manga, and novels.